GONNA PICK THAT BANJO ANYHOW

"My dearly beloved friends," Willie began, holding his index finger aloft to command attention and pronouncing each word with a little flourish at the end and giving "friends" three syllables, "has it occurred to you during this eve-en-ing's performance that your brothers and sisters appear to be afflicted with an embarrassing and unsightly loss of memory, which causes their tongues to twist painfully around familiar words, which causes melodies to go a-*stray* and rhythms to break faith each beat with its brethren? Well, I am here to tell you, brothers and sisters, that there is a reason for this and there is a cure. The cure is to sing. Can anybody *teyell me,*"—his voice rose with televangelistic fervor—"yea, can you *teyell me* what the name of this blessed song might be?"

" 'Mama Don't 'Low,' " Gussie bellowed.

"PREcisely, darlin'! *Amen,* sister. And dearly beloved, just what is it that Mama don't allow and how exactly do we feel about it?"

"No *gui-*tar pickin'," someone said, and they got through the first line.

And through the same thing, the words all fitting into the melody, not easily, but with the banjo keeping the tune and the people who didn't sing but just remembered the words prompting the stage, the whole thing came together, simple and complicated as a child learning to tie his shoes, or a brain-damaged adult relearning how to tie his shoes.

Also by Elizabeth Scarborough

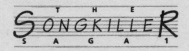

THE SONGKILLER SAGA 1

PHANTOM BANJO

ELIZABETH SCARBOROUGH

▲▲▲

BANTAM BOOKS

NEW YORK · TORONTO · LONDON · SYDNEY · AUCKLAND

PHANTOM BANJO (Songkiller Saga #1)
A Bantam Spectra Book/June 1991

ISBN 0-553-28761-3

Published simultaneously in the United States and Canada

Bantam Books are published by Bantam Books, a division of
Bantam Doubleday Dell Publishing Group, Inc. Its trademark,
consisting of the words "Bantam Books" and the portrayal of a
rooster, is Registered in U.S. Patent and Trademark Office and
in other countries. Marca Registrada. Bantam Books, 666 Fifth
Avenue, New York, New York 10103.

PRINTED IN THE UNITED STATES OF AMERICA

OPM   0 9 8 7 6 5 4 3 2 1

This book is fondly and gratefully dedicated to Tania Opland, Keith Todd and Tory, Kat Eggleston, Steve Guthe, Danna and Bennie Garcia, Rittie Ward, Bob Crowley, Janice Endresen, Allen Damron, Bill Moss, Tim Henderson, Mack Partain, Emilie Aronson, Ruthstrom and Robertson, the Kerrverts, Joyce Constant, the Baileys, Mark Simmons, the SMAGS in Fairbanks, Rob Folsom, William and Felicia, Victory Music, the Berrys, the Farrans, Suzette Haden Elgin, Valerie and Al Rogers, Eileen McGann and in general for all singers and pickers of traditional and not-so-traditional "folk" songs, for the singer/songwriters who make sure the folk of these times don't go unsung, and for the interpreters and performers everywhere who make the songs live, and the fans who (like me) love them for it.

ACKNOWLEDGMENTS: Thanks to Bill Staines for the use of a portion of "Louisiana Storm" and to K. W. Todd for "The Oregon Trail." All other songs were authored by trad. or anon. or me.

A WORD FROM A WAYFARING STRANGER
▲▲▲

A good storyteller, I have learned, does not make the whole entire story center around herself, as if she was the most important thing *about* the story. I've seen many a fine songwriter who once wrote and sang wonderfully understanding songs about the lives of ordinary people fall flat on his ass when he gets a little famous, gets away from regular folks, and pretty soon all he's able to write are songs about how god-awful it is to be on the road and how he is so a-lo-ow-ow-ow-ow-ow-own.

So I want to make it clear that though I'm in it and I have a little part of it, this story is not about me. It's about me telling about what happened when certain parties decided to deprive the world and these United States of America in particular of what is broadly, inaccurately, and disputedly called folk music.

About these certain parties; lawyers would probably call them the parties of the first part, but I call them devils. For one thing, they are, as you will see in this story and the other two parts of it that follow, mighty powerful and also mighty evil. That fits devils down to the ground. More than that, they're mysterious and magical and we—my friends and I—only learned what happened on their end in little bitty pieces here and there most of the time and had to fit it all together as we went along. Because to begin with, I would say the common attitude among us was that we all were inclined to like magic without exactly believing in it, which was different from later when we were forced to believe in it but didn't like it much at all.

It wasn't your little Tinkerbell fairies or nice old bats with magic wands, none of that stuff. Not even wise magicians like Merlin or witches like that woman with the twitchy nose who used to be on television. So though I could tell you they were goblins or gremlins or all-powerful wicked wizards, I think I'll just call 'em what my grandma from back in the Carolina mountains would have called them: devils. Not necessarily the hellfire-and-brimstone kind that get you if you don't believe a certain way. Buddhists have devils same as Christians, same as a lot of folks. Most everyone has something like that. So just say these were basic, generic, all-around-ornery devils who were opposed to anybody having any kind of belief or good feelings in themselves that helped them get by. That was why they hated the music so, you see. That was why they set out to destroy it.

And that is why it's been up to me, who never has been able to carry a tune in a bucket, to go before the others, back into where just about all the music has been pulled out by the roots. My job is to tell how it happened, to fertilize the soil, to make the people ready for when the songs come back, fresh cuttings transplanted from the old soil where my friends and I have spent these last harrowing years harvesting the songs from their own history, trying to save them from the oblivion where the devils sent so many of our own songs.

I don't go on the radio or TV talk shows, now that I'm home, or anywhere where the devils can find me and keep me from talking to people. I use my gift of gab I got from bartending and the performance training I got from dancing plus what I learned from hanging around all those musicians lately, and I travel around among the ordinary people, the kids, the bums, the working folks—anyone who is bored or lonely enough to have time to listen. I turn myself into someone else, someone as fascinating as a snake charmer, someone who is a worthy enemy of all those devils, and I make myself heard.

What follows, written down, is the important part of what's been happening since I've been back, staying with a friend and with an audience as long as it seems safe, then moving on to carry the story farther, to break just a little more ground. It's not in my voice because mostly it's not about me except as I'm reflected in the eyes of other people. It's about them, what they say, what they do, what can be guessed from the things that happen and from the lifting of an eyebrow or a quirk of a mouth. And of course it's about the songs, which, when you hear them, speak for themselves.

So think of me, and of yourself, as if we were birds on a branch or flies buzzing in the air around that first schoolyard, where a funny old woman is talking to a bunch of kids, telling them about something that happened a few years before.

CHAPTER I

▲▲▲

"One time all the devils in the world had a meeting to decide what it was they could do to make folks even more miserable than they already were.

"First thing happened was the Chairdevil stood up and allowed as how they all ought to be congratulated for doing such a fine job so far." The woman paused to heighten suspense while the children who were huddled around her in the noisy schoolyard strained so that they wouldn't miss anything she might say next.

The children were fascinated by the woman, not only because of what she said, but because of how she said it. When she talked, she moved her face more than people usually did and she moved her body too, so that she seemed to *be* the Chairdevil calling a meeting to order. This was the second story—she'd told another, a short one, at morning recess, a silly one about animals, just to whet their appetites. The boy had been impressed then too by the way she spoke different voices with each character, seeming to turn into a new person as she spoke in each new voice. She never left out important words, even if they weren't suitable for children, and somehow, all of this combined to make her words come as alive in his mind as anything he had seen on TV. She moved more than he would have thought possible for such a small person, and all without shifting from her sheltered position in the middle of the group.

And she was funny-looking. Oh, you could tell she had once been pretty enough to be a corporate executive herself, but she'd let lines get in her face, though her eyes were still snapping bright and her cheeks red as apples after the grocer sprayed them with a hose. Her legs were still fine and shapely, the boy noticed that too, right off, but her waist was too thick. And her hair was a mop of gray—not white, not silver, not violet or blond, but plain old elderly gray—curls. Nor was her voice quite what he was used to. When she wasn't pretending to be someone else, it had a snap and a twang and sometimes a sugary drawl. She didn't call them children, she called them kids, and instead of trying to learn their names, she carelessly addressed them all as hon or darlin' or kiddo. His mom would have a fit if she knew he was listening to someone like that. Everybody knew better than to talk like that these days. You learned better just listening to the educational shows on your TV-PC. This crazy old woman might as well have been a spaceperson for all the similarity she bore to the women even his grandmother knew. He couldn't *wait* to hear what she was going to say next.

" 'We've made great strides in this century, fellow devils,' the Chairdevil said. 'Why, our nuclear bomb, nuclear reactors, and all our other nuclear knickknacks by themselves can not only blow up the world and melt down into mass catastrophe but can make those greedy, hysterical suckers out there square off against each other like nothing has since the apple Our Founder sold First Couple.' A round of polite applause greeted this, but it was pretty much old stuff. The Chairdevil was a fairly conservative fellow in his way, and liked to stick with the tried and true.

"After a bit he waved his hands for the others to stop clapping and continued, 'And for those who have their heads too stuck in the mud to notice a little thing like world destruction, some of you enterprising souls have added teensy little wars in miserable little places. I'd mention them individually, but I can't keep track of them myself. Just let me say that just because the war you promote isn't a big budget job between major powers doesn't mean it isn't important. The little stuff adds up and I want you to know it is by no *means* overlooked.' The Doom and Destruction Devil and the Stupidity and Ignorance Devil exchanged knowing glances and settled back with sighs full of long-suffering and neglect. The Chairdevil theoretically did know that the cumulative effect of their very successful efforts to see hunger and hostility clamp down on one regime in one little country after another regime in another little country made all the difference—*all* the difference—in the world, but the Chairdevil just naturally went for the flamboyant. Simple things like astronomical death tolls didn't impress him. He liked things to go boom. In some ways, he was surprisingly democratic. He enjoyed seeing great civilizations crumbling, the rich and privileged, the sheltered and pampered, dying just as miserably as poor folks. It was one of his more endearingly infuriating characteristics.

"He departed from his notes then, laying them down and saying in a casual, off-the-cuff way, 'And I really like what y'all have been doing with the terrorism thing too. Very clever. Very tricky. Pick off the civilians. Pick off the so-called innocents. Why should they be left out? Keep reminding our minions that it's up to us to set the example. If our people commit one little suggestive atrocity, our lead will be followed and amplified on tenfold.' He looked kind of humble and grateful after that and everyone else tried to look the same way.

" 'On the domestic front, I think the pestilence department should be congratulated on all those diseases that have made it more dangerous than ever for the livestock out there to reach out and touch anyone. I like the sanctimonious thing S&I has been promoting to go with it too.' The Stupidity and Ignorance Devil held up both huge hands and made them shake each other in the air like a prize fighter. Now *he* was one that always got a lot of pleasure out of the little things. 'And by the way, S&I should continue to be congratulated for inspiring all those enterprising people out there who even when there are no nearby minority groups of any sort for them to hate never forget to hate them anyway on general principle and continue to foster generations of hatred by never failing to beat their kids, their parents, and each other with enthusiastic ferocity.'

"All the other devils certainly agreed that they could drink to something like that and they clapped some more and said 'Bravo' and 'Hear hear' and so on, making an awful racket until the Chairdevil shushed them again.

" 'It has come to my notice, however,' he continued,

'that while we're doin' just dandy in the department of adding little complications to people's lives, we have been remiss in the taking-things-away department.'

"Well, the devil in charge of the root of all evil got himself in an uproar over that and he stood up on his high horse and told the Chairdevil that he objected, because hadn't he caused recessions, depressions, inflations, and a doozy of a stock crash that sent the world's money supply on a roller-coaster ride and made several prime ministers and premiers, one or two presidents, and a couple of kings wonder who they couldn't start a measly little war with, just to raise steel and oil prices a mite and get rid of more of the excess population?

"But the Chairdevil waved him down and said, 'Now, Root, you know that's not at all what I mean. Anyone can see you have been doing a fine job and it would take a real nincompoop not to be so plain depressed about the way things are going in the world that they eliminate themselves. But the fact of the matter is, there *are* a lot of nincompoops in the world. And you know what nincompoops do when we do all this stuff we do so well?'

"The other devils had several suggestions but the head devil just kept shakin' his head. 'What do they do if they work a hard dirty job with low pay, plenty of danger, something like mining or herding cattle or working in cotton mills or farming? What do the damned fools do to keep going?'

" 'Get drunk? Take drugs?' asked one devil.

" 'That too, but what else?' the Chairdevil asked.

"After a long stupefied silence, he told them.

" 'They sing,' the Chairdevil said. 'Remember we're talking nincompoops here. How about parents kept up all night by a puling squawling shitting peeing slobbery useless baby? What do they do when the kid's howling wakes them up again?'

" 'Beat it to death?' one of the devils asked.

" 'Beat each other to death?' Root asked.

" 'No, the biggest one beats the smallest one to death unless the smallest one has a butcher knife or a gun,' a colleague told him.

" 'I know!' the youngest devil said. 'The big one beats the little one to death and *then* beats the baby to death.'

"The Chairdevil shook his head sadly. 'No such luck. They sing.'

" *'Sing?'* the devil committee cried all together as if they'd stuck each other with pitchforks.

" 'Ever hear of lullabies?' asked the Chairdevil. 'It's been the same every time we've got them right where we want them. Put them on death row for stabbing some uppity truelove who isn't so true after all and they sing. Shanghai them out to sea and they sing. Put them on a chain gang busting rocks and they sing. Send them off to war and one side sings one kinda songs, the other side sings another, and all the blasted pacifists sing another, and a lot of the time they even all use the same tune! We haven't come up with a single scenario yet, no matter how miserable, unfair, heart- or backbreaking that some damn fool doesn't make up a song about it or remember an old one that hasn't even ever been played on the radio.'

" 'That's disgusting,' said a she-devil with a delicate shudder.

" 'That's insulting,' said another.

" 'Perverted, I'd call it,' the one sitting next to him said.

" 'Wait up a minute, something's not right here,' said another one finally. This one was the one in charge of drink and drugs and general debauchery. 'I get down there quite a bit, and lately I can't say I've noticed anything like what you're talking about. Mostly people don't sing much anymore. It's a specialty, like everything else. People sing on the radio, and in concerts, and on television, and sometimes at the movies, but they don't sing at work unless their work is singing.'

" 'Exactly,' said the Chairdevil. 'That's exactly what they do. If they were all still singing the way everybody used to, do you think we'd be able to have ourselves a meeting like this? Or make ourselves not only nuclear bombs so that they can blow each other up but reactors so they can get blown up right there in their own neighborhoods? All our really good stuff has come up since they gave up singing on their own and started hiring somebody else to do it for them. But the point is, the damn fools still haven't pushed the button, nobody big has invaded, raped, and pillaged anybody else big for a long time now.'

"Now all the devils exchanged knowing looks. They knew he had finally gotten at what was really bothering him. The shows the musicians gave were getting in the way of the really big show he was always longing to see.

"He went on. 'Those songs aren't as strong as they used to be—fortunately, people have progressed nowadays to the point where they'd much rather work for a company that dumps crap into a river than work for free to clean it up. Practical people know that it is more realistic to have their foot on somebody else's neck than to lend a hand, which would probably be bitten by other, equally practical and realistic people.

" 'But that's beside the point. Even though those songs don't get sung as often and by as many as used to sing them, the ones we've had to put up with for all these millennia are still polluting our atmosphere, destroying the ambience we work so hard to create. Furthermore, these hired singers are making up new songs all the time. Despite the example Our Boys made of Victor Jarra in Chile and of Sam Hawthorne and his ilk during the McCarthy era, more and more misguided fools want to sing that wretched kind of song than are able to make a living at it. They have to go. The songs have to go.'

" 'Just a minute, Chairdevil,' said the Debauchery Devil. 'Some of those singers are my best people.'

" 'Fine. Then they'll be reunited with you real soon.'

"And the devils all took a vote and everybody but the Debauchery Devil raised their hands and then finally the Debauchery Devil's hand went up too."

▲▲▲

"What happened then?" asked the boy cautiously.

Though what the woman had been saying was funny, she didn't look or sound funny now. Her eyes had a far-off expression, like his mother's when she was thinking about flying to the coast for a merger. Her voice didn't sound sweet anymore and as much as he'd mistrusted that, he preferred it to the one she was using. It made him think of something baked so hard it got little cracks all over it, like Oklahoma on the Geographic Special.

"Well," she said, taking a deep breath and looking away from them for a moment to look at her hands. Her hands were small, wrinkled around the knuckles, veined on the backs, and still looked as if they could make kites, cut out paper dolls, or pour drinks, which was what they'd been doing most of their life, though the boy had no way of knowing that.

▲▲▲

"Well, the devils wanted to dive right in and start after the singers of those songs but the Chairdevil held up his hand for silence.

" 'Can't do it,' he told them.

" 'Why not?' they wanted to know.

" ''Cause it won't work, not that way. Didn't I just tell you what happens when we attack them directly? You have to understand that these are not reasonable people we're dealing with here. They're as crazy about martyrs as your average religious fanatic. Attacking them directly only encourages them. Besides, the songs protect them.'

" 'You mean there's spells in the songs?' S&I asked.

" 'Hell, yes, there's spells in them,' the Chairdevil hollered back, temporarily blowing the cool-and-in-control impression he was trying to create. The Stupidity and Ignorance Devil had that effect on everybody sometimes. 'What do you think I've been telling you? Why do you think they're so dangerous? They are spells, charms, and a do-gooder conspiracy so old—well, not as old as we are, but old enough—so old that hardly any of the singers know what they're about anymore. Not all of them are important, of course. But all of these people seem to sing at least some of the dangerous ones along with the others. Naturally, the singers we most urgently need to eliminate are the ones that know the most powerful songs, which will free us to pick off the others at our leisure. But those who know the spelled ones are difficult for us to cope with, personally. So we'll have to be careful about this and use minions. Our best people.'

" 'Demons?' one asked.

" 'Terrorists?' asked another.

" 'I got it! Generals!' said another. 'Or is it mass murderers or banshees or ghouls we need here? Monsters maybe.'

" 'Shoot,' said the Chairdevil. 'We'll need all of that kind of thing before we're done. And worse.' "

▲▲▲

"Worse?" the little boy interrupted the story to ask. "What could be worse than mass murderers and monsters?"

"And demons," his sister reminded him.

The storyteller lowered her voice and leaned forward as she told him. "Why, they called out the worst forces all their hells had to offer, honey: bureaucrats. Bureaucrats and politicians."

And with that the recess bell rang and the woman smoothed her short skirt around her fine legs with her old hands and left them to go to class.

▲▲▲

She was back the next day though, in the same place, the place the boy's eyes had gone to as soon as the teacher let them out the door. It was sort of in the shadows. She was so small she could easily be mistaken for one of the children from a distance. They hunkered around her as if they were playing marbles. It was nice to have an adult, even a small, old, strange one, talk to them. The mother of the boy and girl didn't have much time anymore and the housekeeper only spoke Cambodian. Their father had left a long time ago. Some of the other children wished their fathers had left too. They came to school sleepless from listening to fights all night or with bruises peeking out from under their sleeves or on their stomachs when their shirts rode up during playtime.

The woman didn't wait for them to be quiet. She just started right in and they had to shut up if they wanted to hear the story.

She took up exactly where she left off. "Since the devils

decided to use such a fearsome sort of army as bureaucrats and politicians, they thought it would be best to start trouble in one area and then gradually expand it until songs were gone all over the world. They decided to start with these here United States of America and with Canada, settin' up trouble between the two of them, which was not all that hard to do."

Jennifer Thomsen raised her hand. "What about Mexico? Mexico is on our other border," Jennifer said. She was just showing off for the woman how good she was in geography.

"That's a real good question, honey. But you're a little smarter than those devils were. Those devils figured since nobody sung songs in English down there in Mexico, they could deal with Mexican singers and Central and South American singers later. Besides, the Latin American devils had a lot going on already and were wiping out singers right and left. What with all the coups and revolutions down there, everybody with any brains whatsoever, including singers, tended to get wiped out just for the fun of it. But I'm glad you brought that up, because I'm going to start by telling you a story that takes place around the Mexican border. It's about a cowboy. You kids like cowboy stories?"

They said they did, though the boy wasn't really sure what a cowboy was. Maybe it was like the picture in the old book of the Minotaur. A cow on the top and a boy on the bottom. Maybe he'd seen one on PBS sometime, on a special about zoological curiosities, but right now he was indignant. He had been promised something else. "You said you'd tell us about the bureaucrats and politicians."

"And businesspersons," his sister, who wanted to be just like her mother when she grew up, prompted eagerly. "Oh, please, I want there to be businesspersons making shrewd deals and finding wonderful tax loopholes and all . . ."

The woman chuckled. Times had changed some since she'd started this line of work. But if she was going to accomplish her mission, she couldn't start in preaching right away about what she thought her audience needed to hear. She needed to please them first, tie in their interests with what she knew was good for 'em. "Okay, sis, you got *it. Plenty of heroic businesspersons—though I'm warning you, this is a real story and they don't always win—"*

The girl nodded gravely and the other children wriggled with anticipation. If the good guys didn't always win that just added to the excitement.

"Don't leave out the bureaucrats," the boy reminded her.

"No sweat, buster. Cowboys and bureaucrats, politicians and businesspersons it is. Now, I want you to remember that devils are a lot older than you or even me, and they carry grudges a long, long time. The reason the head devil knew so much about using politicians to get at the songs was he'd tried it once before, when he used a tin-eared politician to invoke an evil spell upon the land called a blacklist. He destroyed many singers then, turning them one against the other for reasons that had nothing to do with music, silencing some forever, causing some to all but die of despair. Until only a very few, including the great Sam Hawthorne, who you'll hear about a little later, were able to withstand his power."

"Wait," said the boy. "If this blacklist was an evil spell, how could that Hawthorne guy have beat it? Was he a devil too?"

"Depends on who was telling it, kiddo. But no, that wasn't why. Hawthorne was young and strong then and very smart and very dedicated. And then of course there was his magic banjo, but I'm not going to say another word about that right now. Bureaucrats and businesspersons you wanted and bureaucrats and businesspersons is what you're gonna get."

CHAPTER II

▲▲▲

The President was greatly troubled and he called his advisors to join him at his ranch for barbecue so they could talk things over. "Boys," he said, "oh, and ladies too," because the President, who didn't really think a lady's place was in the cabinet unless that was where she kept the dishes, sometimes forgot he had a few yes-women along with his yes-men, "despite our valiant efforts, this country still seems to be going to the dogs. Rampant socialism and liberalism still flourish within our boundaries. In spite of what I tell them is good for them, people keep whining about the environment and socialized medicine. They cry because there's not enough money to go around but have repeatedly backed our enemies in Congress in thwarting our efforts to start a nice long profitable war that will let us annex lucrative mineral rights in a few two-bit countries that are going to the Reds anyway. Damned cowards are afraid of the bomb. As if the Reds had the guts to use it."

"No way, Bruce," said Secretary of Defense General Mortimor Boron. "Look, boss, you shouldn't get yourself in a sweat trying to please those civilians. They wanted a space program too and when we gave them one that would not only get our people out there but give them a little firepower, look how people acted."

"I know, Mort, I know, but we have to at least keep up appearances."

"Exactly," said another voice from the hot tub. "That's why we picked you, Bruce. Who better than a former model to keep up appearances? And you mustn't be so discouraged. You've done a very good job. We've learned the power of communication these days and with your help most of the people can be convinced that we know what's best for them. Even the media has stopped being so damned critical. At least the ones who don't want trouble with the FCC or the IRS."

The President smiled his engaging, sincere grin. "Well, the people did want to see Big Business taxed. I thought threatening to make all cameras and recorders count as taxable recreational equipment instead of business expenses would bring the networks around and it did. Your average journalist may be an egotistical jerk, but the people who are really in charge are reasonable, responsible citizens."

"As I say, good work," said the man in the hot tub. "But there is one troublesome area, mediawise, that we still need strong measures to cope with. There is a certain kind of musician in this country who stirs up trouble, criticizes our best efforts, spreads liberal commie ideas, leads the opposition with sarcastic songs that lead to slogans and buttons and picket lines. These people have been free to cross borders from one country to another, a lot of them coming through Canada, bringing foreign doctrine and criticism of U.S. foreign policy, industry, you name it, with them. Our people pay to have their government insulted."

"We've suspected as much for some time, haven't we, Sam?" the President asked the head of the CIA, who nodded and watched everyone through his sunglasses.

"We suspect that may be one way drugs are coming into this country," said Sam, who strongly resented anyone interfering with a CIA monopoly.

"Right. Well, not only do these foreign nationals enter our country and spread their poison, but there are people born and raised in these United States, many of whom do not pay their fair share of taxes, if you ask me, who travel freely from city to city stirring up trouble and discontent."

"Who are these low-life bastards?" the head of the FBI growled over his cigar, which drew frowns from the Surgeon General.

"They're your so-called folksingers, Mr. President. Though, of course, a lot of the crap they spread isn't even folk music. They just make it up whenever they have a new party line."

"Why aren't these degenerates in prison?" the President demanded.

"They enjoy it too much," said the General. "Why, remember when they raised so much hell that they lost us the Vietnam War, back in the sixties? Hell, a criminal record was as important as a guitar back then."

The First Lady cleared her throat, "In all fairness, dear, I have heard some very persuasive antidrug songs from these people."

The FBI man shook his head, "No good, ma'am. The drug problem originally started with these people. Why, if white folksingers hadn't glamorized nigger—excuse me, ma'am, black—"

"I think we can all speak freely here, Ed," the President said.

"Black junkie blues, schoolchildren would not today be endangered."

Not from the competition anyway, the CIA man thought. They'd be supporting America instead, just like they were buying bonds.

"What do you suggest, Nick?" the President asked the man in the tub.

"Actually, Bruce, I suggest you leave it to me. I'll put together a task force and I think I can safely promise we'll keep these people out of your way from now on so you can continue with your important work."

"Fair enough," the President said.

▲▲▲

Julianne and George Martin had come to the end of their road—at least for two weeks. They pulled their van into a parking place behind the Trendy's Pizza Parlor in Odessa, Kansas, and climbed out. Julianne ran a comb through her tumbled blond hair and hauled fifteen pounds of hammered dulcimer out of the back of the van so she could get at the microphone stands. George picked up the PA and an amplifier. She twitched a finger loose from her load and pried the screen door open a crack, inserted a toe to widen the crack, and bumped the door back with her hip. A man wearing a bowling shirt and carrying a double pepperoni pizza almost ran George down as he hauled the amplifier through the door.

Julianne set down her load and wiped the sweat off her face with her forearm.

"You think this place is wired for electricity?" George asked.

"This is the back way, silly. Come on, let's find the manager." They threaded their way through a short hall with worn linoleum and piles of boxes, cans of tomato paste, into a room even hotter than the outdoors. A ceiling fan kept the flies circulating nicely.

George looked at the Formica counters and tables, the metal chairs, and the plastic hanging lamps with Trendy's written in red plastic across the shades. "What kind of gig is this anyhow?" he complained. He was not at his best at the end of two-day drives. He'd developed a pain in his right shoulder and had a headache from the sun.

Juli shrugged. "It's the kind of gig that's between Denver and Tulsa is all I know. Lettie Chaves said Mark Mosby made a hundred in tips here besides the fifty they're paying. *And* there's a trailer with a bed and free beer and pizza."

"We don't drink beer," George reminded her.

"That's not their fault," she said. Julianne was annoyingly fair sometimes. "It'll be a place to spend the night, a new area, and gas money. Look, I'm perfectly willing for you to do the booking but—"

"Okay, okay. I give. It's the Carnegie Hall of western Kansas. I think that's our man over there. The one in the Trendy's tractor cap." George doubted they would do as well as Mark Mosby, though Julianne's sparkle sometimes brought out generosity in people who looked as if they didn't have an ounce of energy or a penny's worth of fun in them: people who looked like he felt now.

Tractor Cap answered Julianne's smile with a grunt. "You the Martins?" he asked.

"That's right," she said.

"I'm sorry. I tried to phone but I couldn't reach you. We can't use you after all."

"What?" George asked.

Julianne said, "But why not? I'm sure if you put up the pictures we sent you in our promo packet you'd increase your business tonight and—"

"I put those pictures up okay, and I had to take them all down again. They're back in my office if you want them. That guy saw them and that's why we decided not to have music."

"I don't understand," Julianne said. "What guy?"

"The man from SWALLOW. You know the—"

"We know," Julianne said wearily, sinking into a chair and resting her clenched fists between her knees. "Good old SWALLOW—the Songwriters and Arrangers' Legal Licensing Organization Worldwide."

"That's right. They said they license all the songs sung all over the world and if we hire live musicians, they'll be singing songs whose writers or arrangers are protected by SWALLOW so we have to join up with their licensing service to be entitled to have their songs sung here. Then he told me how much the fee is. Do you *know* how much he wanted?"

Julianne and George nodded grimly. "We know," George said.

The Trendy's manager shrugged. "Well, I'm sorry but our profit margin is too narrow for that."

"Ours isn't really terrific either," George said, "and we just drove a hundred miles out of our way to play here."

"I'm sorry about that, Mr. Martin. And I'll be glad to give you supper to pay for your time. People did enjoy that fellow we had here last month. But we just can't afford trouble. That fellow said if you played here and we didn't pay, he'd sic the organization's L.A. lawyers on us. It's hard enough keeping in business. You know how it is."

"Yeah, sure," George said, but Julianne, who wanted to salvage something out of the situation, jumped in, "We understand, sir. And as you can tell, we're familiar with this particular problem. But the fact is, we don't do any material that SWALLOW represents. Ours is all either in the public domain or original stuff we've written ourselves and—"

He shook his head. "I brought that up and the guy said that maybe that was okay when the organizations were just the two that used to exist for this country, but since licensing has gone international it takes in a lot more territory. He said for one thing, if we even want to have a jukebox in the place, we can't have anyone doing original stuff not licensed by SWALLOW, and that even with traditional songs, lots of people use arrangements made up by SWALLOW artists. And I guess, from what you folks say, you aren't licensed by SWALLOW, huh?"

George and Juli shook their heads.

"Like you say," George told him. "The fees are very high. Also, they won't take everybody. If they don't like a song, they won't license it."

"Is that so? Well, I'm sorry about you going out of your way like this, folks, but I can't risk losing my franchise. So how about that free pizza? You like pepperoni? That's the special tonight."

It was okay, once the Martins, who were both vegetarians, picked off the pepperoni. George was so mad he drove all the way to Tulsa that night after all. The van overheated two miles from their friend Barry Curtis's house and they had to call Barry at three A.M. to come out with his pickup and get them and the instruments while AAA towed the van into the nearest service station.

Barry and his wife Molly were both at work by the time Julianne woke the next afternoon. She pulled on a T-shirt and padded into the kitchen, trying to remember where the Curtises kept the coffee. Her name jumped out at her from a stick-it note on the refrigerator door.

"Juli and George. Call Poor Woody's," and listed the number. Juli had a bad feeling about that message. What had happened to them in Odessa had happened to friends of theirs in other places. SWALLOW was scaring a lot of potential small gigs out of hiring live music.

▲▲▲

Sure enough, three hours later the manager of Poor Woody's hung up in Juli's ear. George went back to bed, and pulled the pillow over his face. Barry patted Juli's shoulder. "Sorry, Jule. Maybe something will turn up."

"It was a three-week gig, Barry. We needed that money."

"Why don't you call Lettie and see if she and Mic have heard of anybody who's hiring hereabouts?"

"Someone SWALLOW hasn't scared off first?"

"Worth a try. Anyway, if you tell Lettie what's happened to you, by the time she finishes saying what she'd like to do to the bastards, you'll start feeling sorry for them."

Her mouth tightened in what he had to take for a smile. "Thanks, Barry. We'll pay you back for the call as soon as we get work."

"No problem. We get to hear you play for free often enough," Barry said, and settled into a threadbare platform rocker with a new fantasy novel and a scruffy gray cat on his lap.

Julianne dialed the Chaveses' number, expecting to hear Lettie or Mic answer by the third ring. Instead, the answering machine clicked on. "If you have an urgent message for Lettie or Mic, dial 206-555-4444."

She dialed. A woman answered. "Hi," Juli said. "Is Lettie Chaves there?"

"No, sugar, I'm sorry. Lettie and Mic are up to Vancouver pickin' up a friend. I'm Lettie's mama, can I help you?"

"Mrs.—"

"Call me Gussie, sugar, everybody does."

"Okay, Gussie. I'm Julianne Martin. Just tell Lettie and Mic George and I are at the Curtises in Tulsa and sure would like to hear from her."

"Julianne Martin? Why, I'm so pleased to talk to you, hon. Lettie and Mic are always goin' on about you and George. How you doin'?"

"Oh, fine," she said and then, prodded by the interest and warmth in the woman's voice, "well, not exactly. Three weeks worth of gigs just fell through and we were hoping maybe Lettie knew of an opening someplace around here close enough we could get there on five bucks worth of gas."

"I'll have her call you back the minute she gets here. Now don't you worry. Everything'll work out. You wait and see." Trust a friend's mother to come up with platitudes.

Oh, well, at least they *had* friends, Juli reminded herself. She'd been taught by her mother, the expensive child psychologist her mother had sent her to after her father died, and her guru to count her blessings so, dutifully, she did. She lit the gas jet on Barry's old stove, made herself a cup of chamomile tea, carried it with her to the living room where she scissored herself onto the floor. She did ballet stretches as she'd been doing since her dancing days, then rolled her head in circles and rotated her shoulders. Two weeks of riding across country, eating goopy truck-stop nachos and peanut butter sandwiches, drinking too much caffeine to stay awake when they couldn't stop for the night due to the highway regulations of one state or another. George had the right idea going back to bed.

Her forehead throbbed and she knew that pretty soon a tight band would close around her scalp and she'd have one of her headaches again. But then nobody ever said it was easy.

Barry read on, totally absorbed, but the cat uncurled from his lap, stretched one paw at a time, and hopped down in front of Juli, its calm little face upturned, waiting for her to make a lap. She obediently did so, hoisted it onto her thighs, and petted its lumpy fur. Poor thing was allergic to fleas, she remembered Molly explaining. Its name was Pyewacket, or was it Helva, or was that Lettie's cat? No, Lettie's cat was Tan, Satanna, or one of them. It was hard to keep straight all of their friends' cats and dogs, there were so many of them. People like the Curtises and the Chaveses were always taking in strays, cats, dogs, musicians.

First they'd come to the club and grin all through your set, clap hard, and chat a little at breaks. They might be the only ones all night to leave any kind of a tip, though it was always only a dollar or so, but they came back every night of a gig. Long about the third night they'd ask what the accommodations were and after that there was a bed, a bath, a stove, and foster animals instead of a sleeping bag on the floor of the van and a spit bath in the john at whatever restaurant or bar they were playing that night.

Of course, some of the people who were attracted to musicians were kind of weird—wanting to nose into their private lives and live vicariously what seemed to be a more glamorous life-style. But the friends she and George had made and kept weren't like that—they were great. Most of them, like Molly and Barry and the Chaveses, were considerate of the musicians' privacy and gave them plenty of space. George tried, for purposes of both friendship and publicity, to write a newsletter every once in a while to let people know what was happening on the road. And Juli usually loved to talk anyway, and to hear about other people's lives, about the day-in-day-out troubles and triumphs that she'd thought were so boring when she first went on the road.

One day she and George hoped to be able to afford to drive a mobile home or a bus around the country, but in the meantime they were lucky to have people like the Curtises, who were always glad to see them but who treated them as casually as if they were roommates and took little notice of their coming and going. When Barry and Molly or some of their other friends went on vacation, sometimes Juli and George got to house-sit for them, and had a place all to themselves. It was like playing house. But God, she got tired of playing house in other people's houses. Still, it just made no sense to maintain a place of your own when you were never in it.

Once upon a time, she had heard from older veteran musicians, gigs had come with room and board. But that hadn't been the case most places for a long time. So friends across the country, the Curtises and others, who worked straight jobs and had an extra room were godsends. And then there was Lettie, who had a small record distribution business for privately produced records, which she not only sold but promoted to the few folk radio shows and all the festivals she and Mic could attend, kept club lists, and wrote reviews for folk music journals. Her husband Mic was willing to drive all night so he and Lettie could attend a festival, where he introduced everyone to everyone else whether he knew them or not, was quickly on first-name terms with all of the luminaries at any given event, and was just as quick to turn them on to the music of less celebrated friends. Other friends were musicians themselves, but not on the road. Some helped friends with bookings or were willing to type newsletters. Then there were people who organized concerts and festivals, open mikes and referral lists, printed newsletters or journals—several folks she knew of were involved in that in Chicago and Lettie said her mom knew of a guy who did that kind of thing in Tacoma too.

Juli's reverie was interrupted when the door banged open and Molly Curtis jogged in, her dark brown hair escaping from its braids to cling in damp wisps to her sweating face. Her legs were bright red under her blue running shorts, her tank top soaked. She thrust a paper bag into Julianne's hand, "Here, girl. You looked like you needed this and they had your favorite flavor at the 7-Eleven." Inside were two plastic cartons of vanilla almond frozen yogurt with a couple of plastic spoons.

Juli grinned up into Molly's dripping face. "You're wonderful," she said, but her gut was in knots from exhaustion, tension, and caffeine and she knew she couldn't eat a thing.

She pulled the plastic spoons from the bag and tapped them together idly, then deliberately arranged them between the fingers of her right hand. "Hey, you know, I was working on a story to tell about magic spoons while we were on our way down here," she told Molly. "What do you think of this rhythm?"

Tapping the spoons across her left hand and clicking them against her thigh and forearm, she ticked out a rhythm. They didn't make as much noise as her metal or wooden spoons. "Well, you get the idea. It goes like this, ba da da, ba da da, ba da dad dad dad dad da, ba da da, ba da da, ba da pow *pow* POW!"

"Amazing what that girl can do with frozen yogurt," Barry observed.

Molly threw a stack of letters at her. "Here, girl, stop playing with your food and read your mail."

Juli tore open the letter from their accountant, a friend named Pete Zimmerman in Chicago. This must be the tax refund they'd been waiting for since April. But it wasn't. It was a letter. "Dear George and Julianne, Don't get upset. I'm sure we can work things out and there has been some misunderstanding. But you need to be back here by July 10 for an IRS audit. They claim you owe $30,000 in back taxes and fines from 1987 on. Unless you can show you maintain a permanent home, they're disallowing your travel expenses as business deductions. Call me ASAP and we'll work out strategy. Love, Pete."

Without a word to the Curtises, Juli threw the opened letter on top of the pile of mail, left the yogurt melting in the cartons, and strode back to the spare bedroom, where she threw herself on the bed next to George and buried her face in the pillow.

▲▲▲

Meanwhile, the Chaveses had been having a good time driving another musician friend down from Canada.

Mic drove and Lettie sat in the back seat while their guest, Hy MacDonald, regaled them with bawdy stories of his travels from Scotland through Australia and New Zealand, and his previous successful tours in the U.S. Hy did not look like a man who wrote and sang romantic, mythic ballads full of Celtic folklore and imagery that made sensible young women with good careers in banking want to climb into his lap and light his cigarettes. Short, thin, and balding with limp sandy hair covering only the back two thirds of his scalp and his front teeth yellowed from nicotine, he looked more like a particularly nervous banker himself, Lettie decided. But she and her husband were the last ones to judge by appearances.

Mic looked more like a Scottish folksinger than Hy did. With his first name and his freckled face and red hair, he was often mistaken for a kid of Irish or Scottish lineage whose mother had married a Mexican. In fact, the Chaves name, which dated in Texas from before the Alamo, was pure European Spanish and Mic, whose full name was Miguel Alejandro, was the heir to generations of Texas's aristocratic Spanish heritage—no money, but plenty of pedigree. But now he talked as rapidly and enthusiastically as the most verbose Celt, swapping Hy yarn for yarn.

Lettie was the shy, seemingly aloof, intense one of the pair, the more compulsively creative. And who knew where she'd gotten *that* from? Well, her mom had been a dancer when she was younger. Lettie had seen the pictures. But ever since she could remember, Gus had worked as a barmaid. At least she was finally out of the oil fields, able to indulge her lifelong ambition to get the hell out of West Texas now that her little girl was secure with Mic. She'd moved her cats and her shoe collection to a little rental house in Tacoma and tended bar across the street from the place where Craig Lee's Triumph Music cooperative held open mikes. The pickers all came in to the bar to jam after the open mike shut down, and to be spoiled by Gussie. Even the Seattle city slickers who thought Texans were all oil-rig bums and hicks had thawed to Gussie's West Texas drawl and down-home warmth. And Gussie had adopted Washington and especially the musicians as matter-of-factly as she took in stray cats.

Which was how Lettie and Mic got acquainted with Craig and had gotten drafted as "roadies" for Hy to bring him across the border for the Triumph Concert that would kick off his cross-country tour.

"And then there was Roger in this foolish puce spandex jogging suit—" Hy was saying as they drew up to the customs window. It was late, so the lines weren't too bad, but they'd already swapped three stories and Hy had sung them a piece of his new song while they waited.

"Where are you going?" the customs man asked.

"Tacoma," Mic said.

"Where you coming from?"

"Vancouver."

"Place of residence?"

"Amarillo, Texas, for us," Mic said, indicating Lettie with a wag of his fingers.

"Aberdeen, Scotland," Hy said, and handed over his passport for inspection.

"Your business in Tacoma?"

"We're visiting my wife's mom," Mic said. "And we're taking this gentleman to a concert he's performing."

The customs man ran his flashlight across Hy's passport and peered at it more closely, then flashed the beam inside the car, where it picked out the guitars sitting in under the hatchback. "Will you pull in over there by that white line, sir, and you and your passengers get out of the vehicle and enter this building through that door?"

"Yes, sir," Mic said, and as he pulled away, he rolled his eyes at Lettie in the rearview mirror. Oh, well, they'd expected a little hassle since Hy was neither American nor Canadian. They were unprepared, however, when a uniformed man with a lug wrench and crowbar demanded the keys to the car and began popping hubcaps.

"Had some problems tonight, have you?" Mic asked the customs official behind the desk casually.

The man ignored the question. "Which of you is Hyslop MacDonald?"

"That would be me," Hy said.

"We'll need to retain your passport for a while, sir. Meanwhile, if you and the other gentleman would step into that cubicle and remove your clothing and hand it out. And you, ma'am, if you'll use that other cubicle and do the same."

"What's the problem, officer?" Mic asked, although he doubted that it would do any good and would probably make the customs people nastier.

"The problem, sir, is that you're attempting to assist a known political subversive and probable drug trafficker into the United States."

Mic and Lettie looked at Hy, who shrugged. "Maybe they think I'm Irish."

CHAPTER III

▲▲▲

Even the worst of luck is bound to change sometime. In a later batch of mail George unearthed the flier from Josh Grisholm scheduling an upcoming appearance in Tulsa. The Martins had met Grisholm at the Dumas Folk Festival, introduced, as usual, by Mic Chavez. Josh was not only a great writer of funny topical songs and the best-known living player of plucked autoharp, but he had made money at folk music since the pop folk groups started playing his songs in the sixties. He had a good agent, a small record company, and a national reputation. Maybe what he didn't have yet was an opening act. It was worth a try. Juli had been corresponding with him since that first meeting, and his letters, though short and infrequent, were witty and warm. A letter wouldn't work at this point however, so Juli called his agent, who gave her Grisholm's number at his present gig.

Josh was glad to hear from her and even gladder that the two of them were in Tulsa. "God, Juli, it would be terrific if you and George could stick around long enough to open for me," Josh said. "Give me a chance to talk to Dave Meeker, the guy who's producing this concert. When he called the other day, he asked if I minded having a rockabilly band open for me."

Juli smiled into the phone, appreciating the way Josh made it sound as if *they* were doing *him* a favor.

George had been wandering around the Curtises' house making peanut butter sandwiches and catching up with the new cartoons taped to the refrigerator since the last time he was there while Juli talked on the phone. The conversation was brief. He heard the plastic clatter as she recradled the phone. "No dice, huh?"

"No problem's more like it," she said, grinning with the sunniness that was more customary to her than the gloom of the last few days. "Three hundred dollars *and* a meal for a forty-five-minute set. Not too bad."

The prospect of playing the concert worked like a tonic. They rehearsed feverishly in the intervening time. The afternoon of the show, George wore his blue mattress-ticking shirt with the white stand-up collar, Sears jeans, and a pair of red suspenders. Juli shook the wrinkles out of a calico skirt and used it for a petticoat under a front-buttoned blue dirndl, pressed a white cotton blouse embroidered with white thread birds, and belted them together with a striped sash her sister had sent from Bahrain.

They spent the afternoon pretuning the instruments. A few days before they'd changed all the strings on the guitars to give them time to mellow out before the concert.

The concert was scheduled for eight-thirty. Before the show, they joined Josh for a drink in his hotel room. The room was standard Holiday Inn, but the space between the bed and the wall was filled with two guitar cases, four autoharp cases (Josh always kept an extra instrument tuned in case he broke a string or needed to change to another key quickly, as he often did with the autoharps), and a smallish suitcase. The little table held toothbrush glasses, an ice bucket, a can of Diet 7-Up and a can of Diet Pepsi and a couple of bottles of booze.

Josh greeted them with a brief hug and a perfunctory buss on the cheek for Juli. "Did you bring your instruments up with you?" he asked, pushing back a receding mane of wiry salt-and-pepper hair with both hands.

"They're down in the van," George said.

"Sometimes I wish I still drove to most of my gigs. The airlines keep thinking up new ways to lose and damage instruments all the time. Last time they broke that special hammered dulcimer I had made—the one with the bass notes? It's like playing Russian roulette every time I get on the plane—"

"And that's not even counting what might happen to the passengers," George said. "Like the crash coming back from Piedmont carrying Lila Whittaker, Karen Parsons, and Jed Sikorsky."

"Let's not think about that just before the show,

okay?" Josh said with a pained tightening of his jaw. He poured drinks for all of them in the toothbrush glasses and when he turned back to them he seemed a little less tense. "So tell me, how's it going with you?"

George muttered something noncommittal but Juli plunged in, telling Josh about the sabotage of their schedule by the SWALLOW agents. It was good to get it all out of her system and she ignored the drink as she paced around the room, hands flying, while she told Josh the whole frustrating story, sure that someone with his business acumen and experience would have valuable advice. She was brought up sharply only when George emitted a loud strangled sound that made her glance toward her audience and see the acute discomfort on George's face and the glower on Josh's.

She gave a sickly grin and sank onto the bed, "You see what I mean about having a bad time, Josh. Ain't it awful?"

Josh rose and turned his back to them again as he poured another drink. "This is a little awkward, Julianne. You realize, don't you, that all of my songs are registered with SWALLOW?"

"They are? Well, you wouldn't want them doing that kind of thing, would you?" Juli asked hopefully.

"Well, I admit they get a little high-handed once in a while. I was pretty hot when they wouldn't register that spoof I did of the CIA raiding Belize. But I sing it anyway and they haven't said anything so far. As for policing the industry, it's what I pay them for. Of course, I admit it seems a little overzealous going after small clubs, especially considering how stiff the fees are, but the distinctions are a little hard to make under the trade laws."

"But it's just not fair, I mean—" Juli began, despite the warning kick on the ankle from George.

"Well, no. And I admit, I hate the censorship side of the organization. They're pretty stiff but that's what happens when organizations get too big. But with so many video companies and music publishers being owned by international conglomerates, it gets complicated trying to cover everybody under each country's set of laws. You have to be reasonable about it. Back when the only real venues were in this country and Canada, the organizations we had to protect songs were good enough, but these days . . ."

He shook his head and sighed into his drink.

"But, Josh—think. It's censorship. Exactly what you try to cut through with your songs. You would never have stood for it back in the sixties."

He gave her a wry smile with precious little humor in it. "It's like Dylan said, sweetheart. 'The Times, They Are A-Changing.' And how. Everything is more complex now."

"I don't see why we need any of that anyway," George said.

Josh shrugged. "You've been struggling a long time, George. What if one of your songs actually threatens to make you some money? Except that where you'll make money isn't off your own little folk recording of it, but of other people doing it on video, computer networks, cable, in concerts, on the radio and network television. Big companies and big name entertainers can be pretty casual about paying royalties to a small-time songwriter. SWALLOW collects on your behalf. Also, they make sure none of your material is ever performed or published without proper attribution and they prevent your songs from being overexposed."

"Overexposed?" George asked. "You mean by having nobodies perform your songs? Having maybe people who have to play in pizza parlors mutilate your material? Well, gee, Josh, I can sure understand how you would hate to have that happen."

▲▲▲

"How dumb," the boy's sister said, interrupting the flow of words, gestures, pictures, freezing Josh in midtirade in the minds of her schoolmates. "Didn't those silly people know that it was just business? How could they expect a successful entrepreneur like Josh to sympathize with their cut-rate operation?"

"Oh, knock it off, Muffy," her brother said. "Obviously they looked upon him as a mentor. It was logical for them to expect him to advise them. Never mind her, lady. What

I want to know is, were those devils you talked about behind all the trouble?"

"Well, sure, honey. Right at that point, SWALLOW was just starting to show its hand with the little people who couldn't fight back, and the little clubs that had to close out music because they couldn't pay up. Stuff like the censorship, which later included almost anything with words a body could understand, only got worse later on. But right at this point, does anybody here see what's happening?"

"Certainly," Muffy said. "SWALLOW is very effectively separating the bulk of labor from its obvious leaders, the ones who would have the bargaining power to gain concessions that would benefit the less powerful workers. But what I don't understand is why they would want to make their prices so high and not protect everybody? Wouldn't that make them more money and then Josh could be friends with Juli and George and they wouldn't lose jobs and all that icky stuff?"

"It surely should work that way, okay," the woman agreed. "Any organization that was really out to protect musicians wouldn't think about protectin' 'em right out of jobs, would they? See what I told you? You can almost smell the sulfur smokin' behind that SWALLOW outfit. Now then, shall I stop for today or do you all want to hush and let me finish?"

"Go on," the boy said.

▲▲▲

Juli was trying to think of something to smooth over the thundering silence George's outburst had cast over the conversation when someone knocked on the door.

Josh answered it.

"Dave, how you doin', buddy?" Josh shepherded the other man into the room so heartily you'd have thought Dave was paying him millions, instead of merely a thousand or so, and was carrying the paycheck in his hand.

Dave was about forty-five, fine-featured, and handsome. His silver hair set off a cinnamon-colored tan and nicely echoed the silver of the thin concho belt at the waist of his expensively weathered jeans and the silver and turquoise watchband peeking out under the cuff of his equally expensive-looking work shirt. He looked much more like a star than Josh did. In one hand he clenched a briefcase doing a good impersonation of a saddlebag.

"Hate to bother you, Josh," he said, "but I've been looking for that opening act, the Martins, and—"

"These are the Martins, Dave. Julianne, George, Dave Meeker."

Instead of taking George's extended hand, Meeker set the briefcase down on the bureau and began pulling out sheaf after sheaf of papers. "Glad you got here early. This may take a little time. We need you to fill out the withholding form, of course, though we don't withhold for one-night stands ordinarily, and the workman's compensation papers—do both copies please, and print—and the waiver in case anything does happen—that's for our insurance company—and this contract, and of course, we'll need your equity card number." To Josh he said, "I'm sure that having these people open for you will make a more integrated show on the whole, Josh, but really, it is much easier to use a company band so we don't have to go through all this paperwork and tax hassle every time. Before long, our insurance carrier is going to forbid us to use outside talent at all."

"I hope that doesn't include me," Josh said.

"Well, no, of course not, but since the company has acquired production rights nationwide, once you sign we can consider you to be on the payroll, especially if you do whole tours with us. The hard part is filling in with local talent between major acts, and these warmup acts. We try to have a few bands in each city. Of course, the alternative would be for you to take your warmup act with you on tour, at your own expense of course."

"I'm sure there'll be no problem," Josh said. He was growing a little red in the face, but he was handling the situation with tact and without an ounce of the biting sarcasm so often prevalent in his songs. Julianne could see him forming snappy comebacks and swallowing them. The work situation may not be so bad for him right now because of his established reputation, but there were obviously a few drawbacks.

She hated to add to his difficulties, but faced with one particular question that occurred right beside her name at the top of each questionnaire, she had to. "Josh, there is just one tiny problem. It keeps asking for equity number and we're not—I mean, we don't have one. Does that matter?"

"What do you mean you're not equity?" Meeker demanded.

"You have to admit the dues are pretty stiff," George said. "And it's not like they generate work for us—in fact, the organizing they've done has scared off a lot of the gigs we used to play, Elks halls and county fairs and so on."

Dave ignored him and turned to Josh. "Josh, Josh, I thought you knew these folks, babe."

"We're fellow artists," Josh said. "I never asked them about any of this crap before. They're wonderful performers, write terrific songs—"

"I don't care if they're Malvina Reynolds and Woody Guthrie come back from the grave. If they ain't Equity, we can't use them. I'm sorry, Josh, but you ought to know that. We could be picketed, sued, for using non-Equity people, besides being in violation of those new federal laws." He rattled the sheaf of paper at each of them in turn. "And it is law, you know. Not just Equity. Laws made to protect you people. Any place that hires you or anyone else without complying with all of the requirements is committing a violation."

"Yes, but it was Equity that forced those stupid laws through Congress without consulting any of us . . ."

"They could hardly consult you if you weren't members," Meeker pointed out, wagging his turquoise ring in her face.

"Well, what do you care anyway?" she asked. "Is your company going to buy up every lodge hall in the country?"

Josh laid a heavy hand on her shoulder and squeezed, but to Meeker he said, "Sorry, Dave, I never gave it a thought. Most places I play with the house artists but my friends here needed a break and you don't have anyone appropriate to open—"

Meeker had the grace to look abashed. "I'm sorry too, Josh, but it's really cut and dried—nothing to do with you or me or these people. The law is the law. We have to have these papers filled out to satisfy federal regulations, and in order for the papers to be processed properly, the Martins would have to be Equity members. So I'm afraid it's back to the company band, no matter how you feel about it." He shoved three stacks of forms back into his briefcase, tied the concho-anchored thong that held it shut, and departed two steps ahead of the Martins.

But as George stepped out into the hall, Josh caught Juli's hand and said, "I'm sorry, Julianne, but Meeker does have a point. Look, I'll *pay* your dues. Here's the money. Join the Equity, then I can help you. You know that folk musicians have always supported the unions."

"Josh, I'm sorry, but it's a lot the same kind of problem as SWALLOW," Julianne told him. "Since the musicians' union merged with Actors' Equity, the organization doesn't do a thing for musicians except restrict us. Particularly people like George and me. People who belong to other unions have a steady employer, work the same place for years. SWALLOW and the Equity are fine for big-name people like you who are so much in demand that clubs will go through any amount of hassle and expense to get you, or production companies like Meeker's will try to monopolize you, but the pizza parlors, beer joints, and Unitarian fellowships just aren't ready to go through all that legal rigamarole just to give a job to a few starving musicians. I mean, get real, who wants to fill out workman's comp papers and deal with paying out matching social security for a fifty-dollar one-night stand?"

"It's for your own protection, Juli," Josh said, pressing the money into her hand. "Join up. You're not going to get anywhere if you don't."

"We're not going to get anywhere if we do either," George snapped, poking his head back in the door. "Come on, Jule. I thought I saw a help wanted sign at McDonald's on the way in."

Josh sighed as he watched them go. He did not look forward to playing with a rockabilly band and he was sorry the kids had to be let down. But he certainly wasn't going to blame himself for their lack of foresight. At least Juli hadn't refused the money.

▲▲▲

"There," the woman said, "how's them apples?"

"Huh?" the boy asked.

"How'd you like that story? Lots of high finance and businesspeople—"

"Yeah, but the ending wasn't happy," the girl complained. "When do the Martins invest the seed money Josh gave them, make a killing on junk bonds, join the Equity, get lots of jobs in big places that can afford to pay that other club, and live happily ever after?"

"They don't."

"But that man, Josh, told her . . ."

"He was wrong, I'm afraid. They did try to join the Equity later, with the money he'd given Julianne, but the Equity was more interested in interrogating them about gigs they'd played illegally, and fining them for it, than they were about making them members and getting them jobs."

The little girl who knew about geography sniffed. "Too bad the Martins didn't know about the laws Equity was passing in time to use our government's mechanisms for protesting laws they didn't like."

"Oh, they and a few other folks did. They signed petitions, wrote a few letters. But mostly when it all started they were on the road, pooped from trying to keep up, make a living. The devils had their people in key positions in the Equity, the courts, and Congress. Those minions knew exactly the right way to get to the musicians with boring language and stupid wrangling. If, say, the devils had hired people with guns or gotten the police to lock them all up for disturbing the peace or something, why, it would have been just like the head devil said. The singers would have written a passel of new songs about the 'great struggle' and would have defended themselves eloquently. Every good singer is at least half actor and thrives on

drama. What they can't take is being ground down, bored into oblivion by bureaucracy. So for starters, the devils had their minions introduce sneaky little bills that had to be nagged down over and over by boring petitions and writing letters to the same tired congressmen about the same old bills with thus-and-such new attachments each time. That's just the kind of fighting singers are real bad at."

The boy shrugged. "It sounds like a mere labor and management dispute to me. Josh got to be management—"

"Only he wasn't," the sister said. "He belonged to the Equity and wanted them to. He directly opposed management interests in general by insisting the Martins do something that would cause extra work, time, and money for the employer, when he could have used the company's band instead."

The woman thought these were the damndest children she had ever run across, or she would have thought so had she not met other kids like them lately. The way they argued business deals and who was squashing whom was maybe no worse than in her day, when kids shot each other with toy bazookas when they played soldier or toy pistols when they played cowboy, but the enthusiasm of these children was far more ruthless, in a cold, anemic kind of way.

"You're both wrong," she said. "Josh and the Martins were both labor, only they forgot that. The devils and the bureaucrats had successfully managed to make them think they had different businesses. The Equity laws defeated people like the Martins and the immigration laws, under the guise of controlling drug traffic, kept out people like the Scottish singer the Chaveses were bringing in, until there were just a few big-name people left singing anything at all. Which made everybody separate and a little mad at each other. Which made each and every one of them all that much easier to pick off when the devils were ready to pounce. The immigration laws not only kept people like the Scot out, it kept all the American singers in. Even Canada wouldn't allow them to play there anymore, much less Europe, once it was learned how the U.S. was 'protecting' the rights of its performers."

"But what happened to Juli?" another little girl wanted

to know. "If she was so beautiful and so good surely she rose into a management position in some large corporation and—"

"I'll get back to her," the woman promised.

"After the cowboys," the boy said. "I wanted to hear about the cowboys spe-siff-ick-lee."

His sister rolled her eyes at the woman. "Now you've got him talking like you."

He stuck his tongue out at her and looked expectantly at the woman.

"Can't imagine why you're interested," the storyteller teased. "Cowboys are nothin' but no-account agricultural laborers, after all."

"You promised," he said indignantly.

"Well, okay, if you're sure. Tell you what. Tomorrow's Saturday. If you meet me at the park by the slide I'll see if I can recollect that part too."

▲▲▲

They didn't recognize her at first because she was pushing a toddler on the swings and at the same time minding a baby in a pram. She was dressed like the other mothers in bright colored doeskin, soft exercise clothes—in her case the polo shirt and matching sweatpants were a lavender blue that chased the shadows from her eyes and made them the same color, made her old gray curls look like designer hair.

Since the children's various nannies and baby-sitters tended to sit together for their own gossip session in the park, it was no trouble to get away to the play area. As soon as they arrived, she picked up the toddler and sat down on the swing herself with the kid in her lap.

"Now then," she said. "Where were we?"

"The cowboys," the boy said, glaring at his sister, daring her to ask for anything else.

But the boy and his sister and the other kids soon forgot about each other or anything but the woman swinging and rocking the baby, weaving a story, using their imaginations to give life to her memories.

CHAPTER IV
▲▲▲

After thirty years traveling the country singing the folk songs of the land, Willie MacKai was right back where he started from and if anybody had been fool enough to ask him how he felt about it, he'd have told them he liked it that way, right after he told them to mind their own damn business. Willie had been brought up in this ranch country, shooting rattlers off the hot rocks, breathing the dust into his nostrils, learning not only the traditional cowboy songs but the songs of the Mexican vaqueros who worked for his father. His father had been foreman of the spread where Willie worked now as a guide and a guard for room, board, and whiskey and cigarette money.

He'd been a mess when the boss had taken him on and he knew he only had the job thanks to his old man. He'd counted on that, since his dad had worked for Lafitte Ranch most of Willie's life and was known to be so indispensable that when the old man died, fifteen new hands had to be put on to take his place. Willie also counted on his own past reputation. The boss had always enjoyed watching him perform. That had almost worked against him though.

"I dunno, son," the boss said. "Place has changed some since you was a kid. I need somebody who's going to stick around. Not much high life out here, no women except Conchita the cook and she weighs three hundred fifty pounds if she weighs an ounce. Not what you're used to."

"What I'm used to ain't what I want anymore, Lenny," Willie told him. He was slumped half down in his chair with a whiskey in one hand and his hundred-dollar hat in the other, fanning the hat back and forth—not to cool himself; Leonard Lafitte's office was air-conditioned. Just nerves. "I need to settle down, have a place to live and a steady job."

"No woman?"

"No *one* woman," he said, grinning like a lobo. "Can't see depriving all them others."

He was being careful to keep it light, not to beg, but Lenny was shaking his head. "Naw, Willie, you're too good at what you—"

Willie set the drink carefully on the edge of the mahogany desk. The shine of the wood showed through the layer of dust. "Sure I am. I'm too good. You know how much good bein' too good's done me, Lenny? I'll tell you. I haven't worked in six months. I had to sell grandma's farm she left me to pay bills two years ago. I have thirty-five dollars to my name. You know how long I've been on the road, Lenny? Thirty years, that's how long. Thirty years of never missing a gig, no matter how hard I had to travel to get there. Thirty years of working even when I was sick or hurt. Thirty years of helping some young guy who thought I was terrific, wanted to be just like me, and watching him make the money and get the fame and forget he ever knew me when I could have used a break too. Thirty years of singing songs I think are true and strong and make this country a better place to be in. And watching left-wing bastards take all the bows for telling the American people that they're shit. It's been thirty goddamn years too long, Lenny. I want me a real job."

Lenny rubbed his bald spot with the heel of his hand, pulled a set of keys out of a drawer, and slid them across the desk to Willie. "Your dad was the best man I had, Willie, and it ain't been the same around here since he died. I know you been doin' something else but I also know you're a chip off the old block. Job's yours, son, and I'm happy to have you. Just hope *it* makes *you* happy."

It had, for a while. For a while, nothing felt very different. Willie covered miles a day in a Jeep, patrolling the borders, the line shacks, the fences. He kept his eyes open and his gun loaded for parties of the new wetbacks—not harmless poor Mexicans in serapes and sandals, but well-fed–looking people in brand-new Nikes and designer jeans, carrying their worldly goods in waterproof Gucci nylon overnight bags. He hadn't found any, and used the firearms mostly for snakes and signaling, or occasionally having to put an injured animal down. But roaring across the miles spanned by Lafitte Ranch, going back to his messy den of a house at night to drink in front of the television, not having to sing over a bunch of rowdy drunks and singing only when he felt like it, which wasn't often anymore, it took him a while to realize that the life he'd lived since he quit college was over.

It had been two years since he worked. The only performance he gave these days was the line of bullshit he fed the stockholders he took on hunting trips for havalina and whitetail deer. He'd always said he could fall back on hunting if he had to, survive the way he had survived as a twelve-year-old kid, when it was his job to put meat on the table. Well, here he was, buttering up two or three rich men who didn't have to hunt to put meat on their tables and who seemed to consider him a cross between a native porter and the local quaint character.

Well, fuck 'em. He lit another cigarette, poured another drink, and slumped back in the chair facing his television. Despite the air-conditioning, it was hot in his little house. He wore a pair of cutoffs and nothing else. His tan had darkened at face and forearms, faded everywhere else. The pool was for family members only, and besides, he worked a lot of fourteen-hour days now. You'd think a man could sleep, working like that, but he sat up half the night watching television, just for the voices. Ranch work wasn't what it used to be. Most of the other men were married, living in the town Lafitte built for them to live in with their families. Some were taking night classes at the ranch town's college extension branch, bettering themselves. Like he had. For all the good it did him.

He was halfway through his third whiskey and diet cola when the phone rang, and Mark Mosby, who he hadn't seen in five years, told Willie that he needed to talk to him so urgently he was driving down from Austin immediately.

"What's it all about, buddy?" Willie asked him soothingly, responding to the teary note in Mark's rich baritone voice. Mark was one of those "sensitive" guys who tended to cry when they got upset. Willie only cried when he got real tanked and maudlin.

But Mark also tended to get secretive when he was in trouble, and now he said, "I'll tell you all about it when I get there. I—I guess I'll need a banjo lesson, for one thing. But for now, give me the directions to the ranch . . ."

▲▲▲

Mark Mosby barreled down the highway from Austin with a troubled mind and a strangely jangling banjo in the seat beside him. He wished he'd gotten the case for it so it wouldn't be so distractingly noisy. Was it his imagination or did the accidental reverberation of the strings make up a tune that vaguely resembled the old Woody Guthrie song "Hard Traveling"? Not that Mark thought traveling was especially hard. He liked it. Driving was a sort of meditation for him and if he ever needed to meditate, it was now. According to his watch it was barely six o'clock, not yet twenty-four hours since he'd decided to give himself a treat on a gigless night and go to a concert.

He didn't usually treat himself to concerts by other pickers. They made him uncomfortable. For one thing, he wanted to be up there singing himself, wanted the applause to be his. For another thing, he'd rather be a player than a spectator. For another thing, he just couldn't help getting a little jealous of any other musician, especially an acoustic musician, who had a wide-enough audience to draw a concert crowd. He knew he was good enough to fill the halls, if only he could get producers to listen to him, to promote him. His voice was better than the voices of most concert stars and his accompaniment better than average. Furthermore, he was a showman, and would have been an idiot not to see how people responded to him, especially women. Yet somehow all the big breaks had eluded him—at least so far. So normally it made him twitchy to watch someone else perform.

This time, however, was different. Sam Hawthorne was a legend to anyone who cared about folk music. See-

ing him perform at least once was practically compul-
sory.

Sam was the master of the singalong. His specialty was
rallying and inspiring people—he'd led civil rights and
antiwar marches in the sixties and nobody doubted his
guts. The man had all but been martyred by the blacklist
during the McCarthy witch-hunts. That was part of the
reason Mark thought he might just be able to stand to see
Hawthorne. Nobody in their right mind could envy a
man who had been through what Sam had.

The auditorium was crowded. It had been sold out for
a week. Mark only got through because one of the security guards was a fan of his and slipped him in.

It wasn't like he was depriving a ticket holder of a
seat. He hung out with his guard friend, watching the
river of people flow down the corridor and channel off
into the rows of the auditorium. Smoking wasn't allowed
inside, and Mark had a two-pack-a-day habit. So he had
a smoke in the corridor while watching the five-hundred-
dollar hats, fringed leather halters with beads and bosoms
spilling from them, tight designer jeans, thousand-dollar
boots, college sweatshirts, jogging clothes, and T-shirts in
various colors bearing the logos of various folk festivals,
most prominently Kerrville and Dumas, file past.

As soon as people had settled with a sigh of clothing
and a thump of chairs, feet, and bodies, Hawthorne loped
on stage, his banjo dangling from one improbably large
paw, the expression on his face a far cry from his trademark half-neighborly, half-fatherly smile. Without looking at the audience, he began frailing his banjo. It was an
old tune—which tune? Dammit, Mark knew. He didn't
do a lot of traditional music himself but he had heard
other people play it hundreds of times—

Turning onto the county road that led to the ranch,
Mark remembered. It had been another Woody Guthrie
song, "I Ain't Got No Home."

But Sam didn't sing. He played a couple of lines on the
banjo, then began talking. "You know, I don't always
agree with everything the government of the United
States of America does—" a big laugh from the audience
at the understatement. "But one thing they have done

that I think is mighty fine is that they have established an institution that preserves the history of this great, though often misguided, land of ours."

Mark thought this was a very strange way to begin a concert, and figured Hawthorne was about to get preachy again about some cause or the other. Mark really wasn't much for causes himself and waited impatiently while Sam stared off into space.

The banjo idly pattered away while Sam spaced out. Mark knew that Hawthorne was pretty old, but it was sad to see the tall, defiant figure so stooped and weary. The spot on him was the wrong color too, because Hawthorne's skin looked gray. Feet shuffled, people coughed and murmured, and finally somebody yelled, "Take it, Maestro!" Sam snapped out of it with a visible shudder, belatedly remembering his audience. His prominent Adam's apple traveled the length of his long neck and back up to the tip of his short gray beard. "Over the years we've all put a lot of work into the Folk Music Archives of the Library of Congress. Dusty Barlow's final recordings were there, as well as many the two of us did together, as well as the work of many, many other traditional and contemporary singers. Songs collected by Frank and Anne Warner, Vance Randolph, Charles and Ruth Crawford Seeger, the Lomaxes, many others, found a home there. The people who once sang these songs onto the field recordings are long gone. Many of the songs have never been collected from the recordings. Many that have been collected and recorded by people like Woodie Guthrie, Leadbelly, the Seegers, Dusty Barlow, and many, many others as well as yours truly are now out of print and have for years been unavailable anywhere but through the Library of Congress.

"Ladies and gentlemen, just before I came on stage I received a phone call by a friend who knew I wouldn't be watching television right now—though some of you may have been watching the news before the concert and know what I'm about to say. A series of explosions started fires in the basement of the Library of Congress buildings—the cause isn't known yet, or the extent of the damage except that—and this is why I was called—between the fire and the explosion and the water damage, it's believed that the portions of the Library containing the Folk Music Archives were totally destroyed."

More murmuring, then Sam cleared his throat into the mike again and said, "We haven't had such a tragedy since the War Between the States, when the North burned the historical treasures of the South and the South did likewise, insofar as it was able. In Europe, war upon war has destroyed thousands of the world's most precious art treasures, libraries, historical monuments, wiped the work and memory of generations of women and men from the face of the earth." His voice broke again and he brought his hand to his throat and dropped it again. "The Library of Congress always reminds me a little of some great cathedral of learning—the ceilings are painted and the doorways are gilt and the entry hall is big enough to have great fancy-dress balls in. The Folk Music Archives wasn't in a big fancy room with gilt on the doors. Most of it was stored in little bunches throughout the basement. The public part was also in the basement, a couple of little cubbyhole rooms tucked away in a corner so remote you almost need a road map to find it. It was crammed with books and tapes and some electronic equipment so old it probably had a certain antique value. The most valuable thing, however, was of course the rare and priceless songs it contained."

After another pause, he continued, "But I want to say, on the hopeful side, that many people still know a lot of the songs, and furthermore, that there are fine writers of songs who are giving us new ones all the time. Right now, I can't think of any songs about fires, but I would like you all to sing with me a song about a flood written by a young man named Bill Staines. It's called 'Louisiana Storm.' "

He plucked the banjo with deceptive simplicity—his was the book and record on banjo playing from which most of the other pickers in the business had learned. The tune was oddly upbeat for a disaster song, and Mark thought Sam might be using it to bring himself and the audience back to a more positive state of mind from which the concert could continue. Sam gave particular emphasis to the verse, "If I ever live to be a hundred/One thing I will remember well/That one time in my life/ Well, I seen enough water/To put out all of the fires in hell," and the audience, or those of them who understood what he was talking about, sat silently until then, but as his voice began to crack they sang with the determination of protest marchers, "Let the sun shine down/Down on Lou'siana. Let the sun shine down/Let it dry up all of the rain." The guard was singing along and Mark joined in, full voice, his rich baritone carrying over the other unamplified voices, turning a few heads his way.

The audience's singing visibly buoyed Sam and his spine straightened, a ghost of the familiar grin touching the corners of his open mouth. Every other strum or so his fingers flicked the banjo head so that it sounded like the drum in a marching band. *"Again!"* he called out, and bellowed the chorus once more, throwing his head back and lifting his voice so it sailed over the heads of the crowd. His Ichabod Crane body bent slightly backward, as if to gather the emotion he wanted in the song and hurl it through the microphone.

For a moment Hawthorne was ageless, and Mark was conscious only of the ropes of sinew standing out in the strong forearms that had relentlessly plucked tunes from the banjo in his hands for the last fifty-five years. But Hawthorne was in his mid-seventies. A large part of his life's work had just been destroyed.

Sam's strong old heart had survived blows as hard in the past, but in the past, the heart was younger.

Mark didn't think about how much Sam was sweating at first—even with air-conditioning, Austin in midsummer was hot, and with stage lights, it was a wonder smoke wasn't rolling out of Sam's ears. And when the old man stopped singing on the fourth repeat chorus, Mark assumed it was to make the audience sing louder. But when Sam stopped playing, and grabbed his left shoulder with his right hand and held on to the mike with his left hand, Mark dropped his cigarette.

Hawthorne gasped once and tried to pull the banjo off his neck but instead fell forward, banjo, mike and all. People rose from their seats to stare and someone, pre-

sumably the concert producer, ran onto the stage and
shouted for a doctor, but no one came forward immediately.

Meanwhile, Mark, who had had life-saving training as
a swimming instructor, was already halfway to the stage.
He almost crashed head-on into a youngish man from the
other side of the auditorium. "You an MD?" the man
asked. Mark shook his head.

"I am," the man said, and turned Sam over roughly,
pulled the banjo off over his head, kicked the microphone
out of the way, and shoved the banjo toward Mark. Mark
stood there holding it while three RN's and a medtech
who had just fought their way forward from the bar in
the back of the auditorium joined the doctor. The four of
them took turns breathing into lungs that had once filled
union halls and schoolrooms with unamplified song.

Mark was still standing holding the banjo when the
ambulance crew arrived. The doctor meanwhile slugged
Hawthorne in the chest in a way that would have excited
the envy of many a mine boss, bigot, and FBI man. The
emergency medtechs brought the portable defibrillator
and zapped Sam right there on the stage. In between zaps
they started IV's and loaded Sam onto the stretcher,
wheeling him out the door.

Mark looked after them, long after the crowd surging
toward the door obscured his view. Someone screamed
and he realized suddenly that sounds had not been registering for some time. As abruptly as if the volume on a
television had been turned up, he heard the sobs, the
shrill questions, the shouted demands for information. A
brawny kid in a "Hook 'em Horns" T-shirt was arguing
loudly with Mark's security guard friend. It sounded like
he wanted his money back.

The hall emptied and the parking lot roared with the
sound of departing cars. Mark walked out into the heat.
It was eight o'clock and still broad daylight.

The car was stifling hot and Mark couldn't get out of
the parking lot for forty-five minutes. Vehicles sat idling
in both lanes of the access road, out onto the four lanes of
highway and beyond. By the time he had crept through
that to reach the only hospital in Austin with an emer-

gency room and found a parking place, it was almost ten o'clock. Time for Hawthorne's concert, had it not been aborted, to end.

▲▲▲

Some time ago Mark had turned off onto the ranch road, a well-packed gravel and tar affair now squishy with the heat. Though it was nearly seven P.M. now, the sun still shone and Mark still drove with the windows open—air-conditioning clogged his sinuses.

He saw the longhorn in plenty of time. He just figured it would be used to traffic on a ranch road and have sense enough to lope away.

He thought that because he'd been raised in Houston and knew of the contrariness of longhorns only from hearsay.

He was only doing about forty miles an hour anyway and saw no need to slow down as he drew even with the beast. What he hadn't noticed, in his preoccupation, was that the longhorn trotted closer to the road as he approached. Just as he should have been past it, it was in front of him.

The last thing he saw were beady little red eyes glaring meanly through the windshield as he pulled hard left on the steering wheel and felt the van hit what felt like a ski jump. He was thrown against the open window, and a spike of blinding pain sent him spinning down a long tunnel of pulsing black light. As he fell, the tinkling strains of "Ride Around, Little Dogie" sprinkled after him.

▲▲▲

Willie poured another drink and was three quarters of the way through *The Comancheros* when someone knocked on his door. "Señor MacKai," a soft, slightly accented voice said from outside the door. Willie padded over to it and opened the inner door, leaving the screen closed to keep the flies out.

"What's on your mind, Benito?" he asked. The kid was about eleven years old and looked up to Willie as he would look up to a black sheep uncle. Willie was used to being idolized and normally encouraged it. Tonight, while he was feeling about as worthless as tits on a boar hog, starry eyes just made him tired.

The boy had other things on his mind than worship, however. Panting with excitement he said, "Señor, I am out exercising the horse Mosquito, you know? And I hear a noise like thunder, three claps, very loud. Maybe a big gun firing, do you think? And now, you smell? A fire, no?"

Willie sniffed the wind like a wolf scenting prey. An oily, acrid, smoky smell stung his nostrils. He wet a forefinger, held it up. Wind was from the south. What there was of it. Which fortunately wasn't much. Pausing only to shove flip-flops onto his feet and throw a gun into the Jeep, he grabbed his drink and roared off down the southbound road. Probably just wetbacks burning old tires or something but even so, you had to check. He hadn't looked at his watch when Mosby called, but he'd watched two movies since then so it must have been at least three hours ago. His head was still fuzzy from the booze, but cleared rapidly with the combination of pumping adrenaline and the evening air.

He smelled burning hair and flesh at almost the same time he saw off in the distance down the long flat road the flames of the wreck, sparks catching on the dry branches of a scrawny cottonwood, smoke obscuring the starlight.

▲▲▲

The awful smell of cooking hair and flesh grew stronger as Willie pulled up to the wreckage of the van, and Willie wondered if he'd even recognize Mark. The heat flowing from the wreck hit him like a flamethrower and he skirted it, trying to see inside. It wasn't the same van Mark had been driving the last time he saw him, but a similar one, white like all the others, windowless in the back. You could see the van's frame through the fire now, smell the fumes of the burning carpet and plastic. Willie covered his mouth and nose with one hand and stumbled on around, almost falling over the charred, smoking corpse of the longhorn lying near the wreck.

The foul-smelling smoke hit him in the gut and he

bent over to puke out most of the evening's bottle, thinking it would be a cold day in hell before he ever ordered a steak again.

Straightening, he spotted something gleaming in a patch of yucca just beyond the wreck, and walked toward it.

Oh, God. Oh, Lord. Looked like one of Mark's instruments had made it, even if he hadn't.

But then, beyond the cactus-cradled banjo, he saw the boot, and the leg encased in denim, and the rest of Mark sprawled beyond.

He knelt beside the younger man, staring at his back to try to see if he was breathing. You weren't supposed to move somebody who'd been hurt like this, he knew. Might break their back or something. But hell, you had to tell if they were alive. He touched Mark's face, still warm and wet with perspiration.

Abruptly Mark sat straight up. His eyes flew open and his hand poked at his mouth.

"Shit, I broke a tooth," he said.

Willie shook his head slowly. "You're damn lucky that's all you broke, my friend. What happened?"

"How the fuck should I know? A goddamn steer charged the van—"

Willie laughed, his sense of humor activated by relief. "I'll have to have Lenny speak to his livestock. Can't have them breaking people's *teeth* every time they decide to commit suicide. Come on, pal, let's get you back up to the house."

Mark seemed okay except for the tooth, a little bleeding from one ear, and a giant red swelling circling into his matted dark hair. Staggering together, he and Willie headed back for the Jeep.

They were almost there when Mark snapped his fingers and lurched away from Willie to return to the yucca bush and pluck the banjo free before climbing into Willie's Jeep.

Back at the house, Willie unearthed an almost-clean towel and wetted an end of it to wash the blood from Mark's ear.

"You got to watch it on these back roads, son," he

teased Mark. "These attack cows will just leap out and get you. I'm going to give a call up to the house and have them come down with another van, take you in to the doctor. Okay? It'll be faster than waiting for an ambulance to come here and that way you won't have to bounce around no more in the Jeep."

"No, no, no," Mark said. "I'm okay. Be fine. Just—"

"The hell you are," Willie said, and picked up the phone to call, but the line was busy. He set it back down and told Mark, "I'll try again in a couple minutes."

"Gotta tell you about Sam," Mark said. His speech was a little slurred.

"No, buddy, you got to rest. Let me fix you a little drink to relax you and you just take a nap while I get us some help."

"Willie, goddamn—lissen t'me."

"Okay, okay. What's on your mind besides that goose egg growing there. Let me put some ice on that." He looked in the freezer. "It'll be a few minutes. I used the last one in my drink. Just a sec." He grabbed the towel he'd used to sponge the ear off with, fished what was left of an ice cube out of his drink, and wrapped it in the towel, applying it to Mark's head.

"I'll try them again. We'll get you to the hospital in Brownsville."

"Forget it. I'm fine. Little headache's all. Had too much hospital already."

"If you got insurance, boy, this is a good time to use it," Willie said. "Looks like you lost your ass this time. Everything but your banjo."

Mark swallowed some of the drink Willie put in his hand, and rallied a little, making a conscious effort to enunciate. "Naw, unpacked the van last March when I came in off the road, started staying at Joann's place."

"You off the road?"

"Had to. Couldn't afford it anymore. Not enough money in the gigs to pay for the gas to get there."

"I sure as hell know what you mean about *that,*" Willie said emphatically. "But you never used to have any trouble getting gigs."

"Look, Willie, about Sam . . ."

"Sam who?"

"Hawthorne."

"What about him?"

"He's dead. 's his banjo."

"How'd you get it?" Willie asked.

"He—gave—it—to—me," Mark answered. "Got to tell you."

"Let me try to reach the house one more time and then I'll listen to what you say while we're waiting for them."

The line was still busy.

Mark was hard to understand at first, but he was a stubborn man and made sure Willie heard everything about the concert and afterward. He was concentrating so hard that Willie knew what he had to say was important to him, and so Willie concentrated too, until his own mind filled in the details and he was able to visualize what Mark told him.

▲▲▲

Mark had carried the banjo into the hospital emergency waiting area. It looked like the aftermath of a battle. Stretchers lined the walls, people threw up in emesis basins, or bled quietly into makeshift dressings while they waited their turn for treatment in one of the rooms. Mark half expected to see Hawthorne among them, with the paramedics still doing CPR.

A woman was busily typing up forms at the receptionist's desk, behind a glassed-in enclosure. Mark tapped on the glass and asked for Hawthorne.

She glanced at him, her eyes barely flickering with the kind of feminine response he usually elicited. "You family, sir?"

"Yes," he said, knowing that he'd get nowhere if he said no.

She told him which room Sam was in and that they were preparing a bed for him in the cardiac care unit.

If they were getting a bed ready, Sam had made it then. Still carrying the banjo, Mark strode down the hall before anyone could ask any more questions and opened the door to the room the lady had indicated. He thought he'd leave the banjo with Sam, or with the nurse, see how the old man was doing, and leave.

A forest of IV stands stood over the bed, and the steady beep of an electrocardiogram machine dominated the room. A nurse stooped near a crash cart, checking the drugs and supplies, replacing items that had been used.

Sam lay pale and still, a thin greenish oxygen tube spanning his face like an overgrown plastic mustache. Mark stood by the bed and watched Sam breathe for a moment, then started to turn to the nurse.

Then Sam's eyes opened and he glared up at Mark.

Mark, who was never very sensitive when it didn't suit him, kept his voice pitched low, so the nurse wouldn't be able to hear. "It's okay, Mr. Hawthorne. I'm not a reporter. I—I brought your banjo to you."

The older man blinked and relaxed a little. "Sorry, son," he said, and his voice rasped from the effort. "I'm not taking requests right now."

"Well, I've got one anyway, sir. There's a whole lot of people getting rain checks on that concert. You get better now, hear?" And Mark gently laid the banjo on the bed and started to leave.

"What might your name be, son?" Hawthorne asked.

Mark returned to the bedside, so that Sam wouldn't have to strain to speak and also so that the nurse wouldn't hear and realize Mark wasn't family after all.

"Mark Mosby."

"You're a picker."

It wasn't really a question but Mark said, "Yes, sir."

"Well, son," Sam said, clearing his throat painfully. "You may know my wife died a few months ago. My brother and sister are in England. I always thought when I died, I'd leave Lazarus there"—he blinked toward the banjo—"to the Archives. But—" he coughed, then said in such a low whisper that Mark had to lean over the bed rails to hear him, "suppose you hang on to it for me."

"Sure. Don't worry, Sam. I'll be right here in Austin. I'll call tomorrow and see how you are. As soon as they let you out of here I'll—" but the old man's eyes had closed and Mark's ear picked up a change in the beat of the background noise. He called the nurse and she punched a button at the head of Sam's bed that brought other doctors and nurses racing in.

Mark had fled the room then and stood holding Sam's banjo, watching the door to the room for what seemed like hours, until the doctors and nurses came out too. This time Sam was with them, the sheet pulled up over his face. He wasn't going to need the bed in CCU after all.

▲▲▲

The night Sam Hawthorne died, a woman in Fredericks, Maryland, got a posthumous phone call from him asking her to organize a folk festival.

"Mae, Sam Hawthorne here," the famous clipped Yankee voice announced when she picked up the phone.

Even groggy as she was from nightmares about the explosions at the Library of Congress over in D.C., which was only about an hour's drive away, Anna Mae would have known who it was. Only Sam Hawthorne ever called her Mae.

"Sam, did you hear about the Archives?"

"Yes, Mae. Yes, I did. And that was partly what I'm calling about. I'm afraid I didn't take the news so well, and not to beat around the bush too much, Mae, you might say it killed me."

"What?"

"Heart attack. Hurt like hell and what's worse, I never finished the concert. But that's not the important part. The important part is that Dusty and Bill Beresford—you know Bill—"

Anna Mae nodded dumbly at the telephone and then realized what she was doing and said, "Yes. Bill's the archivist of the folk collection. He was working late and was killed in the blast."

"That's the fellow. Good man. Fine picker too. Anyway, you know I've always kept an open mind about religion, but it seems as if the bunch of us are sort of stuck at the airport metaphysically speaking. Don't seem to be getting anywhere. Well, we don't mind so much because the company's good but we've been talking it over and we think something's going on down there. Why don't you have a little get-together in our collective honor and see what comes up? I hate to give you such short notice, but you've always been a good organizer. I remember the fine work you did at the Annapolis festival that one year."

"Thank you, Sam," she said, glowing with the warmth the special friendship with that remarkable man had always given her. "You know I'll do my best."

"I know you will, Mae. My best to everyone. Sorry to have to cut this so short but you understand . . ."

"I understand, Sam. Thanks for thinking of me."

"Take care of yourself, Mae. And watch out. Oh, and about Lazarus . . ."

"What about Lazarus? Sam? Sam?" Anna Mae had listened for a long time. When she woke up, she was still listening, and for a moment she thought it was a dream, but the receiver was still in her hand.

▲▲▲

Back in Texas, Mark Mosby, dying of a slow-leaking brain hemorrhage, finished his story in the best dying cowboy tradition before he joined Sam and the others. "Couldn' b'lieve it. Didn'know what to do," Mark told Willie. "Slept . . . woke up 'bout three . . . called you." The injured man was lying on the couch and looked up appealingly at an increasingly nervous Willie. Mark should have gone to a hospital right off, Willie thought. The boy's eyes looked funny—one big and dark, the other one shinier and greener than was natural.

"I'm going to try the house again," Willie told him. The line was still busy. Willie poured another drink, sloshing the liquid over the sides of the glass and onto his hand. Drying the hand on his cutoffs, he said, "Buddy, you hang in here a minute. I'm going to try to drive up to the house and fetch help."

Mark lay very still and said nothing, the empty drink glass resting on its side by his hand, the banjo at his feet.

CHAPTER V
▲▲▲

Willie banged through the screen door. It should have taken him no more than two steps to be at the Jeep but the damn fool thing refused to stand still. It swayed in the heat and quivered away from him each time he lifted his foot to step forward. He squinted his eyes, trying to zero it in but it wouldn't focus—he was either drunker than he thought he was or he must have gotten more shook up by the accident than he had supposed. He took a deep breath and stepped forward with all the deliberation of a Zen master.

And jumped three feet back through the open screen door, slamming it behind him as from the corner of his eye he caught the flash of diamond-patterned scales slashing down and forward into the light pouring through the door.

Had it not been for years of conditioning, the sixth sense of someone raised from boyhood in snake country, he might have remained in the path of that long body slicing the air where his chest should have been. By the time the snake landed with a heavy plop to coil onto the seat of the Jeep, however, Willie had the screen door between them almost without thinking about it. No sober man could have done it better.

"Sorry to bother you, buddy," he said as he backed into the room, his eyes never leaving the Jeep, "but I gotta get my pistol. Big ol' rattler tryin' to drive the Jeep out there."

He meant to make one of those cool understatements of danger that men in that country liked to make, but Mark wasn't much of an audience. He lay still and paler than ever—his habitual tan was barely noticeable now.

There was no reason for Willie to worry about him really, except perhaps that he had made his living from his ears and his instincts for years and something in the way Mark lay suddenly looked wrong. He touched the shoulder hunched toward the back of the sofa and Mark fell over on his back, his mouth open, eyes half-slit.

"Mosby? Shit, boy, this is no time to get puny on me. Come on, snap out of it," he said, but he knew that wasn't going to work. He tried to remember what he knew about first aid but it extended mostly to snake bites. He could help best by getting the boy to a hospital. But when he lifted the receiver this time, thinking to dial direct into Brownsville, the receiver crackled back at him, giving him an ear full of static. Dialing didn't improve the situation. He tried the house again and this time, instead of the busy signal, he continued to get static.

He picked up his pistol and walked to the screen door. The snake's dark shape lay coiled on the seat like a cowpie, its head waving a little, as if looking for him. Willie pulled back the hammer.

"Oh, sure, that's the way," the snake hissed. "Kill me too, like you did that poor slob. That's all you're good for."

"You're as dumb as you are ugly," Willie said. "Mark's just a little busted up."

"Oh, yessss? Go check."

Slowly Willie backed into the room and shook Mark. "Hey, buddy. Buddy, you okay?"

Mark's body fell off the couch and Willie saw that his eyes were open around the bottoms, showing only the whites. "Oh, shit," Willie said.

"Killer, killer, killer," the snake taunted. "Drunken murderer. Don't you know whiskey is poison on top of a head wound? He would have lived until you took him to the hospital if you hadn't poisoned him with that so-called snake-bite medicine. Killer, killer, killer."

"Well lookee who's talking," Willie yelled back. "I mean, talk about the pot calling the kettle black, goddamn rattlesnake calling *me* a killer. Jesus Christ, snake, I didn't kill anybody and your kind ain't good for nothin' but. Mark'll be okay. I just got to get him help. That's what I'm trying to do right now, except you're in the way waitin' to bite me."

"Oh, blame it on me if you want to. But you're rid of your rival now, aren't you, MacKai?"

"You mean Mark? He's my friend—or was. And I didn't kill him. He just—he just—uh—died."

"You might as well have put that bullet in his head, smart ass. Why didn't you drive him straight up to the house? Were you afraid your boss would see how pie-eyed you were? Were you more worried about your job than your friend's life?"

"I just figured all that bumpin' around was no good for him. Bring him back here, let him lie down, have a drink . . ."

"Oh, yesss, a drink's the answer to everything, wouldn't you say?" The snake's head rose into a question mark at the last question.

Willie blinked twice and raised the gun. "I'd say I'm a lot drunker than I thought I was to stand here takin' this horseshit from a goddamn snake. So long, slick." He shot it dead to rights and it died in an appropriate bath of snake blood and shredded upholstery.

Willie opened the bullet-punctured screen door and was about to lift the reptile from the seat with the barrel of his gun when another flash of fang and scaled body dove from the flat roof above the door. Once again, he put the door between him and it with more speed than either of them believed possible. The snake's fangs tore at the screen.

Withdrawing its fangs from the mesh long enough to rare back to strike again, the second snake hissed, "As my mate was saying before she was so rudely interrupted . . ."

Willie blew that one away too, and tried the phone in the house once more. This time it was dead.

He slammed it down and carefully sidled toward the Jeep, opening the door to scrape the dead snake off the seat with his gun barrel. The serpent landed in the road with a puff of dust.

Willie slid onto the bloody Jeep seat, then decided he shouldn't leave the door standing wide open. Mark wasn't going anywhere, of course, but he didn't want any more snakes getting into the house. As he closed the door, however, the vibration set the banjo strings to humming and it sounded like the seven notes from the chorus of an old song about the War Between the States and a sweetheart who didn't want to be left behind. "Won't you let me go with you," the banjo seemed to say and Willie took it into his head that he just couldn't leave Hawthorne's banjo lying there, even though his own guitars were both in plain sight.

The strings thrummed the same seven notes again as Willie grabbed the instrument and slammed through the door again and out to the Jeep.

He turned the key over and the engine started. The main house was about thirty miles down the road. His house was by way of being a fancied-up line shack.

Halfway down the road the Jeep died, the gas gauge needle sunk deep into the red E.

It occurred to Willie that he was not having a very good night. It occurred to him that everything that was happening sure made for a powerful string of unpleasant coincidences. It also occurred to him, however, that just such strings of coincidences tended to stack up against him when he was particularly loaded. Not that he felt particularly loaded at the moment. No, it was more like it was the rest of the world that was drunk and he couldn't make heads or tails of it without another drink.

Banjo in one hand, pistol in the other, he climbed out of the Jeep and started walking in the direction of the big house.

As if it had been waiting for him, a horse trotted up. He recognized it at once. He had personally named it the Strawberry Roan, although it was actually dun-colored, because of its disposition, which matched that of the horse in the Curley Fletcher poem, made into song just after the turn of the century. The line "You could see with one eye he's a regular outlaw" fitted the dun better than any saddle ever was likely to.

In keeping with the rest of the drunk world though, the horse seemed inebriated too. Uncharacteristically, it trotted meekly up to Willie and nuzzled him, all but wagging its tail and inviting him to hop aboard.

"No thanks," Willie said. "My mama learned me

never to accept rides from no strangers; and, horse, you are actin' stranger than all get out."

The horse knelt in the road.

Willie was suddenly weary in every fiber of himself and even the banjo and the gun felt like mighty burdens. Seeing the horse just kneeling like that, asking to be ridden, well—Willie liked to think of himself as a man who was never one to say no to temptation. He climbed aboard, the horse's sweat and that of his own legs mingling. Slinging the banjo around onto his back with the strap across his bare chest and sticking the gun barrel into the waistband of his cutoffs, he grabbed a hank of mane and tried to turn the horse with his knees. He wanted to ride toward the big house, of course, but the dun-colored Strawberry Roan had other ideas.

No sooner was Willie safely aboard than the horse broke into a gallop. Bucking Willie had expected, and recalcitrance, but this was like riding in the backseat of a car going 120 miles an hour and having no way to get to the controls. He just hung on for dear life and tried to enjoy the ride. It was a little hard. He found he was not prepared for all eventualities. True, he had the banjo and the gun, but he had forgotten to bring his cigarettes.

▲▲▲

"I don't think this is a very nice story. I don't think it is suitable for children," the boy's sister said. "It is not a moral story."

"Sure it is, honey," the woman said. "I just haven't gotten to that part yet. It's about as moral as any story you're ever going to hear."

"Didn't the cowboy know cigarettes and liquor were bad for his health?" the boy asked worriedly.

His friend Jonah slapped him on the arm. "God, Scott, how dumb can you be! Haven't you ever heard of self-destructive tendencies? Willie knew he was a damn fossil —there aren't any cowboys anymore. So he didn't care if he died of lung cancer or exploded his liver or shot his own peepee off carrying that gun in his pants like that."

But when they looked up from their argument, the woman and the baby she had been minding were gone.

▲▲▲

A week or so later, at a shelter for the homeless, the bag lady who had been haunting the Seattle streets got to the point in her story where the cowboy was carried away on the dun called Strawberry Roan.

The woman who supervised the shelter at night, a society matron with crisp silver waves and a round Nordic face, so unlined that it would have seemed lifted or redolent of Retin-A had it not been so animated, spoke up. "Excuse me, Gussie, did you say something about the Strawberry Roan? My second husband and I used to sing a song called that, written by a friend of ours." She sang a bar or two of a melodic, pastoral-sounding love song in a clear voice and then said, "But I've forgotten the rest I'm afraid. And I don't have the tune quite right."

"You sure don't, lady," said one of the winos, a man who just called himself Pete. "It don't go nothin' like that and it ain't no love song. It goes like this—" and he whistled a simple, repetitive tune through a few times over until the curly-headed bag lady patted him on the arm.

"That's real good, Pete. Where'd you learn that?"

"Offa old Tex Ritter movies when I was in the VA hospital," he said. "But it ain't no love song. It's about a horse."

"I'd heard there was one about a horse," said the society lady, whose badge said Mrs. Kathie Jorgensen, "but I never knew how it went."

"I can recite it but I can't sing it," Gussie said.

"I might be able to," Kathie Jorgensen said. "If Pete could whistle the tune again. Then I'll get a pencil and write it down as you say it."

Gussie looked uncomfortable. "Maybe afterward, kiddo."

"After what?"

"Gussie's telling us a story, Kathie," a man with graying hair, a blunted face, and thick tongue and narrowed child's eyes, said. This was Tony, an aging man with Down's syndrome. He'd outlived his parents and had been living on the streets for the last five years. His childlike manner was sometimes sly and sometimes mean but now it was fraught with anticipation, eager to be bamboozled and

convinced that there was something more wonderful in the
world than what he saw around him. "Go on, Gussie. Go
on."

▲▲▲

Well, it didn't take any time at all for Willie MacKai to
get real good and sick of that ride. Bareback with bare
legs is all right for kids, but Willie hadn't been a kid for
thirty years. The dun galloped back down the road, past
the Jeep, past the cabin where poor Mark Mosby and the
two dead rattlesnakes lay, on and on till it passed the
smoldering wreck of Mark's van and raced into a bloodshot sunrise all clouded and begloomed with what Willie
learned very soon was a hell of a hailstorm that pounded
him and that dun with bitter-cold missiles and lashed
them with wind and wet but still the dun galloped on and
on, past the point where any sensible horse would have
dropped dead.

Three times Willie decided he was already dead and
gone to hell and this was it, riding through those tomb-
cold hailstones on the back of a crazy horse, feeling saddle sores pop out on him like zits on a teenager and seep
like acid out to encompass other parts of him in close
association with the horse. Three times he decided that if
he was dead there was no reason not to just jump off and
he tried, but his sweat and blood and the horse's foamy
sweat and blood stuck his legs to the horse's sides like he
was one of those centaur things the old Greeks used to
talk about. The mane snarled around his fingers, trapping
them. All in all he decided it was less trouble just to stay
put and see what happened.

Willie lost consciousness before the dun's hooves hit
the edge of the ranch property. While he was uncon-
scious, Willie didn't feel his sores and bruises, didn't feel
the hail tearing at him, didn't feel when it stopped. All he
felt was the rocking of old S.R.'s back, steady as a hobby
horse.

Through the rain, wind, and hail, he dreamed he
heard the jangle of the banjo strings and it seemed to him
as if they were playing "Stewball," the song about the
racehorse.

When the rocking stopped, Willie was still on the topside of the damn fool animal, though he was bleeding like a stuck pig from his sores and smelled like horse. He was also dry as a bone because he'd ridden the dun plumb out of the storm straight through a day so hot it had sunburnt the top of his head where the hair wasn't as thick as it used to be and on into night again. But the minute he opened his eyes, despite his many sores, bruises, and cuts, Willie felt sorry for all the terrible things he'd been thinking about S.R. and all the awful names he'd screamed at that horse under his breath.

For right there before his very eyes was Lulubelle Baker's Petroleum Puncher's Paradise Bar and Grill. The sign was neon and went halfway around the building and the rest was lit up with Christmas lights and beer signs. This time when Willie tried to get off he just slid right off. He patted the old dun Strawberry Roan on the neck. "You're a fine beast, S.R.," he said. "A horse after my own heart. Wait a minute and I'll bring you a beer."

The pat was too much for the horse, who had done more than any mortal, nonpossessed horse could have done in four days. He fell over sideways with a thump, between a bright blue pickup with a window full of bumper stickers and an antique yellow Volkswagen bug.

CHAPTER VI

▲▲▲

Lulu, oh Lulu open up the door. Lulu, oh Lulu, come and open up the door. Before I have to open it with my old forty-four. I bin all around this world

—"I Bin All Around This World," Trad.

Willie scratched his sunburnt head with sunburnt fingers cramped and sore from holding on to the dun's snarled mane. He tried to amble casually into Lulubelle's but all he could manage with his stiff knees and saddle sores was kind of a jock-itch waddle.

Inside, once his ears got adjusted to the noise and his eyes to the darkness and his nostrils to the welcome and familiar miasma of smoke and liquor fumes, Willie plainly saw that Lulubelle Baker's was all that such a place was supposed to be. It was filled with song, of a sort, something that was probably supposed to be Jimi Hendrix–style electric guitar but sounded like an alley full of cats having a love-in. It contained a bar with gleaming bottles of spirits, and reveling drinkers and lots of lingerie-clad women. And girls and little girls and young boys, which made him think he'd just have a drink and call the boss and be out of there, because he somehow didn't think the young ones were there with their mommies and daddies because it was a family kind of joint.

The women and children popped in and out of view as they passed through clusters of men into the glow of a lava lamp or the come-hither lights from the gambling machines. Mostly everything and everybody was obscured by the smoky haze. Willie inhaled deeply and made his way to the bar, with difficulty, since there was barely room for a man to walk normally, much less one whose temporarily bowed legs were taking up enough room for two.

He ordered a whiskey, picked up a bar napkin, and sponged off the worst of the sores where they showed under the tattered legs of his cutoffs.

"Oooh, darlin', don't that smart?" cooed a solicitous female voice in his right ear. "Why don't you let li'l Lulubelle kiss it and make it well?"

He turned to answer her—he'd either have to speak in her ear too or she'd have to read lips. There was no way even *he* could project over the caterwauling guitar and the bleeps and burbles of the computerized machines, the clinking glasses and the shouting. He didn't much want to either. He was bone-tired, and clumsy because of it. He clean forgot the banjo strapped on across his back and as he swung around to talk to the woman he felt something catch him up and she yelped.

"Ouch, dammit all to hell, you just about put my eye out. That kind of thing costs extra, sweetcakes. Better take that contraption off your back or you'll be busted before you get started."

"Not nearly as busted as you yourself, ma'am," he said, tipping an imaginary hat in one of his more feeble attempts at low Texas gallantry. Then he flipped the banjo around so that it swung across his chest and belly instead of his back and at least he could be in charge of the damage he did. "Hope it didn't hurt you none. Would be a real shame to put out such a purty eye."

She pouted at him. She was young, for the madam of such a place, but probably she was fronting for someone —the mob or something, he supposed. Even with all that green and blue eyeliner she didn't look more than twenty-two. Without it, she'd be more like eighteen, he reckoned. The eyes in question were huge and brown, the skin tanned and glowing like sunset, the hair streaked blond, strawberry-blond, peachy-red, and amber. Her tits were huge, her legs were long, and everything else was temptingly small and delicate, including the red lace teddy that left something, though not much, to further negotiation.

"You used to be able to do better than that, stud," she complained, apparently about the compliment.

"When was that, darlin'?" he asked. "I don't believe I've had the pleasure."

"If you had, you'd sure as hell remember it, honey," she said. "I just meant, I heard tell you can do better than that. You *do* have a reputation," she said, sidling up to him now and breathing in his ear so he could smell her cheap musky perfume through the smoke. She moved all the time when she talked, sort of throbbinglike. He felt heat rising from her skin, as if she had a fever. Beads of sweat broke out on her face and in her cleavage, and dried right up. She licked her lips with the tip of her tongue and he knew that if only he could have heard it there would have been a faint hiss from the moisture turning to steam. On the one hand, that was kind of exciting. On the other hand, he was not drunk enough to want a woman with a disease.

"Well, sure, darlin'," he said smoothly, although even he wasn't sure that his notoriety had spread among womankind quite that far. He'd been out of circulation for a while, after all. Too bad his reputation as a musician wasn't as widespread and apparently illustrious. " 'Course I can do better, but cut me some slack. I think I did purty well for a man that's just pulled a friend out of a car crash, watched him die, killed two snakes, and been rid all over creation for a couple of days bareback on a loco horse."

"I can see where that might tarnish even a silver tongue like yours. Let's go upstairs and see if I can't find something to polish it up with, what say?"

She sashayed in front of him without waiting for an answer and he followed, carrying the second glass of whiskey he'd bought for medicinal purposes.

The banjo twanged and he thought he could just make out a medley of "Brandy, Leave Me Alone," "Cocaine," "Scotch and Soda," and "Mandy Lane." Of course, it was probably just his ears playing tricks on him, all the beeps and hums providing the notes he was thinking about, inspired by the atmosphere at Lulubelle's. He was *almost* certain it had to be his imagination and the orange glow of a beer sign that made Lulubelle's eyes ignite with red light when she turned to make sure he was following.

▲▲▲

"Whewee," Pete said. "That's what I call a hot date."

"Gussie, this is great," Mrs. Jorgensen said. "What an imagination you have! I hope I can persuade you to stick around and help me write a skit for our Christmas presentation. But right now it's time for lights out."

"Lights out? After that?" Crazy Ruthie the Dog Lady, who boarded her pack with the woman who ran the costume shop, protested. "I won't be able to sleep a wink!"

"Me neither," sighed Tony, who was wearing an even dopier grin than usual.

Mrs. Jorgensen looked at her watch. It kept them from seeing her hand tremble. She was more interested in Gussie's crazy story than she wanted to show. Her misspent youth may have been misspent, but it had been completely hers and she missed it more bitterly than she was willing to admit to anyone, especially herself. "Okay, a few more minutes but that's it."

"Thanks, Miz J. You're a doll. If a person can't party no more, least he can do is hear about it—" Pete mumbled, a reminiscent tear running down his spiderweb-veined cheek.

▲▲▲

Lulubelle led Willie down a long hall. Some of the doors were open and it reminded him a little of parties he had attended during the sixties, people doing all kinds of drugs, having all kinds of sex, eating and drinking all kinds of intoxicants. One whole roomful of people was soaking in a hot tub full of liquid chocolate and looked like a human candy-bar commercial.

Lulubelle opened a door and led him into a smallish room with a bed, a couch, a TV, and walls and ceiling covered with the kind of mirrored squares you could buy at the hardware store. The place smelled like a clearance sale at the perfume factory, underlain by the odors of oil, dirt, sweat, pot and cigarette smoke, and booze.

"What's your pleasure?" she asked, starting to shimmy out of her teddy.

"Hold on, there, darlin'. I'm not sure right now I can even afford to be on the premises. This is some operation you've got here."

She wound her fingers from the back of his neck to cup his ear and brush his cheek. Her hands carried the salted-fishy smell of sex. The banjo stirred with his pulse to a four-bar blues.

"Oh, in your case it's real reasonable, lover," she said. "I don't need cash money. Any old thing'll do. That banged-up old banjo oughta fetch something at a pawn-shop. You can give me that."

"Sorry, darlin'," he said, and he started to launch into an explanation of how it was Sam Hawthorne's banjo, etc., but then he decided he didn't really want to do that after all and said, "I'm a mite attached to it. 'Sides, charming as you are, that horse and I just about did one another in. I'm not exactly up to it."

"But, honey, that's my specialty," she laughed.

"No thanks," he said. A chance to stand for a few minutes, a whiff of smoke, and a stiff drink had revived him some after all that fresh air and exercise. He would have thought he was in a dream except that he hurt so realistically. And he might have been in DT's except that he had it on good authority those started after you *stopped* drinking, which he had not.

"Be that way then. But I was about to pour myself a li'l ol' drinkee-poo and put my feet up and I still intend to do it with or without you. Want a nip? It's on the house."

"Well, if you put it that way. You wouldn't happen to have a cigarette, would you?"

"Sure 'nuff. Here you go, my favorite brand."

She handed him a packet with what looked like a forest fire on the wrapper. He thought he'd been on the ranch too long. "What kind's this?" he asked.

"Brimstone Lights," she said. "I like the unfiltered kind, myself. Twice the tar and nicotine as the other brands."

He lit one, inhaled and coughed, his eyes and nose running. The banjo tinkled faintly to the tune of "Fire Down Below."

"Where did you *get* these cancer sticks?"

"Company brand," she said. "The folks that own Lulubelle's are into a lot of other things."

"Yeah, between you and me it's a wonder they ain't into jail."

"Now, now, sugar, don't *you* go gettin' all judgmental on me. Besides, even cops got to have a little fun once in a while. Want to watch some TV?"

He knew he should be doing something else but he wasn't sure what. He was damn sure in no shape to sit another horse or even ride in a car for much of a distance. Or walk for that matter. But there was Mark, lying dead in that cabin, and the wreck on one end of the road and the stalled Jeep on the other. He owed it to the boss to call in. "Mind if I use your phone first?"

"Don't have one," she said. "Our clients hear about us by word of mouth. You might call it sort of a grass-roots movement."

"They used to talk about that a lot in my old business," Willie said. "I was a folk musician, see . . ."

"I know," she said. "I've been a fan of yours. You did some of the damndest drinking songs I have ever heard and, uh, brought in lots of business."

"Yes, ma'am, I did. But like I said, I don't recall having had the pleasure of meeting you before."

"Oh, I was around, but you might say I've admired you from afar. You were good. That Huddie Ledbetter now, he was another of my favorites."

"Leadbelly? You couldn't have known Leadbelly?"

"Couldn't I?" she asked. And when she turned to face him he saw that it was only the dim light that had made her skin glow so youthfully. In good light it was more like polished leather with little cracks and flakes. Her limbs were downright skinny and the boobs were obviously the work of a plastic surgeon from the hard aggressive way they stood out. The strawberry hair was dull as straw that had been in the bottom of a horse stall for a couple of weeks and gray at the roots and her teeth had lines of yellow nicotine where they'd been capped. He felt a little more comfortable with her then, more like he didn't have to put on so much of an act. Well, not quite comfortable. In the glow of the lava lamp on the TV her eyes were still red, like a cougar's by moonlight. Willie was not one to be sentimental about the beauty of cougars.

"Well, you sure don't seem old enough to have known Leadbelly," he said, not entirely lying. Hell, even if she was in her mid-fifties, which was, taking into account the hard life she'd been living, his outside guess, she would have barely been a teenager when Leadbelly died in '49.

"Sure did. You might say I was his muse."

God help me, he thought. Another overaged groupie remembering how she screwed the stars. Then, because he had a penchant for absolute fairness at unexpected moments, he admitted to himself that he had always thought it was the women like her that made being a star fun in the first place. "I'm sure you were, darlin'," he told her.

"It's about time for the news," she said, and the TV came on, although he hadn't seen her tap a remote-control button.

The update on the fire at the Library of Congress came after the President's request for an increased defense budget and there was a brief mention of Sam Hawthorne's funeral back in Boston.

The channel flipped once more, though again, he didn't notice Lulubelle doing anything to flip it, and a blond female announcer said, "Tonight's top headline is the crash of a U.S. Airlines commuter jet from Los Angeles to San Francisco. The plane carried over two hundred passengers and crew, many of them performers and music lovers bound for the San Francisco Folk Festival. Among the confirmed dead are Josh Grisholm, and Nedra Buchanan, best known for her collaboration with the enemy during the Vietnam War. The ill-fated festival was also to have featured the late Sam Hawthorne, who died two days ago at a concert in Austin, Texas, and fiddler Bill Beresford, who died in the mysterious fire bombings that destroyed the lower levels of the Library of Congress buildings."

Willie guessed that *would* have pretty well wiped out the headliners, okay. He shook his head, wonderingly. Weird how so many people in the same profession were dying off all of a sudden. And what about the snotty way the newscaster sounded when she told about it, as if she was saying "good riddance"? Even to Willie, who was a fairly conservative man politically, the dismissal of Nedra Buchanan as a traitor seemed unduly harsh. Buchanan was a gifted singer from a long line of Scottish historians and folklorists and she had also marched for civil rights and world peace and nuclear disarmament and a number of other liberal causes. Willie didn't usually agree with her, but he respected her for her determination and strength of purpose, as he had respected Sam, who he also thought was crazy as a bedbug.

"Well, well," Lulubelle said, "looks like you were smart to get out of that business. Not only is it unprofitable, it's getting dangerous."

"Sure seems that way, don't it?"

"No seems about it, honeybun," she said, and the channel flipped again.

"Police are seeking a ranch hand today in connection with the death of an Austin man. The body of Mark Mosby, thirty-eight, was discovered . . ."

"Well, they make it sound like they think I killed Mark! He just died—somethin' from that accident. I've been tryin' to get to a phone to tell somebody when that damn fool horse ran away with me and—" Willie broke off suddenly, wondering just how much trouble he might be in and just how much he ought to be telling this very strange hooker about it all but Lulubelle was paying him no nevermind at all.

"The ranch hand is also wanted for the theft of a horse bearing the Bar B Bar brand of his employer."

"Now, goddamn it all, that's it! I mean, that just takes the cake!" Willie said, pacing as furiously to and fro as his sores would let him. "Hell, I didn't steal that horse. It stole me!"

"So, you're a wanted man," Lulubelle said as the

screen went blank. "My, my, a real desperado. I always knew you were a bad one, you devil you."

"It's all a mistake. I can straighten it out as soon as I see the boss," he said with more confidence than he actually felt. Nothing seemed very straight at the moment. "Jesus, it seems like the whole fucking world is fallin' apart. First Sam, then Mark, then Josh and Nedra and what with the destruction of the Archives and all—god damn, that's most of everybody and everything I've stood for . . ."

Lulubelle giggled. "Aw, c'mon, sport. What did those big shots ever do for you anyway?"

"Mark was no big shot. He was my friend."

"Yeah, and look how he paid back your friendship! Did he try to help you when he was getting the gigs?"

He appreciated the sympathy for a few minutes before he realized that she shouldn't have known about any of that. "Wait a minute. Just how closely have you been following my musical career anyhow, lady?"

"Musical career? Hell's bells, darlin', I don't care nothin' about your musical career . . . except for the sentiment in your drinking songs and the way it boosts business. I'm tone deaf. Can't tell a dirge from a jig, if you want to know. But I have followed you otherwise, your love life, your marriages, your drinkin' and smokin' and the inspiration you've been to countless others to do likewise, and I have always mightily admired you. Takes a real actor to make being so miserable look like so much fun most of the time and has won quite a few converts to the cause."

"I don't know shit about no cause, Lulubelle."

"Why, honey, I am on *your* side. You just hold on awhile here and you can watch all the assholes who ever made you feel like nobody flushed right down the tube."

"Wait a minute, you mean you knew this stuff was going to happen?"

"Sure, and I can show you another thing or two too. Wait a minute. I got something here that will just make you *die.* You will be so friggin' glad you got out when you did . . ."

She slid a videocassette into her VCR and the screen

filled with the image of a handsome young man in black
neoprene trousers that looked a little like a wetsuit, a soft
garnet-colored open-necked sweatshirt piped with black
satin, and garnet-colored aviator glasses. Lulubelle settled back against a threadbare satin pillow embroidered
and fringed with gold thread that said Deep in the Heart
of Texas. She tucked her right ankle under her left but-
tock and swung her right leg up and down, curling her
scarlet-tipped toes like a kneading cat. "Oh, that Nick,
he's a pistol, he is," she said.

The man was starting what seemed to be a speech, or
maybe a progress report, and at first Willie couldn't make
heads or tails of it.

"The program has been coming along nicely. Our
weather bureau has provided the coup de grace for many
of the major festivals, providing heavy rains, cyclones,
hurricanes, earthquakes, and, in one particularly inven-
tive instance, a blizzard, to complement the efforts already made to see to it that there are dwindling numbers
of the subjects left to warble their disgusting nonsense to
whoever might still be deluded enough to listen.

"The Public Pestilence Service, meanwhile, has been
busy in the more heavily settled areas near mountains,
coal-mining areas, and universities, where remnants of
the families who have been identified as carriers of this
brand of so-called music are most concentrated.

"Thus those members of the family who insist on
clinging to the old songs have been dying off and the
information has been rendered extinct by the simple ex-
pedient of introducing new motivations and interests to
the children of these vector families. The elders who
proved too hearty to succumb to the deadly diseases have
been afflicted with Alzheimer's, while blasting programs
at local mines have served to deafen many of them.

"Meanwhile, the academics involved have found that
they can't sponsor such outmoded subject matter as
ethnomusicology or folklore without losing grants. En-
rollment in their classes has dwindled sharply and the so-
called scholarly organs that once published their papers
have gone out of business. Also, the academic population
was easily infected with the same diseases we used on the

commercial performers—AIDS, the new airborne strain of herpes that settles in vocal chords and attacks joints, other kinds of arthritis, as well as some of the exciting new three-year viruses.

"Our most important strategic coup thus far was accomplished by one of our terrorist minions at the Library of Congress, but other collections have been quietly but effectively obliterated. We expect to have polished off all of the major offenders by the end of the year and to have implemented the program for eliminating recordings and books containing the offending material so that it cannot be relearned.

"The death of a major opponent, Sam Hawthorne, was a happy side effect of the operation at the Library of Congress. With the death of Hawthorne and the destruction of the material at the Library, we have succeeded in wiping from memory a large body of the most powerful songs. Those contained in the Library and those known to Hawthorne are no longer of any major importance and it is an easy task to simply mute them in the minds of those remaining performers. In a short space of time no one will sing these weakened songs and they will be truly dead. This is, of course, a major victory for us. To a lesser extent, the repertoires of other prominent figures will be similarly disposed of as their ability to transmit is destroyed, and we expect the project to peak by the end of the year, at which time other impediments to our influence can be tackled."

"Who *is* that guy?" Willie asked as the picture dissolved.

"That's Nick. Didn't I tell you he's a pistol? Did you ever hear anything so rich?"

"Did he say what I thought he said? Did he have the collections at the Library of Congress blown up?"

She nodded.

"Sam's death?"

"Well—no. Can't take credit for everything, though, well, hell, why not. Sure. Slugged the old geezer right in his sentimental ticker."

Willie took a deep breath to keep his whiskey down.

"How about the plane wreck with Nedra and Josh? That an accident?"

"Nicky baby has something to do with 'most all so-called accidents, darlin'. What's the matter? You look like you ate somethin' bad. I showed you that to give you a laugh. Don't tell me—"

"No, no," he said hurriedly. This was more a nightmare than a dream by now and he had no idea what kind of a thing Lulubelle Baker was but he knew enough not to antagonize her. "Just that these here saddle sores are gettin' sorer all the time."

She pulled a little vial of powder from her cleavage and shook it at him. "I have something right here that will fix you right up. It's new—devil dust—lots better than angel dust."

He might have known an aspirin was too much to expect in this place. "It's okay, darlin'. If you don't mind I'll just use your bathroom and mop 'em off again while I'm in there. Then I reckon I'd better get back to the ranch and see—"

"You can't go back now," she said, her red eyes kindling threateningly.

"Oh, just long enough to clear my name, darlin'," he called back casually.

"I jest showed you that 'cause I thought you'd get a kick out of it," she wailed in a wounded fashion. "Nicky'd be real unhappy if he knew about it but I told him, shoot, Nick, some of those singers are my best folks and I felt like you'd like knowin' how we gave all those do-gooders their come-uppance."

"Who's Nick? Is he some kind of organized crime boss?"

"Not crime. We don't care one way or the other about law. Just what seems like fun, stirrin' things up some. There now, try a little of this. You'll like it. It won't hurt you, honest."

She held out the vial to him. He held out his pistol to her, barrel first.

"Don't think I can say the same about this, Lulubelle. I want to thank you for your hospitality, for the entertainment, but just now I think I'll be on my way if it's all the same to you."

Her laugh was as bitter as bile. "No skin off my ass, darlin'. I was just bein' friendly, for old times' sake. Outta the goodness of my li'l ol' black heart. Go on and make a fool of yourself. Run your goddamn mouth. Nobody's gonna believe an old soak like you anyway. And you missed the chance of your life to make beautiful music instead of that racket you used to make."

The banjo twanged "Goodnight Irene" all the way down the steps, through the crowd, and out the door where Willie stepped into the brightness of a hot Texas morning, blinked to adjust his eyes, and found himself in the middle of an empty plain beside an exhausted horse. He knew it was exhausted because he could see its chest heave once in a while and because it didn't stink any worse than it did, which it would have if it was dead.

▲▲▲

News of Josh Grisholm's death sent Julianne Martin straight to her spiritual advisor, Lucien Santos. Fortunately, Santos had been able to see her right away. He was immensely popular, as he should be, since he possessed a psychic gift greater than any of the others Juli had entrusted herself to for healing after George was gunned down at the job he had taken at a convenience store to try to pay off the IRS. Santos's past life regressions and transchanneling were so eerie that he'd rapidly become the most popular psychic counselor in Joplin, Missouri, winning many converts and thoroughly alienating the rest of the psychic community in Joplin. Professional jealousy, Julianne figured. Because Santos was not only very gifted, he was also very wealthy.

Even before George's death, Santos had relieved much of the sense of pain and loss she'd felt at having to give up doing music full-time to work at waitressing. She had seen Santos once, then, and George had gone around tight-lipped for a week. When she'd finally gotten him to talk he said, "Jule, we can barely afford rice and you spent seventy-five dollars to have that guy tell you you used to be a jongleur in the court of Eleanor of Aquitaine.

I wish you'd have hit Ellie up for a loan while you were back there to pay her messenger boy."

She'd thought George was probably jealous too. Lucien was a good-looking guy, tall, fit, redheaded, and with the most penetrating brown eyes that seemed to absolutely burn with warmth when he looked at her. She didn't tell George that Lucien hadn't charged her the full seventy-five dollars, but told her he saw better things coming for her and he was so sure of it, he'd let her pay him the rest when her good fortune materialized. That was pretty nice. Certainly not the mark of a charlatan. And when George was killed, Lucien was so wonderful that Julianne thought he probably was developing a thing for her. But maybe not. When she'd withdrawn into herself for a while and not consulted him, he hadn't seemed to mind, and was always glad, almost relieved, to see her. He never had charged her full price and he had done her so much good.

Not only did she feel much better after she saw him, but she was in awe of his quite exceptional powers. Through him she had actually talked to George several times, received messages, been able to tell George the things there hadn't been time for before his death. When she was with Lucien, it was like George had never died, as if the bottom hadn't ever dropped so suddenly out of her life. When Lucien transchanneled for her it was sort of like talking long distance to the other side, and in her past-life regression, she knew what she learned was not her imagination or a dream. Wide awake, under only a very light trance, she had *seen* herself in Eleanor's court, and in a later session, in a later life as a troubadour for Mary Queen of Scots. Even just in ordinary counseling, Lucien never had to fish for what her problem was or resort to vague generalities as so many other practitioners had to.

She composed herself on the couch, deep-breathing as she'd learned in yoga class. Lucien deep-breathed for a few moments too. This room was so restful, with a tape of soft panpipe music playing in the background, the warmth of a small woodburning stove, sandalwood incense perfuming the air. Chimes tinkled at the window and crystals glinted soothingly from odd spots around the room. Lucien always turned down the lights and now, through her closed eyelids, a spot of bright warmth penetrated from the flame of a fat red candle Lucien burned to give clients something to focus on during sessions.

Lucien's voice was a warm baritone, with a faint trace of foreignness about it, she wasn't sure what, something Spanish since his name was Santos? Or maybe Portuguese? It completely disappeared when he was channeling. "Oh, Julianna," he said, softening and broadening the a's, "once again, you are grieving."

"Yes," her voice sounded far away to her, as if it belonged to someone else.

"Someone you liked very much, admired, maybe even loved, has passed to the next phase."

"Yes."

"And this person's death, coming so soon after George's death, makes you feel isolated and cursed and so very much alone."

"Yes."

"This was Josh Grisholm, wasn't it? The one who died? He was an extraordinary performer and, I believe, a great influence on your art."

She nodded, tears rolling down her cheeks from the sympathy in his voice.

"But, Julianna, you know he isn't far. You have learned that much with me, surely. And we've talked in our sessions about George. How by pairing with another musician rather than a patron who could appreciate your uniqueness you put false boundaries on your art, on the type of expression you allowed yourself, repeating your patterns from former lives and former failures and manifesting failure for yourself because George, in life, had such negative patterns. Now you are doing so much better, working at a steady job, getting in touch with yourself, focusing on your inner power rather than diffusing it as you did when you and George did music together."

"But I miss it," she said. "And Josh's death reminds me how much I miss it. Also, I've learned so much from you that I want to use the music to share what I've learned. Lucien, it *feels* like the right thing to do and now, with Josh's death, I realize how short life is, how little time is left to teach and to learn."

She opened her eyes and saw Lucien nodding, smiling through his red mustache and goatee. If it hadn't been for the way he wore his long red hair in a braided ponytail, he would have looked more like a Freudian psychiatrist than the more nontraditional counselor he was.

"Well, then, Julianna," he said as if he had known what she was feeling all along, "then now may be the time for you to begin what you have learned you must do. Let's see if anyone on the other side has any guidance for you." His head dropped to his chest. "Has anyone out there got messages for Julianna?"

After a moment, George's voice addressed her directly. She caught her breath sharply, feeling a reluctance she only now recognized to hear George's voice, so familiar but also, somehow, so alien, when she wasn't able to see him, touch him. Sometimes to have him with her only in such a limited way seemed almost more painful than comforting. But she didn't like to seem uncaring so she had never expressed that thought to Lucien. Odd that he hadn't picked it up.

"Juli, hi, babe. How's my girl?"

"Fine, George. How are you, honey?"

"Oh, you know, it's always great around here. Harp practice, heavenly choir rehearsals."

She sighed. "Must be some good jams there lately with all the musicians who have crossed over. Is Josh there?"

"He's on his way. Processing in now, I think. Look, babe, I just wanted to tell you that your feelings are absolutely right and I'm glad Lucien is giving me the chance to tell you. You've been so lonely and the waitress job has been such a drag for a creative woman like you. You need to get out, go to a festival again, meet some of our old friends. Now, listen to me. In the mail today you'll be receiving the announcement for a festival in honor of all of us who have gone before. You should go."

"Hon, I can't. I don't have the money for a bus and I have to work and . . ."

"Manifest it, baby. Hitch if you have to but go. Stop with all this whining and crying and start moving."

She winced. George was a lot more critical and bossy now that he had crossed over than he had been in life. But then, once a person got to the other side, they surely *knew* what was a mistake for the living and what wasn't. He was just trying to help her.

"And, Jule?"

"Yes, George."

"When you get back, you should start working with Lucien on developing your own powers. We can feel your vibes clear over on this side. You could be great help to others, hon. Oops. I'm being summoned. I think they may want me to show Josh around. Talk to you later, babe."

Julianne nodded as if he could see her.

Lucien shook himself and sat up straight, opening his eyes. "Well, who was there?"

"George."

"Did you kids have a nice chat?"

"Well, yes, but he wants me to go to a folk festival and I . . ."

"That might be a good thing, Julianna. To put a closure on all of this garbage from your past about music. Go. Confront all those people and exorcise them. And then perhaps you can begin to explore other options, allow George to rest and break out of the patterns of your previous lives and start living this one."

Lucien wished her such luck on her trip that he didn't charge her at all for his services. And since she was so hurt and confused and still so much at a loss, and since it gave her a direction that made her feel as if she was actually taking charge of her life, she sat down and wrote a song as soon as she got home, packed a tote bag and her spoons, and began a daily vigil for the invitation George promised would come in the mail.

CHAPTER VII

▲▲▲

Willie stood blinking in the pounding sun. When he saw a mirage, he saw a dandy. Well, maybe. A bawdy house where the whores watched folk music terrorist programs on the six o'clock news wasn't a whole lot less probable than talking rattlesnakes, but that wasn't sayin' much. If he accepted the fact that he'd just escaped a devil woman, where'd that get him? Here was where, alone miles from civilization with nothing but a half-dead horse, a pistol to shoot it with, and a banjo that seemed to think the whole thing was funny since it started tickling itself with "The Old Gray Mare She Ain't What She Used to Be."

His nostrils tickled faintly as the dust rose with a hot wind. Off in the distance, a dust cloud plumed up in the north. If anything could have surprised him by now, which it couldn't, he would have been surprised since he was near no road that he knew of. In fact, now that Lulubelle's was gone, he wasn't sure exactly where it was that he was supposed to be except out in the middle of an enormous expanse of parched Texas landscaped with nothing but rocks, dust, dry grass, mesquite, and tumbleweed. But wherever he was, he now saw that a beat-up blue Chevy pickup was bearing down on him, the sun glinting on the windshield.

It screeched to a halt a few feet from the horse's tail. The door banged open and the driver lumbered out, jerked off his battered black hat, and threw it in the dust.

"Goddammit, MacKai, I heard there was a bad case of horse abuse out here but I never expected to find you here."

"I don't think it was probably 'horse' that they said, Brose, but it's real good to see you anyway."

"What'd you do to this animal?" Brose Fairchild asked.

"More like what he did to me. You wouldn't believe it. Who the hell called you from way out here?"

"Beats me. Someone who wanted you to catch hell anyhow."

"You gonna try to save this cayuse or shoot 'im?"

Rivulets of sweat ran from the clown-red wool of Brose's hair down his face, which was dusted with large brown spots, bigger than freckles. The shape of his features was the same as those of his long-gone papa, a black "travelin' man." The red hair and beige color he got from his mama, a stripper from Kansas City who had been professionally known as the Wild Irish Rose.

Once Willie and Brose had toured together, Willie doing cowboy songs and sixties folk, Brose playing blues licks on six-string and twelve-string like nobody on the circuit had heard live before. Then he'd blend the blues into an Irish waltz and finish off with a reel. But he'd gotten sick of it somewhere along the way, and now he worked as a sort of troubleshooter for the animal protection agencies, locating and rescuing animals no one else thought worth saving, taking them back to his ranch and nursing them to health.

He and Willie hadn't seen much of each other in recent years, nothing at all in the last two.

"If you don't look damned silly, with that banjo around your neck and that gun in your pants," Brose said. "And how is it you're gettin' it to play 'Cool Water' all by its little ol' self?"

"It was Sam Hawthorne's banjo," Willie said. "It's been doin' this ever since Mark brought it over to the ranch. I sort of figure that must have been the secret of Sam's success, having it so well trained it played itself so he could just kick back and sing. Now then, let's shoot that horse or load it and get back to your place and I'll tell you about it."

"It's your horse, MacKai. You decide. You want to try to save 'im, we'll try." Brose had saved a lot of beasts that, from a farmer's or rancher's viewpoint, weren't worth the trouble. Lots of people had considered him not worth the trouble too, at one time or another.

"It's not exactly *my* horse. In fact, some people are claiming I stole it."

"Same difference," Brose said slowly. "You stole it. You decide."

"Aw, shit. Let's have a try at saving him. I ain't real sentimental about horses ordinarily but ol' Strawberry is an ornery independent cuss and I identify with that. Certain parties played a dirty trick on both of us and that's a hell of a thing to do to a good horse, not to mention a good man."

He and Brose rubbed the horse down with a gallon of alcohol Brose poured over the horse's heaving sides. Then Brose took a turkey baster and forced bottle after bottle of Gatorade down the beast's mouth to replace the fluids and salts it had lost. Finally, they used a special winch Brose had built into the back of the truck to hoist the horse into the truck bed. Brose tied a tarp over the top of the truck bed to shield the animal from the sun and the men climbed in the cab, Willie with quite a lot of difficulty. The hot seat nearly fried him and he had to fan it with his hand for a moment before he could stand to sit down.

"Now then," Brose said. "What you doin' takin' up horse rustlin' in your old age? I thought you was workin' on your pappy's boss's ranch."

Willie told him everything starting with the accident. Including the talking rattlers.

"Sounds like DT's okay," Brose allowed. " 'Cept like you said, two minutes between shots ain't long enough for withdrawal to cut in." Privately, he wasn't so doubtful of Willie's story. Working alone on his place with injured animals, Brose had begun noticing things, seeing and hearing things he wasn't prepared to talk about to most people. Those rattlers may not have actually talked to Willie, but Brose knew Willie let things get to him more than he admitted most of the time. If he was, say, in shock over Mark's death, and surprised the snakes by blundering in a way a man born and bred to snake country might not normally blunder, well, then, no wonder if his own guilt put words in the snake's mouth he meant for himself.

The rest of the story got wilder though, with Lulubelle Baker and her crazy television programs. When Willie had finished Brose asked, "That what you plannin' to tell the cops?"

"I don't even want to *think* about the cops," Willie moaned.

"If they thinkin' 'bout you the way you say, you better dull that story down some if you want to tell it to them and keep out of the psycho ward."

Now, Brose was no slouch at making up big lies himself. He'd been doing it most of his life, one way or another, to survive and to entertain himself, get himself laid, and sometimes to entertain other people. He and Willie had spent enough time on the road together they knew each other's lies, the kinds of lies they told, when they were most apt to get elaborate. This was not Willie's kind of time. Of course, Willie was a more accomplished actor than Brose had ever been, but still, Willie MacKai was unlikely to waste a windy of that magnitude on an audience of one man he knew had a well-developed built-in bullshit detector.

Besides, Willie never lied about no whores. Willie never would admit to needing whores. His stories about whores would be more like how they didn't want to be with any other man after being with him, not how one of them was patting him on the back for being so damned bad.

And there was all that weird business with the guy on the tube bragging about doing in the Archives and Sam Hawthorne and being behind those diseases—sounded like somebody had been doin' too many drugs to Brose. But Willie never did drugs and his paranoia didn't lean in the direction of diseases, not as long as Brose had known him. It was more in the direction of communist plots and there had not been word one about communists in the whole story. Still, Brose didn't see any reason why someone couldn't change the kind of crazy he was. But though the story might be embroidered or Willie might plausibly have gone nuts sitting around with nothing to do but count cows, Brose believed that Willie believed what he was saying. And maybe it was true. Nothing surprised Brose much anymore.

"So," he asked. "You done any testing yet, see if what she showed you is for real or not?" They were back on the highway now, the truck making good time. It looked like a wreck but a friend of Brose's had fixed it up good in exchange for a couple of retired ponies for his kids.

"How do you mean?" Willie asked. He had been trying to lean up on the side of one thigh against the door to keep his rear from making contact with the bumps but it wasn't much use.

"Sing one of the songs you learned from Hawthorne."

He started with the popularized Leadbelly song "Goodnight Irene," one Sam was well known for singing, since the banjo had been plunking it only a short time before. But for once, not only would the lyrics not come, but they would not fit into the tune properly. He remembered the title, or thought he did, and tried to fit it in to the verse, but it didn't work and he found himself singing, "Goodnight, Irene, goodnight, Irene," until he began to wonder if maybe the song didn't go "Good morning, Irene," or "Good afternoon, Elaine," or maybe he had made it up and it probably wasn't a very good song anyway, if he couldn't remember it. He tried all of his usual tricks, and though the melody was still in his head, sort of, it would not transfer itself onto his vocal chords.

So he tried "Wild Bill Jones" and "Darlin' Corey," and "Banks of the Ohio," and "Adelita," all with no more success. He kept struggling and struggling.

"Ah, come on, man," Brose said, "you shittin' me. You can't remember 'Goodnight Irene'?"

"You know the goddamn thing as well as I do. You try," Willie snapped.

Brose opened his mouth, then shut it again, and snapped back. "Can't. I been tryin' all the time you been tryin'. It's bound to be on some old record. In some old book. Or one of Sam's old cronies back East will know."

"Will they?"

"Sure. Them folks back East not only memorize a song, they even read music and write stuff down and write down three hundred and fifty-seven versions under twice that many titles and all different tunes. They're nuts about it. If they don't remember it, they can dig it up."

They kept trying to remember other songs, and some of the songs in their own repertoires returned but none of the ones either ever remembered hearing Sam sing would come back, not in the least. And the banjo was no help. Once in a while a song would drift over the strings, but it was never the same song the men were trying to sing. It was as if the damned thing was haunted by the ghosts of songs that were as insubstantial and elusive as any Halloween creation in a transparent bedsheet.

Both men were hoarse from singing through the dust and heat by the time they drove up the corduroy bumps of the long road to Brose's place. The house was unprepossessing since tidiness and do-it-yourself repairs were not exactly Brose's strong points. Three fat cats of assorted colors waddled out to meet the truck, then stopped and scratched fleas while a pack of dogs yelped and wagged their way across the packed clay and tufts of brown grass to jump up on the truck sides.

A tight cluster of cows, most of them limping or blindly bumbling into one another, had stampeded toward the fence as the truck approached, and between the barking and the loud "MaaAAAW" of the cows and the bleating of the sheep and goats, it was quite a welcoming committee.

"Quiet'n down, y'all," Brose bellowed, then stooped to scratch ears before crawling in the back of the truck to check the horse.

Various other former patients wandered through the yard, with or without the benefit of fences, a plucked-tailed peacock, a flock of half-feathered chickens, and a llama among them.

"Well, he's still alive," Brose said when he'd checked the horse and climbed back down from the truck bed. "I'm gonna give him some more fluids and let him rest a minute, then we'll drive on into the barn and unload him."

They waded through the debris in the house and Brose

unbuckled the string of belts that held the refrigerator door shut and extracted two cans of Dos X.

"You know anybody to call?" he asked. "Somebody else who might know those songs?"

"I've got a bunch of numbers in my address book back at the ranch, but I came sort of underdressed for the occasion here," Willie said, but his words trailed off to a mumble toward the end. He took a long slug of beer and said, "Buddy, I appreciate your help and this is real interesting and all, but I'm so whipped I can hardly wiggle. Could I talk you out of a shower and a place to crash for a while?"

Brose grunted and nodded toward a metal cabinet shower covered with a curtain in the side of the hallway. The bed was piled with laundry and after his shower Willie shoved it to one side and flopped down on his stomach beside it.

He wasn't aware of falling asleep until something stirred in the room and he awoke to see Brose, smelling of soap, deodorant, and aftershave, wedged between the foot of the bed and a full length dimestore mirror and looking a little like a red-haired refugee from an Arabian Nights story. The red woolly mane sported a black fez with a foot and a half of red silk tassel brushing the shoulder of a white embroidered shirt. Yards of wide red sash joined the shirt to a pair of black pants only lightly dusted with animal hair.

"You joined the Shriners, buddy?" Willie asked.

"Nah, go on back to sleep. I'm just goin' to a gig."

"What time is it?" Willie asked. His watch was on the drainboard back at the line shack.

"Sunday," Brose said. "Go back to sleep."

"Sunday? When was it you picked me up?"

"Friday. Go back to sleep. Forget it. I called your boss and told him the animal shelter sent me after his horse and in my opinion it had eaten some loco weed and damn near run itself to death."

"How did he sound?"

Brose shrugged. "Pissed off to have cops all over his place scarin' his livestock, since he don't recall invitin' them over. Also he's a little puzzled as to how a dead

man got left on his property. I think he's worried about
you more than anything. He's inclined to blame the
whole thing on commie wetbacks."

"I like that idea. Wish I could buy it," Willie said, half
to himself. "Got any coffee?"

"Some. Couple of days old, though. Well, so long.
Don't wait up, mom."

"Hold on, hold on. Where you going really?" Willie
was not normally so curious on awakening. Usually, he
was not fully conscious till three cups of coffee slid down
his throat. But two days of sleep and a strong wish not to
be left alone with the general weirdness surrounding
Mark's death worked better than caffeine.

"A gig, I told you."

"I didn't know you still played."

"Lots you don't know."

"And what's with the outfit? Your band call themselves the Forty Thieves maybe?"

"Maybe. You wouldn't be interested. It's just a wedding reception, for Christ's sake. Go to sleep. Make
coffee. Just get off my back, man."

"Hey, no offense," Willie said.

"Look, it's not star stuff, okay? I play Balkan music
with a little band. Bunch of people I met through work."

"Balkan music? You mean like Polack weddings, that
kind of thing?"

"Ukrainian, Czech, Hungarian, yeah."

"Funny, you don't look it. I thought you were a blues
man?"

"The jig who played jigs, right? Well, I just got tired of
singin' the blues all the time, man. And playin' the Irish
top forty. I wasn't playin' nothin' at all until one day
some client came into the shelter and recognized me from
when you and me was giggin' together. He said somethin'
in front of Burt Sherry and Burt got to asking me about
it. He said they had this little band, played weddings and
anniversaries, family reunions, retirement parties, that
kind of thing. I didn't think too much of it but one time
they were short a picker. Burt asked if I wanted to sit in.
I went along just to see what it was like."

"You must have liked it."

"Naw, you know, it's just all them Balkan blond chicks really dig a man in uniform," he said, straightening his sash.

"Well, damn, I'd like to see this," Willie said. "You taken up the accordion?"

"Come ahead on and see."

Willie looked down. He hadn't bothered to put his bloody, horsey cutoffs back on. "I haven't a thing to wear."

Brose grinned and pawed through the laundry. "It ain't formal. Here," he tossed a pair of jeans at Willie. "These ought to fit."

Willie pulled them on. "Where'd you get these? You lose weight for a while?"

"One of the kids from Dobie House left them last time he was here."

"You take in stray kids as well as animals?"

"Sometimes." He opened a closet door and dug inside, emerging with a rumpled white shirt on a hanger. "This *is* from when I lost weight one time. When I married Lila Jean. I weighed a hell of a lot less by the time she left."

"You got any people bandages or is your first-aid kit only for horses?" Willie asked. They found a roll of gauze and some antiseptic ointment that barely, painfully fit beneath the teenager's tight jeans.

They met the other band members outside the Moose Lodge. All but one guy had on an outfit like Brose's, and that guy had forgotten his fez.

Willie brought the banjo along, just because he didn't want to leave it. They set up on a little stage covered with white crepe-paper bunting. There were two accordions, a mandolin, and Brose's guitar. Ladies in pearls and silky pastel dresses were arranging cold cuts and raw vegetables on plates around the wedding cake. An ice sculpture of a giant wedding ring melted slowly into the punch bowl.

The bride had long, lustrous dark hair and a clear complexion spread over about a 280-pound, five-foot ten-inch frame. The gown almost concealed how pregnant she was but nobody seemed to mind. The groom, a husky fellow several years younger than his new wife, looked as madly in love as brides are supposed to. As the reception line dwindled the accordions wheezed into action and the newlyweds bounced into a polka. After a few bars, the father of the bride cut in and pinned a hundred-dollar bill to her dress. One after another, the other men in the wedding party cut in and also pinned bills to her dress until she looked like a large dancing money tree.

A lot of the dances were line dances, women dancing like beads on a necklace, doing a totally different kind of dance from the men, who danced together in their own lines. When they broke into couple dances, grandparents danced with brisk young relatives, teenagers with toddlers, all age groups mixing and making sure everyone had a chance to dance. The older men were the best dancers, and the most tireless.

The bride spotted Willie and pulled at his hands. He was still having trouble walking but that didn't stop him from showing off a mean polka, though it was more of a Mexican-style one than a Polish one. The bride jounced along like a big sexy beach ball, grinning happily and sweating through the light sprinkle of glitter powder across her cheeks and chest.

Willie was sweating too. The only ventilation in the crowded hall was from the doors, which were propped open to the hot afternoon, and an overhead ceiling fan.

Then someone shouted out what sounded like a request but the song title wasn't in English. The band struck up a tune and the bride's father started a sort of line dance, catching up the bride, the groom, the mother, and Willie in the sweep of people bobbing through the hall. When the dance panted to a halt, someone called another name, but this time the accordions groaned, the mandolin dithered, and a mumbled consultation took place among the musicians. Willie disengaged himself from the line and ambled toward the stage. Brose caught his eye. "How many damn songs do you suppose Hawthorne knew anyway?"

The bride's father shouldered his way to the stage. "Hey, what's the problem, fellas? How come you don't play what my guests ask for?"

The man Brose had introduced as Burt Sherry said, "Sorry, Fred. We seem to have forgotten it."

"Forgotten it? I know you know it. I heard you play it at Charlie Andreas's girl's wedding. I could have hired some kids to play the other stuff . . ."

"Hey, nothing to get excited about. We got sheet music at home. We just usually know it so well we don't bother anymore. But tell you what. Hum a few bars and we'll fake it."

But Fred couldn't hum it, the wife couldn't hum it, the bride never listened to anything but classical outside of weddings, and none of the guests could remember either. The band played a few more popular numbers, but the party broke up early, despite the introduction of a second tub of iced beer. And Fred paid only half of what he owed them.

The banjo tinkled "Nobody Knows You When You're Down and Out" as Willie slung it across his back. Burt Sherry was still arguing with Fred while the others packed up their instruments. A hot gust of wind swept into the hall from the open door and blew two of the tissue paper bells down from where they were thumbtacked to the ceiling beams. The ladies' skirts filled like sails and the swish of taffeta, lace, silk, chiffon, and nylon rivaled the rattling leaves of the big cottonwoods as freshly manicured, damp-palmed hands tried to subdue the garments. "Burt, I *will* think of that song—" one of the accordion players said. "I can sort of hear it back there behind my eardrum, I just can't . . ."

"I know just what you mean. Look, I was going to go home and water the lawn but what say we all go back to my house and look it up, have a beer?"

Brose grunted and started to back away but Burt said, "Come on, Brose. You can check up on those pups you gave the kids. Evvie-Ann has been asking about you."

The old Brose Willie used to know would have made some remark but the one in the fez just looked uncomfortable and nodded. The last stragglers from the reception sat in their thrumming cars, patiently awaiting entrance to the highway while Brose and Willie walked toward the truck, the wind whipping up dust and dandelion fluff, old leaves and new bugs, filling the air with ozone and a whiff of smoke—too much for a trash fire—maybe a big brushfire from a roadside clearance project.

They followed Burt's Mustang and the van shared by the other three farther away from the center of town, out toward Lake Austin. They reached one of the new shopping centers and a condo development in which each unit looked like someplace Shakespeare could have lived, except that it was cloned several hundred times over and stacked and bunched together. Somehow among all of these, down three roads, past linear acres of parking lot, two swimming pools, and a golf course, Burt turned into a parking spot and motioned them to park opposite, next to what would probably soon be yet more condos but was presently a baseball diamond.

Willie didn't much care what they did. He had caught up enough on his sleep that he could keep his eyes open, but the world was still as blurry as if he'd had too much to drink and his bones felt like so many cooked noodles.

He tried to figure out what the hell it was he was doing here, driving up to a Tudor tract house in the middle of Texas with a black ex-blues man in a fez and a couple of accordion players.

A woman with yards of model-quality legs stretching from the hem of her cutoffs to the mottled carpet looked up from her vacuuming when they came in. "Hah there, swee'pea," she greeted Burt in a thick West Texas twang. Then she saw the rest of them. *"Brose,"* she said, "how you bin? The kids are out messin' with that flop-eared dawg you give us."

Brose grinned. Willie shook his head in wonder. Brose had changed his style but not much else.

"Honey, you seen my Croatian songbook? Funniest thing happened today . . ." Burt's voice rose above the greetings of the others. For the first time Willie noticed that his accent wasn't Texan. There'd been so many people from the East move in a few years ago, when computers were all the thing. Then the bottom dropped out of oil and a whole big segment of the Texan population migrated elsewhere, some of them to the East, so accents were more homogenized than they had once been.

Evvie-Ann high-stepped across her vacuum cleaner to a big hutch meant for fancy dishes but filled with books. "I think it's in here, sweetie pie. And, oh, look, this here come in the mail for you today. Them're the guys you played with back in Pittsburgh, aren't they?"

She brushed a lank lock of dishwater-blond hair from her forehead with her hand, leaving a dark smudge on her brow. Burt meticulously removed the staple from a dot-matrix–printed flier photocopied onto flimsy white paper.

"Yeah. Brose, you knew some of these guys, didn't you? Josh Grisholm, Sam Hawthorne, that Buchanan woman that used to be in all those protest marches? They're having a sort of benefit concert for them next week."

"Sure 'nuff?"

"Yessir. Looks like a big deal. God, I wish I could go. My old band, the Povatitsas, are going to play, and a bunch of the other ethnic bands, Italian, Irish, Fillipino, American Indian. And whoever survived the crash and whoever else they can talk into coming I guess."

Brose caught Willie's eye. "Let me have a look at that, will you, Burt?"

▲▲▲

Crazy Ruthie the Dog Lady allowed as how she might like that Brose fellow, but she'd had enough of silly Willie for a while and who the hell was the woman Sam Hawthorne had called after he was dead?

Gussie didn't look pleased to be interrupted in the middle of her story, but Crazy Ruthie was so used to people not looking pleased at her she didn't even notice. "I want to know what kind of a nut gets crank calls from people claiming to be dead and then goes back to sleep?"

"Whaddayou care?" Pete asked. "You ain't had a bed or a phone since you can remember."

"That's got nothin' to do with it."

"Why don't you shut up and let Gussie talk?" Tony asked. He hadn't been feeling so good lately and the gentle smile was more often a snarl, except while he was listening

to the story. "You're nothin' but a flea-bitten old bitch, you pain in the ass."

Crazy Ruthie said she would sic her dogs on him when she saw him again and Pete hollered at both of them but Gussie said, "That's it."

"What?" everybody asked.

"I was tryin' to decide how to tell you about Anna Mae Gunn and that's what a lot of people said about her. Not old, not flea-bitten, but maybe a hard-bitten bitch, and absolutely and quite intentionally a pain in the ass. General Mortimor Boron, who was her friend Sylvia's boss, hated her. So did her own boss, but he was better at keeping secrets since he was by way of being in the secret-keeping business, so he was smarmy nice to her in spite of not being able to stand her."

"Well, if she was such a pain why did Sam want her to organize the whing-ding?" Crazy Ruthie challenged with her chin stuck out so it almost touched her nose.

"Yeah, if first Mark, then Willie had his banjo, why didn't Sam ask one of them to do it?" Pete demanded.

"Dummy," Tony said, "Sam was dead. He knew that first boy he gave the banjo to was dead."

"That must have been it," Gussie said. "Thanks, Tony. Of course, Sam would have known since they'd be dead together and everything. And he'd never ask Willie MacKai. Willie's a nice enough fellow in his own way but he was doin' good to organize himself into openin' a pack of smokes, much less organizin' anybody else. And Sam wasn't the kind of man who got to know everybody real well and earlier in his life, somehow, he'd gotten to know Anna Mae Gunn. She would never win any popularity contests, but she had organized the Annapolis festival for three years running and done a little agenting on the side, besides being a fine singer of Native American chants. And she was tough and thorough and a large part paranoid, which was a very sensible way to be in those days and qualified her real well for the job, though even she couldn't have known just who was watching her movements and just how interested they would be."

▲▲▲

General Boron didn't know much about Anna Mae but he didn't like small, dark, foreign-looking women on principle. Never mind that Anna Mae's darkness was because she was half Native American. She was always swift and sharp, didn't smile much, and had a hysterical intensity that let the General know without ever talking to her much that she was a troublemaker. His secretary, Sylvia, was more what a woman ought to be, tall and elegant and silver-blond. What she saw in that skinny rubber band of a woman he had no idea. So he was both interested and annoyed when the Gunn woman popped into the office and handed Sylvia something and Sylvia went to the copy machine. He casually made a trip to the latrine, and on the way glanced at what was emerging from the machine. As he expected, it wasn't official business.

He'd have to discuss this with Sylvia. The Gunn woman was messed up in some kind of Indian squabble a few years back and she was subversive. He couldn't see why Brett kept her around. She was a goddamn spy and he was sure of it. When he read the flier, he was even surer, and he called Brett at once.

The call was interrupted by Sylvia, who wanted to know what the invoice for all the gasoline and gelignite was for. "Field maneuvers," he told her shortly.

Too damn bad but something would have to be done about Sylvia too. The General grabbed his hat and left the office, strolling casually down the mall until he reached an outdoor pay phone and dialed a coded number. "Nick? Boron. I've found something that relates to that little project of ours. My secretary and some friend of hers are behind it. I think it's a matter for the civilian authorities though. You got a man? Good, good. Glad to be of service. Have 'em fire off a round for me."

CHAPTER VIII

▲▲▲

A kid stood loitering by the fence post where the corduroy road turned off from the county road to Brose's place. The kid had a shaved head with some kind of drawing on it, and wore jeans with no shirt or shoes.

Brose leaned out the window. "Hey, Morris, what's goin' on? Need a lift?"

"Oh, I coulda got me a lift, okay. In a cop car. Just thought you might like to know, my man, that the heat's down at your place. Somethin' about a horse and some dude who—" He peered around at Willie. "Uh—just thought you needed to know."

Brose picked up the pistol Willie had brought with him and began inspecting it while he thought. "You come down here alone?" he asked Morris.

"Naw, me and Bubba and Joe-Ed got a ride from South Congress, thought we'd come see you just for the hell of it."

"You know the drill. Where the feed is, the medicine. Me'n Willie gotta go do something. You guys stick around and take care of the critters?"

"Well, sure but . . ."

"Don't eat everything in the fridge and be sure and belt the damned thing back up, okay?"

"Okay."

"You got any money on you?"

"Some."

"How much?"

"Angie's new squeeze laid fifty on me to get lost."

"Lay it on me and get lost here."

"Rent?"

"A loan. Snot-nose kid like you don't need fifty dollareses nohow."

Willie had been quiet through all of this. Brose looked back and in the shadow of the cab saw Willie's eyes flicker, shining like those of a cornered fox. He caught Brose's glance and rubbed his jaw with one hand. "Sorry to drag you into this, pal. Fact of the matter is, though, I'm not sure how *I* got into it. Or what it is. I cannot believe the police saw that wreck and saw Mark's body and assumed I had something to do with his death. What the hell do they think I did, pulled him out of the wreck, then bopped him with a blunt object? *Why?* I mean, maybe that rattler was right and givin' him a drink wasn't exactly recommended in the first-aid book but hell, I didn't know nothin' about it and I sure didn't know he was so bad hurt. Besides, I just poured the stuff for him, not down him."

Brose nodded and didn't say anything more until they were halfway across East Texas. Part of the reason he didn't was that Willie had gone back to sleep, his chin sinking into his chest until he caught himself suddenly and threw his head back, snorting, where it lolled against the back of the seat. Brose kept the CB tuned to the police channels but heard nothing. They hadn't exactly talked about where they were going but Baltimore seemed as good a place as any. Brose knew a woman who might help them out. Willie no doubt knew several more. The important thing was to get there in one piece. People had gotten killed coming and going to festivals a lot these days. That's what this one seemed to be all about.

He took the back roads and drove throughout the night, then woke Willie up.

"Let's pull into an all-night grocery someplace before you go to sleep," Willie suggested. "Get us some coffee. In case they have my picture on TV. Shit, when I think of all the times I wanted my picture on TV and then to get it this way. Hell of a time to suddenly get photogenic."

They sat in the truck and drank the first cup of coffee before Brose returned to the store for a second cup, which he handed to Willie. "Thanks, buddy. No more for you?"

"I'm goin' to sleep. 'Sides, that shit's bad for your blood pressure, or ain't you gettin' old like the rest of us?"

"Older by the minute," he said. "You got any tapes in here?"

"Glove box."

"Bother you if I play one?"

"Nope."

He popped a tape into the player. It got halfway through the first number before the singer's voice deepened and slurred. He tried to pop it but it wouldn't budge. When it finally did, tape looped across his hand in a bright brown ribbon. He threw it on the floor and kept driving.

They changed places many more times before hitting the outskirts of Baltimore two days later, somewhere around four in the morning, when they saw the hitchhiker.

Willie's first impulse was to stop and pick up the wet, weary-looking woman. His second impulse was to forget it. He did not really believe Mark was dead, though he had seen the body, seen the wreck. He did not really believe a rattlesnake had accused him of murder and an ornery horse had carried him to meet a whore who was apparently part of some grand conspiracy. He did not honestly believe his problem with the police was anything that couldn't be cleared up by knowing the right people or that Lenny would be even angry enough to fire him once he understood that none of it had been his own fault, that all this stuff just seemed to happen—if it had happened, and if it hadn't, there was nothing to explain, was there? Except how was he out here on the road to Baltimore with a man he hadn't seen in three years, a banjo, a gun, and a collection of broken Styrofoam coffee cups and paper nacho trays? Whatever was going on, dream or real, he wasn't entirely sure he was ready for the next installment.

But the headlight beam threw into harsh relief the drooping blond head and the shoulders slumped under the weight of a backpack. And as he drove a little ways past, he thought there was something familiar about the woman, which, considering the number of women he'd known at one time or another, wasn't too unlikely. So he pulled over and honked. Brose roused, mumbling. In the

rearview mirror Willie watched the woman's head snap
up and the way she shifted the wet backpack as she broke
into a run.

She slowed as she approached the car and saw the
outline of the two men. Brose wasn't fully awake so Willie reached across him and opened the door, keeping the
gun close, just in case.

"Hi," she said, peering in at them but backing away
slightly, cautious. Brose was a pretty rough-looking character unless you happened to be an injured animal.
"Where you guys headed?"

The feeling that there was something familiar about
her grew stronger as Willie said, "Fredericks, Maryland,
wherever the hell that may be. How about you, ma'am?"
He never called women darlin' under circumstances
where the lady in question might possibly suspect him of
being a rapist-pervert. At least not before they'd been
formally introduced.

She took two fast steps closer. "Hey, Willie? Willie
MacKai? Is that you?"

"Sure is, sugar, but who's askin'?"

She was already scooting into the truck cab, butting
Brose to one side. He woke up just enough to grumble
and put his arm around Willie and his head on Willie's
shoulder. Willie patted his shoulder absently.

"Julianne Martin. Remember, Juli and George? You
told me I played the spoons like a hula dancer. I said I
didn't know hula dancers played the spoons."

He remembered, vaguely. He met a lot of people, a lot
of musicians. "Oh, sure, *that* Juli Martin. Brose, wake
up. We got company. This here is Julianne Martin. Well,
hi, Juli." He wasn't sure whether to ask about George or
not. Maybe they'd split the sheets.

"Are you going to the memorial festival, Willie?"

"Yes, ma'am. Josh, Sam, Nedra, they were good
friends of mine. Why, Sam was the man got me into
singing the music of our land to begin with. And one time
back in the sixties when I was playing some club in New
York and some drunk charged the stage, little old Nedra
Buchanan picked up a chair and brained him with it.
And Josh Grisholm, ah well, God, we're all gonna miss

Josh. I never heard tell of anybody could cut the bullshit artists down to size like ol' Josh could."

Juli nodded solemnly and wiped the rainwater from her face.

All of a sudden Willie wondered what the hell he thought he was doing. Was he going to try to *warn* these people at the festival of something some crazy whore had told him? What would he tell them, that he had seen a really wild videotape? For Christ's sake, he'd been speaking out for thirty years and nobody had listened to him, in spite of all he'd done. Why should he bother now? What did he owe these people anyway? He almost asked it out loud, asked Brose and Julianne Martin, but he hadn't had enough to drink to be that bold.

"Wow, this is really incredible," Juli said, chasing off the uneasy silence as the headlights chased the tufts of mist. "George and Lucien told me to come and now I know it was meant to be. My God, Willie MacKai. I haven't seen you since Dumas in—was it 1982?"

"That's right. You and George went on just before me. Do you mind my askin' where George is?" He thought it seemed pretty funny that George would tell his wife to go to a festival by herself even if she had to hitch across country to do it.

"You didn't hear about it, huh? About George, I mean?"

The smooth way her voice slid past her husband's name sounded sorrier to Willie than if she'd sobbed and all of a sudden he forgot about himself and his problems and said softly, "No, darlin'. I didn't hear anything. I've been out of touch. What about George?"

She told him very calmly about George being shot to death during a robbery.

"Jesus, Julianne. Darlin', that's just awful. I don't know what to say."

"Oh, it's okay now," she said. "He's doing fine on the other side and anyway, as Lucien says, we brought it on ourselves. It's just that I miss him and I miss playing music, even though I know now that that isn't my true path. But anyway, I wrote this song and both George and Lucien wanted me to come so here I am and now that

I've run into you guys I know it's a sign that it was the right thing to do."

"Uh-huh," Willie said. He was watching the road closely now and preoccupied wondering if he ought not to warn her now of what he knew, so although it sunk in that something was wrong about what she was saying, he wasn't listening closely enough to know what it was. He was more worried about how crazy he'd sound and she was still young and pretty and he didn't want it to look foolish. He'd have to think how to phrase it so she'd be properly impressed and a little scared—he sure as hell didn't want to be the only one who was scared. There was also the fact that he was a wanted man and even though it was a mistake, he didn't think it was all that great an idea to go advertising it around.

"You got any idea where this shindig is being held?" he asked.

She slung her pack up in front of her and dug around. "I don't know but it looked to me like it was pretty impromptu from the flier. I never heard of the producer and she didn't say who else was coming but it might be fun anyway, like an old-fashioned sing."

The banjo faintly tinkled "There's a Meetin' Here Tonight." Juli's silhouette dipped to examine it. "For heaven's sake. I could swear that banjo played by itself."

"Just a trick of the car bumping I suppose," he said.

"Mind if I look at it?" she asked.

He shrugged.

She picked it up, watched the vibrating strings for a moment, then turned it over and examined it, as if looking for a tape recorder, thinking it was a joke or something. "This is pretty amazing," she said.

"Ain't it just?" he agreed. "Impresses the hell out of me, darlin'."

"I can't figure out how you're doing this, Willie, and it's really fantastic the way you've fixed this thing up so it looks so much like Lazarus, Sam Hawthorne's banjo."

"Is that what he called it?"

"Um hmm. I read all about it, how he designed the first one that you could play without retuning all the time and how Manny Golden, the head of Uprising Records, had one special made by an Appalachian instrument maker. I remember because I was in college at the time and was fascinated by folk medicine and magic and the banjo maker was supposed to be from a long line of white witches. The interviewer from the *Folk Music Journal* asked him if that was why he was such a good instrument maker and the guy said sure, all his instruments had a spell to them. Hey, you know, I'd always thought this little quote here, 'May the circle be unbroken,' was Hawthorne's idea, but now I wonder, maybe it's part of the spell, do you think? The whole blacklist business ruined Manny and he died in the middle of it all and Sam has never talked much about any of it."

They drove off the beltway at about nine and pulled into a service station to call the contact number. A machine answered in a woman's low, rather nasal voice and gave directions to a small farming community outside of town. The directions said which country road to turn off on, mentioning that acts should sign up by five o'clock that evening.

"It does sound pretty casual," Juli remarked doubtfully. "Not like what you're used to, Willie."

"No indeed," he said. The festival he had been associated with had had only the top names, and not enough room for all of them, with the program carefully planned out so that the most expensive performers got the best slots, exceptionally talented people without names just sitting in the audience, playing at the all-night jam sessions, and hoping to win songwriting contests. The festival got so big, just before it collapsed due to a lot of bad weather and financial overextension at the time the oil boom went bust, that his name and photo were no longer considered a big enough draw for the promotional pamphlets.

▲▲▲

They took a break at the first highway rest stop. Willie and Brose stretched out under the tarp in the bed of the truck, leaving Juli curled up in the cab. Willie was dreaming:

He was at the old Flugerville Festival with its rows of

crafts booths and thinking how peculiar it was that one of the booths had been let out to an Irish instrument maker but some hippie girl whose eyes he couldn't see for a big hat and whose body he couldn't tell much about because she wore a loose huipil tried to sell him a doll dressed in Guatemalan handweaving. He knew it was a voodoo doll and had either a little microphone in it or some kind of drugs but since he didn't know which, he wasn't about to buy it. The girl's eyes burned red clear through her hat brim and the guy onstage was singing Hoyt Axton's song about the devil being a joker, lying, and in general acting like the old mule who'll be nice to you for two weeks just to get the chance to kick you. Someone was playing that one, on the banjo, and in his sleep Willie could feel his mouth moving to the music, the words slipping over his vocal chords and lifting his tongue and passing through his lips, and then he realized that he was the singer, and he was seeing the red-eyed hippie girl from onstage and her little voodoo doll was playing banjo except that the neck was strung with glittering pins and the tuning pegs were the heads of hatpins. And he heard a flapping above him and he thought, thunder, and he looked out over the audience, smiling, clapping people wearing leather bras and Mexican embroidered clothes and concho hatbands on wide straw hats, or Flugerville T-shirts or no shirts at all, all of them grinning and laughing and talking. All of them on benches around the stage except those lined up at the booths where vendors sold beer and hot dogs, barbecue ribs and sweet corn on the cob, cinnamon buns and popcorn, fajitas and nachos and soda pop. Some of the craft vendors were still doing business too, selling beaded earrings that shimmered like rainbows on waterfalls, tie-dyed shirts, Mexican and South American clothes woven in patterns of red, orange, green, purple, bright blue, birds, flowers, fish, cats, llamas. There was Indian silver work, Hopi, Navajo, concho belts, belt buckles, earrings, leatherwork, all manner of instrument makers with dulcimers and guitars inlaid with gold and pearl birds and dragons and eagles. There were songbooks and tapes, musical spoons and bones, face painters, hatters with rows of feather-banded Stetsons in felt and straw hung from hooks in pegboard, *covered with awnings that flapped with the wind. Why, it wasn't thunder after all, just the awning. Because the sun was still shining bright and pretty, even though it was time for the evening show and he was it. And then there was a shadow over it and the flapping was louder and he looked up to see what looked like a silhouette of the Angel Gabriel blowing sax, accompanying the banjo, but as the angel flew closer, it grew enormous and it was still blacker than the ace of spades, its crow-black, feathered wings flapping and making a mighty breeze and he could just make out the face and it was painted up like Lulubelle Baker's.*

And the banjo changed to start playing "House of the Rising Sun," and he couldn't remember the words because, of course, Sam Hawthorne had done that one once. That wasn't any angel up there, it was an angle, the Angle Gabrielle-Belle, and it was more like a cupid than an angel, a great big bare-assed cupid with a quiver on its back, except that it shot big hypodermic syringes and he knew they were full of dope and probably poisoned, like darts, with all those cruddy diseases you caught nowadays if you messed with women like Lulubelle. And she shot and he felt it hit him like a thunderbolt and thought, hell, maybe I got that Angle wrong, maybe it's Thor—shore is thore— and then it knocked him over again.

He was rolling around in the truck bed with the tarp flapping over him as Brose, who had given up sleeping in the heat that made Willie stink like a billy goat and made him sweat so bad that even his toes were sweating, put the truck in gear and jolted onto the highway.

They found the turnoff just after one o'clock. A few cars, vans, and trucks were ahead of them, but no big crowd Willie could see yet. A black-haired woman stood by a cattle gate. A sign that said PRIVATE PROPERTY NO TRESPASSERS was posted on the fence beside her left leg.

"Hi," she said, leaning over to look into the truck cab.

"This the Gunn place, ma'am?" Brose asked. "Place where the music festival is this weekend?"

"You folks pickers, are you?"

"Yes, ma'am," Brose said. "I'm Brose Fairchild and these here are—"

Willie leaned over the rim of the truck bed, "We're

Brose's Bouncin' Balkan Band, ma'am. And who might you be?"

"I'm Anna Mae Gunn. This is my place. I've heard of you, Brose, from the old times when you played blues with some South Texas cowboy, but I hadn't heard about your band."

She nodded curtly at Juli and Willie. She didn't look thrilled to see any of them. Her eyes were narrow under heavy black brows, her nose hawkish, and in a rounded face her mouth was thin, bitter-looking. Funny woman to be having a festival. But then, this was a memorial festival. Maybe she had a talent for grieving. "Go ahead on in, and welcome," she said formally, straightening up. "I'm just screening people right now. Set up your camp somewhere outside the bleachers. There are some fire pits dug for cooking already. Sylvia Bemis will sign you up for a spot tonight."

"Many other acts come through?" Willie asked.

"Check with Sylvia," she said abruptly, and swung the gate open for them.

They drove through it, and Anna Mae waved them down again. "Just one thing," she said. "We'll be bringing supplies in but we'd just as soon once you get here you stay here. I guess I can have on my property who I want and I'm not expecting a large crowd, but this is by invitation. I don't want strangers following you back to see what the traffic is all about."

Willie thought this was a peculiar way to run an entertainment business, but when he caught her eye for a moment, he realized she looked like he felt, spooked. She broke eye contact and she turned on her heel to greet another car.

The stage was the patio deck of a farmhouse, with logs and a few pieces of lawn furniture set all along the driveway. The side pastures had been cleared of whatever stock might be kept there and several vans, tents, and pickups with campers on the back were there. Rent-a-privies were lined between the camping area and the audience seating.

Brose parked near a fire pit. "That thing ain't going to do us a lot of good," Willie remarked, gesturing at the fire pit. "I hate to say it, buddy, but except for this here package of Oreos and half a paper plate of cold nachos, we ain't got a whole hell of a lot of stuff to camp with." Normally, he would have been touchy about the Gunn woman's admonition against leaving the site, but under the circumstances, he didn't blame her. He figured the same thing was on her mind as his. Well, maybe not Lulubelle, but some of the things he'd learned from her seemed to have occurred to Gunn.

Since they were early, they captured one of the best spots, with a tree and a little brush for shade and privacy. Brose picked it out, figuring they could sleep the same way they had on the way over. Willie didn't mind living rough, but he wasn't real used to doing it before he was going to perform.

Cars kept rolling in beside them and parking, and for a while they talked sleepily and watched who was coming. Then Willie said, "Well, friends, since there ain't no camp to set up and no coffee to brew, I reckon I'll catch up on some more of that napping. Seems to be the best thing going." He stretched out in the cab and Brose and Juli retired to the truck bed this time.

Sometime later, he awakened to the tickle of fur on his outstretched bare arm, brush, brush, pause, brush, and opened one eye to stare into that of an orange cat that perched with all four paws on the sill of the truck-cab window, the tail flicking softly against him as the cat tried to decide if there was room enough for them both in there. He was fully prepared to wallop the beast if it started talking to him but it looked down at him as if he were so completely out of its class it wouldn't bother if it could. Watching it, he became conscious of the sound of guitars and banjos being tuned, voices raised in greeting, song, argument, and sales pitch.

"It takes a worried man to sing a worried song . . ." some obviously worried man sang.

"Only a nitwit would credit the Lomaxes with that song. Frank Warner got that song from Yankee John Galusha in the forties . . ."

"Who gives a shit about that old stuff that's been done

over and over anyway? You gotta add something
new . . ."

"Have a beer?"

"Stop border harassment!" A wide West Texas voice
brayed, "Free the Chaveses! Yes, sir, sign right here.
What's it *about*? I'll tell you what it's *about,* mister. It's
about the goddamn feds lockin' up my little girl and her
husband and a better man never lived than our Mic, let
me tell you, just because they gave a friend a ride."

"Whoa!" Willie came awake and opened the cab door
so fast the cat had no time to vacate before he swung it
wide and jumped to the ground, right into the leavings of
the last tenant of the pasture.

He looked around at the gathered instruments, the
musicians talking, tuning, necking, and generally hanging
out. A tiny woman with a frizz of gray hair and shapely
tanned legs sticking out of khaki shorts was handing fliers to passersby, gesturing with the papers when she
wasn't waving them in the face of a bare-chested biker
type.

"Sounds to me, woman, like you are bad-mouthin' our
northernmost neighbors," the man said between belliger-
ent pops of bubble gum.

"No, you asshole, not the Canadian feds, *our* feds. Oh,
the Canadians do it too, the other way around, but our
damn fool government started it. Claimed it was for
drugs. Well, I'm here to tell you my Lettie nor my Mic
never did so much as a teeny little pointy leaf of marijuana a day in their lives. Why, you should have heard
Lettie when she caught me smoking with that no-account
Harold Beconovich in the parking lot outside the Bide-a-
wee Motel . . . what the sam h—"

"Augusta Turner, you delicious little morsel of feisty
female, it really is you!" Willie exclaimed, picking the
woman up, locking his arms around the Flugerville Folk
Festival logo that engulfed most of her torso, and
whirling her around two or three times.

She broke loose from him long enough to twist in his
arms and give him an enthusiastic bear hug, "Willie
MacKai! As I live and breathe! I might have knowed
you'd be here." The wind tore the papers from her hands.

"Damn! Help me catch these things, Willie. Won't do to go litterin' Miz Gunn's pasture."

He helped. The papers flipped up against tents and legs, slid under cars, and plastered themselves onto trees. "What's all this about now, Gussie?" he called to her across two jam sessions and a tarot reading. "What's this about Lettie and Mic?"

She snatched up the last errant paper they had any hope of catching and slumped down against a tree. He flopped down beside her. "Busted for smuggling drugs, of all things. Can you believe it?"

"I'm sad to say that of a large percentage of my acquaintance, yes, ma'am, I could believe it, but Lettie and Mic? No way. Who was this friend? Maybe he carried them in."

"That's what the feds claimed but, Willie, it was Hy MacDonald, this Scotch singer who's a friend of theirs. The customs people didn't do nothin' to Hy but send him back to Scotland but they locked up my children pending trial by a federal judge and I am not a rich woman, Willie, and I do not have the money to bail them out. And anyway, Hy MacDonald has written to me and to friends of mine and says it was absolutely a frame. He says he had nary a thing on him, not even a bottle, and yet they were calling him a drug runner and a political trouble-maker right out there in the customs station before they'd even searched anything. Of course, I don't know the man, but I do know my Lettie and my Mic and I do know Craig Lee over at Triumph Music and he's been to Hy's house in Scotland and to hear him tell it, Hy's the goddamn deacon of the goddamn church over there and, besides, wouldn't be caught dead smokin' anything but Players and gettin' high on anything but good scotch whiskey—patriotic man, Craig says he is."

Willie could easily believe that. He had the same feelings himself. He was religious too—though he favored bourbon over scotch, he never had cared a whole lot for drugs. For all the big deal made over it during and since the sixties, marijuana was still to him what it had been as a boy raised in a Bible Belt South Texas town a spittin' distance from Mexico—weed was what kids fooled around with and the Mexicans smoked because foreigners did them things. It was nothing a grown man old enough to drink good whiskey should concern himself with. He said so.

"Well, and I wouldn't be so surprised, still and all, if it was pot they claimed to find, though Lord knows Lettie's got more sense than to take it across the border even if she did it, which she doesn't. But, Willie, it was cocaine they found. Not a lot of it. But they claimed they found it in Lettie's purse. With a copy of her catalog."

"The owner of a record distribution company is a better target than a foreign musician, huh?" he mumbled, half to himself, so that Gussie said, "Huh?"

"Look, Gussie, there's a little more to this than it looks like. As a matter of fact, I ain't in awful good graces with the law myself right now. Mark Mosby upped and died on my doorstep the other day and now they're wantin' me to assist 'em with their inquiries, which does not sound all that good, especially considerin' some of the other weird shit that's been happenin' in my immediate vicinity these days."

"That's the dumbest damn thing I ever heard tell of," she said indignantly. "Well, second dumbest. No, come to think of it, that takes the cake but both are just plain stupid to anybody that knows any of y'all, though Lord knows there've been times when I've wanted to wring Mark's neck myself, nothin' fatal you understand, just to get his attention."

"Too bad nobody's asked you to be a character witness," Willie said wryly.

She snorted disgustedly and stared at the ground. The tanned skin of her face and arms looked as fragile as a Civil War–era newspaper. She shouldn't look so damned *old,* he thought. Gussie was only a few years older than he was.

He stared out across the parked RV's to the next pasture. A few head of cattle stood together in one section, several horses in another. The orange cat was now on the roof of someone's camper, sunning itself. In the opposite pasture, the one on the other side of the audience area, Anna Mae Gunn directed as a truck backed up next to a big stone barbecue pit he hadn't noticed before and two men started unloading big slabs of meat. Smoke rose from the pit. Elsewhere on the grounds, a soft-drink stand had been set up and a tent that advertised home-made pies.

▲▲▲

Brose and Juli stood talking to a woman at a card table up near the stage. Willie was suddenly worried about what they would say, worried about the banjo, worried about being there. "Say, Gus?"

"Yeah?"

"I'd be grateful if you'd keep what I told you about Mark to yourself. See, there's quite a bit more to it than that. It's kind of weird but unless I'm real mistaken, it ties in with what happened to Lettie and Mic."

"Do tell? Matter of fact, Willie, there's been a thing or two besides that happen that I'm not lettin' out for general consumption, but if you've got a minute, I'll tell you about it."

"I got all day, far as I know," he said.

"Well, then, about a month or so after the kids were arrested, I went to Spokane for a week to talk to a special lawyer Craig Lee recommended. I was wore out with worry and didn't want to hassle with the drive, so I flew out there and got a neighbor of mine to watch the house. I left my car with my girlfriend Marty. She lives over near the Sea-Tac airport, so it was no problem for her to pick me up either.

"Well, she met my plane and drove me back to her place where my car had been parked out in the street outside her house. I caught a cold in Spokane that was damn near pneumonia, complete with sore throat and laryngitis. I'd only barely been able to talk to that lawyer in squeaks and whispers and little notes all week long and couldn't hardly talk on the phone at all. I was looking forward to my bed, pettin' my cats, and readin' my mail so much it hurt. But when we got to Marty's my car wouldn't start. It had worked fine the last time Marty drove it, the way I asked her to. I thought I was sunk. It was about midnight by then, and the garages were closed, and it was raining. Marty and I stood outside trying to jump-start the damned thing from her pickup. Marty's real clever with cars, but she sure as hell couldn't get it to run so finally she gave in and called an all-night service station down on the corner. It had a garage and she thought one of those boys might know what to do and she got the boy on duty to say he'd come up and have a look.

"Well, there went all that bushwah about teenage boys and cars. That poor dumb kid couldn't figure it out any better than Marty, but he put on a good show and bulled it through. I don't think he'd have bothered on my account, but Marty's a cute little thing. You know how it is, Willie." Willie nodded. He did indeed know how it was. "Well, the kid tried rolling the car down the hill to compression start it, was what he called it I think. Damned if it didn't catch on fire just as he reached the filling station. He was a sight better with fire extinguishers than he was with cars, lucky for me, and he got the fire out, but meanwhile somebody called the cops and the fire department and they came over and did absolutely nothing but have me fill out a lot of dumb forms. So there I am with double pneumonia, a dead car that it was going to take a minimum of a week and a few hundred dollars to fix, and I'm still a good forty-five minutes from home.

"I was about near to cryin' but Marty said I should leave the car there and she'd have it towed to her favorite garage the next morning and meanwhile I could stay with her or she'd take me home. I wanted to go home so bad I could taste it, so we got back in her pickup and off we went.

"Well, it was still pourin' down rain and foggy and blacker than a banker's heart. We started jokin' about how bad things were goin' and how they couldn't get much worse, so of course they did. All of a sudden the road in front of the car blacked out and the dash went dark. The lights had gone clean out."

Willie had been pacing back and forth like a dog on a short lead, and now he stopped and looked at Gussie wide-eyed. "You mean *both* cars went out on the same night? Sounds to me like somebody didn't want you to get home, darlin'."

"Wait. You ain't heard nothin' yet. Marty steered us over on the shoulder and put on her blinkers. At least they still worked, thank merciful heaven. The car kept runnin' but the lights still wouldn't work. We were about to take the next exit off or try to flag somebody down when Marty remembered this mechanic she'd met while she was out dancing had a place somewhere near the Federal Way exit. He had been a pretty cute guy, lucky for us, so she had his card. Also lucky his place was real easy to find because no sooner had we pulled up in his drive than the car went dead too."

The hairs on Willie's arms were starting to stand at attention.

"Well, the fella hotwired it for us and got the lights working and stumbled off back to bed. We pulled up to my place about two in the morning.

"I was just startin' to say goodnight to Marty and thank her for all her trouble and tell her how sorry I was my bad luck seemed to be catchin' when I noticed that though my living-room light was on, the porch light was off. Marianne, my neighbor who was watchin' my house, knew I was comin' home too and had specifically told me when I called her earlier that she'd leave on the porch light. But I figured maybe the bulb had burned out or something.

"I asked Marty to spend the night, since that car of hers might break down at a less convenient place next time, so she tagged behind me into the house.

"I noticed right off that the cats weren't watching for me from the window but thought they just didn't recognize the sound of Marty's car. Then I saw that the porch door was unlocked and I remember saying to Marty that Marianne must have been in an all-fired hurry to leave. The mail was on the kitchen table, quite a pile of it, and I couldn't remember having left so much opened mail there with it, but lots of the letters were open. When I picked one up, I saw it was postmarked after I left. Also, a couple of file boxes of old papers were sitting on the kitchen counter, open. I usually keep them on the back

porch, and when I looked back there, the door was ajar
and there was water on the floor. I figured maybe it had
rained real hard and flooded the floor, and Marianne res-
cued the file boxes, even though I didn't remember leaving any on the floor, to keep them from getting wet.
Probably left the door open to dry it out. There was
nothin' valuable back there and there was an inside lock.

"One of the cats jumped down from on top of the
Frigidaire but the others all seemed to be hiding. I noticed the bedroom door was open when I came in, and
that made me kind of peeved at Marianne 'cause I told
her I didn't want them in there. They pee on the bed if I
leave them alone too long. So I went in to see if they had
and noticed that both the closet door and the window
were wide open too and it was chilly and blowin' cold
rain onto my bed. I knew then somebody had broke in
and I called Marty in and told her. What bothered me
most was that my oldest cat, Chessie, was gone too. Goddamn burglars got no consideration. Can't even close the
damned window behind 'em. I swore if that little old cat
was hurt I'd find whoever broke in if it was the last thing
I did and wring his goddamn neck.

"Well, li'l ol' Chessie had gone and hid under the
house and the other cats came home once they heard me
callin'. The cops came by for all the good they did. They
asked if I had any ex-husbands or boyfriends who had it
in for me, like since I work in a bar I'd hang out with that
kinda sleaze-bags. I told 'em if it was that simple to figure
out who broke into my house, I wouldn't have needed
them. The funny part was that nothin' was gone, not a
blank check or the insurance dividend check that was in
all that mail. I didn't know what to think, Willie."

"Some kid, maybe?" Willie offered, though he didn't
think all the other trouble she'd had was coincidence.

She shook her head. "Nope, and I don't think it was
one of the sex nuts who get their kicks out of invadin'
somebody else's privacy either, like the cops thought. Because about a week later, I went to play one of the tapes
in my car, and it snarled all up in the player. I got out the
album. I always tape my albums for the car, you know.

Anyway, it was scratched clear across both sides. And, Willie?"

"Huh?"

"So were all the others. And all of my other tapes did the same as the one in the car, just snarled right up. I tried to play them on the way out here and they were useless. They did somethin' to the CD's I had from my last birthday too. They won't play any more than the others. Not even your albums, Willie. That's one reason I decided to come out here and campaign for Mic and Lettie. I haven't heard any good music in weeks. You know all the radio shows they used to have with folk music had to go off the air. But I can't imagine why that thief would ruin my record collection and not take anything. Why, a customer of mine that works at Boeing says they're developing some new space technology that needs scrap vinyl. They're payin' pretty good prices for it and Bill, that's my customer, has been raiding garage sales for old records. So I'm surprised the burglar didn't just take 'em."

She huffed to a stop and Willie said, "Maybe you can sell the wrecked ones and get a little money that way, Gus."

"I don't want their damned money. I want my records to play like they're damned well supposed to and I want my kids back."

Willie tried to make light of the whole thing. He didn't want her to be as scared as he was. "Know what I think, Gus?" he asked. "I think you missed your chance to be a radical in the sixties and are now atoning for very sensibly votin' Republican by becomin' a full-blown hippie now that you're old enough to do what you want."

"Well, apparently that's what somebody else thinks too, but I'm not any different than I ever was and I did *not* vote Republican, you cute little fascist you. I could understand it if I *was* some kind of radical, but even if I was Abbie Hoffman come back from the grave I don't see why the federal boys would be so spiteful as to ruin my record collection. And I'm not Abbie Hoffman, I'm just Lettie's mama and they can't hold that against me. Of course, I'm tryin' to get her out of the hoosegow. What mother wouldn't?" When he didn't say anything for a long time, Gussie asked him, "Well, Willie, what do you think? Does this have anything to do with what you were talkin' about?"

"Maybe so, maybe not. I think so. But I got to work it through a little more before I tell you about it, darlin'. As for you, I think you'd be best off keepin' your mouth shut and your eyes open and see which way the wind blows."

He was so serious and worried-sounding it scared her a little, though not, of course, to keep her mouth shut. If somebody, anybody, was out to get her or hers she would by God go down kicking and screaming with all her might and they would know they'd been in a hell of a fight. Nevertheless, for Willie's sake, she nodded and said, "That's what I'm here for."

▲▲▲

Tony went into a coughing spasm and Kathie Jorgensen stopped staring at the stain on the mattress of the cot her strange new boarder had been leaning against while she told her story. "The Gussie you're talking about," Kathie said, her voice quiet and deliberate, as if she was trying to piece something together. "That's you, isn't it?"

Gussie made a face and shook her head. "Not exactly. Not anymore." She shifted position, stretching her noodle-numb legs in front of her and bouncing them up and down until tattoo needles began stinging them.

Kathy started to ask another question but noticed the way the other boarders were turning away, almost as if they were embarrassed. When you got an evasive answer about somebody's identity, it was against street etiquette to pursue the subject. But Kathie didn't live on the street and she had the feeling this story concerned her in a personal kind of way. "You knew all these people then, really?"

"Sure did."

"And these people you're calling devils?" Kathie asked.

"That's what I call 'em," Gussie said. "You got to make your own mind up about some things, honey."

"Well, what I don't get," Pete said querulously, "is how come if you were just you, in one little place, how come you

*know so blasted much about what everyone else was
thinkin' and sayin' where you weren't?"*

*"Hey, don't get your bowels in an uproar, kiddo. It's
just a story. I learned it this way, from the people who told
it to me. If I want to say I'm one of the people in it, what's
it to you? But I got to tell all the parts or it ain't no fun.
And like I say, I ain't exactly the same woman now as I
was then. So I switch off like, like they do on TV, so's
you'll get all the important parts."*

*Crazy Ruthie hit him with the end of the dog lead she
wore around her waist when her dogs were staying the
night at the costume shop. "Yeah, let 'er tell it her way.
Just like on TV. God, it's been years since I had one of
them. Go on, lady, then what happened?"*

▲▲▲

When everybody had finished registering and was milling
around the stage, somebody came out and messed with
the microphone, then the Indian-looking woman stepped
onto the patio-deck stage and introduced herself, saying,
"Welcome to my place and to this gathering. I'm called
Anna Mae Gunn. I advertised this gathering as the
Maryland Memorial Folk Festival for all the great ones
we've recently lost from our ranks, Sam Hawthorne, Josh
Grisholm, Nedra Buchanan, and so many others, all the
departed spirits who left their immortality on disk, tape,
and record at the Library of Congress Folk Music
Archives, now gone. Festival doesn't seem quite the
word. Your names have been chosen from the charter
lists of other festivals. Most of you are musicians, a few
are collectors, friends of the music, distributors, but by
and large we have invited no audience, no reviewers, or
other members of the press.

"Maybe a better word for this gathering is a ceremonial of the sort some of you will be familiar with as an
Irish wake. For me, I think of it more as something that
cousins of my mother's people, the Athabaskan Indians
of central Alaska do, called a Stick Dance, where two
villages get together and sing and dance their folks up
over the top, to the good place where spirits come to rest.
I have reason to feel that with all that's been happening

lately, the people we've lost need the comfort of our support.

"We who do this music, who love this music, come from all over, we travel all over. Despite a lot of stuff that's been happening to try to keep us in our place lately, musicians, especially those who carry the songs of the people, have always wandered—maybe just from one encampment to the next, from one holler to the next, from one town to the next, one castle to the next and back again, bringing news, telling stories. But somehow, with all that wandering, we seem to disconnect from home folks and attach to one another, even at distances, as a large, spread-out, sometimes loving, sometimes brawling tribe. Sort of gypsies without the benefit of a specific ethnic minority heritage to make us worth being studied by cultural anthropologists with government grants.

"But as a tribe, as a profession, as a group of people who share the bond of our music, we have suffered the loss of many of our leaders, our best spokespeople, our chiefs. I welcome you and offer my place as a place for our tribe's Stick Dance, our tribute to our dead by joining our songs to their spirits as they seek their rest from this life.

"One more thing, then I'll hush and let the music start. As many of you may know about us Indian people, when we have a ceremonial feast, which this is, it is a free demonstration of hospitality. The meat, the corn, potatoes, and water are on me. Other folks with the facilities have brought pop and beer and other things to snack on. Proceeds from the pies back there go to help out the families of our friends. They made big money according to our standards, but most of them still couldn't afford health insurance. And well, I can't either. I don't want you to come on my property as my guest to sing at this do and go hungry, so help yourself to the food, but please remember I'm only half Indian. The Scottish part of me won't be at all offended if you have something extra you want to drop in the coffee can to cover the costs. Thanks."

The first act was a jug band composed of jug, washboard, musical saw, kazoo, banjo, and a fellow who played a Coleman stove with a salad fork and promised to play a ladder the following day. They made a lot of racket that sounded a lot like "When the Saints Go Marching In," in the spirit of the Indian feast.

Then there was the gray-bearded man with his hair parted in the middle who stood up and sang a cappella sea chanteys, and a couple with the help of a concertina. Gussie stuffed her fliers in her Mexican basket purse embroidered with the little burros and the sombreroed boys and listened to the songs with such a big grin on her face you'd have thought she'd died and gone to heaven. She didn't know any of the songs at all, and he admitted he liked to do ones he had learned from old sailors themselves or from what he called field recordings instead of copying the same old ones everybody did. But he taught them the crewmen's part, and Gussie crowed along on those choruses confident in the knowledge she'd be drowned out by people with better voices. She loved sea chanteys as only a woman who'd grown up on the prairies could. For her they were alive with romance; sea spray and rolling waves and even battling storms wearing oilskins sounded wonderful when you're baking in 110-degree heat, battling ticks and chiggers. Her love of chanteys was one of the things that had led her to seek the job in Tacoma, where she could see Puget Sound every day. The Sound wasn't quite the ocean, but it was a damn sight closer to it than the Brazos. This chanteyman made it clear to them all though that sea chanteys were serious business and that being a sailor was just as rough and dirty a job as working an oil rig or punching cows or even waitressing, for that matter.

She felt so good singing like that. Cleared the lungs, she always felt, like her kids said yoga did.

Next up was a casually clean-cut middle-aged man who played mandolin and sang in a twangy voice odd versions of old songs she'd heard the Kingston Trio and Peter, Paul and Mary and other famous groups do long ago. It took him a while to get started going good, because he flubbed the first line of the first song several times. Finally he said "damn" in a soft voice and went on to another one. Then he'd stop in the middle of a verse and seem to be disoriented for a moment, unable to remember the words. The way he sang the words, she thought he was putting on being more ignorant than he was, or making fun of people who didn't know good English, and she had about half decided she could do without him.

But then he started talking, telling about when he was a kid with parents who spent their lives collecting songs. He told of sitting in mountain cabins with his mamma and daddy and his mountain aunts and uncles, listening to them sing. Old, old people who lived in the hills with no water but who gathered family for miles around when he and his folks came to visit with their recording machines and Mamma's little notebook. He told how a lot of mountain songs really came from England, Ireland, and Scotland and how the people's speech, which he didn't imitate when he talked, was believed by some scholars to be the same as spoken in those countries at the time the mountaineer's ancestors came over and hid themselves in the hills, isolated from outside influences. Others in the audience may have heard it before but it was all new to Gussie. The idea that "ignorant" English might be closer to the way real Englishmen spoke than the way it was taught in school intrigued her. She'd never apologize for saying "ain't" again. As if she ever had.

Four women about Lettie's age, playing guitars, base, keyboard, and a variety of percussion instruments, sang women's songs, most of them funny, one or two way too close to the bone to be funny. They had to leave the same night to return to their jobs, they said.

An angry no-longer-young man was next. He sang a lot of the old union songs and war protest songs through his nose and glared at everyone a lot and said he thought this "get 'em into heaven" stuff Anna Mae was spouting was a lot of crap but the barbecued beef smelled good.

Finally it was Brose's turn, him and Willie and that girl, Julianne Martin, Brose said her name was when he introduced her. Gussie remembered talking to her a long time ago, right before she heard about Lettie and Mic's arrest.

Sylvia, the MC, introduced the three of them as a Balkan band, but Brose pulled up a folding chair and played his old-style blues, playing faster and faster and adding more and more riffs here and there until the tune turned into a jig. He used to sing sometimes, but he didn't now.

Julianne played spoons with him. Willie didn't join in at all, but as Brose finished, Willie slid in between him and the microphone, a banjo in his hands.

The banjo seemed to be mumbling to itself even before Willie struck a chord, and he started playing the tune to "Mama Don't Allow." Julianne tick-a-tacked it on her spoons and Brose flatpicked it on guitar and Willie caught the eye of one of the jug-band members and whistled through his teeth, motioning with a jerk of his head for the band to join them.

As they stepped up, thumping and tooting along, they began to lose the melody but Willie motioned with his thumb for the sound woman to raise the volume on the instrument mike, and even with the one hand not on the banjo, the banjo relentlessly plunked out the tune. The jug band picked it up and repeated the refrain, over and over, and Willie stepped forward and opened his mouth as if about to sing, then stepped back again, shutting his lips tight and shaking his head. Stepping back up to the mike again, the banjo still ringing, he squared his shoulders and raised an admonitory finger, his voice now sounding like a preacher's or a bogus doctor in a snake-oil medicine show.

CHAPTER IX

▲▲▲

"My dearly beloved friends," Willie began, holding his index finger aloft to command attention and pronouncing each word with a little flourish at the end and giving "friends" three syllables, "has it occurred to you during this eve-en-ings performance that your brothers and sisters appear to be afflicted with an embarrassing and unsightly loss of memory, which causes their tongues to twist painfully around familiar words, which causes melodies to go a *stray* and rhythms to break faith each beat with its brethren? Well, I am here to tell you, brothers and sisters, that there is a reason for this and there is a cure. The cure is to sing and this instrument of song I clutch in my two hands will lead us on. But this instrument, for all its beautiful larynx, has no tongue. Can anybody *teyell me,*" and his voice rose with televangelistic fervor, "Yea, can you *teyell me* what the name of this blessed song might be?"

" 'Rollin' in My Sweet Baby's Arms'!" someone shouted.

"Hallelujah, brother, that's the *spirit.* Not the exact phrase I was lookin' for, but good try."

" 'Mama Don't 'Low,' " Gussie bellowed.

"*Pre*cisely, darlin'! A*men,* sister. And dearly beloved, just what is it that Mama don't allow and how exactly do we feel about it?"

"No *gi*-tar pickin'," someone said, and they got through the first line. Followed by, with shouted prompting from the audience, "But we don't care what Mama don't allow, gonna pick that guitar anyhow. Mama don't allow no guitar pickin' in here."

"And what else?"

"No banjo pickin'—"

And through the same thing, the words all fitting into the melody, not easily, but with the banjo keeping the tune and the people who didn't sing but just remembered the words prompting the stage, the whole thing came together, simple and complicated as a child learning to tie his shoes, or a brain-damaged adult relearning how to tie his shoes. The banjo ventured a little side riff of "We Shall Overcome."

At the same time, Gussie didn't know what made Willie laugh and carry on so about that old Sam Hawthorne song, except that it was a good one for singing along and built up a lot of energy between the stage and the audience, almost all of whom were waiting to go on stage.

They went through every instrument on stage with a solo, except that even during the solos the banjo kept the tune. Spoons, kazoo, washboard, washtub base, a fiddle someone had just whipped out, even the Coleman stove defied Mama's orders and played anyhow, but Willie kept the song going to clapping, finger snapping, stomping, singing, humming, whistling, and singing again, making up more and more verses as if he was afraid to stop.

Finally he did, and when he stopped Gussie's throat was raw and her hands stung from clapping. The song must have gone on for twenty minutes but Willie still stood in front of the microphone, which wasn't like him. He had quite a few faults but refusing to yield the stage wasn't generally one of them. He was breathing a little fast as he said, "Anybody else noticed that it's actual fact that someone ain't allowin' us to sing around here? How long has it been since any of you sang in public, never mind for money?"

"I had a gig two months ago!" someone said.

"Not since March," somebody else said.

"Me, I ain't worked at singing the folk songs of our land for well over two years," Willie said, the banjo, now slung across his back, rattling out "This Land Is Your Land." "A few days ago I found out why, and because of it and maybe because of something a friend left me, I stand here before you tonight as a marked man."

People were getting impatient. They were here not just to hear music, but to play it themselves, and were not the least bit interested in listening to a quasi-sermon by someone who seemed to have fallen prey to a particularly weird trip. "You should be more careful who your friends are, fella, and she wouldn't have left you with a thing like that—" the angry no-longer-young man jeered.

"Actually," Willie said, bringing the banjo forward again, "it was a guy—"

The heckler made an even nastier comment and Gussie edged over to him, ready to brain him with her Mexican basket bag if he didn't dry up.

"And what he gave me was this banjo. Anybody recognize it?"

Anna Mae Gunn was standing beside Gussie when he held up the banjo, and Gussie heard her make the sort of stricken noise a doe might make when she's hit by a bullet. Anna Mae pushed past Gussie and elbowed her way through to the stage while Willie was playing guessing games, and took the mike away from him. Willie made a bow, waving his arm as if there were a plumed hat at the end of it, but he tried to argue quietly with her. Anna Mae said, "I know," as she turned back to the mike and said, "Well, better get on with the show. Anyone who'd like to talk more to, uh, to this man—see him backstage. Meanwhile, we have a gospel group from Mobile, Alabama, up next, that right, Syl?"

She waited onstage while it cleared and the gospel group took its position. Willie went docilely enough, but his expression was more dangerous than Gussie had ever seen it as he waited for Anna Mae to exit. Anna Mae tried to brush past him but he grabbed her arm. Gussie didn't know if Willie was drunk or not, but she had two of the people she loved in jail already and she was going to do her best to keep his familiar face from making an ass of itself, so to speak.

"I wish you hadn't of done that, ma'am," he was saying, still trying for control. "I know it sounds crazy, but what I was trying to tell them was important. It has to do with—"

"I have a good idea," the Gunn woman said.

Gussie strode up between them, gushing, "Miz Gunn, I just think it's wonderful what you're doing for people here. Why, I was just telling Willie before the show—

have you met? My goodness, I am always amazed at how much people can have in common and not know each other. This is my friend, Will—"

"I think you'd both better come inside with me," Anna Mae told them. "We have to get a couple of things cleared up."

She took them inside to the kitchen, then led them downstairs to the basement, which had been converted into a home recording studio with egg-carton–shaped foam for soundproofing, tape recorders, microphones, and soundboards. They could yell all they wanted down there, which was evidently what the woman had in mind.

She shut the door behind them and she and Willie started shouting at the same time. "What in the hell do you mean—"

"By pulling me offstage," Willie said.

"By flashing around Hawthorne's banjo like that. Where did you get it? Don't you know you could get us all busted that way? Don't you know that's a thing of power?"

Gussie, used to breaking up arguments between drunks before they escalated too high, hollered, "Whoa, goddammit. Simmer down. One at a time, now." They both stopped sputtering and glared at her. "Miz Gunn, this gentleman you're hollerin' at here is Willie MacKai. He was one of the founders of the Flugerville Festival, has been a musician for thirty years, and I do believe that was probably the first time anyone was ever so rude as to boot him offstage."

"Thanks, Gussie, but I can speak for myself," Willie said belligerently.

"If nobody ever has before, then they've never had as good a cause," Anna Mae said. "Now I'm going to repeat my question very slowly and distinctly so you'll understand that I want an answer; what the hell are you doing with Sam's banjo?"

"Playing it, dammit. Leading songs with it, like Sam did."

"Not like Sam did, buster. You'll never be able to do anything like Sam did. How did you get it?"

"That's my business."

"For Christ's sake, you sound like a couple of two-year-olds," Gussie said. "Am I going to have to crack your heads together to get you to calm down. Now, Willie, you were all set to tell a couple hundred of Miz Gunn's guests how you got that banjo, don't you think she maybe has a right to know too?"

His mouth writhed in such a nasty way that she had no desire to know what he was thinking, but she was pretty sure it didn't have anything to do with the spirit of sweet reason.

Finally he passed a hand over his face, watching Anna Mae over it. She glared back. "You're one of them, aren't you?"

"Do you know how crazy you sound?" the woman said, her black eyes boring into him. "One of who? What is that shit?"

"One of the people Lulubelle Baker warned me about. One of the ones who's tryin' to frame me for Mark Mosby's death, which you were no doubt responsible for. One of the ones who destroyed the Folk Music Archives."

"Yeah, sure, I did all that stuff. I do it all the time, and then put on folk festivals single-handed to use up all the extra time and money I have left over."

"Maybe it's a trap," he shot back, his jaw thrust forward.

"Yeah, and maybe you're Sam Hawthorne and I'm just too blind to see it, in spite of the fact that Sam and I have been friends for fifteen years. Otherwise, you better tell me right now how you got ahold of Lazarus."

"Or what?"

"Or I call the cops and tell them I just threw a drunk off my place who looked a lot like somebody wanted for murder in Texas."

Gussie started to butt in again and explain to her that that was a mistake, that for all his bluster Willie MacKai would no more murder anybody than he'd grow wings and fly. Trouble was, she was pretty sure Anna Mae Gunn no more believed such a thing than she herself did. Gussie was just trying to talk Willie into telling Anna Mae what he would have told her of his own free will if she hadn't flown at him like that. Of course, if the Indian woman and Sam had been good friends, then maybe she was grieving more than ceremonially and wasn't thinking too clearly. Or maybe she just liked to make scenes and cause trouble. A lot of people in show business were like that. Anything for a little drama.

Someone was knocking on the door. Anna Mae and Willie stood squared off but Gussie walked right between them and went to open the door. Let in some air if nothing else.

A gangly man stood there, his Adam's apple taking a dive into his collar and bobbing back up as he took in the attitudes of the other two people in the room. "Excuse me, ma'am, I wanted to talk to Ms. Gunn a minute," he said. Gussie was about to tell him it wasn't an awful good time right then and maybe he should come back but by that time, instead of turning tail, he walked right in as easy as if he'd been invited and stuck out his hand to Willie. "Willie MacKai, isn't it? I'm Faron Randolph. Let me tell you, sir, I just sort of came by chance because my wife had some research to do in Washington, D.C., but if I had known you were going to be here, I'd have come on purpose just to see you. My dad took me to the Flugerville Festival one year all the way from St. Joe just to see you. 'Now, son,' Dad told me, 'you pay attention to Mr. Willie MacKai there because he is something you don't see too often, a true folksinger, singing songs taught to him by American cowboys and Mexican vaqueros since he was a boy and also doing all those popular songs city singers have written to sound like folk songs.' He told me to pay special attention to the way you played the guitar, Mexican style, and asked me how many times I'd seen Bobby Dylan playing it *that* way. I was going through my time when I thought Bobby Dylan was the best thing since sliced bread."

All the time Faron Randolph spoke Willie's jaw was untightening and his teeth were unclenching and his eyes were getting more and more unsquinty till they were wide and friendly looking. For a while Willie nodded judiciously at what Faron said, then he took to just plain smiling outright. He never could resist a fan.

"But say," Randolph said, "I notice you're not playing your guitar today. That is a mighty fine banjo you have there. Looks a lot like the one Sam Hawthorne used to play. Wasn't that a terrible thing?"

"It surely was, brother, it surely was. I have *seldom* felt so bad about anything in my entire life," Willie said with heartfelt sincerity and a quick sharp glance at Anna Mae Gunn. "And as a matter of fact, this is Sam's very own banjo, Lazarus, I'm told he called it. A good friend of mine was at Sam's side when he died and Sam told him to hold on to it for safekeeping since none of his other friends or relations were handy. Tell you the truth, my friend Mark watched Sam Hawthorne die and it troubled him a lot. I kind of think now that he may have come out to see me because he didn't like a few other things he saw either, but he never got to really talk about it too much because on the way over, he was in an accident—"

"No!" Faron said.

"Yessir, or at least I took it for an accident. But now . . ." He let the sentence trail off meaningfully. "Well, I had no idea how bad Mark had been hurt and neither did he. But after we'd been talking for a while, he got kind of fuzzy-tongued and slow and I thought he was just sleepy. Next thing I knew he was dead, and there I was with Sam Hawthorne's banjo as sacred a trust as it could be to me from two men I counted as friends, for though I never knew Sam real well, I played with him a few times and he was always an inspiration to me."

"Don't that beat all?" Faron said, half to himself.

Willie sensed he was losing his audience. "But I appreciate your kind words and your asking about it. That was a real interesting set you did. You don't happen to be related to Vance Randolph, by any chance?"

The young man nodded. "On my daddy's side. And thanks, but I really blew that set. Don't know just what was wrong but I couldn't seem to remember the words to songs I've known most of my life."

"In case you missed some of it, that little problem was the point of my whole set until it was—ahem—cut a mite short by certain parties."

"You seemed to be having trouble at first with your song, but you broke through it," Faron continued.

"Well, I had Lazarus and Gussie here to prompt me. This is Gussie Turner, by the way."

Faron waggled a couple of fingers at Gussie. She waggled back.

Avoiding Anna Mae Gunn's eyes, playing the genial host and celebrity, Willie said, "Gussie's daughter and son-in-law, Lettie and Mic Chaves, are two of the nicest people you'd want to meet. Lettie runs a record distribution business for privately produced records and Mic just generally makes himself agreeable, public relations, that kind of thing."

"You're Mic and Lettie's mom?" Faron asked Gussie. "I heard what happened to them. They're good friends of my in-laws." He shook his head sympathetically.

Anna Mae Gunn reached over and touched the banjo's tuning head. The instrument emitted a drone. She looked as if she were seeing Sam in his coffin, as if she knew in her heart for the first time that he was gone. Willie took a deep breath, exhaling his tension and anger, and said, "I'd have told you if you'd given me half a chance."

She looked back at him with eyes bleak and black as the aftermath of a forest fire.

"Mind if I was to play a lick on that banjo?" Faron asked.

Willie lifted the strap over his head and Faron lifted it over his own. He sat down cross-legged on the floor and strummed the strings lightly. They gave back a chorus of "Come in, Stranger."

He picked the rest of it, adding a few licks of his own here and there, and started something else, opened his mouth, closed it, and handed the banjo back to Willie before he stood up again, shaking his head.

The door had been left open and Anna Mae's friend Sylvia appeared in it now. "Just about time to finish up concerts and start the campfires. You want to make any announcements?" she asked Anna Mae.

▲▲▲

The sky was dark already, but clear with stars and a half moon shining bright and pretty—Gussie remembered that later, how clear it was. The clover scent rose sweet from under her feet and soft plumes of dove-gray smoke tickled the blackness as they rose from the campfires that twinkled like fireflies in the pastures on either side of the house. Peepers chorused from the river and cicadas from the yard, drowning out the hum of the microphones as the last note of the last act died drifting through the pasture.

Anna Mae called for a finale, and asked Willie and Faron, Brose and Julianne, the angry young man and the chanteyman, the gospel singers and the jug band, to come back onstage to sing "Amazing Grace." Only once they got up there, leaving very few people in the audience, nobody could remember the words. Faron Randolph's lips moved, as if he was swearing to himself, and then he stepped up close to Willie and Lazarus. His Adam's apple took another dive into his shirt collar and resurfaced, then he began to sing:

> "Amazing grace that we're gathered here
> A couple hundred strong
> To sing for souls of mem-o-ry dear.
> If we can recall the songs,"

He stepped back, scratching his head, but Julianne caught the idea and squeezed in next to Willie,

> "Amazing grace, how sweet the sound
> Of voices raised in song
> If words are lost, more can be found . . ."

Her voice faltered and she made a face and shrugged. Willie stepped back up to the microphone, Lazarus plunking the time like a gaited horse, and finished, "So raise them voices strong," grinning at his own departure from the general reverent tone.

It was time for a chorus and Willie knew it, the banjo was plunking toward it, the audience was straining their necks with the will to sing it, and he felt it bubble up in him but the bubble just would not surface in his brain. He was sweating from the heat, perturbed from the argument with Anna Mae, and weary from sending out search and retrieve messages to his brain to bring back those song lyrics alive. It was very dark by then but by the alligator clamp lights rigged as stage lights he saw people in the front row looking puzzled and moving their lips as if mumbling to themselves, and he knew they were trying to remember the words too.

Then the strings surged under his fingers and a memory came back to him of standing in a starchy white shirt and a hot jacket in church beside his grandma and hearing old Mr. Armbruster, who had once been a circuit preacher to the Indian Nations and who still had a carrying kind of voice, bellow out the first verse even when everybody else was on another one, "Amazing grace, how sweet the sound, that saved a wretch like me. I once was lost but now am found, was blind but now I see."

The audience followed him a step behind and then wouldn't let him stop. They had to sing it three more times, just like Mr. Armbruster, so as not to forget it. Willie was wringing wet with a queer combination of satisfaction at having remembered it and the frightening knowledge that he had forgotten it in the first place and that the finding of it was not all his own doing.

"That sure was a fine performance, Willie," someone said. "Have a drink on me? I came well prepared." He didn't see the face in the dark but accepted the offer gladly.

"Don't mind if I do, friend."

"What'll it be?"

"Seagrams and seven," he said. A plastic tumbler was placed in his hand. "That was mighty quick," he said.

"Like I said, I come prepared," the voice said. Willie just assumed it was a man, but the stranger's outline was vague and androgynous in the dark and the voice was husky and half-lost in the general commotion of people making their campfires and settling down for the evening sing. Still, the voice seemed familiar—a lot of voices did. A man met a hell of a lot of people in thirty to forty years of singing to and with crowds.

"MacKai, I want to talk to you," another voice said. This one Willie recognized. It belonged to the sour-looking fellow who'd sung three or four absolutely legitimate old ballads that it was no wonder Sam Hawthorne didn't do. They were miserably gloomy and violent, even for murder ballads. For comic relief the guy had thrown in two Leonard Cohen songs and a long dismal Phil Ochs protest number about how everything was going to hell. To Willie's mind, the song had been too true to be entertaining. Ochs had been a better prophet than a showman.

Willie took a long pull at the tumbler. "Okay by me. What's your problem?"

"What's yours?" Sourpuss asked. "What do you and your friends mean changing the words of a sacred song?"

"Huh?"

"The words to 'Amazing Grace.' You and your friends changed them. I saw you laugh about it! What do you mean doing something like that? That song has been sung in worship for years by good people who liked it the way it was—"

"Yes, brother, it surely was. That's what I was thinking about when I sang that last chorus." He said it evenly but he was getting a little tired of being hollered at.

"That may be, but those other verses are not the ones collected in the version I have—"

"No?"

"No, according to the Judy Collins songbook."

"With all due respect to Judy, who is a great writer, she's hardly one of your good humble folk singing in the church choir anymore now is she . . ."

"It's a sacred song. You have no right to change the words just because you can't remember them."

"Well, brother, I see your point. Why don't you sing the other verses for me just to jog my memory—write 'em down for me."

"I will—I mean, as soon as I remember them. I couldn't quite recall them but I have them at home."

"Fine. Until then we'll do as we see fit about addin' on a little. Which church do you go to anyway, friend?"

"What's that got to do with it? I'm agnostic."

"They got a lot of good hymns in that agnostic church, have they? Well, you better try to recollect some. I got a few things to say at the campfire tonight might make you want to sing every one of them. You come on along if you want to but I'd appreciate it if you didn't interrupt our madeup verses until you can remind us all of the original ones."

He finished the booze in the tumbler and was about to start toward one of the campfires. Lazarus thrummed with "Brandy Leave Me Alone," as the familiar husky voice said, "You sure told him, Willie. Refill?"

"Don't mind if I do," Willie said, and as he moved toward the fire, felt the comforting presence of the person with the drinks move along behind him.

He settled down onto a log someone had dragged up and pulled the banjo in front of him. The crickets sang and the fireflies danced beyond the edge of the fire and from somewhere there rose another voice, singing something he didn't recognize.

People crowded around the fire just so the light illuminated about half their faces, except when the wind carried more flame one way or the other. Then smoke would twine toward one direction and the people would fan themselves and cough. Julianne said, "If you say, 'I hate rabbits,' the smoke will leave you alone." After that, any given conversation or song was broken at intervals with someone mumbling, "I hate rabbits" in various tones of sincerity or levity.

One of the fellows from the Irish group was there, and the woman doctor named Clarissa who played the bodhran, and they started a tune together on mandolin and drum. It was lively and everyone clapped at the end.

"Sing that one you did for the hospital benefit, Clarissa," one of the gospel singers urged. "You know, the one about Dr. Kildare's ancestor cursing and swearing." The gospel singer was a chubby black man with a soft, educated voice. Clarissa grinned at him.

"You're a better physician than you are a folklorist, Mel. Maybe you'd better wash out your own ears for a change. That's *Lord* Kildare, except the guy's name was really Lord Grey, and he's the villain. The hero is Fiarch McHugh."

"Whatever. It's a great song. Sing it."

The mandolin started tinkling and Clarissa got a good

roll going on the drum, then someplace they took a
wrong turn and the song began to sound like "Drowsy
Maggie," then the "Star of County Down," then it died.
"Sorry, Mel," Clarissa said. "Can't seem to remember
it."

The fellow who had been singing the sea chanteys
hummed and let forth a couple of notes, then let his voice
drop and mumbled, "Cursing and swearing and Lord
Kildare and Fiarch McHugh and *what*?"

Mel shook his head sadly. "They're gonna throw all of
you out of the IRA, you don't be careful."

Willie watched all this quietly, finishing his second
drink and having it quietly refilled from behind by the
stranger, who patted him on the shoulder as he retreated
back to the shadows.

"There's a reason y'all can't remember these songs,"
he said.

"You said something about that earlier," Clarissa said.

"Yes, ma'am, I did. And I'll say it again and keep on
saying it until people believe the truth of it."

Oh, God, Gussie thought to herself, here he goes
again. Poor Willie, his brain must be more pickled than
anybody realized. She didn't know how much to believe
of his story about some whore telling him that supernatural forces were aligned against folk music. Nor did she
know what exactly to make of a banjo that even now was
lightly thrumming "Whiskey, You're the Devil." But she
thought he was foolish to be bringing it up in public like
this, not knowing who was listening or what they might
be thinking of him. Why, they might just lock him up in
a padded cell and forget about him. He'd be better off
taking people aside and talking to them one at a time
maybe . . .

"A man just came up to me and demanded to know
why I only played the one true verse of 'Amazing Grace'
and why we made up the others. Actually, I could have
told him, *I* didn't exactly play the one true verse. This
banjo played it and its strings jogged my memory, after a
few run-throughs, and the one real verse I'd heard the
most came back to me. The banjo was given to me by a
friend who is now dead and it was given to him by its

owner, and I'm sure a lot of you know that that owner was Sam Hawthorne, who was struck down on a stage in Austin after hearing that a large part of his life's work had been destroyed. Sam's death was supposed to be natural. My friend Mark's death was supposed to be either an accident, or my fault, if some people have their way. This banjo is just supposed to be a banjo but can't you hear it, my friends? Let me pause for a moment now and let you listen real careful and you'll hear—"

Dramatically, he lifted his hands aloft, palms up, away from the banjo. Across the fire faces tilted forward, flames dancing shadow patterns across hollowed cheeks, shining on sharp-watching eyes and the bald spots of men of long experience. The banjo strings vibrated with, "I Was Born About Ten Thousand Years Ago."

People looked puzzled or nodded cautiously. Faron Randolph ducked his head as if to hide his grin and Julianne smiled and craned her neck to watch the ribbons of cloud tattering in the wake of the sailing moon.

Gussie thought, it's not him that's being foolish, it's me. Willie never has been much good at talking to one person at a time but he's spent most of his life twisting crowds around his little finger.

And he told about the van accident and about the snakes and about Lulubelle Baker's videotapes. And people began muttering and tuning and talking to each other. Among the mumblings were the words "boozer" and "AA" and Gussie could tell Willie heard.

▲▲▲

A shaft of dirty moonlight filtered through the high, half-painted windows of the old warehouse that had been converted to a shelter. It wasn't much of a light, but it was enough to see by as the bag lady known as Gussie tippy-toed past the snoring Pete, paused beside Tony's cot as he sat up coughing and fell right back to sleep, and finally drew even with and outdistanced the doggy aroma wafting from Crazy Ruthie.

Kathie Jorgensen lay curled in her own sleeping bag near the front door, and didn't notice as Gussie picked the lock and slipped out into the night.

These people had been a fine audience, but they were starting to get too nosy. Gussie shuffled three blocks up Yesler, turned right onto Alaska Way, and up the moving walkway into the ferry terminal. No predators were out in that neck of the woods tonight, thanks be to God, and no cops either. Inside the ferry terminal, she slipped into the ladies', shed three layers of baggy, dirty clothing, washed the worst of the stink off, and pulled a plastic-bag–wrapped pink and lavender pastel jogging suit and a pair of Nikes from beneath the junk in her shopping bag and put them on. She left the bag in the trash for the next scavenger, took the ferry fare from the pocket of her pants, and boarded the Bremerton Ferry. From the dock, she walked into one of the waterfront bars and applied for a job. The bartender hired a woman who called herself merely August, which wasn't so unusual with all the post hippies around, though privately, the owner thought the woman looked as though she might be heading more toward November than August.

She was popular with the customers, though, and those who liked to sit around the bar and visit between buying Lotto tickets took to ignoring the TV to listen to this tall tale she made up while mixing drinks and wiping down the bar. Business picked up, in fact, because all her regulars kept coming back to hear new installments of the story and some of them brought friends back. It chased their blues better than the TV or telling her all their own same old sad stories would have done. Seemed like nobody ever got too drunk or out of line much anymore either. They were too afraid of missing the latest installment to get really bombed, and the regulars helped August keep would-be rowdies in line so she could concentrate on doing her job and telling the story.

She had gotten to the part about the campfire at the folk festival, and how people were laughing at Willie just because he liked a little drink now and then.

▲▲▲

From behind Willie a bottle emerged, the hand holding it shining pale as the moon in the firelight, pouring a ribbon of bright liquid into the plastic tumbler. Willie drank about half of it and set to watching the crowd again, his mouth tight and his eyes swinging contemptuously from one to the other.

Faron Randolph cleared his throat. "You know," he said quietly, as if he were speaking only to Willie. His voice had a startling quality to it, quiet as it was, and people hushed to listen, as if it were a shooting star that they wouldn't see for a long time to come if they missed it this time around. "You know, my daddy and cousin Vance Randolph had a good friend, fellow name of Manly Wellman. Mr. Wellman used to go song-finding with them sometimes. He was a writer, and he wrote about the songs and the mountain folks and especially about a friend of his named John. What he wrote about, people took to be fanciful, what they call fantasy stories, about John meeting up with all manner of evil creatures and wicked conjurers and kind of what I guess you might call the country version of monster and horror movie characters. They were good yarns so they got published by big New York publishing houses. Mr. Wellman never would give John a last name though and most people reckoned that was just to add a little more mystery to the story. Daddy said that wasn't it. He said the reason John was never given a last name was that he was a real person that those things actually happened to and Mr. Wellman never wanted to interfere with him too much by naming him outright, names having a lot of power to conjurers. I don't exactly know what to make of what's been happening to Mr. MacKai here, or of his banjo, but it reminds me a little of John and his silver-strung guitar and I have a feeling *John* would have been able to shed some light on what Mr. MacKai's been talking about."

"The most supernatural thing about this whole conversation, Faron, is that it's jarred more than two words strung together out of you," a voice said from the shadows. The owner scooted forward into the firelight, his face glowing with the intense earnestness of a missionary trying to convert the heathen. Willie recognized the folk-purist asshole who had been railing him earlier.

"The reason these songs are disappearing, now that Sam Hawthorne and the others are dead, is that the rest of you never troubled yourselves to really learn and care about the words except to ape Sam and the real folk interpreters in this country. I'm surprised at you, Faron, with your reputation, for not seeing through this bullshit. Half the people who've been killed off weren't folk musicians at all—hell, Josh Grisholm wrote most of his own songs, and a lot of the others were nothing but little tin movie stars with acoustic instruments as props. They never cared about the origins or meaning of the songs. They never cared to get the story straight. And now the audience is tired of your little fad and is moving on to the next one and frankly, I'm glad. Because now we scholars can get back to our work without being lumped with the rest of you."

"Sing 'Leatherwing Bat,' " Faron Randolph said.

"Huh?"

" 'Leatherwing Bat.' Sing it. It's a folk song, right?"

"Of course it is!"

"And you just said that you, Eric Havelock, and those like you are the only pure people who care enough about the words that you haven't forgotten just because Sam's dead. So sing it."

"I—uh—I don't call it to mind right now," Havelock said. "And I don't sing on dares."

"This so-called jam session is too batty for me, anyhow," Clarissa said. "I didn't take a break from repairing burn patients in the OR all week to come out here and listen to this. Let's play or let's turn in."

They started one of those Irish tunes that sounds like about seven hundred other Irish tunes. Willie made a disgusted face. Well, the music world had never listened to anything else he had to say. Why did he think they'd listen to this? He drank another slug of whiskey and felt like crying, right here in the middle of everything. A hand tapped him on the shoulder.

"I found what you had to say real interesting, Mr. MacKai, and I'd like to talk to you about it," that familiar voice belonging to the whiskey pourer said. "Maybe we could have a private talk."

"I don't see why not," Willie said. "I thought I was among friends here but I see I'm mistaken." He said it loud enough for the others to hear but nobody was interested except Brose and Juli and Faron and Gussie, who *were* his friends and who might have been annoyed at being lumped with the rest.

The man with the bottle was a handsome fellow, his hair whiter than his pale hands. He wore a sweatshirt with a logo Willie couldn't read with only the moon for a reading lamp.

"I've been wanting to talk to you ever since I got here, Mr. MacKai, but especially after seeing the shameful way those people were treating you I just had to speak up," the man said in a voice so oozy with sympathy, Willie was a tiny bit alarmed, wondering if the guy was about to make a pass at him.

But Willie replied politely, trying to sound grateful, "Mighty kind of you, sir." Now why did it always have to be strangers who seemed to understand, he wondered, instead of the people who claimed to care about you?

"Willie—may I call you Willie? Willie, I represent some major interests in the music business. There's a lot of truth in what you've been saying. We both know that. But there's also a lot of truth in what that other fellow was saying. The folk thing has been a trend. America is ready for another trend. I think—those I represent think —you're just the kind of man to lead this trend, to be our first major recording star."

"You do?" Willie sounded a little more cautious but very pleased. "Now what would make you think a thing like that?"

"Well, sir, the fact of the matter is, the average age of America is a little older these days. The time for teenage rock stars is over. There are a lot of lonesome folks out there between marriages, their kids raised maybe, maybe never connected with anybody, who are looking for someone to fantasize about, someone possible to sing to them and lull their fears, tell them they can be somebody even if they have no one."

"Why me?" Willie asked. "Not to question your good judgment and discernin' taste, Mr.—"

"Nicholson. B. B. Nicholson. Sorry," he stuck his hand out and Willie pumped it.

"Not to try to make you change your mind, but I ain't exactly the idol type. There's handsomer fellows, better singers, better guitar players. If getting old is all you need, you got a whole lot of 'em here."

"Ah, yes, Willie, but we want you, not the others. Haven't you read the studies that indicate that people who are too good-looking are intimidating? And any lacks in your voice our studios can augment. As for guitar playing, you won't be needing a guitar or one of those things"—he indicated the banjo—"for the sort of career we have in mind for you."

The banjo had been stuck on "Whiskey, You're the Devil" a great deal of the night but now it switched to "Sometimes I Feel Like a Motherless Child," as mournful and sorry for itself as Willie was feeling for himself.

"Is that so?" Willie asked. "Mind if I bum a cigarette?"

"Be my guest" Nicholson replied, and supplied one. Willie stuck it between his lips. Life missed a beat. The familiar, comforting gesture of lighting the smoke had gotten lost someplace in the transaction. He could have been drunker than he realized, but it seemed to him the cigarette Nicholson supplied was already lit. Willie wished he could see more of Nicholson than that general impression of paleness. The man was thin and chiseled as was the fashion—his axe-blade-sharp cheekbones flashed, his teeth snapped open, snapped closed again when he talked, like icebergs closing in on a ship. The hair he flipped back from his face with an elegant toss of his head rose and fell like a spray of sea foam. He was a smooth customer all right.

Willie's horse-trading instincts were stronger than the liquor. "Just what kind of music is it you'd be wanting me to do, B.B.? You people aren't going to start up a great folk revival, now, are you?"

"I'm afraid not, Willie, though of course we'd like to. I just love those drinking, drug, and murder ballads you do so well."

"Thank you, sir. That's the second time I've gotten a compliment on that lately."

"Unfortunately, your modern-day listening audiences

aren't into that kind of thing. No, sir, but don't let it worry you. The fact of the matter is, Willie, in your case the kind of music doesn't matter really. We'll use a top-forty format, I imagine, to launch you . . ."

"Maybe country would be a better way to go then, if it doesn't matter, like you say. I can't stand top forty. It's not like it's still rock and roll. That stuff on now all sounds alike."

"Country is a dying market, Willie. A year from now, it'll be as dead as folk. People are hipper now. They aren't interested in listening to other people's problems. They have their own lives to get on with. They want something that doesn't intrude. Your music these days has to stimulate them and interest them without making them feel that they have to get involved. Country just doesn't do that. People are tired of yuppies trying to sound like hicks."

"With all due respect, sir, here's one hick would like to have the income to qualify as a yuppie."

"We'll take care of that, Willie. You're a rare commodity because your talent isn't just in recording—we'll help you put your showmanship and charisma to good use with promotional tours, concerts."

It sounded good to Willie, though he did wonder just how in the hell he was going to give a nonintrusive concert. He also wondered why Nicholson was tipping his hand about how much they wanted him and how goddamn unique he was. That was no way to strike a favorable deal.

"Just what's in this for me?" he asked.

"Why, anything you want."

"What if just for grins, say, I was to ask for a million —make it two million—a year with a bonus for every record and each concert—the salary is just to cover the wear and tear on me from travelin', you understand. And get a bunch of my friends here for backup musicians."

"You can have all the roadies you want but we control the musical end of it. Anything else, cars, clothes, money, gigs playing for the President—"

"How about in Europe?" He wasn't very interested in Europe, actually. It didn't have a whole lot to offer compared with Texas, as far as he was concerned, but some women were awfully impressed with it.

Nicholson shied a little at that, however. "Different type of promo involved there, Willie, but we'll certainly see what we can do. To start with we want to make up for lost time by making your name a household word here—"

"An unobtrusive household word?" Willie asked, and at Nicholson's puzzled, humorless look said, "Sorry, just a little joke. It sounds real good, B.B. Shall I give you the name of my lawyer in Austin and—"

Nicholson cleared his throat and said, "Actually, in view of certain developments concerning you in Texas, I don't think that's a good idea. In fact, once you sign with us, it would be a good idea to let our lawyers take care of that whole mess for you."

"You *know* about that?" What swell people. Support-ive, as his last girlfriend said. Real supportive, knowing you're wanted for murder and offering to sign you for a big recording contract anyway. "Buddy, I don't know what to say. I'm real touched."

"Hey, we've got a huge network, information channels and resources throughout the world, and we don't offer this kind of deal to someone we don't really believe in. Don't worry about anything. In fact, we were in the mid-dle of discussing our need for someone like you when your name started cropping up in the news. It's actually what brought you, specifically, to mind. So you see how even events that are real bummers can turn out to be for the best? Anyway, hell, Willie, we knew that with you being in this kind of a bind, you'd need help fast, so we had our legal department draw up a binder. It pretty much just reiterates what we've been discussing here to-night. If you want to go ahead and sign, I can have it sent by courier first thing in the morning and I wouldn't be surprised if we didn't have you cleared in a day or so. An organization like ours wields quite a bit of clout."

"I'm real happy for you about that, buddy," Willie said, clapping him on the shoulder. "Give it here and let me look it over."

He hadn't noticed the attaché case before—funky red

rubber with black and silver trim—but Nicholson picked it up suddenly and with a graceful flourish produced a multipaged document from it, flipping pages until he got to the end.

"Whoa, boy, I guess I had better take my time reading this or see if there's a lawyer handy here."

"Our legal department is pretty sound. Frankly, Willie, we are too big an outfit to try to cheat someone whose assets are as limited as yours."

"Well, but I am part of this deal and I don't sign nothin' I don't read," Willie said, holding the document away from him to try to make out the print.

"Then why not put on your reading glasses and let's go over it together? I can interpret for you. Frankly, Willie, we'd like to have you on board but there's this matter of getting your reputation cleared up. Time is something neither of us can afford to waste."

Willie had never liked high-pressure salesmanship but told himself to simmer down, that this man wasn't selling him anything really, just offering him the chance of a lifetime.

". . . chance of a lifetime," Nicholson was saying. "Now, one thing I want to prepare you for because it seems a little weird to some people, but when you're ready to sign, there is one step further than a simple signature that we ask, and that's for purposes of absolute identification. Once you're on board, you'll be entered into our data banks and our electronic credit system so that you can draw on our accounts anywhere in the U.S. For this, you can see, we need to be damn sure it's you. So we ask for a pinprick blood sample and we use that to take your fingerprints. That way we have absolutely unique identification and protection against fraud."

Willie, strangely, was feeling more sober all the time. He had always been a cash-and-carry sort of man himself and had no use for systems that catalogued you down to your toenails before they'd let you at your own money. But he wanted to sound reasonable so he said, "I'll tell you what, B.B. In view of the fact that I don't want my fingerprints spread around right now, let's just have me sign in regular ink tonight and we can do the other stuff once you've cleared me."

"I'm sorry, Willie, we don't do business that way. We need the identification on the agreement or no deal."

The banjo played "Don't Let Your Deal Go Down." Willie wondered if it meant his deal or Nicholson's. The funny part was, Nicholson had already agreed to fairly outrageous terms and now was balking at a little thing that ought to be perfectly understandable in view of present circumstances. Someone walked behind Willie with a flashlight and the beam glinted red off Nicholson's left eye.

"Actually, we might be able to work something out and go ahead and sign you up and start clearing you," Nicholson was saying, "if you put up some sort of security—say that old banjo there."

Willie backed off a pace and shook his head. "Nope."

"What do you mean, 'nope'? I swear to blazes, man, we offer someone who's been a no-account bar singer most of his life a chance at the big time, money up front, expenses paid, fame and fortune, and ask for a little simple something on faith and you have the gall to say, 'nope'?"

"Yep," Willie said.

"You would throw away a chance like I offer you simply because you're nervous about being fingerprinted?"

Before Willie could answer the flashlight swung back and pinned Nicholson right in the face, so both eyes were red as in the color in a bad photograph and the teeth gaped in sharp and shining surprise. "What's this about fingerprinting?" the flashlight's owner asked.

Willie stepped back behind the beam and tried to look hard at Nicholson but the image blurred.

"I was merely offering one of your guests a job—" Nicholson began.

"Uh-huh," Anna Mae Gunn said, and for once Willie was glad of the woman's guard-dog brand of charm. He couldn't quite bring himself to tell this dude to piss up a rope himself, because he wanted desperately for him to be on the level and prove it, he wanted to be mistaken and for that big chance to really be there. But in his heart he

knew that was about as likely as it was that there would
be tax reforms that involved giving *back* money instead
of extorting more. So he was willing to let Anna Mae do
his fighting for him. He may have been scared half sober
but he was still too drunk to walk straight anyway, much
less throw a punch that would do him any damn good.

"He just wanted my fingerprints in blood first," Willie
told her.

"I'll bet he did. I don't recall checking you through
the gate today, mister. Just when did you get here?"

But Nicholson wasn't interested in Anna Mae Gunn.
His eyes were on the banjo, now thumping "I Don't Want
Your Millions, Mister." To Willie he said, "No wonder
you're such a loser, MacKai. Lust doesn't persuade you,
greed doesn't move you. You lack the basic motivational
elements necessary to succeed in this life. I'm afraid
you'll find simple stubbornness is not going to do you as
much good when you're playing in the big leagues, my
friend."

"Willie," Anna Mae said, "I don't want to start up
with you again but if you still want to do business with
this guy I'd appreciate it if you'd take him off my land to
do so."

"Oh, I reckon we're done."

"That," said Nicholson, "is what you think."

"Get off my land," Anna Mae said.

"Certainly. But, Willie, you're not the only one who's
stubborn . . ."

"Off," Anna Mae repeated.

Nicholson walked around the nearest tent and disappeared, but it seemed to Willie that the red glow of his
eyes hung in the air behind him after he'd gone.

"Sorry," Anna Mae said to him. "But I've met all too
many snakes of that stripe."

"I guess it takes all kinds," Willie said. But he knew
what kind Nicholson was now. Too bad. He would have
liked to have seen the image Nicholson's outfit was going
to concoct for him in exchange for the banjo and, if the
stories were accurate, his immortal soul.

▲▲▲

So Nicholson slunk away, but with a grin on his face, for he preferred to deal with Willie the hard way rather than the easy, and he didn't give him credit for being smart enough to use the banjo effectively enough to ward off disaster.

If Nicholson had left the conventional way, by the gate, just a little later, after the campfire died and Willie staggered off to the truck bed and Anna Mae back into her house, he would have seen the vehicle with the dark headlamps pull up to the gate. A man whose hair glinted gold in the remaining starlight got out of the truck, deftly picked the lock, opened the gate and drove through, carefully closing and relocking the gate behind him before he drove, still in darkness, to park among the other parked vehicles and sleep amid the other sleepers.

CHAPTER X
▲▲▲

The day was bright and hot and more musicians arrived. The Povatitsas, Burt Sherry's old group, a local hula class, six more Irish groups, two teams of bagpipers and highland dancers, numerous singer/songwriters with a variety of accompanying instruments, and a steel drum band. People who had not performed the previous evening filled the afternoon with women's music, children's music, and old union and work songs.

Gussie had gotten up earlier than most and was alert enough to grab a place under one of the cherry trees to unfold her camp stool and lean her back against the tree bark. The fliers were gone and her Mexican bag was much lighter. She felt pleasantly loggy from the night before, and let the music drift through and around her as she sat half dozing. Bits of the conversation she'd overheard before she slept came back to her, and it bothered her, but it was none of her damn business, after all, and Willie hadn't shown his face yet anyway.

Julianne signed up for a solo spot between the steel drummer and the union songs. Gussie felt half hypnotized by the music, the hands that moved so precisely but with such vigor to strike a note from a drum, a set of strings, the way they were able to keep the rhythm going, striking just at the right intervals with pick or fingers, those clever, nimble fingers and surprisingly strong and sinewy arms, on young and old, male and female. You didn't see that many musicians who managed to keep extra flesh on them and it wasn't only because so few could make a living.

Julianne Martin, for instance, standing up there swaying to her own beat, her face rapt as her slender hand moved like a feather over the strings of a borrowed guitar. She was singing some silly little children's song, bouncing from the knees at the bouncy parts, smiling as she sang. A gentler, prettier picture Gussie couldn't imagine, and you could see the young girl she had been shining through to animate her face. You could picture her hair glossy as warm butter and fine as silk, though now it frizzed a little at the ends, as if it had suffered a bad permanent. But at the end of the children's song, Julianne's face sank back into the overly serious expression Gussie was more familiar with.

"Since this is a kind of memorial service we're having here," Juli said, "I'd like to sing a song I wrote for the memory of my husband. I was very bitter about George's death when it first happened. But I've learned some things since from a wonderful man who does psychic readings and healing and has put me in touch with a longer view of our continuing existence. And I've come to understand a lot about me, George, and everybody else since then. This is called 'You Asked For It.'

"In some other life you were rich as a king
You ruled slaves and peasants and treated them mean
In this life you sang songs of the poor working man
But you never tried to work with your hands

"So you asked for it.
The fate that seems so unfair.
You asked for it.
'Cause all along your shadow self was there.
Like gangrene it ate up your energy
Your happiness, money and health
And you were too angry and too blind to see
You were doing it all to yourself.

"I used to feel guilty and sad all the time
For poor hungry people whose lives weren't like mine
But I no longer hate life for what it is not
And I know they have asked for the lives that they've got.

"Yes, they've asked for it.
Being tortured and murdered and starved
They asked for it

They mapped destiny in their stars
'Cause in their former lives
They did not learn to be wise
And what we do to others will be ours.

"I've studied hard and learned all these lessons carefully
It's freed me of my grief and guilt and set my spirit free
For my life and love I'll take res-pon-si-bil-ity
I've grown and will allow good things to come to me

"And I've asked for it
Now I'm happy and wholesome and strong
Oh I've asked for it
For it never is life that is wrong
We choose our own notes as we sing our own song
My song belongs to no one else
'Cause I asked for it and this is what I've gotten for
    myself."

Of course, Gussie reminded herself, sometimes even in
this music the lyrics could be a lot of hogwash.

Willie had sauntered up beside her to lean against the
tree and now he caught her eye with one of his bloodshot
ones. His face was a caution, and in spite of herself Gussie almost giggled. He looked as if he'd taken a bite out of
an apple and met up with the ass end of a worm. "I do
believe that's the single most god-awful song I've ever
heard in my life," he said.

"I suppose you can't tell a book by its cover," Gussie
said, "but I don't see how a nice girl like that can truly
believe that kind of thing."

Faron Randolph had been heading for Willie but had
been arrested by Juli's performance. Now he took the last
step toward them, grinning and scratching his head.
"Sounds to me like what happens when someone raised
Calvinist-style hard-shell Baptist takes up Zen Buddhism
and gets tangled up in their own karma," he said.

Eric Havelock sat on the log ahead of Gussie and now
he turned and said, "So that's what they meant by 'opiate
of the masses,' " all the while looking at Juli as if she

were a particularly interesting microorganism. "I'll be damned."

"If she's right about what it takes," Willie said, nodding toward the stage, "you're gonna have a lot of company, buddy."

They were the only dissenters within hearing distance, however. The applause almost drowned out their disgruntled comments and Juli beamed with the benign smile of a missionary who had just won over the cannibals.

While she was singing, two men and a woman kept putting big slabs of red-basted ribs on the big barbecue grill. The savory smells rising from it rivaled the underlying odor of manure and lines formed three deep until the grill was no longer visible except for the smoke.

▲▲▲

Gussie sat fanning herself. Those other folks could just go right on ahead of her, never mind how spicy-rich the ribs smelled. It might be well after her usual dinnertime but the sky was still clear except for a thin strip of white cloud over the river way off beyond the unfinished condo complex. The heat waves shimmered up from the grill, so the air all around looked like sun-warped plastic. Julianne, sitting on a log and eating sweet corn, licked her fingers and wiped sweat from her forehead with her wrist. "They didn't really need to light the grill today," she joked to Gussie. "Could have cooked everything on the stage without ever starting a fire. I just keep remembering how good sweating is for your pores."

"Uh-huh," Gussie said, but she wasn't feeling all that much like chumming up to Julianne after that last song of hers. If that self-righteous sweet young thing knew even a teeny little bit of what Gus's life had been like, she'd probably say it was a wonder Gus hadn't got herself turned into a cockroach by now.

The little strip of gray on the horizon stretched itself into a long boa over the highway, which was hidden by a rise in the pastureland. But where that strip grew, the air seemed to split and Gussie could just make out a noise, insistent as the buzz of a yellow jacket but more of a thump-thump-thump, the distance-muted blare of a radio turned up loud. The smoky rail rose into the sky, and seemed to draw cloud out of the blue as it did, tainting the clarity with corruption and noise. Then despite the people the rumble and the blare grew louder, the cloud, a dust cloud, she could smell it now, rising a ways down the corduroy road, and over the hill in a heat shimmer of its own a red van bounced blaring and booming into the driveway. It was shiny as a candy apple, despite the dust cloud, and it had one of those special paint jobs, orange flames and black skull and crossbones.

Anna Mae Gunn, who had just walked away from the grill and had been heading in the direction of a blond-haired man Gussie didn't remember seeing the day before, changed direction, handed her ribs and corn to somebody else, and strode over to the van. Gunn's black hair was in two pigtails today, tied with leather thongs and fluffy white feathers. Her skinny brown legs stuck out of hip-slung cutoffs and a Vancouver Folk Festival tank top was knotted beneath the pointed bumps of her braless breasts. She wore brown flip-flops on her feet but still looked as if she was ready to kick ass.

The blaring noise suddenly stopped and a man with spiky bright red hair and a sleeveless black T-shirt and black denims crawled out of the driver's seat. He nearly had to step on Anna Mae to put his feet onto the ground.

"What can I do for you?" the Indian woman asked, her fists on her hips and her feet planted wide apart, as if she expected him to try to knock her over.

"Isn't this where the Maryland Memorial Folk Festival is being held?" the man asked, his voice soft, polite, and mock-innocent in deliberate contrast to his hard-punk looks.

"It is."

He leaned back and hollered into the body of the van. "It's the right place, guys. Start unloading."

"Wait a minute," Anna Mae said. "I'm the director of the festival. Who are you and what do you do?"

"I'm sorry," the newcomer said, his hand fluttering to his chest as if he were a mellerdrammer heroine trying not to lose her virtue to the landlord. "I thought it was an open invitation for anyone who wanted to donate music for the memorial fund for Nedra and the others. I'm Duck Soul. I don't do exactly your kind of music, but Nedra was what you might call an intimate friend of mine and so we wanted to contribute. After all, my kind of music does bring in more bread than your kind these days . . ."

Intimate friend, I'll bet, Gussie thought. Despite the spiky hair, Duck Soul was quite a hunk, muscles rippling from the sleeveless T, chiseled cheek and jaw, electric blue eyes.

Two other fellows who looked like bikers who'd had a good scare began unloading the back. A few of the other musicians, including Brose and Juli, gathered around.

"Wow, will you look at this stuff!" one of the gospel singers exclaimed, reverently touching a piece of electronic gear.

Anna Mae stood glaring while the heedless Soul directed his crew to set up the equipment on the back part of the porch, behind everyone else. There was already a sound system but he added a few things Gussie wasn't familiar with. When his setup was complete it looked capable of launching nuclear missiles.

"Now just you hang on a minute," Anna Mae said. "You can't use all that stuff. I don't know if my house current will take it."

"Oh, dear," Soul said. "Well, we'll just have to see, I suppose, but I'm sure it will work. It's state of the art, you know, and takes less power than you'd think. I would have brought my generator, but I knew this was an acoustic concert so I tried to pack light."

"Aw, let the man have a chance, lady," Brose said. "Ain't it all for the same thing anyway?"

"Hey, man, that's really nice of you," Soul said.

Juli had been stroking the sleak plastic sides of something with lots of knobs and slides and switches. "This is amazing stuff. The technology must really free you . . ."

"You bet your sweet ass it does, baby, but there's a lot to harnessing all this power. The blending can be a real bitch, getting the right mix takes an exquisitely precise touch on the knobs—"

Brose said, "A little hard to sit in, then, ain't it?"

Soul arched a red-tinted brow at Brose. "For some, maybe. But me, I'm good, and I'm fast, and I'm hot. The technology just means I don't have to play my fingers off to the knuckles to get sounds that would blow any of the rest of you offstage."

Uh-huh, Gussie thought. There goes Mr. Nice Guy.

"I don't know about that," Brose said slowly, hitching his guitar up on his belly like a gunslinger hitching up his holsters.

"How about a duel?" Havelock suggested sarcastically. "Electric current against talent and skill."

"Don't be such an asshole, man," Soul said, still easily but with a sharp edge to his voice and a mean glitter in his eyes. "I told you I'm good."

"This is a ritual celebration," Anna Mae said. "Not a contest."

"How about if we were to make it interesting?" Soul asked. "I just came here to play, donate a little time, but you guys have an attitude problem. I'm getting a little pissed at all this snob shit. I got ten thousand dollars for the fund says I can outplay anybody here. Losers match it."

"Hell, man, nobody's got that kind of cash around here," the chanteyman said.

"Or the confidence, apparently. Okay, I'm easy. One thousand from each of you who accepts the dare, but if I win, and you don't have the bread, I win your instruments."

"What will the ground rules be?" Brose asked.

"Anything goes," Soul said.

"Anything?"

"I just said so."

"You're on, my man."

And so it was that male plugs were plugged each into its female plug and balance was adjusted, slides were slid, knobs were turned, and switches flicked. Current flowed. A tuba tooted from the keyboard of Soul's synthesizer.

Brose sat on a stool and played a complicated riff that mostly took place on the neck of his guitar. Duck Sole pounced out a few chords that sounded like a funeral dirge.

Willie, the banjo still hung around him, watched from beside the tree. He was comfortable again. A cigarette hung between his lips and he clutched a diet soda in his hand.

Duck Soul turned his dirge into a wheeze of sound, deceptively wispy, before his fingers lifted and dived for the keyboard and a band boogied out—guitar, bass, drums, clarinet, whatever was needed to round out the sound appeared when the man struck a key.

Brose diddled through one bar of a Balkan dance tune in response, then unslung the guitar from his neck and tried to hand it to Duck's back. Into the mike he said, "Okay, man, you win. Ain't no way one little old guitar is going to compete with all that."

Duck grinned. "Then get reinforcements, man. Anybody. Everybody. Just remember, if I beat everybody on stage, I get a thousand bucks from each one and I take all the instruments. Just to prove to you fuckers that the shit you play is *dead*. Make you admit what real music is."

And he played on, something by Hell's Kitchen or Broken Glass or who-the-hell knew who, Brose didn't, he didn't listen to that shit much. Rock was okay, but it made sense to him when an anthropologist friend of his had described it as usually being a case of the white man ripping off the black man's music in order to arrogate to himself some of the superior sexual prowess he believed the black man possessed. Yeah. What he said. Sounded good to Brose. So maybe Brose played Balkan music and all that shit to arrogate to himself the white man's superior polkas, pastries, and a few blond chicks. At least, according to the prof. Actually, Brose played because he liked to, not because he had a bunch of theories he was trying to prove. Apparently Duck Soul was not dealing from the same deck. Too intense. One man was not going to convince him otherwise, and neither was a whole stageful but here they came, filing up beside Brose, that girl Juli first, the one who'd done the weird song, with her spoons. She was taking the whole thing as a joke, laughing. Well, hell, girl didn't have nothing to lose but a couple of old soup spoons.

The jug band and the Irishers followed her up and the gospel singers who were really a couple of doctors, he knew because they'd given him their cards. One was a sinus specialist or some damn thing and the other was a radiologist. The guy on the washtub bass was a lawyer with some fancy New York firm that sounded like a Jewish family reunion.

The steel drummer added his percussion to the lady plastic surgeon who played bodhran for the Irish group. The steel drummer was a Japanese guy who was a railroad engineer with a useless degree in business law of the Pacific rim. Wasn't much call for that kind of thing where the guy lived in Arkansas so he drove trains instead.

Soul answered their entrance with a driving riff of his own, a one-man battle of the bands even without his opponents. The amps were loud, the drum machine throbbing as if it were the heartbeat of at least the state of Maryland, if not the whole earth. Horns skirled into wild screams and the guitar was a twenty-car freeway pileup. Soul began to sing—anyhow, that's what they figured he was doing because you could hear his voice even though it was hard to make out what he was singing.

When he stopped, barely soft pedaling the drum machine to let them know it was their turn, Brose's ears were still ringing with the sound.

Up front Gussie and Willie exchanged looks. Gussie didn't even wonder why Willie didn't get up there with the others. He looked like his head was killing him now. He would no sooner get up there and stand in front of all those monitors listening to all that noise screeching back at him than he would lay his head on the barbecue grill.

But the beat was infectious and sexy, and it started Gussie to tapping her toe, then stomping her foot, and before she knew it she was on her feet dancing, snapping her fingers, clapping her hands. When Soul stopped she waited expectantly, watching the stage while the drum machine thudded out the seconds.

The kids on stage, some of whom weren't kids at all but closer to her age, conferred hurriedly, tried a couple of things, and couldn't seem to find anything they could all remember. At any other time, Gus thought loyally, they could have blown the machinery off the stage, but from what Willie said, a big chunk of the common repertoire had somehow been hacked away by Sam's death.

Off to one side, Gussie noticed the blond fellow Anna Mae had been headed for earlier eyeing Willie, as if waiting to see what he'd do. The man hadn't taken sides or tried to sing along or seemed moved by the rock beat. Maybe he was a promoter—businessman or something. His hair was cropped close and he had a no-nonsense look about him, and seemed to be sizing up everybody there, but especially Willie.

Gussie had been sweating from every pore, so hot that she thought she'd just drip clean away into a little greasy puddle, but all of a sudden a breeze blew up, unsticking the hairs from the sweat on her bare arms, evaporating the sweat, and raising goosebumps all over her.

Black roiling clouds clustered over to the north, by the river, low on the horizon. And was that rumbling sound the drum machine or thunder?

Anna Mae looked up sharply, scowled, and signaled Sylvia. Together they began hauling a tarp over the trellislike structure that roofed the half of the deck nearest the house and tied the ends to poles. All of the musicians were now in shadow, but the equipment was protected from rain.

"You guys are fizzling out," Soul laughed. "But you're not giving it your best shot. Everybody ain't here. I still see lots of instruments I could win out there in the audience. Come on, my music is better and you know it. Hell, you can't even remember your own songs. How good can they be anyway?"

The others were still arguing among themselves. Havelock wanted to sing a traditional Nova Scotian fishing song but it was so obscure that nobody else knew it to sing backup.

The drum machine pounded to a stop and Duck jumped to his feet and said, "Give up, then, dammit! Admit it! I win."

"How immature and unenlightened," Juli said in the silence.

And from offstage, where Willie was standing, debating about whether to play or not, the banjo lying propped up on the log beside him played "John Henry."

Brose listened for a second, then leaned into the microphone and said, "We ain't licked yet. MacKai, you got me into this shit. You gonna strap that instrument on and get your ass up here or just stand around lookin' decorative all day?" Then, without waiting for an answer, Brose brushed past Soul, who was standing in a victorious pose beside the keyboard, and usurped his place at the keys.

CHAPTER XI

▲▲▲

" 'Scuse me, my man," Brose said over his shoulder to Duck Soul, "but I ain't buyin' into this lowly manchild-versus-the-machine shit and I don't intend to die with no hammer in my hand. You have done arrogated all my superior sexual prow-ess I intend to let you arrogate. 'Less I'm mistaken, our bet ain't about who is the hottest musician or who has the most firepower, instrumentwise. It's about who has the best music. Now stand aside, boy, while my accompanist and I show you how it's done."

He lit into the synthesizer with the skill of a master.

Willie didn't know if he was more astounded at the way Brose was tickling the keys or the way the banjo seemed to actually be guiding his own fingers into the tune of "John Henry."

Brose winked at him.

"I didn't know you could play one of these things," Willie said into the microphone so Brose could hear him over the wails of the synthesizer.

"Lot you don't know about me," Brose said into his own mike. "Anytime you go to teach kids somethin' it's a two-way education."

Just to show he meant it, he added a heavy metal passage that fit right in with the steel-driving man.

Soul, who was finally catching on that he was being outgunned with his own weapon, protested, "S'posed to be a song, bro. Not just a tune. *I* sang a song."

"Did you now?"

The steel drummer, his smallest drum slung from a strap around his neck and his drumsticks in his hands, edged over to them. "I can sing that song. The other guys on Amtrak think I'm a nut for collecting old railroad songs but I tell them it's something my parents learned in the internment camps and that shuts them up."

With a lot of clanging, he bent down to sing into the

mike, faltered for a moment, then sang "John Henry" in Japanese.

Soul started to stammer out a protest but Brose interjected between verses, "Hey, man, it don't have to be in English to be a folk song and anyway, everybody knows anything comes out of bein' incarcerated is cool." He turned to the drummer, who was providing steam-hammer effects in a steady bong even as the conversation continued, "Okay, my man, teach us the chorus and everybody sing along."

Pretty soon Gussie was singing so hard she scarcely noticed the bite of the wind that bowed the tarp over the musicians so that it swelled with the gusts and emptied with a sharp flap. She hadn't known she could sing in Japanese but actually the words were a little like Spanish ones, and she sang with a strong Tex-Mex accent.

Meanwhile a cataract of cloud filmed the bright blue lens of the sky and blotted out the summer sun lingering into the evening. Close behind boiled a great muscle of storm, angry gray clouds moldering to rotten black, bloated with rain and electricity.

As they swarmed over the stage, the little alligator clamp lights beamed out of the darkness, focusing on Brose as the drummer. Juli and all the others stepped back and he drove into the bridge on a keyboard solo, singing into the voice mike in English, "John Henry was a steel-drivin' man, oh, Lord, John Henry was a steel-drivin' man."

The lightning struck like a snake too damned crooked to rattle a warning. Maybe the clapping hands and the amplified keyboard drowned out the first thunderclap but then, maybe it never came. Because one minute it was so windy and dark about all you could clearly see was the little stage lights bouncing off Brose's snaggle teeth and his eyeballs and the next the light seared your eyes so bright it cut clean through closed eyelids and printed itself on your brain, a fork of lightning diving straight for the microphone.

A nuclear bomb detonated inside Gussie's head, an explosion of grating, grinding noise that was more than her ears could bear. She felt her hair stand straight up as her skull split apart with it, then the ground slammed into her face.

Millions of icy needles exploded over her body as the rain hit and she struggled back up to her elbows, trying to support her head with her hands. Her brain pounded louder than John Henry's hammer and the steam hammer put together and the ghostly image of the lightning flash repeated again and again in front of her eyes, superimposing itself on the melee on the stage.

People's mouths gaped open, their faces contorted with fear, and she assumed they were screaming, though she couldn't actually hear them. It was like watching a silent movie. She felt rather than heard the death noises of the sound equipment as too much power snapped wires and blew chips and sent sparks flying. The drummer leaped off the stage and landed jackknifed over his drum. Willie looked as if he were still in flight, his belly supported by Juli's back, one knee cocked as if he were running, the banjo outflung and his knuckles tight around the neck. Brose lay beneath Willie and Juli Brose and little drifts of smoke rose from the three of them, or maybe, Gussie prayed, oh, maybe it was only from the wires that jumped, writhed, and sparked all across the stage, restrained only by fetters of duct tape placed at strategic intervals.

People leaped drunkenly to the ground from the stage and staggered around, or wobbled around the yard, opening their mouths as if they were trying to pop their ears, but Willie and the others didn't move. Sparks flew from the keyboard. Duck Soul hunkered over to one side of the stage, his arm wrapped protectively around a crying girl.

At the edge of the stage Anna Mae stood poised for a split second like a chicken hawk searching for prey as her eyes swept the blast-stunned people, the sheets of rain dumping into the tarp, turning the front yard into streamlets and puddles and pools, and back to the wires jumping onstage. She looked madder than ever, Gussie thought. Damn, that woman can look pissed off about anything. But then with a flick of wet black hair she sprinted into her house.

Nice that somebody has somewhere warm and dry to go, Gussie thought nastily.

The wind still tried to blow at the tarp, but it was so full of water all it did was spill little cascades over the edge. It was tied by two pieces of nylon cord to the poles at the front of the stage, and those poles already bowed with a combination of the weight of rainwater in the tarp and the softening to mud of the ground in which they were planted. Onstage, Willie stirred.

"Jesus, God almighty," Gussie said aloud, though her voice sounded only in one ear and then as if it were coming from a great distance. If the poles gave and the tarp dumped that load of water onto those hot wires, Willie and the others still trapped onstage would be electrocuted. Faron Randolph was hauling one of the gospel singers offstage and Willie raised his head, looked around, then clenched himself across the others to shield them. It wouldn't work that way. Gussie had no desire to be electrocuted but she didn't intend to have to live with the memory of her friends frying in front of her when she might have prevented it either.

She threw down the Mexican bag she'd been vainly trying to cover her head with and swayed to her feet. Stars still burst in front of her eyes between her and the stage as she lurched toward it. Still standing on the ground, she leaned across the front of the deck and tugged at Willie's pant leg. He looked up again, toward her, but didn't seem to grasp what she wanted. In for a penny, in for a pound, she thought to herself, and climbed up onto the deck, picking her way through the wires to Willie, and tried to pull him up by the armpits.

He nearly threw her backward as he hauled himself to his feet but her dancer's coordination paid off and she skipped aside to reach for Juli.

But at that point Brose reared up, dumping Juli onto her feet. He shook his head like an angry bull and rose to his knees, casting a quizzical look first at Willie, then at Gus. Smoke curled up from the black-singed ends of his red hair. Willie leaped from the stage, banjo still in hand, and reached toward them with his other hand. Gussie turned Juli onto her back. Her face was red as if she'd been sunburned, with no lashes or brows and her bangs all singed away. Gus felt a pocket of pressure pop from one ear and heard thunder rumble, more distant now, along with the crackle and hiss of electricity and rain, the creak of tent poles straining.

Brose lumbered to his feet and Gussie shot a steadying hand toward him, but not before the top of his head touched the low belly of the water-pregnant tarp and one of the poles skidded sideways.

He jumped for it as the edge of the tarp gave, folding under a torrent of water that crashed onto the stage, over him, over the wires, splashing toward her and Juli.

She knelt there stupidly waiting to die, watching the water, wondering indignantly who in the hell was going to help Lettie and Mic now. She was still waiting, watching Brose double back to reach for her and Juli, when Anna Mae calmly walked up to her from the back of the stage and asked, "Is she okay?" nodding down at Juli.

"How in the hell should I know?" Gussie asked querulously. "I thought we were both fried."

"I cut the power."

"About time," Gussie snapped, then realized she was shaking like she needed a drink worse than she had ever needed a drink in her life. Angry with her unsteady hand, she grasped Juli's shoulder. Her fingers seemed to have trouble gripping.

"Come on, girl," she said to Juli. To Anna Mae she said, "Looks like it knocked her out."

Willie crawled back up onstage. "Whatever you do, don't give her a drink," he rasped. "Has anybody called the paramedics? There are people seriously hurt out there."

Juli's eyes opened. "Owww," she moaned. "What the hell?"

"It's okay, kiddo," Gussie said. "You can now tell people lightning won't dare strike you because it never strikes twice in the same place."

The limp attempt at a joke was lost on Juli who asked, "What? What did you say?"

"Just funnin' you, honey."

" 'Scuse me? What did you say?"

Juli's voice came out high and funny as she said, "I can't hear a damn word anybody's—oh, God." She rose drunkenly as a cobra dancing to a third-rate flute player. "Oh, shit." She started to shake her head and sucked her breath in with pain. Very carefully she returned her head to a forward position looking as if she was afraid if she moved it again she'd tear it right off. She gently tapped the heel of her hand against the side of her head above each ear. "It's like my ears are trying to pop but can't," she complained.

"Oh, sure, honey, that happened to me too but—" Gussie started to tell her that it would go away in a minute.

But Juli was looking up at everybody, Gussie, Anna Mae, Willie, and Brose, who once again loomed over them all. She smiled sort of half apologetically, looking pained and frightened. She thumped by one ear again but when she took the hand away there was a little smear of blood. "Oops. Maybe that's why I can't hear anything, do you s'pose?" she asked, lapsing almost into baby talk. "I think maybe you better get me a doctor."

CHAPTER XII

▲▲▲

While Anna Mae ran back into her house to call an ambulance, the others tried to find help for their own wounds or those of their companions. Fortunately, plenty of the musicians attending seemed to do medical jobs for a day gig. Sylvia had at one time been a paramedic, the washtub bass player a registered nurse, the gospel singers were a radiologist and an eye, ear, nose and throat specialist. Then there was the plastic surgeon, the woman who played bodhran for the Irish group, and the neurologist who played a marimba.

Willie hunkered down next to Juli. Now and then he had to open his mouth and crank it to first one side, then the other to try to pop his eardrums. Gussie snagged the gospel-singing EENT man and brought him over to Juli. He gave her a cursory once-over, then said he had to go to his car. When he returned, he was carrying a briefcase.

"Got your instruments in there, Doc?" Gussie asked, then coughed. The acrid smell of burning wire did not blow away as easily as regular smoke or the scent of manure.

He nodded. "Yes, and even more important. Got my release forms. Waivers of responsibility if the patient doesn't go in for follow-up treatment." Juli signed in a shaky blue ballpoint scrawl.

He had her sit up on a log in front of the ruins of the stage, one of Anna Mae's tartan couch blankets around her soaked blouse and jeans. Her drying hair was beginning to curl, the charred bangs kinking into tight ringlets at her hairline. Her blue eyes looked naked and defenseless, slightly startled without lashes and brows.

"We'll need to have Clarissa look at your burns," he said.

"Calling in consultations already, huh?" Gussie asked.

"Well, of course, Julianne is entitled to choose her own physician but I just thought . . ."

"It's dead," Anna Mae said, stalking up to them. Her mouth was set in a hard line and her hands were balled into fists at her side.

Gussie stared at her stupidly, then said, "Oh, you mean the phone?"

"Yes."

"Lightning must have gotten it too," Willie said.

"Maybe," she snapped back.

The gospel-singing EENT man, whose name was Harvey something, said, "Looks like it's all first degree but I'm no expert. Let's get her inside. The light's so bad out here I can't see a damned thing."

"It's no better inside," Anna Mae told him. "We're still disconnecting everything so I can turn the house current back on. And I'm not sure my own wiring didn't burn out."

"Well, inside is still going to be better. Somebody needs to round up all the sleeping bags and blankets they can find and somebody else start getting people in. Some of these folks are going to be shocky. We need to dry them out and warm them up."

From the roar of helpless engines and the whine of mud-mired tires, Gussie figured that some people were already trying to liberate themselves from the rain-soaked fields. Brose had a winch on his truck, but his wheels were as stuck as everybody else's. Still, he plodded dizzily from car to car trying to help rock the four-wheel drives out of the mud so they could help the other vehicles. The blond fellow Gussie had noticed staring at Willie earlier was helping too.

Duck Soul peered over Gussie's shoulder, "How's she doing?" he asked, nodding at Juli.

"We're not sure. She probably needs to go to the hospital but the phone's down, and everybody's stuck in the mud."

"Not me," he said, jerking his thumb in the direction of his van, which still sat in the driveway. "I could take her, or any of the others, and make the call too."

"You could drive away and not take your share of the blame for this too," Anna Mae growled.

"Blame? Hey, lady, it was, to put it in insurance company terms, an act of God. Hell, I'm grateful to that guy I was playin' against. If he hadn't taken over my keyboard, I would have been crisped instead of him. I'm just tryin' to help out here. Give me a fuckin' break, huh?"

"Looks to me like you've *had* breaks, mister. Who the hell do you think you are, busting in here with your electric crap? You're sure no friend of Nedra Buchanan's I ever heard of. Who put you up to it? The feds?"

"God, no, lady, my manager just thought it would be like, a good publicity stunt, you know?"

Anna Mae whirled around, *"What?"*

" 'Scuse me, ma'am," Faron said, his finger upraised to tap her on the shoulder again, "but I think we should build up another fire and dry these folks out."

"Okay. Sure," she said, sounding annoyed, then added absently, "good idea."

"Well knock me over with a feather," Gussie said. "I do believe that's about the pleasantest thing you've said to anybody all day." Even as she said it she realized it was a stupid time to be picking a fight with the woman, but she had just about had it with Anna Mae's snappiness, and she said so.

"Most people would be knocking themselves out trying to help and here you are biting the heads off of everybody who consults you, which they shouldn't have to, it being an emergency situation, but seem to be doing out of courtesy since it's your place."

Anna Mae looked for a moment like she was going to hit her, then said, "You don't know anything about it," and stalked into the house.

A closer, louder engine roared and Duck Soul drove past her, looking dead ahead, heading for the gate. His assistants were still onstage dismantling the sound system.

Gussie followed Faron back to the woodpile and began hauling logs to the fire pit.

Nary a trace remained of the rain except the mud and a greasy mugginess clinging to the night air. With the sun down, the air was nippy enough that you could toast your front by the fire and your backside would still be shivering from the wet and cold. Everybody sat around it popping their ears and hugging blankets and sleeping bags. Some had had changes of clothing and towels and these they shared out with the people who had only come for the day.

Brose had given up on the cars and sat staring into the fire, chucking sticks at it. Gussie sat beside Juli and hugged a blanket around her. Before long Juli slouched down so that her head was in Gussie's lap, as Lettie's had been all too often after she fell off her bike or somebody hurt her feelings. Idly, Gussie combed the limp blond hair with her fingers, wondering if the poor kid had asked for this event and if so, which particular transgression she was atoning for this time.

"So, Willie," Eric Havelock said, "what kind of spook do you suppose sicced the lightning on us?"

"Can you speak up, son?" Willie asked. "One of the nice things about that little bolt from the blue, Havelock, is that I can see your mouth move but I can't hear any of your crap."

Hawkins, the chanteyman, was saying to Randolph, "All I can say is, I'm mighty glad this didn't happen at sea. We'd have all been lost for sure."

"Y'know, I think you're onto somethin' there," Randolph said. "I bet that's why there are so few recorded instances of heavy metal folk concerts taking place on ocean-going vessels."

Gussie hooted appreciatively and regretted it when Julianne moaned and sat up, started to rub her eyes and winced from the flash burns.

"Whatchall gonna do when you find out Willie's right is what I want to know," Brose said.

"What do you mean when we find out he's right?" Havelock sneered. "You're not going to let a string of bad luck make you superstitious like little Miss Crystal Aura there, are you?"

"Goddamn, man, are you that fucking dumb or do you just sound that way?" Brose asked. "Lightning strikes and you still don't get it, do you?"

"And I resent the aspersions cast on the character of the widdah Martin," Willie said, forgetting he had claimed he couldn't hear what was going on. "Julianne just happens to be what you might call an advanced thinker. A little misguided maybe, but a few more times having all that luck she don't believe in knock her on her ass and she'll come around."

"You all just stop that right now, hear?" Gussie said. Her dander was up so high she bet her face was as red as Juli's. "For shame pickin' on a little old sick girl who can't even hear what you're sayin'."

"At least we're not talking behind her back," Havelock said. The woman who had been giving him a shoulder rub stopped abruptly after a particularly emphatic pound with the side of her hand that resembled a karate chop. "Jeez, people sure are sensitive around here."

"Is she crying?" someone demanded.

"No—that's a siren. Somebody must have called the ambulance after all."

"Do we still need one?"

"*I* do," Havelock said. "I think my shoulder blade just got busted."

"That ain't all gonna be busted," Brose said, rising to his feet. "Them're *po*-lice sirens, not ambulance. Think I better go find me a powder room."

"Shit," Willie said and scrambled to his feet, the banjo playing "Birmingham Jail" ever louder as the sirens approached, "me too. I'll come along just to make sure you keep the powder dry."

The banjo shifted to a song the New Christie Minstrels used to sing, "Company of Cowards." The two men disappeared into the shadows beyond the fire just as headlights cut through the gloom, across the fire, and toward the house, catching Anna Mae in their glare.

Immediately after the first set of headlights came another and another. Two uniformed officers climbed out of the first car.

Gussie, who had had a great many policemen as clientele in her bartending days, rose to her feet and walked toward them. These kids were all throwbacks to the revolutionary days of the sixties. They automatically bristled around cops. Walking quickly but casually toward them with her hands in clear view she said, "Officers, God are we ever glad to see you. We have injured folks here. Is the ambulance on its way?"

The police didn't answer her. Several more piled out of the car, brandishing nightsticks. One in the first car pulled out a bullhorn. "Okay, we've heard about this riot. You people can't get away with that kind of thing in this county. Come away from that fire and line up against the sides of the cars, your hands on the hoods and your feet spread."

"*All* of us?" Havelock asked, and got whacked for his trouble.

"Just a minute here," Anna Mae said, flying into the light. "This is private property and there wasn't any riot. We were having a private party with entertainment and there was an accident and—"

But another officer appeared carrying the cash box, which was right out on the table where Sylvia had left it when the lightning hit. "Oh, yeah? You always charge for your private parties, lady? I don't even want to tell you how many zoning laws and city ordinances you're in violation of, not to mention harboring fugitives. Assume the goddamn position. You have the right to remain silent . . ."

Gussie gripped the police car hood and swore under her breath. It wasn't enough that these bozos had to arrest her kids, now they were getting her too, and all these other innocent people.

"We have a right to call a goddamn lawyer, don't we?"

"I am a lawyer," said the steel drummer. "Don't worry, they can't hold us for long. Even if Ms. Gunn was in violation, it's a civil thing, not a criminal one."

The musicians and the few audience members who were not musicians were lined up in rows on both sides of the cars. Then, with their hands on top of their heads, they were herded into the last vehicle, a van. Gussie smirked triumphantly when they packed the damned thing and still had more people left over than they could cram in.

"Oh, Captain," a woman officer called from beyond

the beam of a flashlight. "I found that Texas plate you were looking for, right here, just like the man said it would be."

The Captain sauntered into the light. "This fire here, that's another violation," he said, and picked up a log, walked toward the house, beamed the torch into one of the windows, and flung the burning log. A crash of glass and a rush of light and sound as the curtains went up testified to the accuracy of his aim.

"Goddamn you, you can't do that to my property," Anna Mae said, rushing toward him.

"Oh, I think you'll find that I can do just about what I like around here, Miss Gunn. See, I happen to know quite a bit about you and how you came to have this place. Higgins, Montgomery, you see to it that that fire is dispersed."

"Backup vans are on the way, Captain," said a patrolman who stuck his head out of the window of the second car.

"Fair enough. As they drive up, call a fire truck. We don't want this hazard to spread to the homes of law-abiding tax-paying citizens."

"Do something," Gussie hissed to the steel drummer but he shook his head.

"They know this is illegal as well as I do. Can't you see they don't care? I'm likely to get shot resisting arrest. Wait until we're being booked, in a room full of people. Then I'll make them wish they'd all taken up truck farming."

The two policemen were chucking burning logs at the house while Anna Mae screeched at them to stop it, but they acted as if they didn't hear.

▲▲▲

On the back of the rise behind the house, Brose, surprisingly fast on his feet, caught up with the fleeing Willie. "Where you goin'? You leavin' all them folks down there to take the rap for you?"

Willie wasn't even winded. The banjo had switched to another old outlaw song, "Run the Ridges." "Damn, buddy, I think you stepped in something. I got a good whiff of bullshit just then."

"Come off it, man. Where the hell you think you gonna go?"

"Not to jail and have one of those red-eyed things show up as prosecuting attorney, that's for damned sure. You may not have noticed, brother, but things ain't happenin' exactly like they ought to these days."

"I noticed. Why else they be sendin' cop cars to take care of people struck by lightnin'? Like me, for instance. We been friends a long time, Willie. I always knowed you was a fool about some things and I never mistook you for no hero but I never thought you was a coward either."

"Like you said, we been friends a long time. So I'll let what you just said pass. But think of it this way. If they try to go after that Indian gal for harborin' a fugitive and they can't find me, they can't very well say she's harboring me, can they?"

But the argument was curtailed suddenly by Anna Mae's voice crying out over the general cacophony. A faint pulsing glow brushed the tops of their heads from the rotating lights of the police cars, but this was suddenly pierced by a brilliant shot of flame and the shattering of glass.

Brose had been very near to the truth in accusing Willie of cowardice, for in his realistic, everyday life Willie was not big on risks or extra worrisome responsibilities of any kind. However, Willie, like Brose, did have another self, the one that he was when he cheered for the hero of a movie or a book, the one that he used to use when he sang of high adventure and strong hearts against impossible odds.

The plain fact was that the noise and the lights and the crashing and the shouting seemed more like a movie than it did like real life so Willie acted like his movie-fied self. The banjo still slung across his back, he hit the hillside on his hands and knees and low-crawled up to peer over the edge.

Brose landed with a thump beside him. A policewoman was throwing a guitar into what was left of the bonfire while another cop threw a log at the house. Anna

Mae struggled with a plainclothesman twice her size. The smoke and flames played on the faces of the cops, the lights on the faces of the former festivalgoers lined up against the cars—Willie was reminded of World War II movies where the Nazis were rounding up victims for the concentrations camps.

▲▲▲

Gussie had a hard time believing she wasn't in the midst of a nightmare. The strobing police lights, the dancing fire on the stern, malicious faces as they delivered the final blow, one by one feeding expensive guitars and fiddles to the fire. Policemen did not behave like this. They didn't treat people and their property this way for no reason. The strings twanged and somewhere, among it all, she heard other strings twanging "We Shall Not Be Moved," anthem of the sixties passive resistance movement for civil rights and against war. And from the general cacophony she picked out Willie's voice whispering fiercely, "Not now, dammit. Cut it out. If I'm going to be a damn martyr you could let me pick the time at least."

But the banjo kept twanging and the people lined up waiting for the police van folded like dominoes in a supposed Asian political situation, until all sat on the ground with their arms over their heads. And the gospel-singing EENT man had a sob in his voice as he chanted, rather than sang, "We shall not, we shall *not* be moved," and the others joined in.

The police hauled several of them, including Anna Mae's friend Sylvia, into one of the vans and it drove off, siren blaring and lights flashing.

It was just the diversion needed to cover Willie and Brose commandeering the garden hose and slipping down to the back of the house to turn on the faucet. Suddenly from the shadows, a spray of water squirted onto the flames at the window and played over them, hitting in the face the policeman who tried to add another log to the house fire. By now the banjo was so loud it seemed amplified, but the singing was louder. The hose detoured from the house briefly to wet down several of the other cops.

"Over there, in the shadows!" the Captain said, drawing his gun. "Get those assholes."

A shot rang out and Gussie's first thought was, oh, God, they've started killing us. But when she peeked under her armpit, she saw that the policewoman who had been examining wallets for ID had moved back from the cars and now held her arms in the air with her weapon in her hands. The woman's cap was off and her hair clung wet and shiny against her head. She leveled her gun in the direction of the Captain and asked in a puzzled, suspicious voice, "Wait a minute, wait a minute. What are we doing here?"

"You got a problem, Ms. Sergeant?" the Captain asked nastily.

"Yeah. What the hell's going on here, sir? Who authorized this? I been checking ID and so far we have two attorneys and four doctors, a priest, a nurse, three daycare workers, six waiters and waitresses, a sailor, two carpenters, a welder, three teamsters—their union is going to get our ass somehow, sir, you wait and see—twelve social workers, a congressional page, and—get this—a Texas Ranger."

"Drug runners. They're all drug runners, little lady. Why do you think we're doing all this?"

"Doing what, destroying the evidence?"

"Put down your weapon now, Sergeant. This is insubordination."

"Just a minute, sir. She's right," a black officer said. "We got no call to harass these people. Some of them are hurt. What you doin' burnin' property like this? Which department did you say you on loan from anyway?" He felt befuddled and stupid, coming on night duty, after a day of little sleep, and had gone along with the orders with perfunctory verification, had hardly noticed how strange and brutal the new captain's orders had been. It was as if he were moving in a daze, as if he'd been drugged, by his own power, by the fear that always nagged at him when he went into a confrontation, by the authority flashing out of the Captain's eyes, glinting dark maroon in the flash of the patrol car lights. But the little tune tinkling out of the banjo, the way these people

looked and dressed, the instruments, reminded him of
another time, when he was just a kid, and having people
sing him into the white grade school in Biloxi. He felt
real bad being on the wrong end of that song, on the
wielding end of the nightstick.

Another van arrived then and the Captain said,
"Never mind the chatter. Load these people up and, you
two, find out who's got that hose and stop them."

"Don't move," warned the Sergeant, shaking her wet
head. When the water first hit her, she had drawn her
weapon instinctively, as she had been trained to do when
threatened. But as the water ran off and the funny plunky
tune trickled into her ears, she realized that the real
threat lay with the unorthodox orders she had been following. The sense of unease that had grown on her since
she started patting down the prisoners and realizing they
were not, as they seemed, merely some itinerant group of
musical hooligans, but working people, even professional
people, and injured at that—no one had said anything
about injuries. Why weren't ambulances called? What the
hell was going on here? And what was with this new
captain that he issued such orders—illegal orders, she
was sure. She was going to lose her job for pointing her
weapon at him, maybe even go to jail, but if anybody
found out about this raid, she'd lose her job anyway.

The older of the two men who'd been feeding musical
instruments to the fire snatched a Gibson Hummingbird
guitar back from the hissing flames and stared at it, and
beyond it, to the Asian huts he had burned in the sixties
and to other, worse things he'd done because he was ordered, things that he was still living down, things that
spoiled his aim when he was on the firing range. And
here he was again, destroying, uselessly causing pain, because some asshole that outranked him told him to. He
picked up the guitar and carried it back to his patrol car.
Sergeant Emilie Gray, with her gun leveled at the Captain, just watched him. He leaned into the car and picked
up the radio.

"Wait. What are you doing, Del?" Emilie Gray demanded.

"Covering your butt, Gray. I'm calling the chief in on

this and see if he authorizes what our fearless leader here has put us up to. And if he does, I'm calling my congressman and we'll see if she agrees, and if she does, well, hell, I might start a second career in broadcast news."

"Call an ambulance while you're at it, then," Sergeant Gray said. "A lot of these people have been hurt."

"I'd like to remind you insubordinate fools that there's a murder suspect and his accomplice loose on this place, probably at the other end of that garden hose," the Captain said. "If they escape, I'll have your asses for obstructing justice and aiding and abetting a felon in addition to all of the other charges I'm totting up against you—and any of the rest of you who are just standing around . . ."

"Why don't you let me worry about that, Captain?" asked a burly blond man who slowly turned with his hands still on his head until he faced the house, and the raging plainclothesman. "I'm the investigating officer in that case. Detective Sergeant Bud Lamprey, Texas Rangers. The lady sergeant with the gun there has my badge. I've been observin' the proceedings all day now and I was just fixin' to take Willie MacKai back to Texas for questioning as soon as we got these casualties taken care of, before you folks showed up and started nailin' everybody and settin' fire to everything. I gotta say, y'all sure do things mighty strange around here."

While the ranger spoke, the officer Sergeant Gray had called Del was listening to the squawk box. Suddenly he tensed, leaned inside, and turned up the volume. The dispatcher, even through the static, sounded a little excited as she babbled a string of numbers loosely connected by words. Del held out the receiver so the Captain could hear and the two men glared at each other. Gussie had the oddest impression that the anger in the Captain's gestures as he snatched the receiver out of the lead car was not as genuine as he wanted the others to think. She caught the glitter of predator's teeth through curved lip as he snapped a response into the microphone, then turned back to the other officers.

"Those of you who prefer to disobey orders can make up your own minds about whether to obey this one or not, but the rest of us are needed out on the highway. There's been a pileup and the van that just left here is involved."

"What about the prisoners, sir?" asked a cop who sounded disappointed.

"The hell with 'em," the Captain said.

"How bad is the accident?" Clarissa, the plastic surgeon-bodhran player, asked.

The Captain smiled at her. "Turn yourself in at the station later and we'll let you know if anybody survived the fire. Right now it doesn't look like it."

The steel drummer held on to Clarissa so that her fists were out of range of the Captain until he could climb back into his car, followed by the rest of his officers. The prisoners, still uncertain of their status, fell away from the cars as the policemen pushed past them and flung open doors. Del and Emilie Gray exchanged a long look, then Emilie holstered her gun and ran for a car, as did the black officer, who threw a backward glance, which seemed to Gussie a mixture of yearning and apology, at the people standing among the wreckage of the stage, the fire, and Anna Mae's house.

▲▲▲

The sirens diminished to no more than a baby's cry in the distance and two wet, smoke-smudged figures walked cautiously out from behind the house. Like everyone else, their features were hard to make out in the moonlight. The police had been thorough in destroying the fire.

"I'm sorry about your house, Anna Mae," Willie said. "Is the Texas Ranger still here?"

"I'm right here, MacKai."

"Then I surrender. I won't give you no trouble. I didn't do nothing wrong and even if it might be proved otherwise to the satisfaction of some, I ain't lettin' any more innocent folks get hurt on account of me."

"We can talk about that later, MacKai. I've already heard what you have to say for yourself, and after witnessin' that disgustin' display of unprofessional behavior I'm inclined to give you that there's sure as hell *somethin'* screwy about all this."

Anna Mae emerged from her house. "The fire's out. Everybody come on inside."

Her voice was as featureless as her face in the shadows but by the time Gussie and Brose, with Juli between them, followed the others through the smoke-damaged kitchen into the living room, Anna Mae had set out two kerosene lanterns and a slew of scented votive candles in little blue and red glass cups that made the place look like a church and smell like a department store cosmetic counter, with an underlay of burnt wiring and charred cloth from where the kitchen curtains lay in ruins in the sink, as Gussie had seen through the moonlit window on the way in.

Navajo rugs softened the hardwood floors and a real brick fireplace with a wood stove inside of it squatted in the center of the room. Quilts were draped across the couches and Anna Mae pulled one off and handed it to Gussie to wrap around Juli before the couch filled up with people.

"Real sorry about your house," Gussie said. "Damn, you try to do something nice for people and something like this happens to you. Those cops were just as pure mean as any I'd ever seen, all except that lady and those two fellows, who seemed decent enough. That Captain sure had a burr under *his* tail though."

Anna Mae shrugged and sat down with her knees pulled up and her arms wrapped around them in front of Brose. Her face was half-buried in her arms. "You think they're really dead?" she asked Brose.

Brose just stared back at her.

"Don't answer that," she said. "Of course, they're dead."

"Now, Anna Mae, you don't know that," Gussie said, trying to be soothing.

"Like hell I don't. Sylvia was in that van."

"People survive accidents," Gussie reminded her matter-of-factly. She wished she had a bar rag. It was easier to keep calm if you were polishing something and she definitely felt that one crisis would keep leading to another as long as people allowed themselves to be stampeded by imagining the worst, even when they didn't know. She firmly tried not to think of someone like the police captain having power of life and death over Lettie and Mic.

"That was an accident like what happened to Karen Silkwood was an accident," one of the Irish from Ireland said. "They're probably just waiting to come back and get the rest of us."

"Sixties paranoia is a little old hat, fella," Havelock said disparagingly.

The Irishman looked at him and said, "Don't you be sellin' my paranoia short, me lad. I wasn't even born till yer sixties was nearly over and I've been watchin' for goons of one sort or the other most of me life. Whether they're coppers, soldiers, government strongmen, or the bleedin' little people, somethin' there is that's not wantin' the likes of us to leave here alive."

After all that Celtic melodrama, the remnants of the festival crowd did leave alive, if a little muddier. While some of them slept, Willie paced outside and smoked, carefully shepherded by the ranger, who, now that he had announced himself, had to look like he was performing his duty, although he now had more than a shadow of a reasonable doubt about Willie's involvement in Mark's death. There was also the little matter of jurisdiction. Texas was a long way away and if Willie was headed back that way anyhow, the ranger was going to be on a whole lot firmer ground accompanying him back to the Lone Star State for questioning.

Brose fiddled with his truck tires and finally managed to rock the truck out of its trough and drive onto firmer ground. Others began to follow his example.

▲▲▲

Julianne refused to go when the doctors filled a van with the injured for transfer to the hospital. She was okay, really, she said to Gussie and to Clarissa. Feeling her mouth move and her throat contract as she spoke without hearing her own voice was an odd experience, but at least she didn't have to listen to the arguments of the others. After her initial fearful reaction and a good look at herself in Anna Mae's candlelit bathroom mirror, she decided that there wasn't much wrong with her, that having lightning blast a microphone in front of your face would make anyone a little deaf for a while, and it would probably go away.

Anyway, if it didn't, there wasn't anything doctors could do, was there, except charge her a lot of money? Her ears would get better and her eyebrows would grow back and she'd rub a little aloe vera on the burns and take extra vitamin E. No big deal. Right now watching the mouths move and hearing no voices, being surprised by a touch now and then, was a little surreal.

At least she was well prepared to be deaf. She'd learned American Sign Language during her days as a dance major in college, when she'd earned extra money as an interpreter. In fact, the silence made her think of dance, as if everyone were moving underwater. It was interesting, the silence. It would not be permanent. It could not. She was a musician. Even though she hadn't been playing in a long time while she was waiting tables, she knew that really, like Cinderella, she was more than she appeared to be.

She would hitch a ride back to Joplin with Faron or Brose or Willie and see Lucien and tell him he had to heal her. George would help him. She would tell them that whatever her psychic gifts might be, she didn't want to do that. She wanted to keep doing music. Surely this little trial was just sent to her to show her how very much she needed to do what Lucien had mistakenly assumed was just a passing thing. Hadn't he been the one to tell her she'd been a musician in all those other lives? George would help him understand. George would be glad. He'd encouraged her to come here because he knew, really, that she had to rediscover what the music meant to her—had meant to both of them. And just as soon as she'd been without the possibility of music long enough to prove she'd learned its value, she'd get better, her hearing would return. It had to.

Gussie thought about writing her a note, explaining what had happened to the people who'd been arrested, letting her know how urgent it was that they get out of there as quickly as possible. But then she thought, hell's bells, the girl's got enough to worry about already. Anyway, if what Willie thinks is right, they're after musicians and neither one of us qualifies right now, so at least the two of us should make it out of here alive.

▲▲▲

Harry who worked in the shipyard looked up from his Lotto tickets. "Well, did they?"

"Did they what?" the woman called August asked as she continued to polish glasses.

"Did they get out of there alive?"

"Nope, just then the house exploded and they were all blown to smithereens. Of course they got out of there alive, Harry, or what would be the point of the story? Not the ones in the first van of course. I'm afraid Sylvia, the Highland pipers and the dancers, and all of the Irish group but that one guy were goners. Casualties of a war they didn't even know they were fighting. Maybe if they'd known about it they'd have gone in for big band music or Lawrence Welk or something."

"These people you're calling devils now though, August," Lewis the submarine sailor began, "come on, devils?"

"Well, of course they worked through regular people sometimes, like I said, people like the crooked cops and terrorists and corrupt politicians, but who else do you think could cause lightning to strike and why would anyone else be so interested in destroying a dead man's banjo?"

"Doesn't seem to me like they tried really hard," Lewis's girlfriend Vicki said, in between thoughtful sips of a virgin daiquiri, which she always drank because she didn't like booze that much but liked the stories and left it up to Lewis to be the designated drunk. "I don't see why they couldn't just take it away from Willie."

"Well, because it was the concentrated memory of a lifetime of the very songs that had kept the devils from takin' over for centuries and centuries. They couldn't no more snatch that thing offa Willie's neck than the Wicked Witch of the West could take Dorothy's red shoes. But they could make it awful hot all around him."

"Then how come when Willie squirted them with water they didn't melt?" Harry scoffed.

"That stuff only works in the movies. Besides, it's devils we're talking here, not witches," explained Bill Johnson, who worked on the computers over at the naval base.

"And that lady cop and the other two did stop him when they got squirted—I guess you could say they melted in a way," August said, polishing another glass.

"So then what? Did everybody leave except Anna Mae?"

"Oh, she left too. Julianne, the ranger, and Willie rode with Gussie—since the ranger had flown out from Texas and his rental car was good and stuck. He called a tow truck on the way out of town. Gussie drove because she was able to get her front-wheel drive station wagon out the easiest and as long as both Willie and the ranger were with her, she thought she could make sure there was no more police brutality for the rest of the trip.

"Anna Mae rode with Brose, and Faron gave Hawkins a lift and arranged to meet Brose at a truck stop in western Virginia after Faron swung up to D.C. to pick up his wife. We wanted to keep tabs on each other. Knowing people who've just been killed, missing your own death by nothing more than a skinny little cobweb of coincidence, that can make you skittish.

"And then there was that banjo of Willie's. Willie never took it off anymore and Faron watched it a lot, as if he was studyin' on something. Anna Mae had already said it was a thing of power and she set great store by it, because when the rest of them left that night, she deserted her place and her job to go with them."

▲▲▲

Anna Mae didn't even lock her house when she left. Brose asked her about that on the way to the next Nickerson Farms stop, one night when she was brooding and they were well out of the range of any radio stations and he was drowsy and she was about as bad and he knew that if they didn't talk he wasn't going to be able to make it through one more mile and doubted if she would either.

"You're not afraid somebody's going to go into your house and steal all your stuff?" Brose asked her. "Your neighbors watch it good or what?"

She shrugged. "Nope. Somebody's going to take the stuff and the house. It wasn't exactly mine anyway. I was never told not makin' music was part of the deal, though."

"What kind of deal *did* you make, Anna Mae."

She flinched away from him as if he'd rubbed sandpaper across her sunburn. "I'd just as soon you didn't use that name right now, okay?"

"Why not? It's your name, ain't it?"

"Not exactly."

"Exactly whose is it then?"

"You remember the woman they found murdered by the feds at Pine Ridge?"

"Yeah."

"Well, it was her name. Mine used to be Mabel."

"Mabel? No shit?"

"Yeah, Mabel Charlie."

"I'd have changed it too."

"That wasn't why. I'd been to college, see, and I got a job working on the committee investigating alcoholism on the Navajo reservation out in Arizona. One of the guys I worked with was this bright kid who was going to be a lawyer when he got out. He dated a cousin of mine. He was tactless enough to point out to the committee chairman, who was also the mayor of this little town— I'm not going to say where—that the mayor ran the first bar on the highway as Indians came off the reservation. He started organizing a protest against it—that was while the whole Wounded Knee thing and the Alcatraz thing were going on. I didn't really go along with that Red Power stuff much. I'd gotten my education and I felt like the system had treated me pretty well. I told one of the other men on the committee maybe it would be a good idea if the mayor was to resign, because of this demonstration my cousin's boyfriend was arranging. Instead, all of a sudden there's cops come looking for my cousin and the next thing you know, they 'find' her dead in her boyfriend's car. The boyfriend said he'd been driving down the road and saw her in the headlights, lying on the road. He stopped and even though he thought she was dead, he put her in the car to take her to the hospital. They claimed he murdered her. Later, her brother busted him out of jail and they kidnapped the mayor but there was a shootout and both young men were killed. I couldn't believe it. I wrote letters to my congressmen and right after that the one that was sponsoring the antialcoholism program asked me to come to Washington as a lobbyist.

"He was a good-looking, dynamic man and I thought he was really interested in our problems at first. He took me to a lot of meetings where I wasn't supposed to say anything and a lot of parties and eventually let me know about this 'cheap' property he had found that I could buy, where he could come and visit me. He never came, once I moved out here, and never returned my calls, and the lobbying job turned out to be as a secretary. But a lot of other people came by asking me questions about what happened in that little town, and later I learned that everybody my cousin's boyfriend had tried to rally together was under investigation—all because I blew the whistle on them. They told me that.

"I heard about Anna Mae dying because she wouldn't talk, no matter what they did to her, and here I had just told them everything to betray my people because I thought cowboys and Indians wasn't a problem anymore. So I took her name to remind me how stupid I'd been. Every time somebody calls me her name I think how she gave her life to keep from betraying her people and I got a house for betraying them because I wanted to suck up to the all-powerful white men."

"You mean you changed your name to hers on account of you figure you didn't deserve it?" Brose asked.

"Yeah."

"That's weird," he said.

"It's another customary kind of thing some of us do to remember something important," she said. "Sam Hawthorne knew about it, but he'd only call me Mae. Something about that man. I met him at a rally—I went to a lot of those once my congressman boyfriend left me here with my hard-earned property, though this is the first time I've been punished for it. Anyway, I ended up sitting next to Sam at a sit-in and he asked me about the name too. I didn't want him to think I was as good as he was—I wanted him to know all about it so he'd know not to trust me. Only he just said anybody could be fooled.

"That that was what we were doing in the demonstrations, making sure that the bullshit the people trying to control the government dished out didn't fool the public like it fooled me. He said that's what musicians had always done, from before the time of the old minstrels in Europe, that Indian people and African people had had their own equivalents too of a special profession whose job it was to wander around, spreading the news and debunking nonsense. He said it probably wasn't a kid at all who told everybody that the emperor was running around flashing. He said it was probably a folksinger. He said some other things too, recently, but . . ." but she hesitated to talk about that right now. Too much had been happening that she couldn't explain and didn't understand. She was sure the dream message phone call had come from Sam—had to have come from Sam, but what if it hadn't? What if she had been used by these people Willie was talking about, tricked? Maybe they could sound like Sam. She knew even very mundane tricksters like her boss had ways of discovering things she wouldn't have thought he could know.

"That how you got interested in the music then?" Brose was asking. "Through Sam?"

She nodded slowly. "That and the squaw dances. I used to love those when I was a girl. But, yeah. I listened to everything Sam did, even sang a little myself for while, got to know some of the people on the circuit. I booked a few acts into clubs, even ran a club of my own in Baltimore for a while."

"I had my job, and then too, my folks were sitting on a little oil when it was found in Oklahoma."

"So you grew up rich, did you?"

"Richer than most of the people I've worked with, anyway, though that's pretty relative. We weren't Rockefellers. But I believed in the American way. Musta been all of that white blood on my mama's side that confused me. Just because we lived in a nice house and I went to college and the Nazarene Church and nobody talked politics at home, I thought they must have meant somebody else when they talked about the Indians that had fought for their lives and their land in the old days. Well, that piece of land back there? They can have it. I wonder how they found out. I even had Sylvia use her machine for the flier and I got my mailing list a long time ago when I was at one of the festivals that was folding that year. I mailed the fliers out from Virginia."

"Well, those sneaky types got to do something to keep their jobs, same as the rest of us. I don't imagine they stopped watching you very long. If they were curious about any of us, it was probably pretty convenient for them, you have to admit. Maybe they didn't think of having you do it, but they found out about it somehow or other and sicced the cops on us. You couldn't have known you'd be playing into their hands. Besides, even they couldn't have come up with the lightning."

"Damn," she said.

CHAPTER XIII

▲▲▲

Gussie was at the wheel toward sundown, about a mile from the Kentucky-Tennessee border, when the first hailstone struck her station wagon's windshield with such force that the ranger jerked awake and reached for his sidearm.

"Relax," Gussie told him. "It's just a little weather."

The ranger had shifted position, from having his legs stuck out in front of him with the ankles of his boots crossed, his arms folded tightly across his chest, and his eyes staring straight ahead, he switched to the equally tense pose of leaning toward the window and shifting his glance from the passenger window to the windshield every few seconds to watch stones the size of quarters bounce off the glass and disappear. "Maybe so," he said to Gussie, "but I'm responsible for y'all now that Willie's in my custody. Tell me the truth now, ma'am. You seem to know him pretty good. What's Willie messed up in? Some kind of mob or top-secret science stuff?"

"Who? Willie? Far as I know, nobody has ever accused him of harboring thoughts more scientific than how to analyze the workings of a firearm."

"Might he not have pissed off the mob or some gun-running spy outfit someplace? I just can't see where that Mosby fellow's death is enough to get the feds, the Maryland troopers, and those bad actors who showed up at Ms. Gunn's place all on his tail. And all this other stuff —the accident. Maybe it's coincidence but it sure looks to me like somebody wants him dead. I intend to see nothing like that happens before due process of the law says so."

"You think he'll get a fair trial, do you? After what you saw?"

"Hell, he's not even accused of anything yet, except horse-thieving, and his boss got the horse back, I hear.

No, we just are investigatin' Mr. Mosby's untimely demise and wanted to ask MacKai about it. He'll be treated fairly in Texas—it's not like Maryland and that's for damn sure."

He sounded earnest enough but Gussie didn't know him well enough to tell.

The hail smacked like bullets against the windshield and piled up in drifts that weighed down the wiper blades. The tires crunched and bounced over invisible stones. The noise of the storm all but drowned out the banjo, which lay beside Willie and softly plinked out "Razors in the Air," which was on one of the Kingston Trio albums Lettie had damn near played the grooves out of when she was a kid.

"It doesn't make any difference," Gussie told him. "You hear that banjo back there? You ever heard of any banjo playing all by itself like that?"

"No, but I imagine there's technology would explain it. We can dismantle it once we get Willie in custody."

"My God, man. You admit you hear the banjo, you saw lightning strike the stage just as Brose was winning that fool contest, you saw how strange that policeman was acting—even those other cops, once they snapped out of it, realized how peculiar they'd all been behaving. Can't you admit there might be something a little unusual going on here? You've probably heard what Willie said about it all when he tried to talk about it at the campfire. It fits, wouldn't you say?"

"No, ma'am, with all due respect, I wouldn't. Of course, I didn't get there till early the second morning so I missed hearing MacKai talk at the campfire, but he's given me the gist of it. And while it's fine and dandy for you artistic types if you want to believe in magical mumbo jumbo, I'll have to tell you honestly that I don't hold much with that. Somebody's playing some little tricks somewhere and the interpretation you all are puttin' on this is just that—interpretation. Now, I *am* inclined to think old Willie is being framed by somebody for something and I'm probably gonna be hard-put to protect him against that if whatever it is has as much influence in Texas, as you seem to think, as it does in

Maryland. But I—goddamn, lady, watch out! You nearly run off the road."

"Sorry," Gussie said. She'd been trying to pull over and park for the duration of the storm but her lights caught nothing but darkness and hailstones and she couldn't tell where she was. Where the shoulder of the road should have been she saw nothing but a plunge into darkness with hailstones pelting down into it. She was shaking a little as she edged the tires back onto the road.

The road seemed deserted. Since the McDonald's in St. Louis she'd been playing leapfrog with Brose's truck and the van carrying the Randolphs and Jim Hawkins. But there were no taillights ahead of her and her rearview mirror was black and featureless, as if the road were rolling up behind them as they drove over it.

Then suddenly there was a humming noise and the interior of the car was bathed with white light, brightening and focusing into two headlamps like disembodied will-o'-the-wisps looming ever larger in one side of the mirror. For a moment, the lights flooded the front seat with blinding brilliance, then blinked out to be replaced by rumbling wall, a push of air, a shower of stones and rain crashing against the hood of the car. Then as the stones and water cascaded down the windshield, a Christmas display of red and white lights shone blearily through the water, some of them blinking, some just shining, but all of them outlining the back end of an eighteen-wheeler.

Gussie shifted into third gear again, then fourth, and followed confidently in the truck's wake. "I hope he's a-goin' our way," she said, " 'cause I'm gonna follow him until this storm is over."

"Sounds like a plan," the ranger agreed, and took the tractor cap he'd bought at the last truck stop from the dash and pulled it down over his eyes.

The banjo bumped along in the back, twanging almost fearfully in a minor key, seemingly unable to make up its mind between "Roll on, Buddy" and "Hard Travelin'."

▲▲▲

Brose hadn't worried when the fog rolled up between Gussie's old station wagon and his truck. He figured the road was miles long and overhead the full moon and a sky full of stars lit the way so he didn't even need to use his high beams. They'd meet up when the cloud lifted. But after an hour and a half, as Faron Randolph's van drew up in the adjacent lane, Brose rolled down the window and signaled to Faron's wife to roll down hers. "I think we lost 'em," he yelled into the wind.

Faron's wife looked over at him and then back at Brose and nodded, then pointed straight ahead. Her voice blew back to them as the van surged forward. "Fol—" he thought it said. Or maybe it was "Fog."

▲▲▲

Mile after mile, Gussie followed the lights. The snores of the passengers, the rumble of the wheels, the familiar tick of the station wagon's engine, the wind and rain rushing around the car, the growl of the eighteen-wheeler, and the banjo's plaintive twang of "Dark as a Dungeon" all faded from her mind and into the background. She was aware of nothing but the pattern formed by the blinking lights on the rear of the truck.

The pattern wasn't always the same. Sometimes it was one right after another on the top row, reversed on the bottom row, sometimes it was every other one, sometimes just the red ones, at others just the white. She focused on them and followed, at first intentionally. She didn't notice when the hailstorm stopped and no one else remained awake in the car to tell her, or to ask her why she continued slavishly to tailgate the truck. When the truck stopped for fuel, she slid from her seat and filled the car's tank, paid up, and climbed back in the car still watching the flashing lights on the back of the rig.

And then, all at once, the flashing lights flashed off. Gussie found herself, still in the driver's seat, still surrounded by sleeping people, still idling behind the tanker. She was surprised to notice that in spite of the square pattern the lights had formed, she'd been following a fuel tanker. An old one. The letters on the back, clear in her headlights now that the distracting blinking had stopped, must have said Shell at one time, but the S had been rubbed out so it read "hell Oil."

Once she unfocused her eyes from the tanker's rear, it was impossible for several minutes to refocus on anything else. Then, slowly and painfully, she pried her hands from the steering wheel and saw they had blisters and calluses from gripping the wheel. The backs of her thighs, her back and butt were as sore as if they were covered with boils and her neck and shoulders burned with pain. Her eyes felt as if she'd been using pop bottle caps for contact lenses.

Behind her loomed a truck bearing what looked like some kind of pipe, loaded high and extending, illegally and dangerously, past the roof of the cab, wobbling up and down with the vibrations of the truck's engine, like a giant's fencing foil aimed at her back.

Wherever she was, the teamsters in this neck of the woods needed stricter enforcement at their weigh stations, she decided. The logging truck on her right side was loaded as high as the pipe truck in back of her. STYX LUMBER, it said on the side of the cab in neon paint. To the left an automobile graveyard, a skeletal metal parody of the rigs used to transport new cars, blocked any possible view of the surrounding country.

Not that there would have been a lot to see. The trucks blocked out most of the view, but what she could see, bouncing off their metalwork and reflecting in her mirrors, looked like feeding time in the forest, with a three-deep line of bright white animal eyes gleaming in the darkness, winding for miles behind her and, peering from among the smashed metal of the car corpses beside her, coming toward her three-deep one lane over. Ahead of her, from around the tanker, were taillights-red animal eyes winding forward. Very far forward, they seemed mixed and also seemed to rise above where she was and below but she only had a dizzying feeling to rely on, because the huge trucks on all sides of her blocked so much of her vision, as she supposed they also blocked anyone else from seeing her car.

▲▲▲

The Debauchery Devil, still in the guise of Lulubelle Baker, snorted, for a change, nothing more potent than derision. "You're slipping, boss. You told us yourself we would have to use minions to go against the—uh—adversary. And then you barged right in there against MacKai, banjo and all. What's that you always told us about delegating authority?"

"I did delegate authority," the Chairdevil said. "I did not, of course, go myself. I sent a simulacrum and two individuals whose contracts we hold and in whom I have —had—complete confidence."

"Isn't it you who always tells us never send a simulacrum to do a man's work?" the Debauchery Devil asked with what innocence s/he could muster, which was understandably not a whole lot.

"Or a man to do a devil's for that matter," the Pestilence Devil added. "That pet police captain of yours didn't even handpick his people."

"It was a spur-of-the-moment–type deal," the Chairdevil said.

"That is no excuse for shoddy work," said the Doom and Destruction Devil.

"You should talk. What about Vietnam, what about Central America, what about Af*ghan*istan and the Middle East? You've had I don't know how many chances to blow the world to perdition and you just piddle them away . . ."

"I work in mysterious ways," D&D sniffed. "I'm a lot more effective at providing long-term services to more people in more generations over a more extended period *my* way."

They all ignored that because there was, after all, some truth in it and if there was anything their kind disliked, it was truth.

"Hmph," the Chairdevil said. "Well, much as some of you might like to think I'm losing my touch, I am on top of it. By the way, *Lulubelle,* your influence on MacKai hasn't been nearly as great as you led us to believe. Anyone as tight with you as you claim he is should have jumped at the contract I offered him . . ."

"He was just being greedy and holding out for more," the Debauchery Devil said, defending him.

"Hmm, perhaps," the Chairdevil said.

"Cheer up, boss," the Stupidity and Ignorance Devil said, "we're doing fine."

"I suppose you're right," the Chairdevil said. "Lightning has a mind of its own and Duck Soul has almost no mind at all so the combination was never surefire, so to speak, but nevertheless we did achieve some maiming and bodily injury there. Definitely going to convince the safety conscious in that crowd that going to those singing things is at least as harmful to their health as cigarettes, booze, drugs, and our other products. And if our police minion was undermined by mutineers, he did manage to break up that little party and send them flying right back into our clutches. While it may be a little hard to come up with something suitably impressive in the middle of a farm, short of sending the animals on a rampage, and we've done that. And not to be unnecessarily redundant, now that the adversaries have piled themselves into vehicles we have them right where we want them. Because no matter what, the highways are ours."

"Not *another* fiery smashup," the other devils all groaned, unanimously bored with that overused ploy.

"Nothing so crude," their leader assured them.

"I don't see why you couldn't just let that Texas boy scout take Willie back to jail," the Debauchery Devil complained. "After we went to all that trouble to frame him."

"If I've told you once I've told you a thousand times, we don't want these people in jail. Not the musicians. They'll cause nothing but trouble. Besides, the Texas boy scout, as you call him, is yet another of those thorns in our side—an honest cop. No, I've decided to eliminate the problem of MacKai and that banjo once and for all with what you might call a nonviolent solution—I've simply sent them into limbo—with a modern twist or two."

▲▲▲

Willie sat up in his coffin so fast he bumped his head on the lid. For a moment he felt disoriented, and then he reckoned that coffins didn't usually accommodate four, and two sitting up at that. Of course, he had been lying in the back of Gussie's station wagon, which was rigged so the backseat would fold down. The car no longer grumbled forward and that, he supposed, was what woke him, though he had certainly been known to sleep through many a pit stop.

"Where are we?" he asked, wanting to know if, for instance, they were in Texas yet and sitting outside the jailhouse in particular. The sight of the sleeping ranger reminded him of the delicacy of his position and he wondered if he was in any immediate danger of being tossed into the pokey.

Gussie sat silently for a while without answering, then turned and looked at him, the headlights of the truck behind them glittering off her eyeballs. "You tell me and we'll both know," she said. "Willie, I don't even know *when* we are. Back before the hailstorm it was midnight on Tuesday. According to my watch it is now midnight on Saturday. According to the sores on my butt and the shape my hands are in, it's midnight sometime in my nineties."

"Well, goddamn, Gus, it was real nice of you to let me sleep but that's ridiculous, darlin'," he said, checking his own watch at the same time. "SAT" it said, no matter how long he stared at it. So he hunkered down and looked out the windows around them. "We at some kind of truck stop or what?"

"We're in some kind of god-awful traffic jam for what I can make out," she said. "I don't know where we're going anymore. I was just following that truck up ahead of us until we got out of the hailstorm. But with all these trucks around us and it bein' dark and all, I can't even make out where the hell it is we are so all-fired anxious to get to that we're lined up with all these other lamebrains to get there."

Willie fought down an interior uneasiness that made his skin tingle and his gut turn over and decided if he looked and sounded calm and practical maybe it would absorb from the outside in. "No matter. Let's trade places while it's quiet and I'll drive."

Gussie didn't even think about opening the door with big trucks squashing in from either side with barely a foot of room to spare. She dug her heels into the seat, put her palms on the headrest, and boosted herself over. Normally she could have done this gracefully but her arms and knees and backside were so sore she caught her toe in the ranger's ear, which woke him up.

Fortunately, all parties involved were skinny, and Willie slid sideways to make room for her, then lowered himself into the driver's seat. As he put his hands on the steering wheel he saw that his hands had blood from the seat. He twisted to look behind him. Gussie lay on her belly, facing the front seat. He held up his bloody fingers and said, "Jesus Christ, Gus."

"Never knew you could get saddle sores from a station wagon, did you?"

He shook his head and rolled down the window, adjusted the mirror, then adjusted the other one. "Wish we'd stopped at a 7-Eleven. Don't hardly feel natural drivin' without somethin' to drink."

"Don't feel natural to me apprehendin' an important witness and havin' the suspect—er, witness—drive me home," said the ranger, awake, thanks to Gussie, and stirring like a bear from hibernation. "Damn, I'm hungry."

"You're free as you can be to drive if you want to, buddy, but take a look around and I think it might ease your mind about any of us goin' anyplace anytime soon."

"I'd like to know where in the hell this place is."

The banjo accommodatingly started playing a mournful tune. "Fat lot of help you are," Willie growled at it. "I don't know what the hell you're playing."

"I do," Gussie said blearily, raising her hand like a kid who could answer the teacher's question. She was beginning to have no trouble believing she'd been driving for five days with no real rest. "It's by a guy named K. W. Todd who used to come to Tacoma before Triumph had to stop the open mikes. Used to be a street singer in

Seattle before they outlawed *that* too but mostly he's a hotshot songwriter. I got Lettie to carry his album."

"That's real nice, darlin', but we need to know the song, not the life history of the fellow who wrote it."

"Just hold your horses, I'm gettin' there," she said, her memory fading as sleep kept trying to take over. "Somethin' about a wheel, oh, yeah . . . hmmm hmmm hm hmm hmmm hmhmhm—like that . . ."

"We got the banjo for the tune, Gus. What's the name?"

"I'm workin' up to it," she said, then began, "Here's a health to the Deveneau's, Jones and O'Malley's," in a tentative and slightly off-key voice, singing a syllable for each ring of the banjo, "Who rode from the east on a slow-turnin' wheel. Who forded wide rivers, past mountains and valleys, to leave their young lives by the Oregon Trail . . ."

"Whoever heard of a traffic jam on the Oregon Trail?" the ranger asked.

"Do I look like the AAA?" Willie said.

"No, but on the off chance that you are could you tell me where the men's room is?"

From all four sides came a sharp mechanical sigh of air brakes being released.

"You're gonna have to hang it out the window, now, buddy," Willie said, turning the key and shifting into first, "looks like we're moving."

▲▲▲

Molly and Barry were attacking their house with deodorant bombs when Ellie and Faron arrived, Jim Hawkins, Brose Fairchild, and Anna Mae Gunn right behind them.

"Peeyew, it stinks in here," Ellie said, wrinkling her nose with distaste. "What happened? The wiring catch fire?"

Her mother's mouth was tight and her black eyes flashed with fury as she sprayed a vengeful mist of artificial pine at a K-Mart Early American lamp.

The room looked oddly naked and it took Ellie a moment to realize what was wrong. The two tall bookcases and the short one with the stereo on top were empty except for a few paperbacks. Her father caught her eye.

"I'm sorry, honey. Somebody came in and took all of them. Your old Joan Baez records and the Easyriders, all of the Kingston Trio and the ones we got at the festivals, your mom's Allen Damron records, all the Sam Hawthorne, Josh Grisholm, Pete Seeger, Emilie Aronson, Nedra Buchanan, Tim Henderson, Bill Staines, Hoyt Axton, Tania Opland, Tom Paxton, Malvina Reynolds, Bob Dylan—everything."

"But, Daddy, didn't you tape them all?"

"That's what you smell. I can understand, what with the paper telling how the big aircraft companies are offering cash for the material in phonograph records now, why somebody would steal them to recycle, but the bastard who broke in emptied our tapes into the sink, slashed and burned them all. We had to have the plumbing replaced but we've been tenting in the backyard until we can get the smell out of the house."

Hawkins sighed deeply. "You know, there seems to be a run of this kind of thing these days. I keep my stuff with a girlfriend in Connecticut and while I was at sea a couple of months ago her place was broken into and all of my stuff I didn't have with me onboard was taken— records, tapes, extra instruments, all my books—hers too for that matter. Three people I talked to at the festival had had the same kind of thing happen to them—their collections stolen and the tapes missing or destroyed, songbooks and any extra instruments destroyed."

"Misery loves company," Barry said, and handed him a stack of mail. Letters from friends from five states asked if the Curtises couldn't dub certain records or privately recorded performances for the writers, as their copies had been destroyed—in two cases in a house fire but most in break-ins. Two mail-order catalog sources for music and instruments announced in fliers that they were forced out of business as their inventory had been wiped out—in a fire, a seizure, a robbery, all seemingly coincidental but final nonetheless. Folk music publications announced they were going out of business due to bankruptcy, tax problems, losing a headquarters, vandalism, death or disease.

Hawkins passed the letters on to Brose and Anna Mae.

"That's not all. Bessie McGill in Denver just called to ask me to help her get a fundraiser together for four of our musician friends who have no medical insurance and have apparently been messing around with the wrong groupies—they've all been tested positive for that latest sexually transmitted fatal virus thing—the one that mutated from AIDS. What do you call it?"

"Bad's what I call it," Brose replied. "Who were the victims?"

Barry told him and Brose swore under his breath. "Shit, man, that's scary. Carmichael and I had a lot of the same close friendships, you know what I mean. Makes me glad I been out of circulation for a while. Guess we can be expectin' a lot more bad phone calls and a few funerals before long."

Faron cleared his throat. "Have there been any other calls?"

"Several—there was my mother wanting us to come over and pick up her laundry and then there was—"

"Anything from a lady named Gussie or Willie MacKai?"

"No—haven't heard from Willie in years. Gussie Turner, she's Lettie Chaves's mother, isn't she? She's been running the record business while Lettie and Mic are straightening out that mess they got into on the border."

Faron's mouth shut like a snapping turtle's and his Adam's apple took another dip.

"Shit," Brose said again.

"Why? What's the matter?"

"Well, maybe they'll show up," Hawkins said finally. "Although, the way things have been going, probably not."

"We should have kept on going," Anna Mae said. "We shouldn't have taken the exit. We should have just kept following."

"Following what?" Brose asked. "They flat fuckin' disappeared."

"At least we didn't see any wrecks," Ellie offered. "So they're probably okay."

"Maybe," Brose said.

"Maybe the ranger decided Willie was too dangerous to keep in custody and stopped off in Little Rock or somewhere for reinforcements or more bullets or something," Ellie said. Faron had filled her in on the events of the festival and she tried not to let him see how rattled she was to have come so close to losing him.

"I can't believe Gussie wouldn't have dawdled and waited for us, let us know somehow," Hawkins said, shaking his head.

Brose disappeared into the bathroom for a moment, stopped at the kitchen sink for a drink of water, and headed for the door.

"Wait," Anna Mae said. "Where you going?"

"Tacoma," Brose said. "That's where Gussie's from, ain't it? Julianne's from around here, Willie and the ranger are from Texas. If they were headin' for Texas they'd have come through here like we planned. The way I see it, that leaves Tacoma."

"That's a long shot," Hawkins said, "but wouldn't a phone call be quicker?"

"Could be," he admitted, and pulled out his wallet, pulled his calling card out, and punched out the numbers. After a long time he said, "Morris? How you guys gettin' on? How's the horse in the barn? Oh, that's good. That's good. Lookit here, anything I ought to know about? Like warrants for my arrest or bombs in the mail? No, well, you dudes be cool and if you need to go back to town, call this number and tell Ray there's free flop space at my place, okay? There is? *Who?* Duck Soul—what the hell does he want? Never mind. Tell you what"—he covered the receiver and turned to Barry—"Can I have some mail sent here for now?" Barry nodded. "Okay, Morris, I want you to send it to this address . . ."

▲▲▲

Willie could remember when he liked driving. He had driven for his living most of his life, more miles than most truck drivers, probably. He used to tell people he sang for free, he just charged them for driving to the gig. The ranch job too was mostly driving. When he was well rested and not beat to pieces, he didn't really mind driving on the open road. But he hated like hell inching along in a snake-shaped parking lot in the damn dark with nothing but those goddamn trucks all around him just as if he was in a goddamn box canyon with nothing to breathe but exhaust fumes and nothing to look at but those goddamn truck lights flashing just like they were laughing at him.

At least his jailer was awake to keep him company. "I know you don't believe this," Willie told the ranger, "but I was framed."

"Actually, not that I can do anything about it, but that's beginning to look pretty damned obvious," the ranger said. "What I can't figure out is why? Most of the other people in your line of work that have been bothered are fairly well known, aren't they? I mean, there could be money or something involved. Mob connections maybe?"

Willie shook his head. "No, unfortunately, officer, you are dead right. With the possible exception of yourself I can't see why anyone, for better or worse, would come after us. Short of a few jealous husbands and boyfriends, I've never made an enemy in my life that I know of. And no, sir, I was not as well known as say Sam Hawthorne or Josh Grisholm or any of the others.

"See, it's this way, officer. This so-called folk music we all claim to care so much about supposedly originated with simple, uneducated folks singing songs while they worked and partied and went about their daily lives. These were not top hits they'd learned off the radio, you understand, but songs they had known all their lives and like as not their parents had known all their lives. Nowadays, to receive any recognition for singing that kind of a song, you have to have a college education and a degree that says you're a folklorist or an ethnomusicologist entitled to examine these folks like they were amoebas or microfuckingorganisms of some kind. Either that, or you have to make up your *own* brand-new folk songs. I don't do neither, sir. I worked most of my way through college singing and then the singing seemed more profitable than the education. Besides, a person who's going to work as a folklorist, in order to eat while he's collectin', either has to have a little money to begin with or a big fat grant, of which there ain't a hell of a lot. As for writing songs, I'm sorry to say I never had the knack. I'm not a writer, I'm a singer, an actor, a performer. I can hold an audience in the palm of my hand and make them feel the song, make them laugh, cry, make them mad, make them proud of themselves but—"

"Sounds to me like that's enough to make you dangerous to somebody," the ranger said.

"Maybe so. But just offhand I'd say it's the banjo they're after," Willie admitted.

The grill of the truck behind him bore down on the back bumper of the station wagon. He'd once checked out a videocassette of a Stephen King movie and the artist who did the box design had whimsically made the grill of a truck look like a huge set of teeth. This grill looked that way. All teeth and high beams breathing down his neck, pushing him toward the back end of the tanker in front of him.

They moved, but not far and not fast. Slowly Willie inched the station wagon forward, keeping a fine balance between ramming into the tanker and being rammed into by the pipe truck. The temperature gauge crept up toward the red and the gas gauge dropped toward the E. Between what seemed like one turn of the tires and the next, the station wagon began laboring up a hill.

Behind them there was a clank and a grind and Willie saw that pipe no longer protruded out the front of the truck. In the next moment there was a rattle and a bang as one of the wrecks on the transport truck slid back into another one. The log chains on the truck to the right creaked ominously.

The ranger leaned out the window and craned to see around the trucks. The logging truck swerved forward, rocking the trailer back toward the station wagon. The ranger pulled his head back in before he lost it. "Shee-it, did you see that? I think he did it deliberately. Why, if this was Texas, I'd pull that sucker over and throw the book at him. But I'll tell you the truth, I don't know where this is. I never seen anything like this. There's so many cars and so much light and those bastards are so close, I couldn't even see the road. Judging from the headlight pattern though, I think we're on a cloverleaf of some kind."

Willie just nodded and paid very close attention to the vehicles around them. The bark from the logs on the logging truck was scraping off on Gussie's window and they could smell the resin through the exhaust fumes. And if the pipe on that truck in back of them slid backward when the truck went uphill, it might slide right through the roof of the station wagon when the truck pointed downhill. "According to my friend there," Willie told the ranger, nodding toward the banjo, "we're somewhere on the Oregon Trail. You know, that's a funny thing . . ."

"A traffic jam on a cloverleaf in the middle of the Oregon Trail?" the ranger snorted. "Yeah. I'd say so."

"No. I think that's the first time the banjo's played a fairly modern song, a composed one at that . . . hey, Gussie, you still awake?"

"Umph."

"That song that fella wrote about the Oregon Trail, is there anything in it that would give us some idea what the situation is?"

"Well, I don't remember all the words, Willie, but basically it's about all these families coming out and dying of thirst and falling off cliffs and drowning and stuff . . ." Her voice faded toward the end of the sentence.

"Thank you, ma'am, that's mighty encouragin'," the ranger muttered.

Willie chewed on his mustache for a long time. Meanwhile the car kept climbing slow as a snail up the side of an aquarium, playing tag with the rear bumper of one truck and the front bumper of the other. The lanes were far too narrow too, and seemed to get narrower as the station wagon climbed. The logging truck remained scraping against their side and on the left side, the wrecker pulled in so that the loose junked car parts jiggled and rattled against the left-hand windows.

At the risk of having a junked car in his lap, Willie rolled the window down to get some air, then had to take a hand off the wheel to push a piece of twisted chrome back out again so he could roll the window back up before he choked to death on exhaust fumes.

The banjo began chiming "The MTA," a political campaign song about a fellow trapped on a subway when he couldn't pay the increased fare. Willie found himself singing softly to himself the part about the protagonist, Charlie, never returning, and stopped when he realized what he was singing.

The needle on the gas gauge dipped to the middle bar of the E.

"Not that it hasn't been slow enough," Willie told the ranger with some satisfaction, "but this whole shebang is about to come to a screeching halt. We, my friend, are about out of gas."

By this time they had stopped climbing and had been crawling along a fairly level stretch, but all of a sudden the hood dipped down and the clanking and banging of the trucks around them reversed itself. Willie glanced in the rearview mirror to see three of the heavy pipes looming out over the cab, so far beyond the hood of the truck that he could not see the ends of them. If only they kept going as slowly as they had been, the pipe might not break loose. Willie couldn't see the face of the driver, though the night was fading to navy, then gray.

The banjo tune switched to "Roll on, Buddy—" and Willie's mind finished the rest of the line as he'd heard Doc Watson do it, "Don't you roll too slow, tell me how can I roll when the wheels won't go?"

About that time one of the wrecks screamed, slamming into the driver's side as it rolled toward the cab of the truck. The wreck's loose bumper screeched and squealed and tore a chunk out of Gussie's front bumper as it slid forward.

A sound like a rifle shot cracked from the other side of the car and the ranger cried, "Holeee . . ." and dove toward Willie, arms covering his head as the length of chain that had snapped loose off the log load smashed onto the roof and cracked against the window, crumbling it into an opaque spiderweb of fractured glass. With a mighty rumble the logs shifted, slewing sideways as they readjusted themselves to the lost restraint, and the ends of some of the bottom ones jutted out to push the station wagon so that it rocked toward the wrecker. Juli woke up whimpering and rolled toward Gussie, who was propped up on her elbows, wide-eyed and shaking like a leaf.

"Oh, my Lord, oh, my Lord, we're all gonna be crushed like cockroaches," she said.

The car's engine chose that moment to die with a sputter and a shudder, but the wheels continued to roll downhill, a little faster now, propelled by the momentum of the trucks squashing them on three sides.

Willie wished the traffic would pick up in the logging truck's lane. If that other chain broke from the strain of holding those tons of timber up all by itself, they'd be crushed beneath the load. On the other hand, it might carry them with it, right into the back of the fuel tanker, and even if it tore free of the station wagon before coming even with the tanker, if the chain broke and the logs flew into the tanker, they could all look forward to burning to death. It didn't seem like a whole lot of choice.

What the devil could they be doing up there? Construction? An accident? There should be big yellow signs or flag people or guide cars or flares or some of those signal orange cones anyway, dammit. This was no civilized way to run a traffic hazard. On the other hand, if they did have those things, he wouldn't have been able to see them anyhow for the trucks.

Why had Gussie driven this way anyhow? The Oregon Trail, if he remembered correctly, stretched from Independence, Missouri, to somewhere in the Willamette Valley so they could be anywhere along it—although he didn't think there were any cities right on the road big enough to justify this kind of jam. All of these cars were sure as hell not going to a folk festival.

As he wondered he became aware that the trucks on either side gave the station wagon just enough room that the noise wasn't so awful and he could hear the banjo again, in waltz time now, the low notes mournful and mellow, the high ones piercing—what was the tune? He knew it—he used to do it—it was one of those truly awful songs he used to do for fun. Religious, sort of, it seemed. One of those lugubrious moralistic things from revival tent times. Something about a drunkard who had a dream about punishment for his sins and—oh, shit, it was "The Hell-Bound Train."

"Thanks a lot, buddy," he said bitterly to the banjo. "You're a big fat help."

"Who? Me?" the ranger asked, still yelling, even though the noise was no longer so loud. "What do you expect me to do?"

"Get out and direct traffic?" Willie suggested through teeth gritted so they wouldn't chatter with the fear of death that was sending little icy runners up and down his spinal cord. "I wasn't talking to you. I was talking to the banjo, Lazarus."

"Why?"

"Because, in case you hadn't noticed, it has a way of playing songs to indicate the situation you're in. So far it's been right on target. If it is this time, let's put it this way, I don't want to meet the drivers of these trucks."

Another bump flung them toward the windshield, in spite of their seat belts. In the rearview mirror, the grill of the pipe truck leered in through the back window, jammed up against it.

Willie took his hands from the steering wheel. "Well, I guess that's it."

"What do you mean, man? This is a dangerous situation."

"Nope," Willie told him. "It's not just dangerous. It's fatal. You wouldn't happen to have a cigarette, would you?"

"You're awful damned calm."

"Call it a last request," Willie sighed. The icy runners up his spine had grown vines that now permeated every inch of him, and oddly enough that quieted him as much as being doused with cold water will quiet a hot temper. He told the ranger, "I'm not exactly calm. More like I'm resigned. It's bigger than both of us, sweetheart. I should have signed the damned contract that Nicholson character offered me. At least then I'd have gotten some fun out of life before they took me. It don't seem fair that I didn't sign anything and they're going to take me anyhow. Not to mention you poor bastards. What in the world did you do, officer, to end up going to hell in my company?"

The ranger didn't answer because about then the station wagon's front bumper tapped against the back of the tanker—gently, very gently, just enough to let them know they were trapped.

"Um," Willie said, feeling a certain intellectual interest in the situation. "you know, whoever's driving these rigs must be good—they're keeping us fenced in nice and cozy and not runnin' into each other so far."

"*So* far," the ranger said. "Dammit, there's got to be a way out of here—"

"Nah," Willie said. He was surprised at how detached he sounded, "We've bought it. Unless I misunderstand, for the crime of carrying this banjo around and singing a few songs, not for any drinkin', sinnin', or carousin', you understand. They kind of liked that—no, for the crime of singing a few songs, I have landed us all in hell." He looked out the window. "Or maybe it's only purgatory. It doesn't seem to hurt yet." Then he decided he was being thoughtless. "I mean, at least I don't. You hurtin', buddy?"

The ranger shook his head. "No, but I'm sure as hell sweatin' up a storm."

"You could just push the glass on out of that broken window. It's not going to stop anything if that log by your nose decides to come crashin' in."

"Well, I'd like to delay it just a little bit if it's all the goddamn same to you, mister," the ranger responded angrily. "What the fuck's the matter with you?"

Willie shrugged. He was feeling less and less all the time. Shock maybe, mercifully numbing him the way he'd heard it does sometimes. It was better than being scared shitless anyway. "It's just that it's all over, my friend. This is it. We've bought it. Relax and let your life pass before your eyes."

"No thanks," the ranger growled.

"Now, hush. You'll worry the ladies."

Julianne was rolled on her side, staring wide-eyed and

openmouthed at the wrecker. Willie wished she hadn't been struck deaf so he could talk to her.

He couldn't see any sky at all now but it was getting lighter and sometime earlier the truck lights had all gone out. He turned off Gussie's lights. No sense in runnin' down the battery.

He looked over at the ranger. Sweat ran down the man's face and darkened his fair hair. His hand clutched his knee but it was shaking all the same. Poor bastard.

Willie reached behind him and picked up the banjo, "I don't want any more preachin' out of you," he told it. "If this is it, least we can do is keep one another company. We got into this for making music so we may as well give 'em their fire's worth." Inside he was thinking, here's a captive audience if ever there was one and if ever there was a good reason to get someone to feel what he wanted them to feel it was now. Maybe the ranger had done something purely on his own to get himself into hell, but Willie couldn't help feeling they were all in this particular hell because of him.

The least he could do was liven things up a little. What was it they said, heaven for climate and hell for society? Might as well make the best of it.

He automatically started to tune and then realized that it was in tune, had stayed in tune ever since he first picked it up. Julianne had mentioned something about that but more than anything, *that* showed that it was a truly magical banjo.

"Any requests?" he asked.

" 'Nearer My God to Thee'?" Gussie asked in a high, shaky voice. She'd been listening all along but she was too stuporous to care much one way or the other.

"Wrong direction," Willie said cheerfully. In his mind he ran through a few choices, but many he couldn't remember.

Then too, songs like "The Wreck of the Old '97" and "Dark as a Dungeon" and several murder ballads in succession were all that suggested themselves and they failed, he felt, to contribute properly to the ambience he wished to create, even if he could remember them, which he couldn't.

In past hopeless situations, when his dad died, when his first wife took off on him and the second one died, when the album he was sure would climb to the country top forty had sunk without a bubble, he had been able to disappear into sleep or drinking until either the situation or his feelings about it went away enough for him to bear it. Too bad for him that he had just awakened from a sleep that would have done old Rip Van Winkle proud. And thoughtless of Gussie not to equip her station wagon with a wet bar.

But he could escape into music too. Music that might for a time comfort the others and would help drown out the sound of scraping metal and growling trucks, help him forget the trap they were caught in, help him forget the deaths of so many friends and personal heroes, and forget, until he died of thirst, he supposed—he never had had much of an appetite and couldn't imagine himself dying of hunger—the heat building inside the car, and the smell of exhaust fumes and road tar seeping up through the concrete. Funny how familiar this particular hell smelled. But he really didn't want to think about that. If he did, he'd get as panicky as the ranger and the women.

So he struck an idle chord on the banjo and it reminded him strangely of a Mexican love song, one of the ones he had learned from the vaqueros when he was a kid. Seemed weird doing Mexican music to a banjo, but then, Sam had done it with Venga Jalejo so why not? His current audience was not inclined to be critical and those whatever-they-weres were not apt to like anything he did anyway. Which suited him just fine.

CHAPTER XIV

▲▲▲

Faron persuaded Brose to go with him in his van, which was large enough to accommodate them all.

Barry at first insisted that the whole business was too dangerous for Ellie but she said, "Look, Daddy, from what Faron's told me, it's going to be a whole lot more dangerous to just stay home and be a sitting duck. I'm your daughter and Faron's wife—how long do you think this bullshit, whatever it is, is going to leave me alone?"

Faron looked down at the holes in his Nike Wannabes and said, "You know, El, it might not be a bad idea for you to stay here in case something happens to us. Then you could get word to other people—anybody who sings, anybody we know, just about. Tell them to lie low, be careful, don't gather together for a while."

Ellie's dark eyes snapped and her chin, pointed as a cat's, jutted pugnaciously. "Mom and Dad can do that. I swear to God, if you're getting sexist on me after only two years of marriage, Faron Randolph, I'll . . ."

"You'll need this," Molly said, unlocking the top drawer to her china hutch and taking out a small gun.

"Thanks, Mama. At least somebody's practical around here."

"You phone us if you find them, you hear, and if you don't, you phone to say you're okay anyhow."

"Yes, Mama."

"Wait just another ten minutes," Barry said. "Molly, why don't you get them some of that vanilla ice cream we got at the 7-Eleven—that sound good to everybody?"

"Thanks, Barry, but we need to get on the road," Brose said.

"Not that quick you don't. This won't take any longer than a stoplight. Molly, sprinkle a little of that powdered Quik on top—you ever had it that way, Brose? Better than chocolate syrup. While you're doing that I'm going to pack you up some food for the road."

"That's real nice of you, Barry, but we'll be okay, really," Anna Mae said.

"Maybe you will, but my kids need to eat and there's enough for everyone."

Further protests were useless, because Barry was already slapping cold cuts, peanut butter and jelly, tomatoes, bananas, leftover tuna salad, and practically anything else he could find between slices of whole wheat bread, flinging bags of chips and six packs of diet soda into plastic grocery bags, and adding a package of Oreos for good measure.

"While you're waiting I think the rest of you had better write down the names, addresses, and phone numbers of any family members or friends you'd want to know if something happens to you," Molly suggested. "Not to be pessimistic or anything but . . ."

Hawkins stirred his ice cream so that the little grains of Quick dissolved into chocolate ribbons, much as a kid might but actually to give him something to do with his hands and stare at while he thought. He was a practical man by training if not inclination and before his singing career had had a business education and had managed his family's dairy for a time. And despite Gussie's romantic ideas about being at sea, that alone was plenty to teach him that self-preservation in a changeable and dangerous environment meant covering all eventualities as thoroughly as possible.

"You know," he said slowly, after the first sip of the half-melted ice cream, "in any event, we need to start some heavy networking about this. Call or write everybody you know connected with music and warn them about this thing—warn them to keep a low public profile for a while. At the same time maybe everyone should begin sharing all the songs people can remember and record them in every possible way—tape, records, tablature, memory, computer disk—each person store it in as many places as he has friends, with other musicians, of course, but also with any civilian friends who might not be expected to have that kind of thing lying around. Mothers and fond aunts come to mind."

Brose returned to his truck for a few things to pack in the van along with Barry's provisions. He took his tarp, the hairy, flea-bitten blanket he kept for sick animals, and the pistol Willie had brought with him.

They took turns driving and sleeping and didn't stop, day or night. Somewhere northwest of Cheyenne, Wyoming, a late summer heat wave set in. They stopped at a rest stop for ice for the cooler and more soft drinks. Hawkins took the wheel. Faron had driven as far as Fort Collins, then Ellie had taken over for half the night, Brose the other half. They'd seen no sign of the station wagon and though they asked at every truck stop on the off chance that someone might have remembered the car or one of its occupants, nobody did.

The drive through that part of the country was long and monotonous, with nothing to see but flat country where the little bit of greenery burned brown almost before you could drive past. The sun was glazed over as white as a hen egg. Lots of times on this drive you could look off to distant hills and mountains, but they were lost in the haze today, leaving nothing but long flat highway, scrubby parched earth, and featureless horizon. Hawkins, used to looking out over miles of monotonous stuff wetter than this was dry, did not particularly mind. He watched the heat waves dance on the pavement as he might watch others dance on the sea and rolled right over them. The week or two had given him a lot to keep his mind occupied.

He was musing on the behavior of the weather and the cops at the festival when he saw the first sign notifying him of a detour and one of the road signs of a man and a wheelbarrow that indicated road work ahead. A little farther down was a slow sign followed by a stop ahead sign followed by some orange cones.

Through his open window he heard a familiar tune, "Forty Miles of Bad Road," and in about a mile the figure of an orange vested, yellow hard-hatted flagwoman rose like a mermaid from the heat waves. She was even combing her hair, which was waist length and almost as orange as her jacket. Probably she was getting ready to tuck it back up into a cooler hairdo, he thought. A big boom box sat at her feet and blasted out the old tune and she was nodding and smiling and combing her hair in time to it. He would have tried to talk to her, ask her how far out of the way the detour was, how long it would take, what the workmen were doing up ahead, just to make conversation and break up the drive, but she was too preoccupied. She gave him a pearly smile and idly waved her comb off the road in the direction of an exit ramp marked by a line of the orange cones. Bubble-brain, he thought, and followed the cones.

Forty-five shock-destroying minutes later, more cones led up onto paved road. Hawkins saw no signs, but it looked wrong. Highway 84 was a four-lane highway, well marked with signs, including those of scenic tragedies that had happened to the poor settlers who drove wagons along this route when it was known as the Oregon Trail.

Road Work Next 50 Miles, a sign said. More cones and another detour sign led him around a mass of heavy mustard-colored earth-moving and road-building machinery. No people, just machines, but maybe they were on their lunch—no, it was early but this was the early nineties after all—their brunch break. Probably having croissants and espresso or something.

He followed the cones and the detour out into more scrub country for several miles, until they actually reached some small hills, just red rock mostly. The detour wound in and around them, through scrub and black brush.

"Where the hell are we?" Brose asked.

"We're taking the scenic route courtesy of the highway department," Hawkins said.

▲▲▲

"Our private highway department, that is," Nicholson said, chuckling over the receiver connected to the miniature transmitter his police agent had attached to the van, the truck, the station wagon, the car Hawkins had ridden in, and Anna Mae's car. The last two had been left behind but the three critical ones had provided interesting information.

"Why not just involve that van in your limbo too?" the Doom and Destruction Devil asked. "Or better yet, have a fuel truck hit them head-on. It's not as if *this* group has that—that—*implement* of that God-cursed old Marxist archangel with them, after all. You can just slaughter them."

"I thought you were the one who liked subtlety," Nicholson said. "I have every intention of slaughtering them, but have you never heard of poetic justice?"

"I did not think poetry was supposed to be our forte," D&D said primly.

"Oh contrary, mah cherry," the Debauchery Devil said. S/He seemed content to remain in Lulubelle's form, but had changed into tight designer jeans, a hard hat, a signal orange vest, and nothing else to join in the fun. "Some of—"

"We know," Nicholson said with a yawn. "Some of your best people have been poets. My point exactly. We are dealing with poetic types here, not heroic types. That song that damned instrument was playing—the one the old bag with the terrible voice was croaking the words to —gave me an idea. My new, improved, modern limbo is far from the only hazard that ever occurred along that route. Something older but no less reliable appeals to me in this case—some of the wonderful old ways we had of thwarting the travelers these puling nitwits romanticize now in their sentimental drivel."

"I still think it would have been better to leave them in the more populated areas, where our minions could deal with them," pouted the Accounting Devil.

"Don't be greedy," the Chairdevil said. "Your minions in the IRS have been doing a great job but that phase of our operation has gone about as far as it can with this particular bunch. Minions are all well and good. You need them at times, when direct intervention would look suspicious—after all, if people start noticing supernatural events and begin truly believing in us they're going to start believing in the competition too, and that's counterproductive, to say the least. So your indirect manipulation is preferable in most cases. And what we've done already should have been sufficient, if it wasn't for that blessed banjo."

"I know," the Debauchery Devil said sadly. "It's already having a terrible effect on Willie. He hasn't taken a drink since the night you almost signed him with us, Nick. Frankly, I'm worried about him."

"We'll have him handy where you can keep an eye on him soon enough," Nicholson promised. "As for these others, well, where we've led them, there'll be no one to notice if the means we use seem a little odd. It's tempting, you know, because now that those songs aren't polluting the cosmos all the time, we grow stronger and better able to control them all with every dead singer, every forgotten word, every faltering note."

"Yeah, yeah, we know," said the Ignorance and Stupidity Devil. "So what are we gonna do to 'em if we ain't usin' minions?"

▲▲▲

"Are you feeling okay, August?" Vicki interrupted. "You nearly dropped a glass there when you were telling about the ranger sticking his head out the window and you've been shaking like a leaf ever since."

"I know. I'm such a butterfingers," August said, brushing her hair back with trembling fingers. "And I really get caught up in the story."

"Me too," Lewis said. "Keep going, but get me another beer first, okay?"

"Say, is this bunch of devils you're talkin' about by any chance in charge of the outfit that's been doing the new bypass over by Shelton?" Harry asked. "I swear they have the same modus operandi."

"Could be, Harry," August said. "They're still around, you know. They manage to be lots of places at once, but they're never all that far away."

▲▲▲

The Chairdevil enjoyed toying with his fellow devils, especially the Stupidity and Ignorance Devil, who always made him feel clever, so he took a while to answer. "Instead of minions, this time, I'm going to do something creative, low-key, and virtually undetectable to other mortals. I'll be making use of natural hazards that have been lying in wait for a long time. In the past they worked like, you should pardon the expression, a charm. I hope I get to use them all but it may only take the first one. Lye beds, underlying the water supply."

"Sounds chancy to me," the Doom and Destruction Devil said.

"Well, I'm sentimental about it, I admit. It's also especially clever of me to turn that damned banjo against those people. That song it was playing is for a change a complimentary one about us, about a wonderful coup we pulled off about a century ago. The first verse is my favorite and tells about my little trap. You see, there was this party going up that very trail and one of the damn fool mortals was going to be a big hero and thwart us from taking the rest of the party after we carefully parched 'em to dry husks. This guy led them to a particular water hole I happen to have contemporary plans for and voilà, hundred percent fatality."

"Maybe," the Pestilence Devil said. The Chairdevil's brainstorm was typical of the sort of dumb idea a dilettante would get if he took off on his own instead of consulting experts.

"No maybe about it," the Chairdevil said, casting a baleful eye at the Pestilence Devil. "Since that time they've added a toxic waste dump nearby and the well I've had dug taps into that too. Beautiful, isn't it? Historical relevance with modern innovations. Lots deadlier than one of the old curses, like those cholera epidemics you were so fond of in the old days."

"A good cholera epidemic both kills *and* debilitates. All your victims have to do to escape your little curse is not drink the water. Whereas once cholera begins to spread, nobody who comes in contact with it can escape it," the Pestilence Devil pointed out with a craftsman's pride.

"This group's been vaccinated," the Debauchery Devil reminded him, since she was very knowledgeable about anything involving needles.

The Pestilence Devil glared at her. Reminding a devil of the tragic circumstances that could thwart the best-laid curses was, in his estimation, the height of bad manners.

▲▲▲

Black Brush National Park, the sign said. Rest Area ¾ Mile.

Well, that was good. There would surely be a ranger station where they'd charge you three bucks per vehicle to see America's natural wonders. The only wonder he cared about was wondering how in the hell they'd gotten so far off the highway with nothing to guide them back. If the ranger could tell them that, he'd pay him the three dollars just for the information.

But the road kept winding and no little rustic shed appeared, no uniformed, smoky-bear–hatted person of any kind whatsoever appeared—no person at all, for that matter. At last there was, however, a pull off into the scrub, a small building with a roof open under the point and signs that said "Women" at one end and "Men" at the other. Surrounding it was, as advertised, a whole lot of black brush and very little else, except for a stone cairn with a metal pump and faucet protruding from it. A bronze metal plaque was embedded in the stone just below the pump.

Brose rubbed his eyes with his fist and yawned open-mouthed, kneeling between the driver's seat and the passenger seat, where Faron still snoozed. "What's up, man?"

"We took the scenic route," Hawkins said. "Want to look at the monument?"

When Brose opened the side door to the van, Faron, Ellie, and Anna Mae awakened. Ellie groaned and buried her face under the sofa pillow she'd been hugging. Anna Mae lay very still, her eyes shifting to Brose as she asked, "Where are we?"

He shrugged

"We're seeing the sights," Hawkins said.

"Oboy," Faron said with mock enthusiasm.

"Let's see here," Hawkins bent over the plaque. "It

would be real good if it would say, 'Highway 84, take a right and go five miles and you're headed for Portland.' But I suppose that's too much to ask. No, here it says, 'Sacred wellspring of the Hotpapa Band of Shoshone Indians, believed to have protective and aphrodisiacal properties and to have been instrumental in producing visions.' "

"You're making it up," Anna Mae said. "The Department of the Interior would never say 'aphrodisiacal' to the public. And I never heard of any Hotpapa Shoshones before."

"That's what it says right here. Aphrodisiacal and protective. And visions. Sounds like just what we need."

"Well, that and something for the radiator," Faron said. Steam was rising from beneath the hood with the hiss of water on hot metal. "I'll get a cup."

"A magic spring, hmm," Anna Mae said. "Just like those bastards to exploit it. Even way out here."

She grasped the pump handle, lifted and pushed twice before she caught a glimpse of movement over by the privy.

She turned. Hawkins and Brose were already staring at a large man wearing a plaid shirt and homespun-looking pants. Must be a new Banana Republic thing. Rustic-looking anyway. He wore a slouch hat over his eyes but as he approached her vision blurred his outline and she thought for a moment she could read "Men" through the fabric of his shirt.

He paused a couple of feet from Faron and stuck out a sunburned hand, pointing with a shaking finger at the plaque.

They looked down again. A large skull and crossbones covered most of the metal and the legend read, "Poison. Lye Contamination."

Hawkins shook his head. "You from the EPA?" But in the time the man had focused their attention on the plaque, he had disappeared again.

"Where did he go? B-back to the privy?" Brose asked.

Ellie was sitting up in the van door now, staring hard in that direction, the whites of her eyes shining all around

the pupils. "Nope. He just—uh—beamed up. Demateri-
alized. Vanished. Whatever."

"A ghost?" Brose asked.

"It wasn't a Hotpapa Shoshone," Anna Mae said, re-
leasing her hold on the pump handle and staring hard at
the plaque. "It's changed back now but I'm not thirsty
anymore. Anybody else?"

"There's Diet Dr Pepper in the cooler," Ellie said.
"That's good enough for me."

"Goddamn, a ghostly EPA agent," Brose said,
scratching his head. "Don't that beat all?"

"Look, there he is again," Anna Mae cried, pointing
down the road.

The figure looked solid now, except that his image
shivered slightly with the heat waves rising from the
pavement. His hand was outstretched, pointing, like
Anna Mae's, down the road.

They quickly piled back in the van with Ellie and
Faron, started the engine, made a wide U-turn, ruining
some of the nationally protected black brush resource,
and bumped back the way they had come. When they
reached the spot where the ghost had been standing,
there was nothing to see, but a scant half a mile later they
found themselves on an entrance ramp to the highway.

Faron kept humming a line over and over.

"What *is* that song, hon?" Ellie asked.

"Well, the whole tune is gone except for this one line,
and I don't remember the original words, but I do remember that it was originally a kind of coded map for
slaves escaping on the underground railroad. I think I'm
going to call my version 'Follow the Drinking Guard.' "

▲▲▲

Once Willie got going, he found he was in unusually fine
voice and the car had pretty good acoustics. The only
trouble was that so many of the songs would not come
back to him. If he stuck with whatever the banjo was
trying to play, he could remember more, but with great
effort, so after a time he took to making up words to
replace the ones he'd forgotten.

"Will you cut that out," the ranger said from between

gritted teeth. Sweat was rolling down his face although the morning was still fairly cool, even with the windows rolled up.

Willie just shot him a pitying look.

"Listen to me, dumbass, this is serious shit we're in," the ranger snarled, although it was pretty clear that the snarl was half his tough cop act, a thin layer of bravado covering his fear.

Willie kept fingering the banjo and a mournful tune leaked from it, tearful note by tearful note. "Yeah, well, the Spring Hill mine disaster was serious shit too," Willie said, as if that were a snappy comeback.

"You're fuckin' hysterical," the ranger moaned.

Gussie propped her chin up on her arm, opened one eye and said, "No, he's not. There's a line in that Spring Hill mine disaster song Ewan McColl and Peggy Seeger wrote about that terrible thing in the fifties where all those men were trapped and killed. I don't remember the whole thing but I know that line about living on hope and songs, Willie."

Willie nodded and the banjo accommodatingly played the tune.

"This is no mine disaster," the ranger said. "But we may smother anyway. How can those fuckers keep crowding us so close without losing control themselves?" He turned to stare at the shattered glass of his window, which was being bowed in by the weight of a log pressing against it. In a moment the glass would be in his lap. On the other side, the taillight of one of the wrecks dangled outside the window near Willie's ear. The pipe truck crowded close on the back bumper of the station wagon, grinning its leering grin in at them while the pipes jiggled precariously overhead.

The ranger pawed through the glove compartment and came up with a heavy metal flashlight. "Cover your eyes," he told them. "I'm going to break the windshield and climb out on the hood."

"And I thought Willie watched too many western movies," Gussie muttered, shrinking back. "You going to try to do it with that flashlight?" she asked as he took the first swing at the window.

"Any better ideas?" he grunted.

"Yeah, just a minute," she fished for her tire iron in the space between the back of the front seat and where she and Juli lay.

Willie watched with a certain benign detachment as she handed the heavy object to the ranger. Under normal circumstances, Willie liked to consider himself a man of action, but nothing had been normal since Mark's call, and he still hadn't decided whether this was one long nightmare or whether they really had died and gone to hell. It didn't much matter. But just to be on the safe side, when the ranger started swinging the tire iron against the windshield he handed the banjo back to Juli and hoisted himself up between the women.

The glass shattered on the first blow and fell out on the second. The ranger grabbed the frame with both hands and climbed up in the seat, sticking his head and shoulders out over the hood. No sooner had he leaned out than the logging truck veered, the log smashed through the shattered passenger-door window, and the glass fell onto the passenger seat. A foot of log occupied the space where the ranger's head would have been.

The ranger glanced back and grimaced.

Traffic picked up speed as he shoved a foot out onto the hood and for a moment he dangled, with little more than a leg and his butt still in the car.

The banjo, in Juli's hands, began wailing "Another Man Done Gone." Gussie seemed to recall the second refrain said, "He had a long chain on," and wished the ranger did.

The lawman poised kneeling on the hood, facing the wrecker on the right, his hands outstretched to catch the metal frame. Diesel stench and exhaust fumes blasted through the empty windshield frame. The ranger rose to a crouch, swaying to the balls of his feet.

The pressure from the pipe truck in the rear relaxed for a moment so that the station wagon was not being pushed forward quite so fast as before, then abruptly, the pipe rig gave them a little bump and sent the ranger flying off balance, rolling for the front of the car, where he would land under the wheels.

He flung out a hand and clawed for the wrecker and missed, but in his scramble he hooked one of his elbows around the side-view mirror, his body sprawled in front of the steering wheel.

"Oh, God," Gussie said, and did a forward belly flop spanning the front seat and grabbed for his ankle. She could reach only the sole of his shoe. Willie scrambled into the front seat and lunged out onto the hood, tackling him around the waist with both arms.

"Hang on there, buddy," he said. But the ranger took advantage of the leverage to stabilize himself, let go of the mirror, and got a good grip on the wrecker frame. At that point the lane of traffic the wrecker was in moved suddenly forward and his arms were almost jerked off before he let go to avoid being scraped off on the side of the fuel truck in front of them and be pulled off.

Willie was still hanging on to him and they were both dragged toward the hood but now Gussie grabbed the steering wheel with one hand and Willie with the other. The wrecker on the left was replaced by another fuel tanker, and as it drove up, Willie and the ranger caught a glimpse of what was in the driver's seat.

The ranger vomited onto the side of the fuel truck before he allowed himself to be hauled back inside the station wagon. All three sat panting for a while.

Willie patted his captor on the shoulder and said, "Relax, man."

"So, MacKai. You still think we've died and gone to hell?" he panted.

"I didn't say died," Willie corrected him, "maybe more of a reverse direct ascension. But that was a fool stunt. Going directly to hell is one thing. Getting maimed is another. Anyway, you saw what happened. They ain't about to let us out of this with nothing more than a few Steve McQueen moves. And even if you and I could get out, what about Gussie and the girl?"

"We'd get help."

"Where? We don't know that there is any help. Did you get a look at what's driving that second tanker? Take a gander, my friend."

The man leaned out the windshield again and peered

up but the truck had pulled too far forward and all he could see was the smooth side of the tanker. On the other side, the log chain creaked and clanked with the strain of holding the entire load alone.

"You may not get much choice about being maimed either," the ranger told Willie. He had to scoot toward the spot between the seats to avoid the broken glass and the butt of the log occupying the passenger seat. "I think it won't be too long until that chain gives way and we find ourselves crushed beneath a pile of oversize toothpicks."

"Tell you what. You worry about it for both of us," Willie said, and climbed back up in the back, leaving Gussie in the front again with the ranger.

"What *did* you see, Willie?" Gussie asked.

He just shook his head. No need to upset the women. She persisted and finally he made a joke about the grim reaper and rotting zombie corpses, but it didn't sound funny to any of them. How could he explain that what he had really seen had vanquished any doubt he had that they were on the road to hell and while the pavement was as smooth as his good intentions had made it, the company left a lot to be desired?

▲▲▲

The station wagon lurched and Julianne woke from a restless dream in which she was an angel whose wings had gotten singed and she kept lurching out of control. The sensation was intensified because her ears felt as if they needed to pop and her internal gyroscope was befuddled so that even lying down, she felt a sense of vertigo. Her face burned and ached, her eyes still carried bright spots in front of them even in the darkened interior of the station wagon, and she felt hot all over and thought she probably had a fever. She had no idea how many hours they had been trapped, how long it had been since the ranger had tried to climb out the front window. Nothing much had happened since then, and she'd gone to sleep expecting to die.

As she rolled onto her back, her hip touched the banjo beside her. She smelled the diesel and exhaust, felt the blast of wind through the windshield and saw the log poking through the shattered passenger window.

The rim of the banjo bit into her leg as she sat up into a lotus position, but she hoisted it onto her crossed ankles and felt the strings vibrate under her fingers, and tried to tell what it might be playing. Gussie's face was a study in well-controlled terror, her eyes darting from one of the men to the other, reading them, trying to see how she could head trouble off at the next pass. The ranger was still shaking and pale, his face sheened with sweat. Willie sat back against the seat with outward calmness, his face less mobile than she had ever seen it, his whole body poised from movement to movement as if listening—and perhaps he was, to the banjo.

Juli shut them all out as she closed her eyes, rested the backs of her hands on her knees, curled thumb to forefinger on each hand, and shut out the trucks, shut out the broken windshield, but somehow, even as she softly chanted a mantra she could hear only in her mind, trying to gain access to her inner self, the banjo kept intruding, drawing her fingers, demanding to be heard.

It was very much like in Lucien's sessions, except that this time she was doing it alone, using the power he'd told her she had. She knew something was in the banjo, struggling to make itself understood, something so strong it sent a thrill through her nerve endings and up her spinal column. The banjo vibrated against her and she could make out the beat of a tune, though she could only identify the rhythm, not the melody. And in her mind's eye, she saw Sam Hawthorne playing it again, his eyes fixed on them, his mouth moving as if he was trying to tell them something.

"Yes, Sam, yes?" she asked that inner image and it regarded her thoughtfully, shrugged the imagined banjo over its imagined shoulder, and signed to her, "Willie."

She opened her eyes. Gussie had been watching her, watching her lashless, browless eyes close in that pink and swollen face, salt tears streaming painfully down her burn-tender cheeks as her lips moved.

But now the younger woman leaned forward, banjo in

one hand, and tapped Willie on the shoulder with the other. "It's for you," she said.

▲▲▲

Brose twiddled the dial on the radio from one pitch of static to another until at last he found a lone scratchy voice adrift in the noise at the extreme end of the lighted strip of numbers. He turned the volume up high, although everyone else was trying to sleep. He needed to hear over the slap of his windshield wipers and the hiss of rain, the howl of the wind tearing across the broad flat plain of the valley floor. Sometime before the clouds started rolling in, ganging up, and gushing rain on top of them, there'd been mountains not too far off. Now the whole world had narrowed down to the torrents of water pouring over his windshield, the metronome of the wiper blades, and the faint fan of wet pavement his high beams illuminated. He had hummed what he could remember of "Bobby McGee," which wasn't a hell of a lot, for the last two hundred miles.

No other cars had approached for hours, and no one shared his own lane. He reckoned he and his friends must be the only fools in the world going where they were going.

"Storm warnings are in effect for northern and western Wyoming, most of Montana and throughout Idaho and eastern Washington with high winds and flash floods possible in low-lying areas."

"You think that's *news*?" Brose demanded aloud. "Man, I don't need you guys to tell me that. All I gotta do is look out the window here at all this wet stuff."

He drove on and the road became full of little streamlets and he got used to seeing water on the road. So when his headlights picked up the edge of the next rain-covered spot he slowed down so he wouldn't go into a skid but kept driving cautiously. He stopped, however, when he saw that this particular spot was several yards wide. It was probably only runoff, of course, and no more than an inch or two deep, and there was no other way to get across. For a moment he sat there idling the motor, and thought he'd chance it. The van sat fairly high off the ground so it would take pretty deep water to do more than dampen the tires.

Then suddenly, just where the lights faded into blackness, the water rippled toward him and something pale gleamed in it, then popped above the surface.

A human head? Yes. It rose so he could see shoulders, a chest, arms reaching from the water, then the trunk, hips—and finally, the guy waded out and stood right in front of the hood. Young guy, no more than about twenty, but soaked and pale. A fellow motorist who'd mistaken the depth of the stream, perhaps? He didn't look scared though, just sad and kind of worried, standing there shaking his head.

Brose rolled down the window. "Buddy, you okay? Looks like you were luck—"

But the young man gave him one last sad look that seemed full of warning and backed back into the stream, wading until he was covered to the knees, the hips, the waist.

Brose flung wide the door of the van and waded into the pool after the fellow. "Wait a minute, man, this is no damn place to take a fuckin' bath!" he yelled, but the man was up to his neck by then and sank back into the deep. Brose floundered in after him, but his foot stepped into nothingness and his head went under. He surfaced, took a deep breath, and dived again, flinging out his arms to try to make contact with the man, but he could see nothing. Surfacing once more, he saw the man standing beside the truck, beckoning again. In a couple of crawl strokes, Brose was back on solid ground and slogged dripping back toward the truck. By then, the pedestrian had vanished.

As Brose climbed back in the truck, he saw the pedestrian's head sink once more into the flooded portion of the road. Brose reached into the back and pulled his flea-bitten horse blanket up to wrap around him as he sat shivering, looking at where the man had been, at the pool into which he had been about to drive and in which they might all have drowned. As he realized the possibilities, what would have happened if he hadn't stopped for the phantom stranger, his shivering became more intense. "Sheeit," he said to himself.

"Something wrong?" Hawkins roused from his nap long enough to ask.

"Not a goddamn thing backtracking a hundred miles won't take care of," Brose said, and roared backward, made a wide U-turn, and headed back the way they'd come.

CHAPTER XV
▲▲▲

"Okay, who's responsible for the spooks?" the Chairdevil wanted to know. "S&I, is this another of your superstitions? Don't you think you could have checked it out with me?"

"Or me?" Doom and Destruction asked. "Our Acts of God branch is not going to be pleased to have a wonderful flood like that just dribble away without claiming a single victim. We could have had that little group right there if it hadn't been for that—that *being* you decided to play Halloween with on our time."

"Hey, he wasn't mine," the Stupidity and Ignorance Devil said. "Or at least if he is, the hauntings department didn't tell me they was sending him in. Not that last guy, neither. So far as I know, them guys is two unaffiliated free-lance spirits."

The Chairdevil changed the subject. He knew who the first spirit was, of course, and had assumed the fellow was' now one of theirs but if so, he had not, apparently, been acting under orders unless someone screwed up. As for the second, he'd have to think on that awhile longer.

What was annoying him now was that group with the banjo, who should have been reduced to gibbering terror by now. Of course, perhaps even he was out of touch with just how bad modern freeways were, and most of them were musicians and used to driving; still, you'd think the logging truck and the pipes and so on should do it. Really, that policeman was the only one behaving like a normal human being.

Willie was proving quite a disappointment. Nicholson had offered him any number of opportunities to run true to type—shallow, self-centered, self-indulgent, and self-destructive—but something seemed to be delaying the inevitable. Instead of falling apart, as the man had on numerous less stressful occasions, he seemed to be getting his act together, and so far as Nicholson could tell, he wasn't even thinking about booze or getting into the girl's pants. He didn't seem to be thinking about much except whatever it was that fool instrument was playing at the moment.

And the girl! He was going to have to speak to her guidance counselor, who was supposed to have been softening her up for recruitment, turning her wish to dabble in necromancy and her budding conceit about psychic powers into something that could shape itself into greed, power hunger, and the despising of everyone else. He'd had a good start too, he knew from her little song, but something was going wrong here too. These wretched people didn't behave properly at all—every time you thought you had them committed to the course you needed, they slipped away, about as easy to herd as a bunch of amoebas.

Oh, well, that was why they were so dangerous, wasn't it? He should have tried more direct means, he supposed, as he had with the "stars" among them. He hadn't expected such nobodies to be so difficult. Of course, some of that failure to conform to expectations was what kept them nobodies instead of allowing them to become "stars" too. Too bad he couldn't do anything direct about the banjo but any number of his other booby traps should take care of the others. Was that dratted banjo enhancing the power of the little snatches of songs the idiots *could* remember? Whatever it was, he felt sure it was a minor problem. The van full of people would succumb to the road, one way or another, and as for the others, they were already, as the old comic books had so poetically put it, in the clutches of doom, banjo and all. If he couldn't actually kill them and destroy the instrument, he could at least keep them trapped in the custom-designed hell he had created with them in mind.

▲▲▲

That wet, dark road seemed a thousand miles long to Brose as he picked his way back down one lane, on the wrong side of the road. His lights blinked out—a short caused by the rain, probably, but he wasn't going to let that slow him down. He woke up Faron and asked him if he had a flashlight.

"Yeah, sure, but why?"

"So I can see where the hell I'm going," Brose said. His voice quavered with cold from his dunking and tension from the long drive.

"You okay?"

"Just barely. The road was washed out back there. And while you folks were sleeping, I saw another one . . ."

"Another what?"

"Spook. It came up from the bottom of that river to warn us not to go across. Jesus! They seem to mean well but I wish to God they'd just hang out a sign or something instead of havin' to make personal appearances. I waded in after the damn thing before I realized it was a spook."

"Did the ghost knock the lights out too?"

"Nah, that just happened. You got that flashlight?"

Faron dug through the pocket on the door of the van. "Right here."

"Shine it out the window, huh? So's I can see the edge of the road. I don't want no more ghosts comin' up out of the ditches to tell me I'm about to go off the road or somethin'."

The blinkers cast a little light too. Brose remembered that there had been an exit for a truck stop about twenty miles back. When he saw the first halo of neon through the rivulets on the windshield and the darkness and the pulse of his blinkers and the whooshing wipers, he thought they looked like those will-o'-the-wisp things, or the Marfa Ghost Lights down near the Big Bend, mysterious and aloof and awfully still and quiet in such a thunderous gully-washer of a night.

By the time the words on the sign were legible, he had bypassed the exit ramp and had to back up and make another run at it, Faron shining the light every which way to make sure Brose had some notion where the road was.

Three eighteen-wheelers sat like drowsing dinosaurs to

one side of the big diesel pumps. Brose pulled in to one side of them.

Faron said, "Now that we're off the road, let me get my tool kit out and we can probably fix whatever's wrong . . ."

"Not a whole lot I expect," Brose said, and twisted the knob for the lights again, experimentally. Two strong beams flooded the pavement in front of them.

"Sure you had them switched on before?"

"Hell yes, I'm sure. They died all at once. Better check 'em before we leave anyway. Must be a short in there someplace."

"*After* a hamburger and a pit stop," Ellie said, climbing out the back and splashing down into a puddle on the pavement to follow the comforting smell of hot fried food poking teasing tendrils of fragrance through the rain torrents.

By the time they reached the café, they were all nearly as wet as Brose. Anna Mae and Ellie headed for the women's room, Brose and Hawkins for the men's. Faron stood awkwardly by the cashier's desk.

"Excuse me, ma'am, has anybody said anything about the road being washed out down the way?" he asked the ponytailed cashier, who didn't look as if she were more than a sophomore in high school. She had been stooped down below the counter, unpacking boxes of small, cheap teddy bears and sitting them on the shelves beneath clips full of multicolored bandannas that fluttered slightly from the draft blowing around the glassed-in front door.

"No, nobody has but there hasn't been a whole lot of traffic."

"Well, you might want to warn folks. Up the road about twenty miles."

"Thanks. I'll mention it. What weather, huh?" Behind her he could see the waitress mopping tables while three truckers, two men and a woman, sat drinking coffee and talking.

"No kidding."

The others emerged from the bathrooms.

▲▲▲

Anna Mae had fallen into step with Brose, who was telling her about the flood and the ghost. Her head was
down, black hair swaying like the silk fringes on a dance
shawl as she walked, nodding to show she was listening
while she focused on the floor and his words.

Ellie and Hawkins were still asking questions as they
slid into their booth but Anna Mae approached the
truckers before taking her seat. "Hi," she said.

One nodded a greeting, another gave a rather numb
smile, and the woman said, as if afraid Anna Mae was
going to pass out Bible tracts, "Hello," very cautiously.

"Just thought you people might want to know, we
turned back from a flash flood across the road about
twenty miles up the road."

"That's funny," said the larger of the two men, who
was swarthy, Mexican, or Indian maybe, with long hair
caught up in a rubber band at the back of his neck. "I
was just by there, oh, maybe two hours ago. It was fine
then."

"That's why they call them 'flash' floods I guess," the
other man said.

The woman, a carefully coiffed blonde who had the
delicate features and clear creamy complexion of many
plump women, glanced from one man to the other a little
anxiously and fingered the crystal in the neckline of her
pink-and-purple plaid shirt. "Strange weather for this
time of year though—I mean, that hot spell wasn't supposed to break."

"Now, Naomi," said the other man, older and with a
grizzled white crew cut, "I never did know weather to do
what it was supposed to, did you?"

"It's not just that. It's—I don't know—it feels funny.
Like that tanker we saw last night."

"That so?" Anna Mae said.

"Yeah," the older man said, "it *was* a little funny and
Naomi here, she's sensitive to that kind of stuff."

"What kind of stuff?"

"Well, you know, on these long straight stretches, you
can see quite a ways, but it was like, for miles there was
nothing ahead of us and then this rig—"

"Not like any tanker *I've* ever seen," the woman said.

"I don't think those flashing lights it had on the back were regulation either, Opie."

"You said that, hon. She did," he told Anna Mae and the other man. " 'Opie,' she says to me, 'lookit them funny lights on that rig. What does he think he's doin'? That station wagon is followin' him so close looks to me like it would get confused.' I said maybe it was his wife or a friend or something but when we stopped outside of Scottsbluff I pulled up alongside him. Didn't see the driver in the tanker, but the truck was fueling up. And there was a woman in the Ford, okay, but she looked half-asleep and there was three other grown folks with her, all fast asleep. Now, I am a man who always minds my own business, Naomi can tell you that, can't you, hon? But I couldn't help it, I said to the woman, 'Lady, I been watching you and you better get some sleep or you're going to have an accident.' She didn't pay me any more attention than if I was the pump talkin' to her though. Just filled up, stuck her gas card in the pump—it was one of them newfangled kind where you pay the pump direct with your credit card—and waited until the truck left."

"Yeah and I never did see the driver get back in either," the woman said. "Opie tried to raise him on the CB but he was off the air. We followed 'em maybe another five–ten miles or so and she never got off his tail."

"Would have followed 'em longer but—well, I was wonderin' so hard about it that I left *my* gas card back at Kearney and we had to turn back. We sorta looked for 'em when we got back on the highway—you can meet a lot of folks coming and going over and over out here, but if they pulled over again, or were still on the road, we never caught up with 'em. Course, they might have got off the main highway, taken a side route."

"What did the woman look like?" Anna Mae asked.

" 'Bout my age," Opie said. "Curly hair. Was wearin' shorts and had good legs. Course, I wouldn't have noticed except it worried Naomi. She's sensitive about these things, like I said. She's in trainin' to be a transmedium."

Naomi stared modestly into her coffee cup and fingered her crystal in a sensitive sort of way. "Oh, Opie.

There's no training about it. It's a gift, I tell you. I'm just sort of developing it, between runs, and listening to the subliminal tapes, you know?" She looked back up at Anna Mae. "I was just sure I felt something coming from that. Once, crossing where it used to be the Lewis and Clark Trail, Sacajawea spoke through me, I'm sure. She wanted to tell Opie that he was about to have a flat and sure enough—"

"Well, thank you very much. I mean, that's very interesting," Anna Mae said. "You didn't by any chance see it farther down the road?"

"Nope," Opie said.

"Well, watch out for that flood."

"Tell you what, I'll let the bears know and find out if one of the alternate routes is open for you," Opie said.

"Thank you."

"No problem. Thanks for the warnin'."

Anna Mae returned to the table. Brose was giving Ellie and Hawkins a brief version of what he'd seen at the flood. When he was done, Anna Mae repeated her conversation with the truckers. Faron widened his eyes for a moment and stared into his coffee cup with a look of "Oh, well. Now what?" but everyone was too travel-weary to do more than wonder to themselves. Ellie bought a *MAD* magazine and she and Faron stared at it and smirked once in a while. Otherwise, the night and the rain drizzled away while Hawkins, Anna Mae, and the Randolphs sat drinking coffee and made frequent trips to the toilets. Brose snored on the table with his head cradled on his crossed arms.

The rain stopped sometime around four A.M. Anna Mae saw Opie go to his truck and return. At seven-thirty he left again but this time when he returned he stopped at their table and said to Hawkins, who was the oldest-looking white man there, "They're patchin' the pavement up ahead right now, mister, and if you and your friends want to keep goin', they've made a stretch passable. We're gonna honk on now, if you want to follow us."

Opie and Naomi kept on Highway 80 bound for Ogden but Anna Mae decided to take 30 into Pocatello instead. If the truckers hadn't seen Gussie's station wagon again on 80, then chances were they had side-tracked. If they were headed directly for Tacoma, Ogden would be out of their way, even if the road was a little better. She thought as she saw the big rig pull away that she really should have mentioned the ghosts to Naomi. They'd have made her week.

▲▲▲

The rains had hit the whole area hard. The highway was littered with stones, driftwood, and other debris and the roadside was studded with yellow diamond signs featuring silhouettes of flagmen and men with shovels and signs saying Men Working, Slow, Danger, or Merge. Although the rain had stopped, the sky was still overcast and the wind buffeted the van as it rolled through the straight stretches unprotected by trees. Still, there was plenty of traffic headed their direction and with any luck they should be in Boise or even La Grande before nightfall. From there to Portland and on to Tacoma, where the roads would be too well traveled for any more ghosts or the pranks of evil spirits. Except for drunk drivers, there should be nothing to worry about.

An ominous rhythmic thunking sound from the left front end brought Anna Mae back to the present. For a moment, she entertained the vain hope that the noise was made by the tires bumping over the cracks in the road but of course, it wasn't.

▲▲▲

As darkness fell the wind rose howling down the mountain roads, past the muddied mechanical monsters parked for the night, their clawed shovels and tar sprayers poised until they were manned again in the morning by members of the operating engineers local. Where the road wound round the side of one mountain, the wind levitated the yellow sign that said Danger, and later another that said Road Closed and another that said Soft Shoulder and yet another that cautioned Avalanche Area Beware of Falling Rock. The signs lifted on the wings of the gale and swept down the mountainside just before the treads of three old tires and one new one on a beat-up van

rolled over the freshly graveled road. The first sign
landed in the bushes a few yards down the cliff. The
second floated facedown along the stream flowing far below in a cleft between the mountains. The third tumbled
over and over like a weed in the wind and was never
found by anyone anywhere ever again. But the last sign
swooped like a bat to land on a 141-year-old grave whose
marker had long ago been blown or carried as far from its
intended resting place as the road signs.

From the place where the last sign had risen on the
wind, the hiss of small pebbles and soft dirt sliding downhill was drowned out by the wind, though as the bigger
slabs of dirt, rock, and concrete gave way, the rumble
was audible to anyone standing outside, listening for it.
But it could not be heard, for instance, over the growl of
the overworked engine of a large vehicle *and* the howl of
the wind *and* the staticky weather report issuing from the
car radio.

But where the rocks and dirt and stones and slabs
landed on or beside that last sign, they disturbed what
had lain beneath that unmarked ground, and the remembered fear and panic sparked a fragment of the consciousness that sharp rocks and the flailing hooves of oxen had
once torn limb from limb. Soon the wind was joined by
another wailing and while all else sailed downward, hid-
eous disjointed forms lifted toward the disintegrating
curve of highway.

▲▲▲

It should have been Faron's turn to drive, but he had had
to wake up to deal with the flat tire, with the spare that
was also flat, and with rolling the tire to the nearest service area and waiting while they called for a matching
tire from the next largest town. Meanwhile, Anna Mae
had slept so she insisted that she wanted to drive for a
while longer and make up the lost time, and would wake
Faron when she grew tired.

The truth was, she wanted the time to think. So much
had happened so fast and now that she was through reacting, and recovering from reacting, she needed to sort it
all out. She had dealt with only a few of the most urgent

loose ends involved in uprooting her life. From just out-side Maryland she had phoned a neighbor she bought pigs from and told him she was abandoning the farm, that if he adopted the animals for the time being, he could keep any money he got for their sale, she wouldn't be returning. He was good with horses so she wasn't worried about them but she did hope the cats, especially the yellow one that hung around the house, would take to someone new. And she hoped whoever was hassling her friends would not include the neighbor in the harassment. He would be safe, if her assumptions were correct. He was so tone deaf even his hog calls were off-key.

The sleeping she had been doing hadn't been especially restful. She kept seeing Sylvia climb into that paddy wagon, the cops feeding instruments to the fire. Hearing a phone ring and the voice of her boss laughing at her over the cacophony of an amplified banjo blaring twangy noise. She searched for Sam in the dream but couldn't find him. Coming with Brose and the others had been stupid. Probably it was because of her that Willie, Gussie Turner, and the banjo were missing. But in spite of her dreams, the phone call could only have been from Sam, couldn't it?

After all, Willie had Sam's banjo and it was the key to something. It had had power when Sam was alive—that story about the old Appalachian witch-man instrument maker was true. But Sam himself had had a great power, the rare power of a man with a life and work at least largely consistent with his ideals. And though he had never had a pretty face or even a very good voice—these last few years as he grew older and older the microphone had had to take up more and more slack as his range narrowed until it was barely sufficient to carry a tune, the words chopped in time to the beat but more spoken than sung. It didn't matter though. The audiences didn't even need to hear him anymore—they knew the choruses, the verses, all the songs he had urged them to learn throughout his life. The songs had been like oracles for her back when she barely understood any politics that didn't directly affect her—she didn't know who the people were he sang about, or why they were being mistreated, or why they were brave or stupid, or why a particular thing made them happy. She didn't understand the background of his stories or the situations that generated them, but the songs made her curious and predisposed her to his viewpoint. Communist propaganda the witch-hunters had called his songs back in the fifties. And it was like propaganda in that it was persuasive—but it differed in that it wasn't lying. Sam sang about what he believed and whether his songs rang true or not for some people, they were true for him. So whether the banjo had given him power or the other way around, she wasn't sure, but suspected it worked both ways. She wasn't surprised the power had survived him on earth. He had always intended that his work live past him, and since that ambition was being thwarted, she could well imagine that bulldoggedly stubborn spirit haunting the tool he'd used to forge his immortality and calling her long distance just to make sure nobody missed the point. He was not one to stand by while another—power? force? being? agency?—wiped his work from even the memories of the people he'd touched. He wouldn't consider being dead an excuse for slackness.

No, the banjo's power made sense to Anna Mae. The mystery was why it should have fallen into the hands of a confused no-account like Willie MacKai.

The road curved sharply ahead, the faint white line seeming to vanish in the distance, but as she climbed it, it twisted sharply to one side. She blinked and followed it. The same thing happened twice more and she wondered where the warning signs were that told of such curves but kept climbing. Soon she'd be over the steepest part and going down the other side.

Suddenly as she was about to round a curve, a white blob—no, three white blobs—rose up before her. Fortunately, on such a road there was no way to go but slowly. At first she thought it was a plastic bag loosed on the road or something a truck had dropped, but then, when she tried to drive on, it swarmed up on her and the shapes coalesced into recognizable forms—two were broad-shouldered and bovine with horns—oxen. The other looked a little like a Picasso version of a young girl

—the features and limbs did not seem to be put together correctly. The good half of the face looked as if it was more afraid of the van than anybody else could possibly be of a ghost but it also looked bound and determined that the van was not getting past it. The arms, one hanging lower than the other and missing its upper half, were akimbo, the fists planted on a hip and the place where a hip should have been. The figure was wearing an old-fashioned long dress but it was missing in places—where the collar and the upper part of a sleeve and half the skirt should have been was nothing but pavement.

Anna Mae stopped the van and put on the emergency brake. "Ellie, wake up and take the wheel," she said.

"Why? What? Oh, my *God* . . ." she said and then, as Anna Mae opened the door and scooted off the seat to make room for her, "Where are you going? That's a ghost out there."

"Obviously. But the others didn't hurt us, did they?"

"They slowed us up. Those men or whatever they were Faron told me about must have sent them."

Anna Mae shook her head. "Maybe. Maybe not. Take the wheel. I'm going to see what she wants."

"Okay, but what if she wants to kill us?" Ellie said.

"Then I hope you're awfully good at driving in reverse," Anna Mae said, and stepped onto the pavement and out in front of the left headlight. The wind tugged at the hem of her shorts and flapped her T-shirt around her, sent rags of her hair to blind her. The pale figures in front of her swayed like tree branches with the coming and going of the air currents. Why would anyone be afraid of such anemic and insubstantial things? Anna Mae wondered, deciding that she was not. On the Indian side of the family, seeing visions used to be required to reach adulthood and she supposed now she would be entitled to change her name to Woman-Who-Saw-Three-Ghosts or something like that if everything was still being done traditionally. On the Scottish side, a family without a ghost or two was ancestrally impoverished. The only spooks who scared her were those who worked for the government. If she was haunted by Sam's ghost, the ghosts of the people in the paddy wagon, the ghosts of the boy and girl in Arizona who had been killed by the cops because of her own stupidity, if those ghosts made her sweat, lose sleep, and ache with the wish to set time backward and do things right the second time, it was because they were her own private ghosts. This poor pale girl and those men held no terror for her—they obviously belonged to someone else, to another time altogether beyond her control. She did wonder why they had been haunting the road along the van's route, though, so she asked the wispy little apparition, "Why are you here, sister?"

The ghost didn't answer but drifted backward, oxen and all, a pace, beckoning Anna Mae to follow.

The wind gusted up again and blew shivers of distortion through the specters of the mutilated girl and the animals. Anna Mae took one step, and then two, and the first of the oxen, with a lifelike scream of animal fear, slipped from sight. Two more steps to see where he had gone and the other ox and the girl followed. But while the ox fell slowly, screaming, the girl drifted like dandelion fluff on the breeze, skirt belling and hair bannering as she fell.

Anna Mae leaned forward and the ground trembled beneath her. Her foot slipped out from under her as a chunk of pavement broke off and plummeted toward the ghosts. She tried to step backward but another chunk broke off beneath her other foot and both feet flew up in the air, jerking her flip-flops off her feet and sending them below. She flung herself backward and held on to the pavement with her fingernails for a moment before two pairs of hands reached down to grab her arms and drag her back to the van.

Once inside she waited until her heartbeat wasn't swamping the sound of the voices around her before she said, "At least now we know what she wanted. She was a warning."

"Next time," Brose said, "I'd try to find that out without following her back to the happy hunting grounds if I were you."

▲▲▲

"Who *are* all these tacky dead people and who is the idiot who invited them?" the Chairdevil demanded.

"I don't know," the Expediency Devil said peevishly. "But every time we seem to be making progress, one of them gets in the way. It's enough to make you superstitious. Why don't we just lead the bunch in the van in with the others since they're so crazy about being together?"

CHAPTER XVI

▲▲▲

Julianne handed Willie back the banjo.

"That's okay, darlin', you just hang on to it. I don't feel a whole lot like playin' now," he told her, exaggerating his gestures so that she could make out what he was saying by the pantomine. But she pressed it on him anyway.

"Sam wants you to have it," she said. "He's gotten the hang of the other side now and he's of the same opinion he was in life. He asked me to remind you that when the bastards are out to get you there's still only one thing to do and that's to organize. He says Joe Hill is over there with him, so you'll have to do."

"Oh, *well*, if you—I mean Sam—puts it that way," he said half mockingly, then remembered that while Julianne might be a little on the weird and spacey side, the circumstances in which they found themselves were not what you might call apple-pie normal either.

As if to underline just *how* unusual circumstances were, the strings began to throb beneath his fingers, drawing them like magnets to the frets and strings that made certain notes, certain chords. He found himself playing a particular frailing technique he'd noticed Sam using the last time he'd seen him. And words he had no idea he was going to say sprang up to mate with the notes and fill in the melody.

"There's blossoms on the flowerin' tree, rich and wine-sweet
fruit
But when the branch is blighted you must prune it to the
root."

He paused between lines to say, "I'll be damned if I'm not writin' a song. Get this down, Gussie. If Hawthorne's ghost can make a songwriter out of me, Lord knows it might be able to do anything—even get us out of this mess.

"Oh, the roots run deep and deep, my dear, they've burrowed
   deep and wide
All from your sunny homeland to the sea's dark other side.

"And the sea begins a river, love, the river starts a stream
The creek is rain and runoff from a mountainside in spring
If the sea it should run dry, my dear, and the riverbed should
   crack
Then you must find the streams, my love, and trace their
   channels back.
And you must pray for rain, my dear, and you must melt the
   snow
For a sea must start from somewhere for to make its tidal
   flow.

"And humankind is like that sea and like that bloomin' tree
And the songs they are its blossoms and the waves upon its
   sea
That sea must not run dry, my dear, nor rotten grow that
   fruit
And if you'd save the tree or sea, then take it to its root."

He played it through twice more, the banjo accommodatingly slowing down while Gussie scribbled the words on the back of a ruined flier. The second time through, Julianne, who was watching Willie's hands on the banjo, told Gussie the names of the notes and those were added too.

"I guess that's not exactly necessary," Willie said. "The banjo made it up the first time. I reckon it would remember it again."

"Maybe we should make a paper airplane out of this and fly it out of this trap in case we're stuck here forever so somebody else could sing it after we—you know," Gussie said.

"Yeah, I know," Willie said. His hands were still playing the song. With effort he pulled them away. "That's about enough out of you," he said to the fretboard. "I get the message but there ain't a whole hell of a lot we can do about it from here."

The ranger had stopped hyperventilating and looked a little shame-faced. "You keep telling me it plays a song that goes with the situation. Maybe it's trying to tell you how to get out of this."

"I doubt that. Seems to me all that it's saying is that to find the songs again we have to go back to where they came from."

"Don't sound too practical to me," the ranger said. "Who knows where that kind of thing comes from?"

"Oh, people know okay. That Randolph boy, he knows a lot about where the songs come from. Of course, a lot of what you hear at your folk festivals—or used to— are modern songs made up by people, though there's still some that like the old ballads. And then there's your ethnic songs and your work songs that were made up by somebody fairly recently but it sort of got forgotten who did it. Lot of songs got made up by people who were in a certain situation or heard about one that seemed worth making a song about. Naw, it ain't all that hard to figure out where they come from. I just can't tell what difference it's going to make to us right now. Unless . . ." He frowned at the banjo. "Well, hell, I don't know any songs about bein' in our particular situation. I don't suppose you're plannin' on inspirin' another one, are you?" he asked it. The banjo strings stirred with the melody to the last song, a little like "Shady Grove," a little like "The Water Is Wide," with a touch of "Darlin' Corey" thrown in.

"There's lots of truckin' songs in country and western but I don't suppose that would work," the ranger said a little snidely.

"Nah, if anyone under the age of forty-five has heard them on AM radio they can't be folk songs," Willie said. "Too popular, make too much money. Besides, I can't think of one of those either that has this particular kind of truck stop in it, can you?"

"Maybe it doesn't have to have trucks," Gussie said. "Maybe it's just something that relates. I keep thinking

of a children's song, what's it part of? Something about
Fiddle in the middle and I can't get around—"

Willie sighed. " 'Skip to My Lou,' I think, or maybe
it's 'Hello, Susan Brown,' but it don't do us a damn bit of
good. We already know we got a fiddle, or a banjo, anyway, in the middle and we can't get around . . ."

He no longer felt dazed and philosophical. He was
thirsty and his throat hurt so he was pretty sure he
wasn't dead. His body hurt all over from the need to
stretch out—being folded up for miles on end, especially
the same miles on end, was putting cramps in worse than
just his style. In a half an hour, an hour, any singing that
got done would have to be done by the banjo alone because he, for one, would no longer be able to sing. Of
course, he didn't exactly have to worry about losing his
voice for his next engagement and he'd keep croaking
something as long as he could, if only he could think of
the right thing to croak. The banjo was oddly un-
forthcoming—it pretty much had a mind of its own and
that mind wasn't on the problem. When he thought back
on it, it had played warnings and pointed out an existing
situation, never a song to counter what was happening.

"How about 'Will the Circle Be Unbroken'?" Gussie
suggested.

"How's it go?"

"I don't know the tune but it's something like, 'Will
the circle be unbroken, be unbroken, be unbroken, be
unbroken, be unbroken be unbroken be unbroken . . .' "

"You keep that up it's never going to be unbroken,"
Willie said.

"Well, if you're so goddamn smart, you think of something," she said.

"*I* didn't get us into this mess," he pointed out.

"Is that so?"

"Aw, both of you shut up," the ranger said. "That
thing is playin' something again. Don't you think you
oughta listen?"

Gussie, still half-peeved but beginning to be ashamed
of herself for squabbling like a two-year-old, broke off
and cocked an ear.

Willie tried to catch the words to the slippery tune,

"Da da da da da old grey horse and somethin' else a muley and somethin' and da da da I'm goin' home to Juli . . . oh, I get it." With considerable relief, he handed the banjo back to Julianne. "It's for you this time," he said.

▲▲▲

The song pierced the receiver on Nicholson's desk, all but scaring the devils so that they scattered away from the boardroom.

"And if you'd save the tree or sea then take it to its root . . ."

Lulubelle Baker shuddered painfully as Willie's voice finished the song. The others sat by in stunned silence as the conversation in the station wagon was broadcast throughout the room.

"It doesn't matter anyway," the Ignorance and Stupidity Devil said when he recovered, which was sooner than the others since his specialty gave him the advantage of imperviousness to any stimulus more subtle than a solid blow with a blunt instrument. "We've got 'em good now. They're damned and all the caterwauling in the world ain't gonna change it. Right, boss?"

He was rewarded with a hound-of-hell snarl, followed by Nicholson's even more terrifying voice of sweet reason. "Your world view is far too simplistic, Stu. Nothing is ever as cut and dried, as black and white, as settled, as you seem to think it is. If all the caterwauling in the world didn't make any difference, we wouldn't be bothering with these nonentities, *would we?*"

The Expediency Devil, a devil of action who felt that the situation had deteriorated beyond the power of mere bickering to solve, snapped his fingers and transported himself to the cab of one of the fuel tankers.

With a furtive look at the rest of the committee, Lulubelle Baker left her image lolling in the hot tub looking high and depressed at the same time, snapped *her* fingers, and popped out of the boardroom and into the logging truck. She wanted to keep an eye on things personally and the music didn't bother her as much as it did the others. After all, hadn't wine, women, and *song* been her stock in trade for millennia?

▲▲▲

The banjo changed tunes as Willie slid it into Juli's hands, but the music was lost in an eruption of noise. The vehicles surrounding the station wagon blatted their horns as relentlessly as if every single driver had died over the wheel.

▲▲▲

Back on good road in broad daylight in dry weather between La Grande and Pendleton, Oregon, the road, the day, and the place seemed so normal nobody would have thought much could go wrong. It had seemed that way a lot of times before, Faron reflected, and he kept his eyes peeled and his senses razor-sharp and thus was, if not ready, at least not too shocked when the Bicyclists From Hell appeared in front of the van.

There must have been upward of a hundred of them. He saw the first one, a straggler, climbing the hill ahead of him. Someone all in yellow, hot pink, and electric blue vinyl riding an expensive-looking electric blue bike with more gears, probably, than the van had. An orange flag with the number 6 flew from the back of the bike.

He started to pass it at the crest of the hill, but, drawing even with the bike, saw that there was a line of others straggling one, two, three, and even four abreast, all of them pedaling furiously even though they were going downhill where he, personally, would have coasted.

"Damn, will you look at that," he said to Hawkins, who was reading a second-hand novel about Horatio Hornblower he had picked up in a tavern where they'd stopped for gas and to use the rest room.

Hawkins looked up. "Looks like we've stumbled into a marathon."

"Yeah," he said, easily passing number 66 and number 13. He thought it was going to be a hassle passing them, but without quite knowing how he was suddenly in the middle of them—and then they slowed down so he was surrounded on all sides—in the front by tightly girded shiny vinyl buns, on the sides by pumping knees and dedicatedly lowered helmets.

Whether there were more of them or he was just deeper into the crowd, Faron wasn't sure, but suddenly the entire road ahead was covered with them, and on every side and behind him were more.

"Notice something about these people?" Hawkins asked.

"Yeah, there's a lot of them and they're all in our way."

"No, I mean, their faces. Everyone I can see from here has to be at least forty-five to fifty years old, maybe sixty, and in *very* expensive gear. Looks like some sort of heart association. Pedal-for-the-Pumper sort of race, what do you think?"

"I think that looks like an exit and I'm going to take it and lie low until they pass. We could stand to find a gas station anyway and at the rate they're going, we'll idle what's left in the tank away within an hour."

"Sounds like a plan," Hawkins said, and returned to Admiral Hornblower.

But no sooner had they turned off than the bikers began pouring after them, pedaling furiously up the ramp to the overpass.

"Give them a chance to decide which way they're going, then go the other way," Hawkins advised.

"Yeah, I guess there should be gas stations on both sides. Or maybe we can sneak back down onto the highway."

But when they reached the intersection they could see that despite the hordes pedaling up behind them like the Pied Piper's rats, a whole army of brightly and tightly clad bikers covered the highway below and beyond them.

Faron feinted to the left and eleven cyclists behind him dutifully gave left-turn signals. He wanted to change his mind and turn right but his way was blocked by then by a couple of dozen more cyclists who had passed him on that side while he was watching the other. So he turned left and headed down the access road, hoping that a gas station would rear its utilitarian sign and they could wash the van or something until the cyclists were out of the way.

They stopped at the gas station on the left and filled

up. It was a modern one, complete with rest room, and a talkative attendant dressed in a red coverall with a nametag obscured by one of those have-a-nice-day smiling circles, only the grin on this one had been stamped out a little funny and it looked like a sneer.

"Some kind of race today, is there?" Faron asked the man. Miraculously, none of the bicyclists seemed to have followed them to the service station.

"Oh, my yes. Yes, indeed," the man said. "Real pain in the neck—come in for water and air and to use the john without spending a cent. Bunch of rich executive types from Portland, too. They been doing marathons for one damn thing or another all summer, or practicing for them, hogging the roads—the Gandalara Cycle Club they call themselves."

"Sure gets in the way of thru traffic," Hawkins observed.

"Well," the man said and Hawkins would later remember that it seemed to him the attendant was suppressing an echo of the smirk he wore on his button. "There's the truck route."

"How do we get to that?" Faron asked.

"Just follow this road. It bypasses town and joins up with the highway several miles down the road, winds around a little, but don't worry, just stay with it."

The van was out of sight, though surely not out of hearing range, of the service station when the god-awful racket began.

Brose knelt between the seats. "What now?" he asked, having to raise his voice to be heard. "More spooks?"

"Can you turn around and go back?" Anna Mae asked.

"And go through that again? No way," Faron said.

"Maybe one of 'em invaded the truck route and got creamed," Ellie suggested optimistically.

Brose grunted. "There's always hope."

But as they continued all they could see was the back ends of six eighteen-wheelers driving in curiously tight formation. Other than the way they were driving, and the fact that they were honking their horns so loudly that they were surely heard in Portland and Boise simultaneously, they seemed normal enough. And this *was* the truck route, after all. And there were a couple more trucks bearing down on the van from behind, pressing it to join them.

Faron drove forward, barely outrunning the refrigerator truck on his tail. Lemminglike, it started blowing its horn along with the others, until the sound totally enveloped them and Faron had to scream, "Hey, you think I should blow mine too?"

Hawkins held up his book and shouted back, "When in Rome . . ."

Faron grinned and beeped "Shave and a Haircut," with clarity surprising in such a din that Hawkins shouted a comment on it. "It's a perfect E," Faron said. "Everyone else is in low A."

▲▲▲

The banjo strings bumped against the calluses of Julianne's hands like a cat nudging to be petted. She closed her eyes and went into her Zen Buddhist transcendental state that harkened back to ancient, pre-Hindu meditation forms. Relaxing into her inner self, letting the universal consciousness and the great I Am flow through her, she gave herself up to the flow of cosmic oneness to allow its music to fill and envelop her and flow out through the banjo. The strings rippled and vibrated, throbbing beneath her fingers, and as she concentrated on the "now" state she grew in awareness of what her fingers were doing, which notes they were playing, what song the banjo was urging from her lips. She sang, like one hand clapping, for to her both the sound of the banjo and the sound of her voice were equally inaudible, and despite her deafness to the words, the plucked notes rang out piercingly clear and true, transcending her limitations, the car, and the horns in a Taoist statement, pure and crystalline, "Swing Low, Sweet Char-i-o-ot, comin' for to carry me home."

Willie had his fingers in his ears to shut out the truck horns. Still, his grandma had seen to it that he never missed church until he was fifteen years old and graduated early from high school to start college, and he had no trouble recognizing the song simply from the way Juli's fingers and mouth moved, and her facial expression.

Nor did singing, or even playing, by braille alone give him much problem. Like Juli, he had sung many nights in bars crowded with rowdy shouting drunks, video games, televised football and fights. Shoot, compared to some of the places he'd played, this highway was plumb peaceful.

He joined in lustily. With the two voices joined together, Gussie could hear well enough to pretty much be singing the same thing at the same time and so could the ranger, who had given up on any kind of more direct action and who was not an especially musical sort of guy but who had, after all, grown up in the Bible Belt.

Through the broken front windshield the notes pushed back at the cacophony of horn sound and they did not go unnoticed.

The thing in the oil tanker that had replaced the wrecker as their left-hand jailer writhed in agony and plunged its foot onto the gas pedal to escape the horrible sound. It tore an entire strip of the door from the side of Gussie's station wagon but swerved wide of the tanker ahead, where the Expediency Devil wished they had a real-live fuel tanker–driver minion who would not be affected by the banjo's power and could simply drown the damned station wagon in gasoline.

In the logging truck, Lulubelle Baker groaned, "Fuuuck, next thing you know they'll start sprinkling friggin' holy water."

The refrigerator truck passed the van and filled in the space vacated by the demon-driven fuel tanker. The van drew up behind it, beside the pipe truck in back of the besieged station wagon.

Everyone in the van was awake, watching and listening, trying to understand what was happening. Hawkins, who was used to feeling for minute shiftings in the balance of wind, sail, weather, and rudder, who watched and listened across the waves for whales to be saved and for threats to them, who was used to listening and singing above high wind, crashing waves and creaking timbers, the thud of hand pumps and, sometimes, the drone of engines, heard a snatch of the song from the station wagon. It helped that he had his window rolled down and his head stuck out of it. Even so, the only word he heard was "Char-i-o-ot."

"They're up there and they must be okay because they're singing," Hawkins told the others, and listened again, hearing "char-i-o-ot" the second time. For most of the others, that word would have indicated only one song. But Hawkins had been raised by a Jewish mother and an atheist father far from the Bible Belt and places where black slaves had moaned gospel songs to keep themselves going. His earliest and also his most recent interest in music was maritime occupational songs and he concentrated zealously on his specialty.

So when he heard the word "chariot" and the faint, tinny ring of the banjo above the horns, he knew they'd found Willie and the others and he leaned gladly into the fumes and noise, and bellowed back what he thought he heard, based on his own frame of reference.

Stomping his foot to the floorboards and yelling the first word, as he would to cue a crew that the time had come for the first beat, the first haul on a line, the first thrust of a pump, he sang, *"We'll* roll the old chariot along, we'll roll the old chariot *along,* we'll roll the old chariot along and we'll all hang on behind."

The crew in the van were all strong singers, knew the chantey and took it up at once, the notes and beat of the work song, accompanied by hands beating on the van walls and feet stomping on the floor, fighting back at the truck horns. Faron honked back in time with the chantey.

"Oh, a vacant lane ahead wouldn't do us any harm," Hawkins improvised to fit the situation. The song was so often "zippered" with verses from other songs or ones made to order on the spot that adding verses was the most traditional thing you could do with it. And what the hell, even if they were on dry land, this was a dirty, tired, ill-fed crew who had been keeping watches driving for the last few days. They'd even gotten pretty wet once or twice. Close enough for folk music. "Oh, a vacant lane ahead wouldn't do us any harm, oh, a vacant lane ahead wouldn't do us any harm, and we'll all hang on behind."

The refrigerator truck zoomed forward, away from the side of the station wagon.

As the people in the van and in the station wagon sang the first lines of the choruses together, Faron grabbed Hawkins's arm and jerked him back inside the van. They changed lanes and drove into the space the refrigerator van had just vacated. The station wagon was beside them with Willie at the wheel and Julianne singing "Char-i-o-ot . . ."

Gussie had been singing so hard it took her a moment to realize that the horns weren't bleating as fiercely anymore. A rush of fresh air filled the van from Willie's open window and she hunkered down to breathe it in and saw the van, with Hawkins leaning toward them bellowing his brains out. As soon as they heard Hawkins clearly, everyone in the station wagon except Juli changed songs.

Willie and Gussie both waved to Hawkins and the ranger nodded wearily, as if the van were some story a speeder was making up to avoid a ticket.

"Hi there, wanna drag?" Hawkins said.

"Keep singing!" Willie called back.

"Why?"

"Christ, never mind, just try 'And if we sing a song they can't do us any harm . . .' " Willie began and the ranger and Gussie picked it up.

▲▲▲

The banjo changed tunes belatedly and Juli followed suit, changing chariots in the middle of the chorus. Lulubelle Baker was profoundly grateful. Despite the fact that TV evangelists were some of her best people too, she could no more abide spirituals of any kind than any other devil and it was only her soft spot for Willie's old wild ways that kept her driving the logging truck instead of dumping the whole load on them. The sea chantey was better, though. Sailors were among her best people too. Especially the old ones the songs recalled—drunken, whoring, loutish, sometimes opium addicts, even, if she was lucky, criminals, killing off whales and other marine life, spreading corruption and disease among innocent island-dwellers who previously had known nothing worse than maybe a little cannibalism. Damn good thing the Expediency Devil was out of sight in front of her. He would have snitched about her unprofessional attitude. Dry stick. She didn't care. She had a good mind to let fly with the logs, light up the fuel truck, and enjoy the bonfire. She hadn't had so much fun in a long time.

"Oh, another little stop wouldn't do us any harm," Willie sang and in the fuel tanker, the Expediency Devil put on his brakes, wondering what the hell was going on back there. Willie flung open the door of the station wagon and jumped out—and almost fell on his face when his knees, folded for so long, refused to straighten for a moment and he had to brace himself against the door to stand. Gussie leaped out behind him, one hand around Juli's wrist. The ranger was the last, half supporting Juli, who clung to the banjo that plucked away on a melody line for the chantey all by itself.

Hawkins yelled back and Anna Mae and Brose flung open the van's side door to receive the refugees.

"Oh, an off ramp from this highway wouldn't do us any harm . . ." Willie sang and halfway through the second repetition there was a shrieking rebel yell from the direction of the logging truck and the second chain broke, sending logs rolling onto the station wagon, barreling across the road toward them.

The Expediency Devil, who occupied his current position to escape the flames of hell, thank you, and who had no wish to endure other, less metaphorical flames, caught sight of Lulubelle's characteristically irresponsible maneuver in his mirror and stepped on the gas, getting the hell out of there, while Lulubelle cackled like a cartoon witch.

The road shook beneath the stampeding logs. The fuel tanker driven by the Expediency Devil speeded away but the second one still blocked the road ahead. Fortunately, the singers were coming up on the chorus again and as they sang, "Roll the old chariot along," it started rolling, barely in time for them to drive out of the way of the logs, toward what mercifully looked like the off ramp they'd been singing for.

As the logs boomed and bounced, the highway trembled—and disappeared. There was no side ramp, no cloverleaf, just a gravel road through a meadow polluted with the skeletons of dead cars, trucks, and buses, rusting in the light rain that started falling as if the dust of the highway's dissipation had seeded clouds. The van clattered onto the gravel and a flying piece pinged against the license plate and knocked loose the tiny transmitter that had been placed there days earlier by Nicholson's police minion at the catastrophic close to the festival. It fell undetected to the ground. The only reaction from those on the receiving end was relief—they didn't have to listen to all that singing anymore and could concentrate much more on the entertaining spectacle provided by Nicholson, the prissily indignant Expediency Devil, and an unrepentant Lulubelle Baker who was still laughing her head off.

"I'll be," Willie said wonderingly, and carefully omitted the "damned" he would usually have used as part of that exclamation. "It worked."

"Something sure did," Faron agreed.

"Don't stop singing," Willie said.

Hawkins tried one of the original verses, about a little slug of rum wouldn't do them any harm, but no rum materialized and Ellie said sadly that it must work only on bedeviled highways. Nevertheless, Willie took charge of the banjo and kept playing the same song and kept singing it until he had no voice and then insisted that others take over. They finished the last chorus several uneventful hours later as they drove into Gussie's driveway in Tacoma.

CHAPTER XVII

▲▲▲

August paused to tell everybody to drink up, it was last call.

"Harry, can I buy you a coffee for your last drink?"

"Nah," Harry said. "After all that, I believe I'll take a taxi tonight and tell it to stay off the freeway."

"Better yet, a bus," Lewis said.

"We'll take you with us," Vicki told him.

"Yeah," Lewis said, "wouldn't want you picked up by any ghostly taxi drivers."

Vicki said, "Come on, August, it's almost closing time. How did they get the songs back and get rid of the devils?"

"Why, child, what makes you think they got rid of the devils?" August asked. "It's not all solved that easily, in fact, it hasn't properly been solved from that day to this. Still, there's a little more I can tell you now," she said.

"And you could tell us the rest tomorrow night," Lewis said. "Like a miniseries."

"Maybe," August said. "Actually, the end of this is, like a lot of things in life, the beginning of the next part. Because although the musicians got loose from the freeway with the help of the songs and the ghosts, the problem remained that the songs were lost and now the musicians realized they were going to need to get those songs back for their own protection, as well as their livelihood."

▲▲▲

The house looked disappointingly normal to Gussie. Her cat chewed her out in no uncertain terms, trotting along on heavy paws and mewing up at her anxiously. The food and water dishes were full so Gussie knew the cat was lying again about not having been fed in weeks. The light on the answering machine blinked furiously and the metal-made-to-look-like-wood top of the kitchen table was piled with mail.

Nobody was the least bit interested in having a seat but the bathroom was very popular. Gussie put the kettle on the stove for them and broke out three-month-old cans of diet soda from the fridge before she stroked the cat or looked at the mail.

"I need to call my mom and dad and let them know we're okay," Ellie told Gussie.

Gussie nodded absently.

"Hi, Dad. Yeah, we're fine. It was bizarre. I'll tell you about it—huh?" She held the phone out. "Brose?"

"He's in the can," someone called elegantly, and then, "Oh, no, here he comes."

Brose grunted a greeting into the phone. "Yeah? Well, I'll be damned. No, I guess here would be best. Yeah, a wire. Through a bank. What's your bank, Gussie?"

"Seafirst."

"Seafirst," he said. "Thanks, buddy, that may solve a lot of things. Oh—okay," he thrust the phone back at Ellie. "Your daddy wants to talk to you again."

"I need to call in to headquarters," the ranger said when she was done. "Is there somewhere I can talk private?"

She waved him into the bedroom—the cord was a long one.

Anna Mae grabbed Willie's arm. "Now, while he's in there, you have to escape."

"I do?" he asked.

"Yes, or they'll kill you and destroy the banjo and . . ."

An angry exclamation came from the bedroom and the ranger stomped out, glaring at Willie accusingly. "They don't know who the hell you are and have no record of what you were supposed to have done and I've been fired for overstaying my annual leave."

"I wish I could say I'm sorry about that, officer," Willie said. "But you understand—I do have a question though."

"Yeah?"

"If I don't have to call you officer anymore what do I call you?"

"Unemployed, mostly. My name's Bud Lamprey. You got a beer, lady?" he asked Gussie.

She waved him toward the refrigerator and punched the phone machine button.

Craig Lee's voice was the first one on her recorder. "Gussie, call my house ASAP," it said, but there was no mention of time or date.

She heard four rings and was expecting his answering service when a timid female voice said, "Hello?"

"I have a message to call Craig," Gussie said.

"Mama?"

"Lettie?"

"Mama, you're back. We've been so worried."

"*You've* been worried! Who slipped you the file in the cake is what I want to know."

"That woman lawyer you hired, she got us off. Proved that the customs official was crooked and made a deal with them to let us go with clean records—"

"What woman lawyer?"

"You know, Ms. Burns, the red-haired one. She was real good, even though Mic kept sayin' he thought she was on somethin'. But she hadn't been there but about a half an hour and they let us go, just like that. Drove like a maniac, and I *didn't* appreciate the way she propositioned us but some people are a little weird, I guess."

"The important thing is that you're free, darlin'. I'm home. Can I come and get you?"

"Well, no, we're kind of house-sitting for Craig. He was in an accident with a friend and she was hurt real bad. He broke a hip and his hands got all cut up."

"I wish that surprised me," Gussie said sadly.

"What?"

"Never mind, darlin'. I got a houseful of company here right now so if you can come on over for a while I just need to see you."

"Us too," Lettie said.

Gussie's hand was shaking as she cradled the receiver again. Willie, who had been clutching a mug of coffee and pacing the floor, stopped suddenly and slid an arm around her sagging shoulders. "Gus, what's the matter, darlin'?"

Tears slid into wrinkles she didn't normally have. "Lettie and Mic are out of jail, Willie, and I just don't have the guts to get back in that goddamn car and go see them. And I feel like calling them back and telling them not to come either, because I'm afraid something will happen to them."

"I hear you, darlin', I'd offer to drive you over there except I'm afraid of the same thing. But we *did* beat the bastards once so I guess we can keep on doin' it, as long as we've got Sam's banjo and that song. Those sons of bitches may be tough but old Hawthorne, hell, never was nothin' as tough as Sam." He was still hugging her and spread a grin across his face but she knew he was just acting cheerful to keep her from falling into even more pieces than she already had.

So she gave him the best smile she could muster, which didn't amount to much. "Yeah, that's right. And thank God for little ol' Juli. She has some funny ideas but there's something about her . . ."

"Yes, ma'am, there is. And that Hawkins guy, comin' after us with that chantey like we were the great white whale or something. We got a little magic on our side too, and some fine friends."

"Fewer of those all the time, Willie," she said, relapsing into gloom as she remembered the festival and the aftermath.

Willie sighed. "True. Too true."

Gussie felt her blood pressure lower fifty percent when Lettie and Mic arrived later, seemingly unscathed by their brief careers as convicts.

They hugged and talked, and later, Anna Mae and Lettie cleaned and dressed Gussie's blisters and raw spots and Juli's and Brose's burns and all three of them took leftover antibiotics from Gussie's bout with pneumonia, which had run its course before the pills had run out.

When everyone had been reunited, treated, fed, bathed, and otherwise made as comfortable as possible, sleeping bags were hauled from the van, borrowed from the neighbors, and quilts and comforters and sofa pillows spread on the floor, which could not only be stretched out on but blissfully did not move while it was being slept on.

Gussie thought she would sleep like a dead person once her head hit her pillow and, as it turned out, that was the problem. She found she was afraid to sleep for fear she wouldn't wake up again. Juli, beside her, curled up like a child and slept soundly. Lettie and Mic snuggled together on the floor on one side of the bed, Anna Mae wrapped a sleeping bag around her on the other side. None of them moved much from one hour to the next, Gussie knew, because she opened her eyes and checked the luminous hands of her alarm clock every half hour or so. Around four she sat straight up as she heard the glass door to the deck slide open and footsteps creaking on the boards. She was in the hallway before she heard the faint tinkle of the banjo.

Willie sat cross-legged on her wooden bench, a blanket wrapped around his shoulders and the banjo in his lap. Fog rolling in from the Sound smothered everything around the deck except for the rosebush that trailed along the top rail. The tip of Willie's cigarette glowed like a Cyclops's eye through the gray.

She'd gotten so used to seeing the banjo strings moving of their own accord that it was almost as if banjo strings always did that kind of thing, but here in the dark and the fog on her own back porch they looked as ghostly as they were. Willie took a long drag on his cigarette and started to insert it between the strings and the tuning head. The strings jangled angrily, and he set the cigarette on the bench beside him instead. With his fingers on the banjo strings, the tune was fuller and livelier.

"There's somethin' on some kinda tree and da da da da da . . ." he sang.

Gussie went back in the house and dug through the battered Mexican straw bag, which had lost one of its little figures as she dragged it from the station wagon to the van, but still held the flier she'd written his song on.

She joined him on the porch and slid the glass door mostly shut behind her. "Here it is, Willie. Here's that song. It's blossoms on the flowerin' tree. Pretty, huh?"

"Yeah," he said, when he'd sung it through again.

"Real pretty, but you know, I can't understand why Sam would choose to break through from the spook world to give us this particular song. Just pretty ain't exactly his kind of environmentalism. And it sure as hell isn't a socialist metaphor. I mean, he doesn't mention Che Guevara or any of that stuff. I know it's what helped us out back there, I know it's important, I know it has something to do with why Hawkins's chantey got us out of that mess but . . ."

The glass door slid back again and Faron stood barefoot in his jeans, wiping his fogged-up glasses on the hem of his Save the Tyrannosaurus T-shirt. "Maybe I can help," he said to Willie and Gussie. To the banjo he said, "Play it again, Sam."

After the song finished, he stared at his toes a long time.

"Well, do you know what it means?" Gussie asked.

"Yeah, I think so. Only I'm not sure it's going to be a whole lot of help. Anybody got any idea if folk performers in other countries have been getting the same sort of harassment we have?"

"I haven't heard anything about it," Gussie said. "I'm sure Craig would know, even if he's in the hospital. But why?"

"Because the song says to go back to the root—and I don't see what else he could mean besides the root of the songs . . ."

"That's what we thought," Willie said. "But it's still not real clear, is it?"

"No, but if you figure that Hawkins's song worked not only because it was right for the situation, but also because Hawkins, as a working seaman, had learned it and sung it as a legitimate part of his work, that's a root in a way. But an awful lot of songs don't have their roots here. Most of what we think of as American folk music started someplace else—an awful lot of it in England, Scotland, and Ireland. Of course, there's all kinds of ethnic music and especially black music that is pretty much considered indigenous American music because even though it has African roots, the songs are mutations, not direct transplants, and a lot of the characteristics peculiar to it come out of the slave experience. Still, I'm afraid if the only way to reclaim some of these songs is to go back to the original roots, what with all the old-timers in the mountains that have been dying off and all, I'd say we're going to have to leave the country."

"Sure. The only way I'm goin' to be able to afford to leave the country is if I get deported," Willie said.

During the last strains of the song, Brose had slid back the glass door and had been listening to what Faron had to say about it. Now he said, "Don't be too sure about that, buddy. You have friends who have come into some unexpected wealthiness."

"What the hell are you talkin' about, buddy?"

"Remember the bet with Duck Soul, the heavy metal artiste, just before the storm? Well, seems old Duckie may have a lot of faults, but welchin' on bets ain't one of 'em. He sent me a cashier's check for the ten thousand dollars he promised. Barry Curtis should have wired it to Gussie's bank by now. I was thinkin' about using it for the farm but the way things've been goin', I might not get back there alive. Besides, the bet was with all of us, not just me."

Willie's eyebrows shot up to his hairline. "How 'bout that? I'd have sworn he was with Nicholson's outfit but maybe not. Lady Luck is spinnin' the wheel of fortune so fast these days it kinda makes you dizzy, don't it?"

▲▲▲

A week later Willie, Brose, Anna Mae, Juli, Faron, Ellie, and Gussie boarded the emptiest British Airways flight they could book on such short notice. They half expected to be hijacked by terrorists and wanted to take as few people with them as possible when they went.

They weren't too far off. Faced with the banjo and the charm-song Sam had sent, the devils voted unanimously to return to using minions on that particular group and had availed themselves of the services of a "sleeper" terrorist agent, one R. McCorley, employed as a steward by the airline, to plant a bomb under one of the seats.

Hawkins, Lettie, and Mic had decided not to go— Lettie and Mic because they needed to get home and see what they could salvage of their lives, Hawkins because he rather thought he preferred sea travel to air. Even so, the party was large, the plane nearly empty. It was shortly after dark and in the flatlands around Sea-Tac airport the air was clear as a bell, the moon rising outside the oval windows of the airplane.

Willie felt a momentary thrill, a rebellious, desperado rush. His sense of the dramatic was titillated by the knowledge that he was finally fighting for something he cared about, and becoming the cowboy-Robin Hood no amount of carousing had ever made of him. He pulled Lazarus onto his lap from its seat beside him and struck up the chord of a rebel song. "Ah then tell me, Sean O'Farrell, tell me why you hurry so. Hush now, boys, now hush and listen and his eyes began to glow. I bear orders from the Captain. Get ye ready quick and soon. For we all must be together at the risin' of the moon."

R. McCorley, fussing with the safety instruction cards three rows forward in order to cover his movements, stopped, straightened, and all but saluted. The fine Mr. Nicholson and all his kind be damned. There were few things McCorley loved better than blowing people up but one of those things was a good old rebel song, well sung. He slipped the wee bit of a bomb back into his jacket. He decided he would stay on this flight, after all, instead of disembarking at the last minute, as he'd planned. The music and the company looked good, he could use a bit of a jaunt back to the auld sod, and he could also think of a more effective way to use his bomb, if he liked. He was still humming the song later as he disarmed the bomb in the men's room.

Juli felt her back unknot as the steward emerged from the bathroom and took a seat. He seemed to be enjoying the music, and now that she had a closer look at him, he appeared to be a perfectly nice person. Still, there had been something about him . . .

Gussie also shuddered, felt someone walking over her grave, as the saying went. The engines rumbled, the plane slid smoothly down the runway and lifted into the sky. She was not the only one who let out a sigh of relief.

"I hope to God this thing stays in the air," she said.

"I think there's something we can do about that,"
Faron said. "Willie, if you'll hand me Lazarus, we've got
plenty of time to learn a new song. A friend of mine,
Suzette Haden Elgin, wrote it for just such occasions. It's
called 'The Airplane Only Flies Because the Passengerss
Believe That It Will.' I think you'll agree there's a lesson
in there for all of us somewhere."

A redheaded stewardess appeared suddenly from the
cockpit. Only Gussie saw her exchange challenging glares
with McCorley before she shrugged, entered the cabin,
and with apparent spontaneous delight clapped her hands
in appreciation of Willie's last song. "Oh, sir, I think
that's ever so delightful. Would you mind awfully if I
learn it too? Does a stint in the pubs wif a bit of song and
dance meself from time to time, as an 'obby like." They
all urged the redhead, whose nametag said her name was
Miss T. Burns ("call me Torchy, it's me stage name
like"), to take a load off her feet and join them.

EPILOGUE

▲▲▲

Harry was waiting, not at his accustomed barstool picking over his Lotto tickets, but outside the door of the bar as the woman who called herself August arrived that evening.

"Evenin', Harry," she said. "Gettin' a little air?"

"Waiting for you," he said. "I just was wonderin' if that woman had gotten ahold of you yet."

"What woman was that, Harry?"

"Glamorous, L.A-type redheaded woman, said she was lookin' for you to offer you a job in a new place she was opening. I just thought she might have called and arranged to meet you. She's waiting for you in there now. Just thought you'd want to know."

They exchanged long, rather serious looks, measuring on both sides, then August asked, "Harry, can you sing?"

"I don't know, never tried."

"Well, try this one, will you, and sing it for Vicki and Lewis and the others and tell them I have to move along now. Family business, say. But remember it, if you can. I knew it when I was a girl, and lost it, and just found it again not too long ago. Some people believe that most of the words were the last goodbye of a condemned Scottish murderer, though mostly it gets sung in *Irish* pubs, but I reckon it will do for Bremerton."

She sang the first verse, and when she reached the second, he picked it up in a surprisingly strong and true tenor that strengthened and harmonized with her shaky soprano, and they sang through to the end of the second verse, "Oh, all the comrades ere I had/They're sorry for my going away/And all the sweethearts ere I had/They'd wish me one more day to stay./But since it falls unto my lot/That I should go and you should not/I'll gently rise and softly call/Farewell and God be with you all."

He hadn't sung since he was a boy, and enjoyed it so

much he screwed his eyes up tight and sang so loud that inside the bar the redheaded woman plugged her ears up and headed for the ladies' room. The bartender sang the words to the last verse, but when it came to the last two lines Harry joined in, "Then fill to me the parting glass— Farewell and joy be with you all." The sound of his own voice pleased him so much that he grinned as he finished the line as the note faded and said, "Damn, I'm good." And then he opened his eyes and realized that he had sung that last line all alone, there in the parking lot, with only the hum of the street lamp and the traffic noise for accompaniment.

ABOUT THE AUTHOR

Elizabeth Scarborough was born in Kansas City, KS. She served as a nurse in the U.S. Army for five years, including a year in Vietnam. Her interests include weaving and spinning, and playing the guitar and dulcimer. She has previously published light verse and short stories as well as a number of Bantam novels. She is presently at work on the sequel to *Nothing Sacred* as well as The Songkiller Saga. She makes her home near Seattle, Washington.

A Special Preview of

PICKING THE BALLAD'S BONES

Volume 2 in
The Songkiller Saga
by Elizabeth Scarborough

In this next adventure of American folk musicians, the group travels to Great Britain in hopes of learning local ballads. In order to do so, however, they discover they must live through the tragic lives of the characters in the ballads. In the following scene, ladie's man Willie MacKai is shocked to find himself not only sharing consciousness with a woman, but her lover is his own mirror image.

Willie had hoped that the Debauchery Devil's fondness for him might let him end up in his favorite kind of ballads—that is, the bawdy kind. As the kitchen at the cottage disappeared, everything was blurry for a while, but he heard a song he remembered Buffy St. Marie once singing called "The Lyke-Wake Dirge."

> If ever thou gavest hosen and shoen
> Every night and a'
> Sit the down and put them on.
> And Christ receive thy soul.

He remembered those words without really knowing what they meant except that what you had done for or to people in life was supposed to be yours in death. For better or for worse. The Golden Rule and all that. God, was this a trick and he was in hell and it was one long hard-shell Baptist, fire-and-brimstone sermon?

But a clear path opened in the haze surrounding him and he saw a field of grass and yellow broom all around and a pretty girl and a handsome devil of a guy pulling up some greenery in a slow and significant way. He followed the path to the couple and took a step and joined them, blending . . .

Something clacked close to the bed. Willie shot out a hand to throw back the bed curtains and waddled to the window. Wherever he was, it sure wasn't Texas.

Below the window was a lush garden of unfamiliar flowers, with stone walls rising all around, cornering in towers and toothed with businesslike battlements. The place was a whole lot bigger than even the main house at the LBJ Ranch.

But he noticed something else as he reached his slender, shapely hand up to wipe his long golden hair out of his eyes and pluck a strand from off his milk-swollen breast. There were a few more profound differences to his situation than mere geography. He was female. Not only female, but pregnant.

Another clack and a clatter as the stone fell short of its mark and a familiar, beloved voice said, "Sarah, cum awa' wi' me." And though the voice had a Scottish burr instead of a Texas drawl Willie would have recognized it anywhere. It was his own voice.

And down below was a man the spitting image of Willie MacKai from his long, elegant legs to his tousled hair with its gold glints in the sun, his gleaming eye, his proud bearing, and the hint he gave of being barely able to stand still for needing to pace. So if that was Willie MacKai down there, Willie MacKai wondered, why did he seem to be here? Had he sprouted a twin? Then he opened his mouth and a soprano drowned in honey sang out to the handsome devil below, "Ah canna cum noo, love. My father and brothers are back from the campaign and they ranted sae loudly ah had nae time to explain to them aboot our marriage. Be wary o' them—ah had a dream last nicht and ah fear it portends us ill. Ah dreamed we were pullin' heather and birk up on the hill. Gae there straightwa' an' ah'll meet ye as soon as ah may."

Disoriented, Willie asked, "Who *am* I?" and was answered, "Why, Sarah Scott, the sorrowfulest woman in the world and yet—with only a little luck, I could be the happiest. Ah look at him, that laddie, fast and slippery as a moss ranger stealin' frae my window. Was there ever sic a bonny sight as him in the plaidie I wove for him wi' my ane twa hands?"

"No, never. A good man, a good choice. Look at his seat on that horse! You've got good taste, Sarah Scott. He's a very bonny lad—"

"Aye, a flower among men," Sarah added, sighing so heavily her breasts ached and a loving warmth melted within her loins. Delicately, soothing herself as she would soothe a horse, she smoothed her nightdress over her thighs, then let her hands clasp over the dome of her belly. "I canna see how Father overlooked him though he's anely a second son instead of a first and his brother inherits. He's a better man than all my three brothers pu' taegethair, and will mak' me a better husband and my father a better son. We'd be happy in a bower in the broom if need be, if only my family would not stand between us."

"A bower in the broom? With no stove to cook for him and no loom to make him clothes? No stable for his horse and no cradle for the baby? And don't forget the bed. Without those things how can you be happy? He may be able to live wild, but you'll soon be a mother. It's not like you can get a job or go to college. You're going to want to keep house for your man and your baby. Women are like that. You know it's true. You say you'd be happy with little, but would you truly?" Willie knew all about this kind of reasoning from the girlfriends he'd had who'd sworn they'd be happy on the road with no money and later, even without babies, proved themselves dissatisfied with the arrangement.

But Sarah twirled herself (and him within her) around as if physically flinging off care and crowed, "How foolish tae trouble myself with such questions. Aye, oh aye, I could be happy and my bairn would be happy and so would we all if only we were allowed! It's that dream has me fey, 'tis all. That and my time bein' sae near. What shall I wear? The brown dress or the gay green?"

"The green goes better with our eyes and brings out the color in our cheeks. Better go for the green at least until we get our figure back." Willie, as a performer, knew the importance of all aspects of image, even though he'd never had to deal with being pregnant before.

Sarah grabbed the green dress and slipped it over her nightie, which Willie realized also served as their mutual slip. The effect was charming—though a bath wouldn't have hurt them—but there was no time. Sarah's lover was wanting and Willie, in Sarah's body, felt soft and glowy and full of hope, yearning toward the man who waited for his love up on the hill in the den, for his caresses and his loving words.

And this didn't seem unnatural to him. He was a part of Sarah Scott and instead of finding her feelings and her yearnings strange, in her body they felt natural to him, exotic—impossible to feel so incredibly turned on without an erection, he would have thought, but he felt it. Maybe it was because the true love was so much like himself—maybe it was some kind of an urge for his consciousness to rejoin his real body, to be one with himself again. On the other hand, hadn't true love been described that way? He'd never believed in it himself. Lust, sure. Wanting a woman because she seemed desirable, like a partner who could expand his life a little, sure. But that never worked out. And it never started with this kind of need. Had any of those women ever felt for him what Sarah felt, what he was feeling, for the man who waited on yon hill? Yon—he was even starting to think with her accent. But it only seemed right. The landscape outside the window looked very much like what he'd been passing through the last two days. More than that, it felt like home.

"Enough trouble in the world without borrowin' more," Sarah thought. "Father will surely be reasonable—will understand why we must marry now, with the bairn and all. 'Twas just the shock of it cumin' upon him all at once that upset him."

"And what of the bruise on your cheek?"

"He didna mean tae strike me sae hard and he wouldna let my brothers abuse me, for he said I was but a stupid girl and easily set on my back. My brothers laughed at that, for often enough they tried to corner me after I grew bubbies and before they went a-campaigning. He's a rash man and he had mickle drink and strang spirits."

"You're soft in the head. Your father's a hard man and he'll never relent and even if he did, how could it work out?"

"I've my tocher lands that are all my ane and we could live there when the babe is born. Cook says it's a boy and she has the Sight. If it's a boy, Father will forgive me sartain for John's wife and Michael's wife have born only daughters and Robbie's yet tae wild tae settle doon. Father will forgive us once I gie him a grandson tae dandle on his knee."

And Willie thought, maybe this is one of the happy ballads after all? Sarah should know her people better than he, and he felt like whistling as Sarah pulled on their kirtle and tied it up with ribbons so it wouldn't drag in the grass. Willie enjoyed the grace of her swaying movements as she made herself ready to meet her lover. She swayed on sturdy, shapely brown legs from a central pivot of her hips, so broad to balance her. How strange to carry nothing between the legs and so much to balance above, the breasts, the belly. Her fingers briskly touched her head, loosening pins and sending a cascade of Rapunzel braids of long, long yellow hair to the floor. She picked up the end to untwine it, and picked up a brush with a bone back and boar bristles to tame the unbound locks.

A flurry of hooves thundered in the courtyard.

"Oh, Lord," Willie moaned. Not a bawdy ballad.

"Oh, dear Lord—" Sarah answered, flying to her window. Her three brothers, six of their men, and her father were mounted and riding hell-bent out the front gate.

"They heard us! They saw us!"

"Wasn't too bright to arrange a tryst where they could hear you," Willie said. "Need to warn that lad. The old man's laid a trap."

"He has and I maun spring it and warn my love else he think I've betrayed him."

"Can we make it in time?"

"Every day this twelvemonth half I've run and never walked tae meet him. Ah, but I'm sae baig wi child noo. No time to get a horse, no time to ask for help. I'll mak' it because I must."

But even the stairs were treacherous, though she'd climbed down them and up them since she was a toddler. They were narrower now than her shelf of breast and belly and she had to stand sidewise to see where to put her feet. Three times three stairs she climbed down and twice as many took her over the rushes and out into the courtyard and across the footbridge toward the meadows.

"I must reach him first! I must! They'll kill him they'll kill him they'll kill him if only because I love him—"

"You're killing yourself. Slow down. Hear how your heart pumps almost through your breast? Hear your breath roar in your ears? Your lungs will burst if you keep this up. Your legs have failed and your eyes have failed and we're blacking out and we won't reach him in time, poor sorry son of a bitch."

And Willie raised his eyes a little and saw a horse's hooves. He raised his eyes more and saw the booted feet and bare legs of Sarah's lover, so like his own bodily feet and legs, and higher yet he saw his strong-veined brown hands clasped on the reins, his slender waist and his chest in its rough cream shirt with the scarlet scarf at the neck—but then, looking higher, he saw nothing above, nothing at all. It was a headless horseman coming toward them and it was his own body that sat the horse and from within him Sarah screamed a scream drowned in her swoon, but it roused her so that she opened her eyes, and the headless horseman disappeared.

"Too late, too late—" she breathed as she ran headlong forward, tripping on her skirts, her belly and her breasts bouncing painfully, her insides shooting knives into her groin and heart, her legs burning as if her bones were burning brands.

"You'll never make it. You're too weak, the baby's coming, you'll burst with the effort, it's too far—"

"There! The hill is there! Only a little ways!"

"What's that clash like pots and pans at suppertime?"

"Gramercy, it's the clash of swords!"

"And that. The horses are screaming . . ."

"Maybe they've just started. If I throw myself between them, they'll have to stop, won't they? For my sake, as they love me, they must—"

"If they don't, it's all the same, isn't it?"

"Aye." And all thought was swallowed by the drumming in her ears and the waves of pain from her belly and loins.

"Listen."

"Silence."

"Why?"

"They've stopped."

"Who's that riding down the hill?"

"I see now—it's Father and my brother John."

"Do you see him?"

"I do not."

Her father's hand lifted in a greeting, half weary, half jaunty, and she could barely lift hers in return, but as he drew nearer she fell against his stirrup crying, "Father, dear, I'm so glad to see you. I had a most doleful dream . . ."

"Ye've done o're much o' dreamin', lass. 'Tis time noo tae get on wi' real life. We've revenged ye agin yer seducer, though we lost Michael and Robert and six men besides in the deed."

He looked down at her with anger suffusing his blunt features, his thin mouth and his bulbous nose, his flaccid cheeks huffing and puffing still with the aftermath of his effort. His hair was gray and his skin was lined and cracked with the weather but his eyes, under brows like thunderclouds, were absolutely cold. He stared into her and through her as if she were an inconvenience, a wart on his hand, a stain on his sleeve.

"He said to find you," her brother spoke up, mockingly. "He said to tell you he forgave you your betrayal o' him. Ah wish ah found it sae easy."

And brushing her off, her father rode on and her brother beside him.

"They didn't even ask how you were, and you so near your time."

"Gin they cared how I fare, they'd never have let matters come to sic a pass."

"They could have offered you a ride to the house."

"They could have left me and mine alane and I'd

never need a ride. I'd walk from here tae the ends of the earth to undo what I fear done."

"Maybe he's just wounded," Willie said. "I think that might be it. I don't feel anything. I can't believe they've killed him. I can't believe that dream was real."

"I can believe though I'm loathe tae think it."

A hand curled out over the crest of the hill, its fingers spread as if relaxed in sleep. But the nearer she drew and the higher she climbed, the more apparent it was that the body was that of a dead man, his chest cleaved open. The grass was slick with blood in a trail leading to another, whose arm lay to one side, his body with his free hand still clasping the stump, to the other side.

And Willie knew from Sarah's memory that this was her brother Michael. Who had once slaughtered her pet lamb and laughed at her when she wouldn't eat mutton for her supper. He had died from hemorrhage when his sword arm was severed. Beside him was a hired man, his skull cleaved to the bridge of his nose, his brains and blood leaking from the cleft. Her brother Robert was beside him, but she ignored them all, the servants and her brothers alike, and never drew a breath the entire time she walked across the hill until she saw him.

He lay facedown, as if napping, his clenched hands arrested by death in the act of tearing at the heather between his fingers. His sword had fallen to one side and the blood on it was still red, the smell of hot metal and blood simmering from it in the sunlight. The dream was not accurate, Willie was glad to see, for his head was still on his neck and the killing wound was from the sword that still stuck in his back. Willie could not recall having seen brother John's sword, when they met on the trail. John it was then who must have surprised Sarah's lover from behind.

"You took eight of them with you though, buddy," Willie thought fiercely.

"Aye, they bought him dearly but not so dearly as it's cost me." And she pushed and pulled until she turned him over and Willie looked into his own dead face. The mouth was quirked as his quirked when he cut himself shaving. The eyes were glazed as his were glazed before his first cup of coffee. He might have been looking in the mirror but for the blood.

Sarah, on her hands and knees, stroked the corpse's hair and began to kiss the wounds and Willie did not somehow find it morbid when she licked and sipped the blood, as if by doing so she could take her lover into herself once more.

Two ravens sat in the tree above them, casting speculative beady eyes on the corpse.

"Get lost, you buzzards!" Willie wanted to cry, but found he had no voice without Sarah, who wearily made shooing motions with her hands and tried to tug her love by his arm away from where he lay. "I'll bury ye mysel', love," she said, and stepped backward on her long braids of unbound hair. She fell and her belly exploded with pain again.

She scarcely cried out but Willie felt the pain that had only been anesthetized by her deeper pain and he said, "Take the sword from his back and cut off that hair. What do you care? He'll never stroke it again. Make a harness to lift him with."

And with the rope of her hair lapped under the arms of the corpse of her lover, she tugged and pulled and dragged him to the foot of the hill.

Her father and her brother were returning with men and shovels for the burying of the bodies and her father glared down at the top of her shorn head and commanded, "Stop. John, take that body from your sister. She looks about to swoon."

"He's a little goddamn late to be worried about your welfare now."

Sarah looked up at her father and said in a voice made flat with pain, " 'Tis like my dream, Father, all full o' woe and weale—"

"Enough!" her father roared. "I won't have ye greevin' thus o'er this sneakin', seducin' dirty dog. It ruins the aftermath of a good battle. I came home for comfort and rest and what do I find but rebellion and sorrowful speeches. Nivver ye mind about him. I'll find ye a lord tae wed ye to who's twice the man and wi' his ane siller besides."

But Sarah jerked aside when her brother would unwind the hair from the knot across her chest and although he was stronger than she and not above striking her, as he had often done before, he shrank from her now.

Her father dismounted and reached for her gently. "I promise, I'll find ye anaither, worthier lord."

She didn't resist as he folded her in his arms.

"Let go of her, you old hypocrite!" Willie said, and the baby inside her burst from the womb and tore it from her as it plunged out of her body.

She fought and clawed at her father as he eased her down on top of the body of the slain man, and she screamed and screamed and screamed and wrenched at him, till the ring on the middle finger of her left hand was half torn off her finger, torn sideways in her struggles.

As her strength failed, a strain of music came to her and to Willie within her from far off, and Willie knew the song that went to the music.

> Last night I dreamed a doleful dream
> I knew it would bring sorrow.
> I dreamed I saw my true love slain
> On the dowie dens o' Yarrow.

And with remembering the song, he remembered that he mustn't die with her here in Yarrow. "The ring. You must twist the ring twice more, backward—"

She slumped so that her cheek was against her lover's wound and as the song played Willie saw that her love was waiting for her. "The ring, Sarah, the ring," Willie in her mind said and the slain lover waiting for her echoed, "My ring, love, my ring—"

That which was Sarah and that which was Willie tangled together more tightly than ever as she died, drowning in her own blood. Willie heard the song clearly, and desperately dived for her spirit that was abandoning his own, trapped in that dying body, "You can't go yet. Stay and release me. Sarah, this isn't all of you. It isn't all of him. It isn't the end. There's the song, Sarah, the song they made for you and him . . ."

And through her rang the second verse, and with it, the realization that this pitiful short life she had lived and was losing, that her lover's life, was not the end, and that they were at once avenged and remembered in all the time thereafter.

"The ring. Twist the ring. Backward—"

Her arms were limp over her love's body and her hands, dragging in the heather, clutched it in her death throes, the heather against her left hand working the ring slowly around, and ever slowly in a full counterclockwise twist . . .

Picking the Ballad's Bones, Volume 2 in *The Song-killer Saga* by Elizabeth Scarborough, takes the American folk musicians across the Atlantic to Great Britain. The devils have not made much headway here, so that the folk musicians can easily research and learn local ballads. They soon run into difficulty, however, when the Debauchery Devil (also known as the Queen of Faerie) throws in her style of magic.

Read *Picking the Ballad's Bones* by Elizabeth Scarborough, on sale November 1991, wherever Bantam Spectra Books are sold.

Three brilliant literary talents.
Three beautiful fate-bound princesses.
One dazzling fantasy epic.

BLACK TRILLIUM
by
Marion Zimmer Bradley
Julian May
Andre Norton

"A fine fantasy novel...The world-building is superior."
-- *Chicago Sun-Times*

Haramis, Kadiya and Anigel are triplet princesses facing the greatest challenge of their young lives: the defense of their kingdom against a powerful dark mage. The key to that defense lies in the gathering of three magical talismans which when brought together will be their only chance to regain their kingdom and free its people. Each princess is charged with finding one of those talismans, attempting quests that will take them to the farthest reaches of their world. And to succeed, each must also confront and conquer the limits of her very soul....

"Remarkable...*Black Trillium* is an entertaining, well-told tale." -- *Dragon*

Black Trillium
An unprecedented publishing event
and a breathtaking fantasy adventure.

On sale now wherever Bantam Spectra Books are sold.

AN246 -- 6/91